RICHER THAN RUBIES

Tessa Barclay

severn House

This first world edition published in Great Britain 2006 by
SEVERN HOUSE PUBLISHERS LTD of
9–15 High Street, Sutton, Surrey SM1 1DF.
This first world edition published in the USA 2006 by
SEVERN HOUSE PUBLISHERS INC of
595 Madison Avenue, New York, N.Y. 10022.

British Library Cataloguing in Publication Data

Barclay, Tessa
  Richer than rubies
  1.   Rubies - Fiction
  2.   Jewelers - Fiction
  I.   Title
  823.9'14 [F]

  ISBN-13: 978-0-7278-6413-0   (cased)
  ISBN-10: 0-7278-6413-0   (cased)
  ISBN-13: 978-0-7278-9184-6   (paper)
  ISBN-10: 0-7278-9184-7   (paper)

Except where actual historical events and characters are being
described for the storyline of this novel, all situations in this
publication are fictitious and any resemblance to living persons
is purely coincidental.

All Severn House titles are printed on acid-free paper.

Typeset by Palimpsest Book Production Ltd.,
Grangemouth, Stirlingshire, Scotland.
Printed and bound in Great Britain by
MPG Books Ltd., Bodmin, Cornwall.

One

Jo Radcliffe switched off the polishing machine with a little sigh of contentment. It was so good when an idea transferred so well from the computer to the metal.

The piece she was working on had no great commercial value. Only topaz and nine-carat gold – a simple experiment to see what it might look like when worn. She'd make the other earring, of course. And someone might want to buy the pair, although she'd only thought of using them as display items in the studio.

The studio next door was half for display and half for reception. At that very moment her receptionist Lindora put her head round the door to ask, 'Are these people coming or aren't they? It's nearly five and I want to close up.'

Jo rose from her stool to stretch and ease her back. No matter how she warned herself to take a break, to move her back muscles, she knew she tended to crouch when she was closely engaged in her work. She took off her protective goggles, closing and opening tired hazel eyes.

'They're coming,' she said. 'He sounded very keen – and very rich.'

'Ah! That's a point.' Her sister-in-law, now acting receptionist, had looked up the prospective customer on the Internet. He had turned out to be someone who made big deals in the City, an arbitrageur, a regular whizz-kid at thirty-five: Ivan Digby, hitherto an unknown to Jo because she almost never read the financial columns.

She stood know, unwrapping herself from her work apron. She was a tall figure, more likely perhaps to be an athlete than a creative artist. At the moment her toast-brown hair was tied back in a bandanna to protect it from the fine dust of the polishing, but strands had escaped to curl over her ears. She was wearing no make-up, she remembered. If she were to be in a fit state to receive this rich man and his fiancée, she ought to tidy herself up.

1

The buzzer sounded in the workshop. It signalled the arrival of someone at the door of the studio.

No one could simply be allowed to walk in, of course. The studio held examples of Jo's work, some of them prize-winning items from important competitions, all valuable and several unique.

'Let them in and offer them refreshments,' she said. 'I'll just be a minute.'

Lindora rather huffily obeyed. Jo had to remind herself that her sister-in-law didn't like being given orders. 'Of course, it's only temporary,' she'd said when Jo offered a home and a job. 'Just till we get on our feet again.'

She and her husband Donald, Jo's brother, had recently returned from a disastrous business enterprise in Spain. They were now sharing the huge flat above Jo Radcliffe Designs. The building had previously been a garage with storage above, bought for almost a song with the first money Jo had won eight years ago. It had taken her until last year to convert the place to her satisfaction.

First, of course, had been the workshop. She'd slept on the floor in the upstairs area until she'd got the workshop properly arranged and equipped. Here were her workbenches, her computer, her tools and, if she were honest, her heart. She loved her work.

She'd left the upper part of the building until last, and for that had hired the help of an architect and interior designer, because she didn't really care what it would look like so long as it was comfortable.

But now it housed herself, her unemployed brother, and her unwilling receptionist sister-in-law. They were 'resting' – that's to say, they were out-of-work actors.

In the little washroom towards the back of her workshop, Jo used the little hand-vacuum to remove all traces of metal dust, brushed her hair into a decent shape, washed her face and hands and then applied lipstick and a little eye-shadow. There, that would have to do. She'd meant to go upstairs so as to put on something a little more attractive than her shirt and jeans, but had got too engrossed in her work.

She walked briskly through the workshop to the studio. Lindora was pouring tea into fine china cups for the visitors. Everything always stood ready on a broad shelf so as to offer a variety of refreshments, and it was this part of her job that Lindora seemed to enjoy most – the chatting-up, playing the part of hostess.

The first sight of the new clients caused Jo's heart to sink. They

2

were clearly very, very rich. Ivan Digby had that fresh-from-the-masseur, fresh-from-the-barber look, signifying perhaps that the delay in their arrival had been because of a lengthy visit to his club.

His companion was an extraordinarily beautiful young woman. She had that sweet, dewy look that was the height of fashion at the moment, with blonde hair allowed to fall in seeming carelessness about her neck and cheeks. She was wearing designer jeans and a top more suitable for the warm day than Jo's linen shirt. In fact, the top seemed to cling to her lovely bosom more by magic than by dressmaking.

About the pair there was that faint yet expensive scent that signalled exclusively made cosmetics. Something dignified and outdoors for the man, something spicy yet demure for the girl. And on the third finger of her left hand there glittered a diamond big enough to shine star-like on the top of any Christmas tree.

So . . . They had a lot of money. They were here to spend it, and Jo was perfectly willing to help them do that – provided, that is, that they didn't want anything silly or gimmicky. No swivelling chandelier earrings, no personalized belly-buttons.

The prospective client rose from his chair at Jo's entrance, holding out his hand. 'So glad to meet you! You were recommended by an acquaintance of mine who knows a thing or two about jewellery.'

'Thank you. Someone who's been a customer of mine?'

'I believe not so far, but jewellery is his hobby and he's seen and admired your work at exhibitions.' He turned to nod towards his companion. 'This is Miri, my fiancée – you may have heard of her? Miri Gale?'

'I . . . er . . .' Jo was floundering.

'She's on television quite a lot?' He was offering these hints as if it would make her cry out, Oh, of course, how could I be so dim! 'On *Catch My Drift*, the quiz programme?'

'Oh . . . Yes . . .' She seldom watched quiz programmes. 'How demanding! You have to be tremendously clever for that kind of thing.'

Miri gave a little giggle and a shrug. 'Not me, sweetie, I'm the one that comes in and hands them their winnings – jingle-jingle in a draw-string bag, as if anybody really gets their prize in one-pound coins these days.' She wrinkled her beautiful nose, looking pleased yet vexed. 'I thought you'd be a man,' she said, taking Jo utterly by surprise.

'I beg your pardon?'

3

'Well, you know . . . Jo . . . I thought it was short for Joseph.'

'It's short for Josephine.' So perhaps they weren't going to spend much money after all. A strange business – someone as clever in the business world and intending to part with a lot ought to have made some inquiries about the designer they were thinking of hiring. Perhaps they were just shopping around.

'Well, I think it's a bit of a swizz,' Miri went on in a vexed tone. 'I mean, who'd think of a girl being a famous designer, winning prizes and all that?'

'I'm sorry if you're disappointed. Perhaps you'd like to think it over and go elsewhere?' Jo suggested

'We-ell . . .'

'Miri darling, don't be naughty. You know Rupert said Jo Radcliffe was the best designer in London – and he's no fool.'

Lindora, standing by to attend to the clients' needs, thought it time to use her charm. She'd heard the irritation in Jo's voice. She knew these little oddities of her sister-in-law's – a little too independent, a little too cool with people she didn't take to.

'It's so very sultry today – can I offer you something else, an iced fruit juice perhaps?'

'No, no, thank you, we really should be getting down to business,' Ivan said, and opened the ostrich leather document case on the table before him. 'I brought you photographs,' he said to Jo. 'The gems themselves are in a safety deposit box in my bank, because of course they're very valuable.'

He offered the pictures. They were large, in colour, and very clear. And they showed Jo the rubies of the Fieldingley Necklace.

'Good Lord! These are yours? I never thought they would ever come up for sale!'

He smiled in appreciation of the fact that she knew their value. 'Oh, you know . . . These old families . . . Their fortunes vary from era to era, and right now the owner of the necklace – I should say the former owner – is an old lady and very hard up.'

Lindora came to stand at Jo's elbow. Together they inspected the necklace shown in the three photographs. Jo heard Lindora give a little smothered sigh of disappointment, for what they were studying was a not very striking piece of late Victorian craftsmanship.

The necklace was really something like an old-fashioned mayoral chain of gold rectangles held together by segments of gold links and tiny diamonds. In the centre of each of the gold rectangles there was a ruby. The gemstone was not particularly large but each was of a very fine deep red and each matched every other almost to perfection.

'Is this famous, then?' Lindora asked, in a tone that seemed to wonder whether it deserved to be.

'Oh, you bet!' exclaimed Ivan. 'These were some of the very first rubies to come out of Burma after the British conquered the country in the 1850s. I got photocopies of documents when I was negotiating the price. Look, here's the original bill of sale, and press cuttings of the time – that was 1868, you see.'

'Press cuttings!' This was Lindora again, astonished to think there could be 'celebrities' so long ago.

'Oh yes, the whole thing was covered quite extensively in the society columns, because the rubies were important and the Fieldingleys had a bit of a position.'

'I wasn't questioning the provenance,' Jo began, with a glance of reproof at Lindora. But he swept on, immersed in his story.

'Until us British took over, you see, Burmese rubies had only been available inside the boundaries of Burma – the king had exclusive rights to them. So I think there was a bit of competition as to who'd get the first lot, and so the necklace caused a bit of a sensation when it was first made. I can tell you it cost a pretty penny at the time.'

'It's still worth a tremendous amount now, isn't it, sweetie?' Miri put in, anxious to establish the necklace's importance even if it wasn't very pretty.

'Well, forty-five thousand,' he said, shrugging a little. 'The rubies aren't by any means the biggest in the world, dear. You know Mrs Fieldingley pointed that out. But the point is, they're a perfect set, forty of them, and their historical value makes them even more important.'

'*That's* the point I wanted to make with you,' said Jo. 'This necklace is quite famous in its way – among lovers of gemstones, that's to say. Although I'd never seen it, I've read about it. What exactly are you thinking of doing with it?'

'I want you to remodel it for Miri.'

'Remodel it.' She'd expected that. Ivan Digby had bought it for his girfriend, and certainly this sedate, rather heavy piece wasn't at all suitable for the sweetly beautiful girl at his side.

But to alter the work of a master craftsman of a hundred and fifty years ago?

'The rubies are so gorgeous!' cried Miri. 'But you know, the way they're put on the little gold plates here – you don't get the full impact, now do you?'

'And they'll look so lovely against Miri's skin, don't you think? And of course when Rupert said you were good at modern styles in jewellery, and said you'd won all these prizes—'

'Not all that many,' Jo protested. 'Only four.'

'Well, that's a lot more prizes than I've ever won!' He laughed, and gave a fond glance at his fiancée. 'Miri's the one who's got trophies, aren't you, darling?'

Miri smiled and gave a little shrug. 'Local beauty queen, that sort of thing – doesn't really count for much, does it?'

It was Lindora who made the expected protest at this. 'Oh, goodness, I bet they were more than "local" – and now of course to be on television . . .'

'Have you seen the show?' Ivan inquired. 'Not much of a part, of course, but they spend a lot on her gowns – very revealing, and I sometimes think . . . well, it brings in the viewers, so we can't complain, really.'

'I'm not much of a TV fan,' said Lindora, with a little smile of apology. 'Or at least, I ought to say, I only watch drama – because actually, I'm an actress, so that's where my interest lies.'

'Really?' cried Miri, looking at her now with sudden interest. 'You've been on TV? What were you in?'

'Oh, no, in fact, legitimate theatre is our interest – my husband and I – we're Lindora and Donald Radcliffe. We've just come back from a tour in Spain.'

A tour in Spain. Jo made no comment. Her brother and his wife had spent every penny they could scrape together on buying a neglected farm about fifty miles inland from the resort coast of Malaga. It was to be a year-round attraction for tourists and the expat British. Here they would put on plays in English: good reliable crowd-pullers such as Agatha Christie and John Osborne, and of course Shakespeare.

They had spent a year wrestling with bureaucracy for permission to fit out one of the barns as a little theatre. The Christmas of last year, they had launched with a stage adaptation of *A Christmas Carol* which had done well. They had followed that in the New Year with *Twelfth Night*.

'Still seasonal, you see,' Donald said on one of his infrequent telephone calls.

Seasonal it might be, but few of the English contingent wanted to drive fifty miles from the beach to see it. It was hastily replaced by a Christie play, *Death at the Vicarage*. And then by others of a popular type. Before the venture even reached the summer season – which, Donald declared, would solve their money problems – their problems became insoluble, and it ended in closure.

They returned home to the humiliation of living off Jo at her unfashionable premises in Wembley.

Only temporary, of course. Donald was out most days going for auditions and 'making contact'. Lindora was less happy; she really did not enjoy having what she considered a non-creative job.

But at this moment she probably found herself in a very favourable situation. She was chatting to a man who made enormous amounts of money. More important, he had a girlfriend who was looking impressed by Lindora's account of her career.

Ivan Digby had other matters on his mind. 'So, what do you think?' he ventured, looking at Jo. 'Do you feel you'd like to have a go at doing something with this?' He nodded towards the photographs. 'I'd like to give the finished necklace to Miri as a wedding present.'

'But that's not for quite a while.' Miri took up the conversation. 'Ivan's bought this fabulous old place in the country – at least it *will* be fabulous when it's finished, though it's been sort of a ruin for some time. So we're planning to get married there.'

He nodded agreement. 'What we're saying is that you could take your time with this, if you've other commitments, you know?'

'It's interesting.' And indeed it was. Although her conscience troubled her. In its way, it was a fine old piece, and an heirloom to the Fieldingleys. Still, the Fieldingleys hadn't hesitated to sell it. 'I'd like to give it some thought. Perhaps I could ponder for a few days and try out a sketch or two? Well no, I'd probably show you something on the computer, really – people generally like to see things in 3D.'

'That sounds fine.' Ivan and Miri exchanged glances of acceptance. Ivan, however, was a businessman. 'Could we make a provisional agreement? Just something informal. And I'd like it kept quiet for the time being.'

She raised her eyebrows. He went on quickly, 'Well, you know, they're famous stones, and Miri's in the public eye, and I'm not exactly an unknown . . . So I'd prefer if word didn't get out until we announce the wedding date.'

7

'Yes, you see, it's going to be a gorgeous wedding,' Miri intervened. 'We're going to have it at the castle?'

'Castle?'

'Well, not exactly a castle, but it's a huge old place – in Cheshire, you know, with lots of land, and we thought we'd have the wedding in the Great Hall, which is going to be done in the style of – what's it called again, sweetheart?'

'Restoration,' he supplied. 'The place was built for one of Charles the Second's unofficial off-spring.' He smiled. 'Should be rather a fine result, when it's finished.'

'Oh, I can just imagine,' Lindora put in. 'And I bet you're having a wonderful wedding-gown!'

'Sure thing. It's all hush-hush at the moment, but it's costing a fortune because it's by – well, I mustn't say, but he's a big name. Satin, you know, and very low cut here –' she patted her lovely bosom – 'because of course that was Restoration fashion.'

'And that's where the rubies are due to make their first public appearance, at the wedding,' Ivan explained, 'so as you can tell we don't know exactly when, but the way the work is going on the house, there's no hurry.'

'Well, thank you, that's good to know.' She felt that he'd wanted to tell her all that so as to impress her rather than to suit any work schedule of hers. And to tell the truth, she *was* rather impressed. It all had something of a fairy-tale atmosphere. Rich and handsome man, beautiful girl, castle, famous old gems.

The gossip magazines would probably pay a fortune to have exclusive rights to that wedding scene, she imagined. So perhaps it wasn't so fairy-tale after all. Perhaps it was a hard business head at work.

Lindora typed out an informal agreement while the guests had more tea and Jo tried to find out what sort of necklace Miri envisaged. But Miri wasn't good with words, nor did she seem to have much power of imagination. 'I want it to look *fabulous*,' she declared, 'with everything sparkling and looking . . . you know . . . rich and impressive.'

'I'll see what I can do,' Jo said.

When they had said their farewells, Lindora at once set about locking up for the night. It was now after six. Donald would be home soon, with news of his day. Jo went to the kitchen to start preparations for a meal. She knew her brother's tastes of old. If the news was good, he'd want wine to toast his success. If bad, he'd

8

want comfort food – something with lots of carbohydrates and a rich sauce.

He'd gone out to a meeting with an old friend who might have some influence with the producer of a new musical, and then there was tomorrow's audition for a TV series – he and Lindora were still debating whether he should go to it or not.

Jo had always had to listen and respond to her brother's enthusiasm about his acting career. Matters had changed little in that respect except that now there were two actors instead of one, whose dreams and ambitions she had to nurture.

It was clear from her brother's look that things hadn't gone well today. She'd always been able to read his mood from the set of his rather heavy features. He was older than Jo by four years, taller than she and thickset, impressive rather than handsome.

'So I said to him, "Look, Ralph, you know I can sing. I'm not a Pavarotti, but I can get by and anyhow, this show is relying on the special effects rather than the music, isn't it?" Turned out it was quite the wrong thing to say. Seems the guy that's doing the music is a pal of his. So I don't think he's going to put himself out for me.' Donald twisted his fork in the pasta and guided the carbonara sauce towards it.

Lindora was quick to offer sympathy. 'Never mind, forget Ralph. We should think about tomorrow's audition. It's a country-type series, isn't it – should we do work on some rural accents this evening?'

'I suppose so.'

'And listen, darling, the most marvellous thing this afternoon, Jo's got a client – a tremendously rich type – and what do you think? His gorgeous girlfriend is in show business!'

'Show business.' It was a grunt of resentment. 'That always means the telly, doesn't it! Or is it videos for promoting some rowdy pop group?'

Lindora recounted the conversation. The fact that Jo was to re-model a set of famous gems that had been a family heirloom hardly seemed to count with them as they discussed it. 'So he's got pots of money? Is he interested in the theatre, did you gather?'

'Well, Donnie, he's interested in *her*, absolutely besotted by the way he's spending money on her, and *she's* interested in acting, you could tell that by how she perked up when I began talking about it.'

'Really?'

So her brother was cheered up, and Jo was able to give her own thoughts to the rubies in the photographs.

She was going to try out some ideas on paper. Take out most of the gold, let the rubies glow as they ought to with perhaps a little sparkle from those tiny diamonds in the chain. Yes. Space, that was what was needed. The gems were almost smothered by the gold platelets, they needed room to breathe.

And yet . . . She'd seen the name of the jeweller who had originally made the necklace on the photocopied receipt: Giacinto Mellillo. She knew of him, of course. She'd learned about jewellery and its makers as part of her studies at art school. Was it right to break up his work?

Mellillo had been part of a movement in the art of gemstone work in the latter half of the nineteenth century. He had, with others, used – reinvented – a Renaissance style. This accounted for what now seemed heaviness in his work. The Renaissance had been a time of opulence, of ostentation: rich merchants had bought jewellery not only for their womenfolk, but for themselves, to wear over velvet robes and with rich fur collars.

So designs that had inspired the Renaissance movement might well have been rather masculine. Certainly the necklace in the photograph lacked femininity although it had been made for Mrs Adelaide Fieldingley. If Miri Gale were ever going to wear those rubies, they surely couldn't be left in that abundance of gold.

Well, that meant that the rubies would have to be re-set. But did she, Jo Radcliffe, have to do it? She felt reluctant to interfere with the work of a fellow artist. Mellillo's necklace might seem lordly, but it was his genuine reaction to the gems. How would she feel if someone were to pull her work to pieces and rearrange it?

She sighed inwardly. What she needed was another opinion. No use turning to her brother and his wife. They were totally engrossed in their own affairs.

So she went to the telephone to call Ben.

Ben Webber had been a factor in her life since art school. At one time they'd been more than friends, but time and career choices had caused them to drift apart. Ben had been at first a student in the metalwork department of the school, interested in the use of silver, gold, and modern metals. By and by the gems which were set into these metals began to fascinate him, not for their beauty but for their scientific make-up. He had left for a course at the university, and had become a gemmologist – that's to say, an expert

10

on the minerals, the naturally occurring elements, that by some force of nature became precious to man. He was highly regarded in his field and had become once again a friend and colleague of Jo's.

The problem was, he was somewhat protective towards her. He meant well, but sometimes she felt he presumed too much on the fact that they'd been so close all those years ago.

Still, she needed an opinion. And Ben was the logical person to approach.

She didn't want to invite him to her place. Donald and his plans for forwarding his career seemed to have taken over. She suggested a wine bar where they often met.

'The Fieldingley Rubies?' he echoed when she told him. His normally serious expression was lit up by enthusiasm. 'Well, what a great opportunity! If I remember rightly, they're a set of perfect colour and depth.'

'Yes, and by Mellillo – do you remember him from the art course?'

He gave a half shake of the head. 'I thought the rubies were set by – wait – wasn't it Castellani?'

'Well, yes, they have the look of Castellani.' She paused, thinking about it. 'I believe Mellillo worked for him. Didn't he manage the Castellani workshop in Naples for a while?'

They searched their memories. The Italian firm of Castellani had been quite dominant in the 1860s and 70s. It was from their workshop that 'antique' designs began to emerge: Egyptian, Etruscan, Mediaeval and finally Renaissance. The Victorians loved it; the styles became the height of fashion.

'Let's say the piece is either by Mellillo himself or someone in the Castellani workshop while he was directing it,' Ben said, his broad brow creased in thought. He tapped the photographs she'd brought. 'So you have a chain, or a sort of collar, that's a specimen of famous mid-nineteenth century craftsmanship.'

'Exactly.'

He let the thought sink in. Then he said, with a smile of self-congratulation, 'So what? There's masses of stuff from that era. In museums, in collections at stately homes, in jewel boxes up and down the land . . .'

'But this is by one of the really great designers . . .'

'And so is a mass of other chains and torques and lockets! You have to remember, Jo, that the Victorians suddenly realized they were *rich*. They spent loads of money on knick-knacks and trinkets

11

and investment jewellery. This chain that Digby's bought for his bride-to-be, it's just another example of the trade meeting the demand.'

'But of its kind, it's by a master . . .'

'I agree, but it's the fact that it's made from the first Burmese rubies to come out into the West that's important. It's the *rubies* you should think about. Nobody's seen them for more than a century because they've been locked away in some family strongbox. Now you have the chance to show them to the world.'

'You think it would be all right to break it up?'

He nodded, waiting.

She drew in a deep breath. She took a sip of her *caffé nero* to fortify herself.

'I think I'll do it,' she said.

Two

Three weeks later Jo invited Ivan and Miri to view her idea of a new setting for the Fieldingley Rubies. She had it up on screen when they arrived – Ivan at the wheel of a splendid BMW, she noted from the window of the studio.

Lindora sprang to open the door before they pushed the buzzer. It was a sunny, bright day, so Miri was wearing a voile dress that clung to her gentle curves and made her look about seventeen. Ivan too was clad in summer gear: cotton chinos, Bally moccasins, and a short-sleeved shirt that might have come from Armani. The light in the studio was always muted, so Miri removed her designer sunglasses as she came in, revealing blue eyes perfectly made up to match the blue of her dress.

Lindora offered iced tea. They waved it away. 'Thanks, we've just had lunch and really, what we came for was to see . . .'

'This way,' Jo said, and led them into the workshop.

The image of her design was rotating gently on the computer screen. She'd arranged chairs so that they could sit to study it.

'Well . . .' Ivan took his place, staring at the screen.

The design showed a fragile collar of lacy, pointed loops. At the point of each loop, a ruby was set. At the place where the loop returned to the basic chain, a tiny diamond formed a sparkling point.

Miri said nothing. She sat looking at the screen, a little frown between her brows, her lips slightly pursed.

Ivan spoke first. 'It looks very . . . very light, very airy.'

'Yes, that was the idea.'

'A complete contrast to the original.'

'That was what I was aiming for. Miri is so fresh and lovely, it seemed to me that anything in the least bit heavy would be wrong.'

Miri had still said nothing.

'It would lie just above her collarbone, wouldn't it? That would be rather good, because the neckline of the dress is low-cut . . . It looks sort of like gossamer. And plenty of room for it to

13

show . . .' He paused. He turned to look at Miri. 'What do you say, sweetness?'

'Are all the rubies there?' she asked.

'Yes,' said Jo.

'All forty of them?'

'Yes.'

'It doesn't look like it.'

'There are forty little loops and a ruby at the point of each of them.'

'Hmmm . . .' It was a breath slowly expelled. 'Doesn't look much.'

'Miri!'

'Well, they cost a lot, and there they are, spaced out like . . . like little spots on bits of wire.'

'But it's sort of floaty, dear – don't you see? Gossamer.'

'Gossamer?' She frowned. It was clear to Jo that she didn't know the word.

'That's sort of like a spider's web,' Ivan explained.

'Oh, great. Forty-five thousand pounds worth of jewellery and it's to be like a spider's web.'

'Darling, that's only a way of speaking – of course it won't look like a spider's web, it'll be glowing and glittery—'

'And you'll hardly see the rubies because they'll all be spaced out all over the place.' She pouted. 'It's not what I expected. It's got no . . . no pizzazz.'

'Forty perfectly matched rubies have all the pizzazz they need,' Jo said carefully.

'Well, I hate it.'

There was a pause.

'OK,' said Jo.

'What?'

'You don't like it. That's OK.'

'How would you like it altered, Miri?' Ivan asked, anxious to get past this awkward moment.

'Well, the rubies should be closer together, so they'd be more in front.' She placed her hand on the cleavage between her breasts, clearly visible because of the design of her dress – a low, V-shaped neckline.

It was certainly a good place to display anything. The golden tan on the smooth flesh led the eye to that point, where shadow and gentle curves seemed to invite something to nestle.

14

'More like a string of beads, you mean? With maybe little links of gold with the diamonds in between.' Ivan was sketching in the air with one hand.

'Something like that – or there could be a bit of a chain with maybe a cross hanging here.'

'Or a circle with some diamonds in the centre. Or – how about a bit of a surprise – a square of rubies with a gold border.'

'That might be good.' She nodded, looking round at Jo, who was standing between them but behind.

'No.'

'What?'

'No, I'm not making a necklace with a pendant or anything else.'

'Well, it doesn't have to be a pendant, so long as the rubies are more gathered together and towards the front.'

'No.'

'Don't be difficult, Jo,' Ivan murmured. 'Surely Miri's wishes have got to be regarded. She doesn't like this design, all it needs is a bit of tweaking—'

'No.'

'You mean you're not prepared to discuss any kind of alteration?' he said with indignation.

'Of course I'll discuss alterations. But I'm not going to alter it so that it looks like something from the nineteen-twenties that your granny used to wear.'

'Now look here, Mrs Know-It-All, I go to the best fashion shops and nobody can say I dress old-fashioned! You can't tell me I don't know what's being worn and what's old,' Miri retorted.

'Where jewellery is concerned, I think you're not very well informed—'

'Oh, so you're saying I'm an idiot, is that it?' Miri sprang up. 'Come on, Ive, let's get out of here.'

'Miri, wait . . .'

She was stalking out of the workshop. He dashed after her, catching her as she was halfway across the studio. Lindora sprang up from the desk, appalled at what she saw: an angry young woman, a harassed man, and a substantial fee, disappearing out the door.

'Good gracious, what's wrong, has something happened?'

'Clear off, you. Where's my sunglasses? I took them off as I came in and—'

'They're here, I picked them up—'

15

'Miri, angel, hang on. Don't slam out the door like this . . .' He caught her arm and turned her towards him. He tilted her chin so that he was looking down into her eyes. 'Come on, sweetie, calm down. You don't like the design, that doesn't mean it can't be changed—'

'But you heard her! She said she wouldn't do it!'

'But you see, love, she's an artist . . .'

'Huh!'

'Yes, she's an artist, and she's got a tremendous reputation, and you know how good it would look in the papers when you wear the necklace that it was made by an award-winning designer.'

'But I don't *like* her award-winning designs!'

'That's because it's different to what you expected. It's new to you. You have to realize that.'

From the door of the workshop Jo spoke in reluctant agreement. 'Ivan's right, Miri. It's new to you, we're new to each other. It's difficult to design for a complete stranger.' She hesitated. After all, the rubies were worth an effort on her part. 'Don't you think so?'

Miri, thus appealed to, frowned and shrugged in disagreement. Then she seemed to have second thoughts. 'We-ell . . . It *is* true that Desmond is making better dresses for me these days, now that we've got to know each other.'

'There you are!' cried Ivan. 'At first he didn't quite click with you. Now he's doing this wonderful wedding dress that you absolutely adore. Now don't you think that if you and Jo were more sort of in touch with each other, you could work it out?'

'But, Ive, she called me an idiot!'

'No, she didn't, that was you, precious, flying off the handle as usual! Come on now, admit it, you lost your rag just because Jo said she couldn't alter the necklace the way you wanted.'

'I had a perfect right to be angry. I don't like that design and I'm not having it.'

'Then what you should do is talk it over with her, not get in a tizzy about it. Isn't that right, Jo?'

'I don't feel like talking!' Miri cried before Jo could answer. 'I'll only be talked down to if I try! Who does she think she is, telling me what I want is like my granny's ideas? It's just not on, Ive, you'll have to find somebody else to do the rubies.'

'Now, now, sweetness, calm down, calm down. Let's just leave the whole thing for now and take ourselves off somewhere relaxing. What do you say? We'll go to the club and settle by the pool and have some nice chilled wine and think it all over. Come on now, Miri, dear, let's do that.'

Calming and cajoling, he urged her little by little towards the outer door. She allowed herself to be soothed, leaning into him so that he was supporting her, bringing him close so that he would feel protective. It was a perfect little manoeuvre, which seemed totally successful to Jo until over Miri's shoulder he gave her a little glance. Raised eyebrows, a tilt of his chin sent the message: 'All right if I get in touch again?'

She nodded, and out they went.

'Well,' groaned Lindora. 'You handled that well, I must say! He's the kind of man that would have paid anything you asked, but no, you drive him away.'

'Linda, drop it. You don't know anything about it.'

'I know he's got money to burn and a girlfriend that wants to better her career. They could have been tremendously useful—'

'Will you be quiet!'

'I think I have a right to say what I think! Miri and I would have built up quite a good relationship, but now I'll never see her again.'

'I think you will, if that's what's bothering you.'

'You must be joking. She absolutely hates you.'

'For the moment, yes. But Mr Moneybags is thinking differently. He'll be back.'

'Really, Jo, you shouldn't be so conceited! He's never going to come near us again.'

'Yes he is. He gave me the nod, Linda.'

Lindora glared at her. 'How many times do I have to tell you that it's Lindora! It's been Lindora for four years now!'

'Sorry.' She thought it a silly change, an unreal, operatic name. Her brother and sister-in-law had spent months pondering on what to choose; they thought Linda Radcliffe sounded too stiff and business like. Donald thought his wife was sensitive, idealistic, warm-hearted – not at all a Linda Radcliffe, and so Lindora came into being. But Jo often forgot.

Lindora now banged on about preparing for her lunch break. Today she'd arranged to meet Donald to hear how he'd fared at the audition. Jo thankfully closed the door behind her, locked up, and took herself to her own lunch date. The roof of her building had been turned into a little garden with plants in big pots and a parasol. Here she sat down with a bowl of muesli and a glass of cranberry juice.

17

She'd dropped off into a light doze when her mobile rang. It was Ivan Digby.

'Is this a good time to talk?' he asked in a tentative voice.

'Yes, fine, what's the situation now?' She glanced at her watch. An hour and a half had gone by since Miri had been escorted, still fuming, out of the studio.

'Miri's having her hair done at the salon. She calmed down, of course. She always does.'

'I'm sorry I upset her . . .'

'Don't worry about it. She gets upset sometimes. It's me that ought to apologize. I'm sorry she was so rude about your design.'

'Well, she had a right to say what she thought.'

'Yes, but . . .' He paused. 'I really liked your design. I thought you'd caught something of her personality in it. But it's no use pretending she'd ever accept it. She's made her stand, and she'll stick with that. All the same, it doesn't mean you couldn't . . . well . . . try again, does it?'

'Only if Miri agrees, Ivan.'

'Of course. I got the message when you said it helped to know the person you were designing for. I thought . . . you know . . . if you and Miri got together a few times, it would help. Would it?'

'Of course it would.'

'OK then, could we set that up? I thought maybe some time next week – if you'd be available. Perhaps you'd like to come over to our place and have dinner and get on better terms.'

'But would Miri agree to that?'

'Not today, she wouldn't. But hey, let a few days go by, and she'll have forgotten most of the argument, and then I'll persuade her we ought to ask you over to sort of apologize, and I'm pretty sure it'll work. What do you say?'

'If you really think . . .'

'So when are you free? Not the early part of the week, we've got a business dinner to attend, and on Friday there's an end-of-the-week conference at the office, and . . . oh . . . I see we're going down to our place to see how they're getting on, so . . . How about next week? Tuesday? Wednesday?'

Jo's diary was by no means as full as his, so she agreed on a date for the Tuesday evening. When she asked for directions, he said, 'Oh, it's easier if I send a car for you. About seven-thirty? That gives us time for a nice little drink before we eat. Are we on?'

She agreed, feeling rather swept away by his decisive manner.

18

So this was what it was like to be acquainted with one of the young lions of the City. She found it rather intriguing.

Jo wasn't particularly interested in clothes. But it so happened that she had a little array of after-six dresses. She often had to attend award ceremonies, college reunions, events of that sort.

So on the evening of the dinner engagement she stood in doubt before her wardrobe. Which one should she wear? The weather was hot, even now at six o'clock. It was summer, which seemed to call for a pale colour, and certainly something opaque so that she could wear as little as possible underneath.

She turned her head away, reached in a hand, and came out with a hanger on which was suspended a shift of ivory silk. Well done, she thought. She had sandals to match.

A thorough hair brush, cooling cleansing lotion rubbed into face, neck and arms, lipstick, eye shadow applied, and she was ready.

The car that arrived for her was a sleek maroon Chrysler. A uniformed chauffeur had the door open for her when she went out. She had to get in the back, which seemed rather lordly, so she engaged him in conversation through the gap in the partition. It turned out it was a special hire car service.

'All our vehicles are maroon and foreign made,' he said. 'Gives it a bit of class, you see.'

He was round opening the door for her when they arrived at their destination. It was a skyscraper building of very modern design on the edge of the City. A hall porter hurried out from the vestibule to escort her in and to the lift. She took a bet with herself that he'd press the button for the penthouse, and was proved correct.

'I'll let Mr Digby know you're on your way,' he said, and began speaking, presumably into some unseen mobile, as she ascended.

'Hi!' cried Ivan, and Miri echoed the greeting with something of a smile on her lovely features. 'How nice you look. Doesn't she, baby?'

'Yes, very nice,' she said without enthusiasm. She herself had no inhibitions about her see-through dress. Under pale pink floral chiffon gleamed a minuscule silk bra and bikini pants. Ivan was in black dress trousers and a loose shirt with a somewhat Chinese collar – casual but very smart. In fact, they were a handsome pair, and knew it.

The flat was huge. Jo was led across the landing from the lift and straight into a living room with windows all around, shaded a little against the evening sun by reed blinds. Beyond an arch was

19

the dining room, but they went through that too, and came out onto the terrace, which had a tiled floor and a green awning under which a round dining table was set for three with sparkling crystal, silver, and tiny candles down the centre.

A servant was waiting to offer cocktails. Icy cold, of course. The servant drew out chairs. Jo had been placed so as to get a view of London under an umber sunset. Ivan was at her left, Miri at her right.

'What do you think of my gaff?' he asked.

'Not bad. Here's to it.' She sipped her Sidecar.

'Yes, I must say I'm pleased with it. And, of course, once the country place is sorted out, we'll have a weekend retreat.'

'But, from the sound of it, I got the impression it's the sort of place you'd want to live in.'

'No can do. Too far out of London.'

'But these days, can't you do all that forward bidding and stuff by computer?'

'Oh, so you know about arbitrage, eh?'

'I saw the film with Michael Douglas in the red braces.'

He laughed. 'Well, I don't wear red braces and yes, I do use a computer from home sometimes. But Miri can't go to rehearsals by computer, you see.'

'Oh, I'm sorry, I rather thought you might not want to carry on with the TV show.' This was to Miri, who had been left out of the conversation so far.

'You've got a funny idea of what showbiz is like,' she scoffed. 'If I give up that quiz show I fade out of sight forever as far as getting anywhere with my career.'

'What would you really like to do?' Jo was aware that she'd blundered; she'd taken Miri's ambitions too lightly.

'Oh, I'd like to be in films,' she replied, lighting up at the thought. For the first time in the fifteen minutes since Jo arrived, some warmth came into her manner. 'A lovely light romantic thing, like *Sleepless in Seattle*. Or something set in a glamorous place like Paris or Miami.'

'You might have to go to Hollywood for that,' Jo remarked.

'Not at all,' Ivan said quickly. 'We've got some great film-makers here. It all depends on getting something that would really work. And of course that would be for the future – at the moment we've got our hands full with the castle and the wedding.'

From what followed, she got the impression that Ivan had perhaps made some inquiries among film producers and found that though he had money and was perhaps willing to back a production, the choice of actors would not be up to him.

It seemed to her that Miri wasn't entirely comfortable with this discussion, so she asked about progress at the castle. This brought forth a spate of enthusiastic information that lasted through until dessert. Ivan then suggested they move inside.

'It's still nice out here at night,' he explained, 'but you get moths blundering into you, and Miri hates that, don't you, love.'

He left them to the care of his manservant, who was serving coffee. He hurried off to get photographs of the castle. Jo then saw that the castle was in reality a turreted house much improved by the Victorians, the kind of place that Betjeman would have loved as a specimen of architecture. Its name was Chembard, and by the look of it, was costing at least a million to restore.

She wondered what Lindora would have said if she'd seen these pictures. It would have given her hysterics to think that Jo had nearly turned this pair away. And when she came to think of it, Jo herself felt she'd been lucky not to lose them entirely.

Nothing was said about jewellery during the rest of the evening. Ivan talked about the City, Miri talked in a jokey way about her role in the quiz programme. It was clear to Jo that Miri didn't really enjoy her part. And when Ivan was called away to the telephone, she ventured to say something to that effect.

'It's not really what you want to do, is it?'

'Well, it's not what I wanted when I came to London,' Miri agreed. 'I auditioned for a lot of stuff, but you see, I hadn't been to *drama school*.' This was said with something of a sneer. 'I couldn't talk posh, and they didn't want me for the character stuff like in one of the soaps, because they said I'd "unbalance" the cast. Dunno what they meant by that, really. Ive says it means that everybody would've been watching me instead of the main characters, but he meant because I'd be better looking than the rest, and he's not really a good judge on that point, now is he?'

'Probably he was right, though.'

Miri accepted the compliment she'd expected. 'So you see, that was why I fell in with this plan of his – he wants to live in his castle and be the lord of the manor, and I'm to be the lady of the manor, so I'm getting lessons at a sort of finishing school in Hampstead – how to shake hands properly and sit gracefully and talk the la-di-da.'

Jo was struck dumb. She raised her eyebrows. Miri gave a subdued chuckle.

'Yeh, it's a bit of a bind, but if it helps me get a decent part in something, that's OK. And of course, it's true, isn't it, if we're gonna live in the castle, it would be nice to fit in with the "county set". Ive's really keen on that. Take part in local charities, mebbe become a magistrate ... To tell you the truth, I sort of think he sees himself with a title by the time he's fifty.' She paused. 'Sir Ivan Digby. Sounds all right, doesn't it.'

Jo laughed. 'Has he got his entire life planned out?'

'You bet! He isn't exactly a control freak, but Ive likes to know what's gonna happen tomorrow and the next day, and preferably the next year.'

The long-term planner himself returned at this moment, to call for fresh coffee to replace his cold cup. Conversation turned to the work at Chembard, the planning of its garden, and then Jo murmured that she ought to be getting home.

'I'll call for the car,' Ivan said.

'No, no, I can get the Tube—'

'Nonsense, he'll be here in ten minutes.' He went to his office to make the call. He seemed to like repairing to that part of the flat, his kingdom, where he studied the markets and held video conferences with the world.

Miri said, 'He's asked me to fix up getting together with you – you know, just us girls. What I thought was, if you want to get some idea of what I like and what I don't like, we could have a session about clothes. What do you think?'

For a moment Jo was taken aback, yet it was an opening. 'That sounds a good idea.'

'So, like, when?'

'When are you at the television studio – is it every evening while the series is on?'

Miri laughed. 'Good Lord, no! You don't think we go there every night and send it out live? No, no, we record it in batches of ten or twelve, filming all day for about a week or ten days. You have to edit out all the idiot bits and when the competitors dry up – they do that a lot, you know. And the editors see to it that all the music bits and the important "jingle of the coins in the purse" is recorded in, and all that. No, I'm quite free for the next couple of weeks, until we do another set of recording.'

Jo was taken aback. 'Oh ... In that case ... Well, I usually work

22

in the mornings, from about, say, eight, until perhaps noon – well, a break for lunch, let's put it that way. Then in the afternoons, I sometimes sketch or visit art galleries for ideas, but it's flexible. And evenings, of course, I'm free mostly.'

'Not evenings, if you don't mind. Ive likes us just to hang out together in the evenings, or we're going to some big thing like a first night or a gala. Let's say an afternoon, then. Not tomorrow, I've got to be in Hampstead. Thursday?'

'That would be fine.'

'I'll give you lunch, eh? Nothing fattening!'

'Right.'

Ivan returned to say the car was on its way. His glance to Miri told Jo that he'd left them alone to make their date. At Miri's nod, he smiled in satisfaction. They said their farewells.

As she went down in the lift, Jo reflected that she'd spent one of the most remarkable evenings in her life.

The strange thing was that she was feeling rather sorry for Miri Gale.

Three

The girl-talk session proved very interesting. First of all, the bedroom suite – it had to be called a suite, it extended to almost the same extent as the vast living room – was gorgeous. Miri had a walk-in wardrobe with clothes in plastic protectors neatly ranged along three walls, headgear on shelves above, and shoes in cabinets beneath.

'Ivan insisted that I had the proper clothes,' the owner explained in a somewhat apologetic tone. 'And, of course it's great. I'm a bit of a fashionista. But, you know, until I met him, I used to get all my clothes off the peg – and sometimes from discount outlets at that. It's taken a while for me to get used to having things designed for me.'

'By Desmond.'

'Yes, do you know him? He's up and coming, going to be a big name one day. As a matter of fact . . .' She hesitated. 'Ive did a deal with him about the wedding dress. It'll get a lot of publicity and really put him on the map.'

Jo busied herself with taking hangers off the rail and looking at them. The idea of turning your wedding day into financial profit was foreign to her, and not very appealing.

'Do you have a hat designer too?' she asked in a teasing tone.

'Nah! Hardly ever wear hats. I got one for going to the races, and another one for going to other people's weddings. But what I like is little ornaments. Look . . .' She pulled a box off the shelf, opened it, and inside was a little headband of pink sequins with a cabbage rose at one end.

Jo exclaimed in delight, and Miri put it on. 'Lets my hair show,' she explained. 'My hair's one of my assets. Genuine blonde, me.' She took a smaller box out of the first one. 'See, there's a necklet that goes with it – lets the rose settle in just the right spot.'

The necklet was made of sequins on a band of net, with a smaller matching satin rose at the centre. Miri held it round her neck. It looked pretty, fragile, vulnerable.

So why couldn't she accept my ruby design? Jo asked herself.

''Course, this is just for evenings. I got other things for day wear.' She studied Jo for a moment then said, 'See, I've got to use my asssets. While I still have them, I mean! I'm pretty, everybody thinks so. I've got good legs and great boobs. My hair's the right colour. So when Ive gave me a bank account of my own to buy things, I went for whatever draws attention to my good points.'

'That makes sense.'

'My drawbacks are, I didn't get much of an education. I know my voice isn't going to win any prizes and I don't talk elegant. So, Ive is helping me pull myself up in that department.'

'Do you enjoy that?'

'Well, hardly!' she replied with irritation. 'But Ive's right. He's got this outlook, onward and upwards, and he doesn't want a wife that'd be a drawback, now does he?'

It sounded a bit like a Pygmalion project. Take the girl from the back streets, groom her and marry her. Jo sighed inwardly. She was beginning to understand that Miri was a complex character. She had ambitions to be a serious actress, had used her physical beauty to establish herself, but was now doubting whether she'd taken the right path.

What was her relationship with the money-making whizz-kid? Did she love him?

Jo had no doubt that Ivan loved Miri. Exactly what that term might mean to him, she wasn't sure. He gloried in her loveliness, enjoyed playing the prince that wakes the sleeping beauty, and wanted her to be a success in the acting profession. How much of this was interest and care in her well-being and how much was for his own satisfaction?

There was no way of knowing.

They spent an hour taking out clothes, studying them, hanging them round the bedroom to get an overall impression. Miri's shoes were interesting too. She loved high heels and open-cut uppers, all of them by designers of distinction. True, she also owned tennis shoes and trainers, but these were for sessions at the gym. It appeared that Miri almost never wore flats.

Hang it all, thought Jo, she loves daintiness. Why can't she see that her jewellery should have the same fragility?

They broke for lunch. It was set out on the terrace, a salad as

25

beautiful as a collection of gems and served with a chilled white wine.

Ivan appeared when they reached the coffee stage. It seemed his day's work was over.

'Oh, yeah, I'm up and out before six most mornings,' he explained. 'I like to be on the spot when the Far East exchanges get into action.' He dropped a kiss on Miri's head. 'So, how's it going? Had everything out of the wardrobe, have you?'

'Not quite, but almost.' He was looking expectantly at Jo, and she understood she had to praise the clothes. 'I'm no judge, really, but Miri has some lovely things.'

'Right, right! No expense spared. I said to her at the outset, "Look, sugar, I want to see you always at your best, so use the money". And then I asked around and a friend recommended Desmond, and now she has her own personal designer, and I think you'll admit he's done well for her.'

'Yes indeed.'

Pleased to have his management approved, he smiled at Jo. She turned the conversation by asking about his morning's work.

'Aw, you don't want to worry your head about that, Jo. The money's always going to be rolling in, you can be pretty sure of that.' The servant brought fresh coffee, poured for Ivan, and bowed himself out. Ivan went on in an expansive tone, 'I take the world view, you know. I want to be on top for as long as I can, and watching the international scene is the only way to do that. By and by, who knows, I may decide to turn my attention elsewhere. Not politics, I know there's a lot of control and influence in politics, but there are other areas. Think tanks, economic consultancy, that sort of thing . . .'

He had lost Jo. Miri too, by the looks of it. Miri was fiddling with her hair and clearly thinking about something else. But Ivan seemed unaware that he'd lost his audience.

Jo felt a little pang of concern for him. He'd been successful so young, had this extraordinary talent for making money. But did that inevitably mean that he would be able to go on to positions of influence when he changed course? It struck her as putting him on a par with Miri: both had ambitions that might not be fulfilled.

Before she left, Ivan encouraged them to make another appointment. 'Can't do tomorrow, I've got to go to my gym in the morning and my class in the afternoon,' protested Miri.

'Well, how about one day next week?' Jo ventured.

'No, wait,' Ivan interjected. 'Listen, Jo, I know it's short notice – but could you make it down to Chembard this weekend?'

'Oh. Well . . .'

'It's OK, you wouldn't have to live on a building site! We stay in a country hotel a couple of miles off – sort of a stately home, but it's quite good. What do you say?'

She had work on hand, but could dedicate all the next day to clearing it up. To tell the truth, to get out to the coolness and fresh air of the country seemed very inviting.

When Lindora heard her news she was envious. 'Goodness, wouldn't I just love to spend a weekend with them! Meeting them over breakfast for a couple of mornings . . . You get to know them pretty well that way.'

'Well, that's the idea, of course.'

There followed a long session of queries from Lindora about Miri's way of life, the contents of her wardrobe, what she liked to eat and drink. There wasn't the slightest doubt that her sister-in-law would have loved to be in Jo's shoes for the forthcoming weekend.

It was still mid-afternoon. Jo decided to put into action a thought she'd had. She had details of the former owner of the Fieldingley Rubies from the caption stuck to the back of the photographs Ivan had supplied. Mrs Fieldingley lived in Shropshire. An address was given, so by ringing Directory Inquiries she got the number to telephone.

The number rang for quite a while. She was on the verge of putting down the receiver when it was picked up. 'Hello?' said a rather breathless male voice.

'Oh. I thought you weren't going to answer . . .'

'Sorry, I was up in the attic doing some of the packing. Who's this?'

'My name's Jo Radcliffe. I design jewellery. I've been asked by the purchaser of the Fieldingley Rubies to re-set them and I was wondering if Mrs Fieldingley had any photographs of them from the past – being worn, I mean. May I speak to Mrs Fieldingley?'

There was a slight pause while the listener made sense of this. 'You're who?'

'Jo Radcliffe. If you have any doubts about me, you can ring Ivan Digby —'

'Oh, him.'

She heard the disapproval in his voice. But of course, that was

27

understandable. A famous heirloom, parted with, most likely, for reasons of financial distress – it was only natural the family should resent him.

To avert any animosity she asked in business-like tones, 'May I ask to whom I'm speaking?'

'To whom you're speaking!' There was a chuckle. 'This "whom" is Betsey Fieldingley's grandson, Timothy Fieldingley. Grans is out at the moment, talking to the estate agent as it happens. What was it again you wanted?'

'I was hoping to get hold of some photographs of the ruby necklace being worn by the ladies of the family in the past.'

'And why on earth should you want that?'

'Well . . . It's a rather intimidating piece. Rather like the sort of jewellery the king wears in a Shakespearian production, you know?'

'It is? Well, if you say so, it is, I suppose. I've never seen the thing.'

'Never seen it?'

'No, it's been in a strongbox in a bank for years. I believe Grans said the last time the necklace had been out was sometime before World War Two – 1937, 1938 – for some posh society affair, I suppose.'

'I see.' Jo wasn't altogether surprised. It was her experience that quite often owners of very valuable or historic pieces kept them in safe keeping of that kind. 'What was the posh affair, do you know? Was it the kind of thing that would attract press photographers?'

'Um . . . I seem to remember some tale about Paris . . . A World Fair? Something like that. Grans said the necklace was brought out to that . . . I think it was one of her aunts — Aunt Norah, was it?'

'Yes?'

'The whole idea was so that she could catch a husband, as I understand it. Oh, you don't want to hear all this. The point is, I imagine she wore it to big social gatherings in Paris and I'm pretty sure there are photographs, though I can't say I've ever seen them.'

'Do you think you could find them? Would it be a lot of trouble to find them?'

'You couldn't have asked at a better time,' he said with a chuckle. 'We're packing up to go, so I've been up in the attic bringing down all the stuff that collects there.'

'You're going?'

'Not me, Grans. She's going into . . . you know . . . sheltered accommodation.' She heard a sigh. 'It's not what she really wants,

28

of course – been independent all her life, carted her painting gear all over the world. But she's got a heart condition now, and you know, Shropshire . . . This cottage is a long way from anywhere . . . Good Lord, what's the matter with me, you don't want to hear all that either.'

'It's all right,' she assured him. 'I'm really interested. Your grandmother is a painter?'

'Well, you wouldn't know her, unless you're interested in plants. That's what she paints – plants and flowers. Quite famous at one time, in her way. But she's been ill for a bit, and . . . There I go again! Jabber, jabber, jabber. It's being up in the attic, makes you sentimental. So OK, I'll sort out which of the albums have got Aunt Norah in them and I'll let you have the photographs. Can't think anybody else would want them!'

'Oh, that would be great. I think it would be a big help to me. I hope it's not a lot of trouble . . .'

'I just put about five of them into a black sack so as to bring them downstairs. Let me have a day or so, and when Grans is safely moved to her new home I'll send you whatever I find with jewellery in them. What's the address?'

'Have you got a pencil?' She dictated slowly, and heard him repeat it as he wrote it. 'I'll pay for the postage, of course, and let you have the photos back.'

'OK, right, I'll see what I can do. Bye.'

The weekend in the country was a great pleasure. The hotel was a beautiful Georgian building with parkland around it. There was a riding stable, there was a big conservatory-type extension housing a pool and a sort of miniature oasis. Outside in the park there was a lake where swans drifted about in a disdainful glide.

But Ivan was determined to spend as much of their time as possible at Chembard. The house was about four miles from the hotel, on a par with it for size though not as elegant, to Jo's mind. However Ivan loved its turrets and steeples. He escorted her inside, Miri bringing up the rear and all of them looking comical in hard hats.

Of course, the place was going to be marvellous when all the improvements were done. Jo listened to Ivan's descriptions and looked at the builder's plans, trying to envisage it all. At one moment, when she glanced at Miri, she saw her staring around with what looked like a mixture of pleasure and resignation.

29

Perhaps she doesn't really want to live here, Jo thought to herself, and experienced once again an unexpected throb of pity.

Back at work on Monday, she sketched out a few ideas that had come to her over the weekend. Then she turned to things in the workshop that she needed to complete for other clients. She was in a little struggle with a recalcitrant curl of eighteen-carat gold when Lindora came in.

'There's a messenger at the outside door saying he's got some photographs for you.'

'Sorry?' Hearing impeded by the bandanna that kept her hair out of her eyes, she failed to catch the words.

'A man. Not in a uniform or anything, but carrying a big envelope. He says you rang about some photographs.'

'Oh – not a messenger! Probably Mr Fieldingley – yes, let him in, I'll be in the studio in a moment.'

Lindora was turning away when she paused. 'Fieldingley? Some relation to the rubies?'

'Same family. Go on, Linda, don't leave him hanging about outside on the doorstep.'

She detached herself from her soldering iron and switched it off. On entering the studio, she saw a tall, rather shabby-looking man hesitating just inside the outer door and looking about him with surprise.

'Mr Fieldingley?'

He looked relieved at hearing his name spoken in welcoming tones.

'Yes, I thought that since I was coming to London anyway I might as well deliver this stuff. Here you are.' He held out a large manila envelope. 'When I had time over the weekend I glanced through the photograph albums from the attic. Grans kept all this stuff but nobody's ever looked at it. Some person in the distant past must have put the albums together and they've just been forgotten.'

'I hope you didn't tear things out of family albums . . .?'

'No, no, there were duplicates of these. You see, Aunt Norah and the World Fair in Paris were apparently quite important so they got copies of all the press pictures – you know how families are, copies were sent to every relative so as to boast how well she'd done. I gather she found herself the required husband.'

'Oh, I see.' Jo laughed. 'Please sit down. Can I offer you something? Iced tea, chilled wine – it's still so hot outdoors, isn't it.' She was sending a glance of reproof at Lindora as she said this.

30

Their guest should have been sitting and at ease by the time Jo got to the studio.

However, Lindora probably didn't think he was worth the trouble. His clothes seemed very well-worn. In fact, they looked as if they might have been slept in. A deep tan covered what might have been a fair skin. There were wrinkles around the dark grey eyes; Jo thought he'd weathered many a storm in his life.

He accepted iced tea. She said, teasingly, 'Is this an interval of tranquillity in the midst of the removal?'

'In a way. But I had to come into town today; I've got to firm up a deal for next year to go to South America.'

'Really? On business?'

'I'm a photographer. I specialize in technical stuff – constructions in water such as oil rigs and jetties and harbour installations.'

'Good heavens!' That accounted for the weather-beaten look. 'And you're off by and by to some romantic spot in South America . . .'

'Patagonia,' he laughed. 'There's nothing very romantic about Patagonia, and I'll be off-shore taking pictures of barnacles and weevils.'

Jo was totally taken aback. 'I've never heard of anything like that. It sounds awful.'

'It's a difficult job but *somebody's* got to do it,' he said, imaginary quotes in his voice as if he were the hero of some action film. 'No, really, it's very interesting and it gives me the chance to see a bit of the world. I suppose I inherited some of that from Grans.'

'I think you mentioned on the telephone that Mrs Fieldingley travelled a lot. Plants and flowers, wasn't it?'

'Yes, in jungles and on mountain tops – all over. If you were a botanist you might know her name. Famous in her way, but that kind of work doesn't make you rich. Hence letting the rubies go.'

'I see. What a shame.'

'Oh, not to Grans. She's not bothered about jewellery and that sort of stuff. Tell the truth, I think she'd forgotten she owned the confounded things, stuck in a strongbox somewhere.' He sipped his drink, shaking his head. 'But they're buying her a nice safe place to live now, so I mustn't just shrug them off as if they aren't important. And you're going to alter them so they look nice?'

She pretended to be offended. 'Look nice? Mr Fieldingley, please moderate your language! No member of the arts ever likes to think he or she makes anything look "nice".'

'I apologize. You're going to make them look as if they belong in the twenty-first century, that's it, isn't it. Well, good luck. From what I saw in these photographs, the necklace is a real old clunker – but of course, that's in black and white. I expect the rubies look better in real life. Do they?'

Jo gave a little shrug. 'You know, I haven't actually seen them yet. Ivan had colour photographs, and I know them by reputation as being perfectly matched, but I don't get to handle them until Ivan and his fiancée agree my design.'

There was a moment of silence. Then he said, 'Well, I hope they won't be difficult with you about it. They were a bit of a pain in the neck to poor old Grans – tried to beat her down rather unfairly on the price. This chap Ivan – he's got a reputation for being keen on money, hasn't he?'

'He has,' she agreed. 'If you read the financial columns, you see his name and I gather he's a very successful figure.'

'Good for him. Not my kind of thing.' He swallowed the last of his tea and stood up. 'Well, off I go to fix up about Patagonia. Nice to have met you, I hope the pics are some help.'

'Thank you for bringing them in person. I hope Patagonia provides you with a lot of beetles and worms.'

She let him out. As she closed the door on him her sister-in-law said, 'Well, really, why did you waste so much time on a man like that? I could have just taken the packet from him.'

'But I spoke to him on the phone and he sounded nice.'

'From what he was saying, it looks like the family hasn't got two pennies to rub together. No wonder they had to sell their heritage!'

Jo let it go. She took the photographs into the workshop to study under a good working light. But there was little to learn from them. They showed a not unattractive girl in a long light-coloured gown of what looked like taffeta, flared skirt decked with frills at the hem. A low square neckline revealed a slender neck and around it the ruby-and-gold necklace, which hung down over her demurely clothed bosom in an unspectacular way.

There were two other photographs taken at the same event. One showed her stooping to enter a taxi, and the necklace was seen parted from her dress, almost in profile. In the last photograph Aunt Norah was shown in a box at a theatre, wearing a more revealing dress with thin straps at the shoulders. The necklace was clearer but still without appeal as far as Jo was concerned.

32

The last item in the envelope was not a photograph but a small watercolour – what looked like a preliminary sketch. It showed a long, slender spray of reddish-brown flowers tipped with yellow, with two larger leaves drawn in pencil alongside. A scribble at the foot of the paper named the flower: '*Thunbergia mysorensis*, April 3, 1976. Nilgiri Hills, Doda Betta, India'.

Attached by a paper clip was a slip with the words: 'Thought you'd like to see the kind of thing Grans used to get up to. Yrs, Tim F'.

Jo recognized talent when she saw it. The authority of the work was convincing: it told her that this was what the flower looked like growing in its environment. The charm and delicacy were perhaps unexpected in a scientific piece but they added to its appeal in every way.

A simple little preparatory sketch for a more finished picture.

Something in it seemed to speak to Jo personally. She picked up a pad and a pencil and began to sketch.

Something like that. Not the same, of course. But something of that grace and delicacy for Miri's rubies . . .

Four

Miri was pleased. She smiled a little then handed the sketch to Ivan. 'What d'you think, love?'

Ivan studied the fine pencil image. It showed a necklace of little irregular rectangles of gold, a ruby alternating with a small diamond at every third or fourth interval. Then on one side, about four inches from the midpoint, a spray of gems on tiny stalks was formed, very like the spray of flowers Betsey Fieldingley had sketched in the Nilgiri Hills.

The rubies represented the flowers, trembling – or it seemed that they trembled – on their stems. Among them like drops of dew were the remaining small diamonds. The lower point of the spray was curved so that it would rest on Miri's breast.

And yet no one could say that it was a representational piece. The gems weren't made to look like flowers as they might have been in the Victorian or Art Nouveau periods. The spray was simply a little shower of deep red jewels dotted with diamonds, suspended cleverly from one side of a chain of irregular links.

But it achieved what Miri wanted. It called attention to one of the 'good points' she'd listed.

'Well, it works for me,' cried Ivan. 'Should look great on you, sugar-babe! And no one else is going to have anything like it – at least, not at first but what d'you bet it starts a fashion?'

Miri gave him a smile of delight. 'You really think so?' The idea of being a leader was clearly bliss to this fashionista.

'When can we see something more? On the computer? Are you going to do a mock-up in semi-precious stones first?'

Jo shook her head. 'I'm not actually going to make this myself, Ivan. It's quite complicated and delicate, and though I'm not a bad workman, I'd rather it was in the hands of a maker with more equipment than I have.'

'Oh, but—'

34

'I'll hand it over to Hechman's. They've made up some of my designs in the past—'

'But I thought . . .'

'You thought I'd do it here in my workshop. No, it needs tools I don't possess, but I assure you I'll supervize every stage of the process. Really, I mean it, you can have every confidence in Hechman's handling of the design. I'll work it up on computer beforehand with every specification noted and checked.'

'Oh . . . well . . . You really can't do it yourself?'

'I'm afraid not, Ivan. Does that mean you don't want the design?'

'No, no, I think the design is great. No, of course not, Miri and I love it, don't we, dear?'

Miri nodded, though she was pouting at the idea of not having the work done by hand in Jo's little workroom. When Desmond designed for her, the clothes were made on his premises – or so she was led to believe. But Ivan was hugging her and assuring her it would all come out well, so she gave Jo a nod of agreement and it was settled.

'Now, there's one thing I have to mention,' Jo said. This was a big point, hitherto unexamined. 'I'll need to have the rubies first, because they have to be examined and taken out of their setting.'

'Examined? What for?'

'Oh, just to ensure there are no little flaws—'

'Flaws?'

She shook her head at him. 'It's just a check-up before we start undoing the claws that hold the stones into the gold backing. I'll want them set in a different way, so that the light will shine through them and give them more of a glow.' She could tell he was somewhat at a loss, so she went on, 'You knew, of course, that the stones were going to be removed from their original housing – but before we do that we just want to look at them and make sure we won't harm them in any way.'

'We-ell . . . yes . . . Of course I wanted them taken off that terrible chain.'

'And made to look more modern, so we have to take them individually out of their setting one by one, to look at them in a new way. And of course give them a little clean-up, if that's necessary.'

'Yes, OK, of course, I see that. Yes, right, what you're saying is you want me to get the necklace out of the bank.'

'Yes, please.'

Miri clapped her hands. 'Great, super! I'm going to get to see them in the flesh! Well, no, I don't mean that . . .'

'You haven't seen them?'

'No, only the photos, and to tell the truth I didn't think much of them because they looked so old-fashioned. But a necklace worth all that money, for real . . . It'll be a thrill to actually handle it!'

Jo chuckled. 'I'm rather looking forward to that myself,' she acknowledged.

'Would you like to come to the bank and see them released from their imprisonment?' Ivan quipped. 'They've only seen the light of day once, when I had them transported from the Fieldingleys' bank to my own – and even then they were carried by a security firm.'

'You didn't even look at them?' Jo asked, astonished.

'Oh yes, two seconds before I put them in the strongbox. They're not much to look at, you know – dead boring.'

They were on the terrace with after-lunch coffee. Ivan used his mobile to call the bank. After some pauses and discussions it was arranged for them to go to take out the rubies on the afternoon of the following day.

That was a day of thick cloud. The long reign of high summer was coming to an end at last and much-needed rain was beginning to fall. Everything seemed turned to a cool grey: buildings, pavements, the sky. Inside the bank, it seemed even darker although lights glowed where they were needed.

Ivan was met by an under-manager, greeted with respectful eagerness, and his party were invited to sign themselves in. Miri and Jo had to provide proof of identity. They were then conducted to the lift for the basement and led into a large room whose steel door stood open.

Inside was a young woman who checked their identities, even that of Ivan. Miri and Jo were invited to wait sitting at a table in a partitioned cubicle while Ivan went with her to unlock the door of his strongbox.

'Gee,' muttered Miri, 'it's like trying to get a look at the Crown Jewels!'

'I've done this before with other clients. It's a bit scary, isn't it?'

In a moment, Ivan appeared with the custodian carrying his strongbox. She laid it on the table. 'Is there anything else?' she asked in her soft, polite tone.

'Not for the moment.'

36

'Please press the buzzer when you're ready, sir.'

'Thank you.'

He unlocked the box and lifted the lid. He pushed two or three other items aside until he brought out a flat velvet case. He closed the lid of the strongbox. Into Miri's hands he delivered the jewel case. She opened it with fumbling haste.

There they were – the Fieldingley Rubies. The necklace was laid out in a narrow double loop against grey velvet. In that display, the stones seemed rather huddled to Jo's eye, but to her their dark glow was compelling.

Miri picked the necklace out of the box and held it, doubled, against her neck. She was wearing a top of crocheted silk with straps across the shoulder. Against the peach-like tones of her tanned skin the rubies looked charming.

'Ohh . . .' She glanced about for a mirror. Understanding her wish, Jo took Miri's handbag, opened it to find a compact, and held it up so Miri could see herself in that tiny circle.

'Are they . . . I can't really see. Do they look good?'

'Well, on you, gorgeous,' breathed Ivan.

'Very rich and luscious,' Jo said with a laugh.

'Oh . . . Luscious?'

'Inviting. Delectable.'

'Honey, you look like a million dollars,' said Ivan. 'Even with the rubies kind of bunched up and in a mess, the whole effect is wonderful. I can't wait to see you wearing Jo's version.'

For a few more minutes Miri tried to see herself in the compact mirror. Then Jo said, 'Would you mind if I had a look, Miri?'

'Well, you're looking.'

'No, I mean can I have them? To examine?'

'Yeah, come on, treasure, let the expert have a look.'

Reluctantly Miri took her hands from around her neck to hand the jewels over to Jo. Jo took out her loupe, fixed it in her eye, then held the necklace close.

'Hey!' cried Miri in astonishment. 'That looks weird!'

'I'm just giving the stones the once-over. Neat setting, very expertly done. I'll tell Hechman he's going to have to give the work to one of his older people because it's not going to be easy to get them out. I wish the light in here was better . . .'

She was working her way along the chain. There was no clasp, the wearer simply slipped the necklace over her head. But it was clear which was the back and which the front, because the little diamonds at the back weren't of such a perfect brilliance as those at the front. The rubies, on the other hand, all seemed very fine.

Ivan and Miri watched her in fascination. 'Would you like me to ask them to bring a lamp?' Ivan inquired.

'That would help.' She looked up. 'Sometimes we take stones out into the daylight to look at them but since it's pouring with rain out there, that's out of the question.'

Ivan pressed the buzzer. The woman custodian appeared. When it was explained that the lighting in the vaults was unsuitable, she said, 'If you would like to take the jewellery upstairs to one of our conference rooms, that can be arranged. There is daylight coming in on the first floor.'

Ivan closed up his box, was escorted with it back to the strong-room. Meanwhile arrangements were made for an empty room upstairs. Ten minutes later they were all three grouped at a window with the necklace in Jo's hands.

'Oh, look,' cried Miri. 'A decent mirror!'

There was indeed an ornate gilded mirror at one end of the room. She took the necklace from Jo and hurried to look at herself again.

'I'm sorry,' Ivan apologized with a little smile. 'The rubies mean a lot to her, you know.'

'Of course.'

'And when we hand them over to you, she won't see them again for quite a while, now will she?'

She nodded agreement. 'I'll be giving the necklace to Ben for certification—'

'Certification?'

'Well, yes, they'll have to be insured before I can messenger them to Hechman's. You see, even if any insurance on them is still in existence, it'll be based on the original value. I mean, I understood from Tim Fieldingley that they hadn't been out of their bank vault since 1938.'

'I see. Of course they have to be re-insured. I should have thought of that myself. OK, they go to this colleague of yours who's – what? What does he do?'

'He's a scientist, specializing in precious stones. In other words, a gemmologist. It's just to verify that it's all right to be working with the stones, that there are no flaws or faults that might cause fractures. I can't see any through the loupe, but Ben's got proper equipment.'

Ivan nodded. 'Miri,' he called, 'come on, give it back, you're not going to wear it while it's like that so you might as well let Jo get started on the job. Come on, honey.'

Ivan summoned his car from the parking garage in the basement. For this occasion he had hired car and driver from his special limousine service, feeling that it would be good to have another man with them while they carried this precious package.

Ivan and Miri were dropped off at their apartment block, and Jo was driven on to Ben's laboratory, which was in Edgware. She handed the jewel case to him with a little bow of introduction. 'The Fieldingley Rubies,' she said, 'first out of Burma somewhere around the middle of the nineteenth century.'

'You mean Myanmar.'

'Of course I do. First out of Myanmar, and hardly ever seen since. Look after them, Ben.'

'They'll have tender love and care, I assure you.'

'When can I have an assessment? I need to let Ivan know since he'll have to contact his insurance firm.'

'I'll give it priority, then. Mind you, that means an increase in my fee!'

'You're a hard man, Ben Webber. Right, I'll hear from you soon, agreed?'

'Agreed.' They smiled at each other, exchanged little kisses on the cheek, and she went back to the hired limousine to be driven home.

Lindora was agog to hear details. 'What's it like in a bank's vaults? Is it spooky? Are you pleased with the rubies? I know you didn't want to bring them here, but what was it like to actually see them?'

'Anxiety-making, if you must know, Lindora. But I'm pleased, it means the stones will soon be at Hechman's being transformed.'

'And then you and Ivan Digby make a proper agreement about your fee for the design and everything?'

She nodded, already on her way through to the passage and upstairs. The thing she longed for most was a cup of tea. It was after five, the day had seemed long, and it was time to bring it to a tranquil end.

Tranquillity continued. Miri and Ivan went to Cheshire to inspect the building work on their mansion, Jo refined her sketch for the rubies, set it up on the computer, and worked out specifications.

Monday morning, Ben telephoned. 'Can I come and speak to you, Jo?'

'What?'

'Are you busy?'

'Well, I'm working, but it's not urgent. Why?'

'I'd like to have a chat.'

'About what?'

'The work I've been doing for you.'

'Oh, Ben! You've found a serious flaw?'

'Not on the phone, Jo.'

She found she was breathless. She got a grip on herself and said, 'Come right away!'

He arrived an hour later, an hour she spent wondering if it made any difference that one of the stones was imperfect. Thirty-nine rubies instead of forty – did it really matter? Some little alterations to her design, that was all. A day or two's work on her part.

Ben had documents in an envelope, reports and graphs. He held them out. She said, 'Just tell me – one stone or more than one?'

'Sit down,' he said.

'What?'

'Sit down. This is going to be a shock.'

'Ben, for the love of Mike, *tell me!*'

He smiled at her with sympathy, shaking his head.

'All the Fieldingley Rubies are phoney,' he said.

Five

He'd said it would be a shock. That was an understatement. Jo felt as if the world around her had disappeared. Sound ceased. The workshop was dim.

Inside her own head she heard the words, That isn't possible. She said them aloud. 'That isn't possible.'

'It's true, Jo.'

Now she could hear Ben's voice. Her vision cleared. 'No, you're wrong, Ben, those rubies are an heirloom, they've been in the Fieldingley family for over a century.'

'So we're told, and in fact the gold has the initials of the maker engraved in tiny letters, so the setting at least is a century old. But the rubies are synthetic.'

He held out the documents he had brought, reports and graphs from his laboratory. 'I put them under the microscope – at first just one, in profile, to get an idea of what magnification to use. Of course I didn't touch the setting, which by the way is very good, the workmanship is excellent. I used a padded clamp and put the stone in profile under the glass – and the flaws were clear at once.'

'It's *impossible*! We know the stones came from Myanmar and that's one of the best—'

'The stones didn't come from Myanmar. They were made in a factory.' His tone was kind but very firm. 'I looked at them one by one. The diamonds are all right, the colour of some of them isn't the best quality, but they're good enough for their purpose. The gold is good too. It's the rubies that are phoney, every one of them.'

'That means that someone must have got at the necklace . . .'

'The problem with that idea is, the settings look untouched. I mean to say, Jo, nobody has prised the original stones out and replaced them.'

'I don't get your meaning, Ben. They're man-made?'

'Yes.'

'But you can't see any signs of tampering?'

41

'No.'

'But . . . but . . . The Fieldingleys bought the necklace some time in the eighteen-nineties. It hasn't been worn much. They took it out of the bank. The grandson, Tim Fieldingley – he was telling me it was taken out in 1938 when a great-aunt or somebody went to Paris for some important event. I've got photographs – black and white – of the girl wearing the rubies.'

'And so what follows? The necklace was in the Fieldingleys' bank. Are you saying that someone on the staff of the bank did something to the necklace in 1938?'

'Yes – no – what I'm saying is the Fieldingleys must have looked at the necklace and if it had been tampered with they'd have . . .' She let the thought die. 'No, you said there were no signs of that. And I looked, when we were at Ivan's bank the other day – just with a loupe, of course, but . . . but . . . everything looked perfect, the rubies and everything, I was perfectly happy with things.'

'A jeweller's loupe isn't good enough unless the light's perfect. Where were you?'

'In a conference room, with daylight coming in.' She drew a deep, sighing breath. 'But it was a very dull day outside.'

He nodded in perfect understanding. 'Well, look, the graph from my sighting shows imperfections.' He pointed at little peaks on the diagram. 'Those are definitely signs of the melting of the oxide. Admit it, Jo. The stones are man-made.'

She was silent. She knew he was right. It was his role to examine and verify gemstones, and he'd found these to be fake.

After a long moment she said, 'Ivan Digby paid forty-five thousand pounds for that necklace. What am I going to tell him?'

Now it was Ben's turn to be at a loss. He pushed his documents about thoughtfully, then asked, 'Is he a type that understands physics?'

'I've no idea. Making money is what he's been good at.'

'We could show him the graphs . . .'

'I think he's only used to Stock Exchange graphs, Ben. Besides, how do they help? His rubies are fakes, yet we can't account for it. The necklace has hardly been out of the bank since it was made in the eighteen-nineties.'

There was a silence. Then Ben said somewhat abruptly, 'Let me go back and do some more work on it. Something seems to be knocking around in the back of my brain.'

'What, Ben? Can you see how the fraud was carried out?'

'Let me do some more tests and have a think. Give me twenty-four hours.'

He seemed almost in a hurry to go. She wondered if he'd thought of a different test that might prove the rubies to be real.

Jo had little experience with synthetic stones. She knew they existed – of course she knew that. Used in industry, in lasers and for things in the past such as the stylus for a record-player that played vinyl.

She almost never saw them but she felt she would have recognized them if only she had been more alert at the bank with Ivan and Miri. Yet why should she have suspected anything was wrong? These were stones in a necklace from a respectable family, held in respectable banks for decades, seldom worn, brought out now under every possible safeguard of security escorts and custodians.

She was completely mystified.

All day and most of the night she was trying to solve the puzzle. She longed to ring Ben to ask how things were going but knew better: if he were doing special tests, he didn't want to be disturbed.

He turned up in the morning before the outer door's security had been released. Jo had to open up for him. She could see he was eager to tell her his results, and was carrying a document case as if it held the title deeds to Fort Knox.

In her workshop they settled themselves at a table where she sometimes did pencil sketches. Ben said, 'Do you remember any of the history you were taught at college?'

'History? What history?'

'Of the making of jewellery.'

'Well, of course. The surge of creativity when Europe began to be very rich, and when precious stones became easier to find.'

'But do you remember any of the science? About when synthetic stones first came in?'

She shook her head in doubt. 'Well . . .'

'No, you don't. And to tell the truth it didn't chime any bells with me until you jogged my memory yesterday.' He held up a finger to demand her attention. 'Somewhere around 1890 a man called August Verneuil invented a method of making synthetic rubies. There had been lots of attempts before but Verneuil was probably the first to be successful.'

'Go on.'

'At that time there was no way of telling the difference between

43

natural stones and synthetic. Only much later, in the twentieth century, have we had the scientific instruments to detect the telltale signs.'

'Ye-es . . .'

'So what I'm saying is this. When the Fieldingley necklace was made, it was made *from the very outset* with synthetic stones. It's always had fake rubies in the settings. The gold and diamonds are genuine, the rubies have always been man-made.'

She drew in a deep, slow breath. Could that have happened? At length she said, 'So the Fieldingleys were swindled?'

'Yes. In a way, yes. Because, you see, Jo, the *makers* might have been sold false rubies. They had no way of knowing the difference so they never realized.'

'That can't be right. Can it? Are you saying August Verneuil was selling . . .?'

'Not at all. I wouldn't want to blacken his name. But what sort of security do you think they had in those days? Someone could easily have had access to the product. They could have matched the sale of the synthetics with a moment when there was talk about rubies being exported from Myanmar – I mean, from Burma, we have to keep the name straight for the period. It was newsworthy then, you must remember. Opening up the Far East to trade.'

'That could be. These new gems, coming out to Europe and the rest of the world, and everyone eager to wear them – like now, when people want to buy the latest fashions . . .'

'If some dealer put up a good yarn about having a friend who'd brought out the first rubies released by the king, keeping them for a few years, and now wanting to sell them – it'd be very tempting to someone who was making the fashionable antique styles.'

Jo nodded thoughtfully. 'You're making sense. So what we're saying is that there was never any false pretence on the part of the Fieldingleys – they've always believed the rubies to be genuine.'

'Yes.'

'But . . . but how am I going to convince Ivan Digby of that?'

'Well, I took a set of photographs using the digicam attached to my most powerful microscope.' He opened his briefcase.

There were four sheets of photographs, ten on each of two sheets showing a part of each ruby under great magnification. The other two sheets contained pictures of the diamonds and one picture of a gold rectangle showing the initials of the maker, Giacinto Mellillo.

'Look,' he ordered, pointing, 'you can see the striae in the interior layer. The colour is of course very good – the colour in synthetic rubies is always good. But those marks would never occur in natural stones. You agree, don't you?'

'Yes.'

'If you show these pictures to Digby, I think he'll have to accept that the rubies are synthetic.'

'But, Ben! He paid forty-five thousand for what we now know was only worth about two.'

'Well, that's not strictly true,' Ben replied, deciding to be didactic. 'When the synthesizing of jewels was very new, the sheer novelty of the idea gave the results some value – although of course nothing like the cost of real stones. Yet in 1890 these might have been worth a bit more than two thousand, and you have to add in the diamonds and the gold – they're still worth something even now.'

'But not forty-five thousand,' she groaned.

'I'm afraid not.'

'He'll kill me,' she said.

Ben looked shocked until he realized it was a joke. He thought about it. 'Would you like me to come with you when you tell him?'

'Would you?'

'Well, I could probably explain about the process of making rubies better than you could.'

'If he doesn't kill us before we get that far.'

He managed a smile, then suggested that she should arrange a meeting. 'When are you free?' she asked.

'Well, I'm free now, today . . . I didn't know what you'd want to do when I gave you the news.'

'You thought I'd faint and need tender loving care.'

'Always willing to provide that, Jo, if you'd only ask!'

She shrugged it off. This was no time to be thinking about reviving that old affair.

She rang Ivan on his mobile. He was clearly in his office. 'Oh . . . hello, Jo . . . Hold on.' A moment while he spoke to someone nearby. 'Yes, love, what's new?'

'I was wondering if I could come and have a chat with you.'

'Oh? No problem – when do you want to do it?'

'Well . . . when are you free?'

Another interruption from his workplace. Then he said, 'I'll be through here about eleven, eleven-thirty. Then I'm heading home. How about you come to the flat and we'll have a drink and maybe a spot of lunch?'

'Well, that would be . . . that would be great.' She expected to be thrown out before they even got to lunch. 'And Ivan, can I bring a friend with me?'

'Of course, why not? Anybody I know?'

'It's Ben Webber . . .'

'Oh, the guy who's giving my rubies the once-over? How's it going?'

'That's what we want to talk about.'

A voice on the perimeter of her hearing said something, and Ivan broke off to say to someone in his office, 'Well, look on the screen, follow the price until it gets – no, why should it? Just wait till it's where we want it. No, *you* deal with it.' To Jo he said, 'Sorry, we're involved in a big buy here. Bring your pal along, we'll have a chat then, OK?'

'Yes,' she said faintly.

Ben had listened to her side of the conversation. 'Are we fixed up?' he asked.

'We're to go to his flat. Is that OK?'

'Suits me.'

It was then about ten in the morning. They drove first to Ben's laboratory, where he got the Fieldingley necklace out of his safe. One of his assistants fixed it up under a powerful microscope so that Jo could see for herself the flaws in the stones.

It depressed her.

She directed Ben to Ivan's flat with a heart as heavy as lead. This was one of the worst things that had ever happened to her in her career as a designer and a handler of precious stones.

The hall porter recognized her at once. 'Ms Radcliffe, how are you. Mr Digby told me you'd be coming and asked me to bring you straight to him. This way.'

But he led, not towards the lift, but towards a big side door in the hall.

'Where are we going?' she asked in alarm.

'To the health club, madam. Mr Digby and Ms Gale are having a drink by the pool.'

'The pool? They've been swimming?'

'No, no, madam.' He gave a little laugh at her ignorance of the luxuries provided by this magnificent building. 'Mr Digby often lunches in the lunch-bar in the club, a very healthy diet lunch, you see. But at the moment I believe he and the lady are just having a drink.'

They were ushered into a reception area all paved in marble and with replicas of classical statues here and there. A young woman in elegant exercise gear was looking after a switchboard. She waved them on towards a great arch, beyond which was the pool – but it was an ornamental pool with a fountain and goldfish.

People were sitting at tables with drinks or what was probably the diet-lunch. Ivan rose from a table at the far side to wave to them. 'Come on, over here!' Miri didn't get up but smiled a welcome.

As they sat down the barman was already hurrying up. Clearly Mr Digby was a valued member of the club. 'What'll you have? Billy makes a good Manhattan, don't you, Billy?'

Ben asked for whisky, Jo settled for mineral water. She felt she was going to need a clear head.

'Been a busy morning for me,' Ivan said with a satisfied smile. 'Did well out of it, got to celebrate later.'

'We're going out to buy something to drive around in the country,' Miri supplied. 'A specialist dealer in Park Lane has an imported four-wheel-drive in sky blue.'

Jo acknowledged the information with hidden anxiety. Were they going to feel like celebrating when they heard her news?

'So you're the gemstones expert,' Ivan remarked, turning his attention to Ben. 'How're things coming along?'

'That's what we've come to speak to you about, Ivan,' Jo said. 'Ben has been examining the rubies, and I'm afraid we have bad news.'

'Bad news? What? Oh, listen, if one or two of them have those flaws you mentioned, Miri won't mind, really, will you sweetness? So long as they don't spoil the general effect – or we could buy in a couple of replacements, I suppose, if we had to.'

Jo looked to Ben. He began, with solemnity, '*All* the rubies have flaws, Mr Digby.'

'Oh, call me Ivan . . .' He broke off. 'What? What did you just say?'

'All the rubies in the necklace have serious defects, from the point of view of value. The fact of the matter is, they're not natural rubies – they're man-made.'

Ivan sat frowning, trying to take it in. Jo understood what he was feeling. The news had been as incomprehensible to her when she first heard it. So far, Miri, who wasn't really listening, hadn't taken in what Ben had just said.

After a pause that held the beginnings of anger, Ivan said, 'What are you saying? My rubies . . . There's something wrong with them?'

'They're not natural stones from a mine in Burma. They were made in a laboratory, probably in Paris.'

'They're . . . what? They're fakes?'

'Yes, in a way. They're rubies, but they're synthetic rubies.'

'Synthetic rubies. I don't get you. How can there be a synthetic ruby?'

'There are a lot of them about, Mr Digby. They're made now in large quantities for industrial use, and for less valuable jewellery, such as dress rings and—'

'Less valuable jewellery – wait – you're not making sense. Are you talking about the Fieldingley Rubies that were brought out of Burma after some war or other – I was told it was in the Victorian era. No, look, we're at cross purposes here. You've got my stones mixed up with someone else's!'

Both Jo and Ben were shaking their heads. Ivan stared at them, colour mounting under the tan on his cheeks.

'What is this? It's a shakedown, isn't it? What have you been up to?'

'It's a matter of scientific fact—'

'Listen, chum, don't think you can dazzle me with scientific nonsense! What are you trying to do – pass off a load of rubbish on to me instead of my rubies? You must think I was born at daybreak today!'

'No, Ivan,' Jo began, in a tone she hoped was calm and soothing, 'you have to believe us. The stones in the necklace are all imitation.'

'Not a chance! I've got the receipt from the original purchase. Forty matched rubies from Mogok in Burma.'

'Yes, that's what the receipt said, and it probably was thought to be true when it was written. But the fact is that the maker of the necklace – that's a man called Mellillo, or perhaps the owner of the firm where he worked – was perhaps misled.'

'Misled! Oh, that's an old trick, misleading the buyer! Do you think I don't see it a half a dozen times a week in my business? Come on, stop the game, I'm on to you!'

For the first time since the announcement of the poor quality of the stones, Miri spoke. Her voice was almost harsh. 'Don't let them get away with this, Ive! They're just a couple of crooks!'

'Right! But they've chosen the wrong victim this time.'

Ben cleared his throat loudly. 'Mr Digby, please watch what you're saying. I have a reputation to—'

'Where? In criminal records? Ha, you're on to a loser with me, Dumbo!'

'I was going to say, I have a reputation to protect,' Ben persisted. 'I've been an expert witness in court, I'm a consultant to most of the great jewellers.'

'Well, not after this, you won't be!'

Ben took a small address book out of his inner jacket pocket and held it out. 'You'll find the telephone number of Assistant Commissioner Purbright there – ring him at Scotland Yard.'

'Oh, and get some pal of yours waiting by the phone to tell me he's a cop.'

'Ring any police station and ask to be connected to Mr Purbright. Or I'll go with you to Scotland Yard and introduce you to the Assistant Commissioner personally.'

Ivan glared. Then he shifted in his chair, grimacing in perplexity.

'Jo has made jewellery for some very important people,' Ben went on, calm and measured. 'I think you'll find that one of the leaders of the Stock Exchange bought emerald earrings for his wife from her last year. Jo will give you his number. Ring him and ask if he thinks Jo Radcliffe is a confidence trickster.'

'But you're trying something on about the rubies,' Ivan insisted.

'No. It's very bad news, and we both expected to have a problem explaining it to you. But facts are facts. The rubies in the necklace were made by man, probably a man called August Verneuil, in or around 1890.'

'You actually know the name of the guy who carried out this swindle?'

Jo felt it time to take her part. 'No one can say Verneuil used his discovery for anything criminal. He wanted to make artificial rubies. There was a lot of scientific investigation into things like that. But try to think back to those days – what would security have been like at his laboratory? Probably anyone could have walked out with what might have been discarded pieces of crystal.'

Now that Ivan had calmed down enough to listen, Ben went through the details of his scientific processes. He produced the photographs. 'Look, you see these lines – they're striations, striae is the technical term. You never see those in natural stones.'

'And once the stones were cut and polished, no one in those days had the equipment to realize they were man-made,' Jo took it up. 'I did some inquiring last night, and there was a piece of jewellery going up for auction at one of the big sale rooms about ten years ago – but it was withdrawn because although it was made in 1894, the rubies were found to be made by flame fusion, Verneuil's process.'

'So you see, when the stones were bought and set, the maker probably thought they were genuine.' Ben was pointing to his photographs. 'If you look at the shot I took of the claw settings – see – you can see the faint marks of the instruments used for the original setting. There aren't any others. Those stones have never been disturbed since first they were settled there. The *only* time the settings have been touched was when the necklace was first made.'

Ivan said nothing. He sat staring at the pictures Ben had laid out on the table.

Miri began in a faltering voice, 'The rubies are rubbish?'

'Well . . .'

'If I wore the new necklace, I'd be wearing junk?'

Jo opened the jewel case, which she'd placed between them on the table. 'They're still lovely to look at, Miri. The colour is lovely.'

'But it's just costume jewellery,' she insisted. Her eyes filled with tears. She snatched up the jewel case and emptied its contents on the marble table. She shoved the necklace hard away from her in rejection. It skittered across the table-top and on to the floor.

'That's what I think of your marvellous wedding present!' she cried. 'You and all your big ideas! Can't even tell real stones from junk!' She leapt to her feet and stalked out.

'Miri!' wailed Ivan. 'Sweetheart, wait!'

But before he could get up and around the pool, his sweetheart was gone.

Six

Heads had been turning while the altercation went on. A waiter hurried up. He looked at the glass Miri had overturned and the necklace lying on the marble floor. He knelt and picked up the necklace, rather unceremoniously.

Jo took it from him quickly. After all, it was a work of art by a master jeweller, although not to her taste. She replaced it in the velvet case. The waiter mopped the spilt cocktail on the table, glancing from Jo to Ben with hidden interest.

Ben was still sitting at the table wondering what to do next.

'Let me have the necklace,' he suggested. 'If he'll let me split a bit off one of the stones I can put it under the electron microscope . . .'

'What would be the point, Ben? He understands now that they're not genuine rubies.'

'But historically speaking, it would be interesting to see if there are any differences between—'

At the point Ivan returned, looking hurt and angry. 'Walked straight out and hailed a passing taxi,' he groaned. 'She'll be in a sulk for days now.'

'I'm very sorry,' said Jo.

To the waiter, still hovering, Ivan said sharply, 'You – another Manhattan and be quick about it.'

Ben said, 'The stones are interesting in themselves, Mr Digby. They—'

'Not to me, they're not.' He stared gloomily at the grey velvet case lying on the table. 'They're really not real – I mean, genuine?'

'They're genuine synthetic rubies. They're not natural stones.'

'And worth what – a couple of quid?'

'Oh, more than that,' Jo said, shocked. 'The necklace has value because it's a piece by Mellillo. The diamonds are all right, the gold is European, but it's good quality because the firm where it was made produced excellent work.'

'But the *Fieldingley Rubies* . . .' Ivan said the words as if they held a magic of their own. 'They're nothing really.'

Ben was going to argue that from the standpoint of a gemmologist they were very interesting, but Jo shook her head at him. She understood that Ivan was scarcely aware of their presence. He was going through the process of understanding his loss – loss of money, loss of prestige. Loss of opportunity to be a glamorous headline in the press.

His cocktail came. He took a hearty sip. After a pause he said, 'If you don't mind, I'd like the pair of you to clear off. I've got to think what to do next.'

'Would you like me to take the rubies?' Ben inquired, reaching out to take the box. He clearly wanted to get the stones back in his laboratory.

Ivan gave him a sharp glance.

'Not on your life. I'm keeping those babies until I've talked to my lawyer about suing those twisters.'

Jo was horrified. 'The Fieldingleys? You can't do that!'

'Who says I can't? They sold me a bunch of duds! I'm going to get every penny back, and then some!'

'But Ivan—'

'Nobody does that to me, nobody!'

'But wait a minute, they didn't do anything wrong – they probably had no idea the stones were false.'

'Are you kidding? I bet they had those rubies examined before they put them on the market, and knew I was getting a load of rubbish . . .'

'You can't say things like that, Ivan, that's slander.'

'It's what happened and I'm going to make them pay for it. Make a fool of me? I don't think so!'

'I think you're seeing this quite the wrong way, Ivan. I don't suppose the Fieldingleys had the necklace examined before they put it up for sale. Why should they? They knew it had been safely in the bank for years.'

'Besides,' Ben put in helpfully, 'if they'd called in a gemmologist it would have cost them money and from what Jo's told me they're pretty hard up.'

'There you are! Out for what they could get! And along came a mug, or so they thought, and they shoved them off on to me!"

'Please, Ivan, don't take it out on them. Mrs Fieldingley is probably as much a victim as you are.'

'Victim! She's forty-five thousand quid to the good and she's a victim?' Ivan glared at her. 'Look, will you just push off? I quite see none of this is your fault but you're not making things better!'

Ben got up with alacrity. He seemed to have taken quite a dislike to Ivan Digby. He moved off a few paces to wait for Jo. She too got up, although she felt she ought not to leave without persuading Ivan to calm down. But Ivan was already turning away from them, to open the jewel case and scowl at it, so she followed Ben.

They parted outside the building. Ben offered to drive her to Wembley but she felt the need to be alone. She went home by the Underground, lost in gloomy thought.

So far she'd told none of the bad news to her brother and his wife. But that evening after dinner she felt it only right to explain the situation, because Lindora had been looking forward to a very big increase in the family income. Which now was totally out of the question – quite the opposite. The mood Ivan was in now, he might end up suing not only Mrs Fieldingley, but Jo as well.

They heard her out in astonishment. When she fell silent, Donald said nothing. Lindora, however, had something to say.

'You've completely antagonized them!' she complained. 'A man like that, with all the money in the world and a girlfriend that could have been really useful to Donald and me.'

'What else could I do, Lindora? I had to tell him the truth.'

'But you needn't have sided with Mrs Fieldingley! Good heavens, Mr Digby was quite right to have a big grudge against her and there was absolutely no need for you to take her side!'

'But he said he was going to sue her.'

'Well, something ought to be done about it, for goodness' sake! He's got to get his money back, hasn't he?'

'I don't know whether he can,' Jo countered. 'He was sold the rubies in good faith. They thought the stones were genuine.'

'You don't know that! They probably knew very well that they were fakes.'

'Lindora, will you please not get in a state about something that doesn't really concern you! And don't say cruel things about Mrs Fieldingley.'

'Doesn't concern me! You know very well I was hoping that with a bit of backing from a man like that, we could have got something going. I mean, the girl has acting ambitions.'

'Yes,' Donald put in. 'I was working out a little deal that she might have liked, a little one-man show for her at one of the studio theatres.'

'Donald, be sensible! She's not Kate Winslet.'

'I know that, Lindora's explained it to me, but I was putting a script together – *Life as a TV Babe*. Not that title, of course, but about her experiences in show business . . .'

Jo groaned inwardly. Her brother had always had this tendency to build castles in the air. 'You've never even met her, Donald. You can't just concoct a script . . .'

'We were going to get to know her,' he insisted. 'If you hadn't bitched everything up!'

'That's enough! My clients don't come to me so as to build up a life-long relationship! And if I'd known what you had in mind, I'd have told you days ago that you might as well forget it. After all, they're just customers, they don't want anything more than a piece of jewellery from me.'

'Just customers! You've been going off to spend weekends with them, you've been out having lunch with her and taking her to museums.'

'Well, you can take it there'll be no more of that,' she declared, sad to have to say it.

She was wrong there. Next morning Ivan rang from his City office. 'Would it be OK if Miri and I popped in to see you later today?' he inquired. His tone was perfectly normal, even friendly.

'Why . . . yes . . . of course, Ivan.'

Jo was speaking on the phone in the reception studio. At the name Ivan, Lindora looked up from the computer on the reception desk.

He asked if it would be convenient around two in the afternoon. Agreeing, she put the phone down in bewilderment. He'd been so extremely angry yesterday – it had seemed impossible then that he would want anything more to do with her.

Lindora was eager to hear what the call had been about. Learning he was coming with the girlfriend, she became frantically active, clearing away any clutter on her desk, making a special washing-up of the coffee cups and glasses, angling the little ceiling spot-lights so that the items in the showcases looked at their best.

'He's coming to buy something else,' she predicted. 'I half expected it. He's going to buy her a kiss-and-make-up present. Now be careful what you say, Jo, and don't let him get away again.'

Though she sighed, she nodded agreement, then retreated to her workshop. She had a commission from another client that she'd been neglecting, a piece she was making herself from her own drawings, so that took up her attention until lunchtime.

Lindora put herself out to make a pretty little snack. Normally, the two of them fished out what they thought they would like from the fridge, but today it was all prettily arranged on plates with a second course of fresh fruit salad prepared by Lindora's own fair hands. Jo smiled to herself. As if she needed inducements to be polite, even friendly, to visitors.

When they arrived, it was clear that although Ivan was offering an olive branch, Miri was still sulking. Lindora bustled about, offering refreshments. They settled down on the sofa in the studio with coffee. Jo waited.

'Er . . . See . . . Miri and I have had a talk, haven't we, sweetness?'

She shrugged assent.

'She really likes that design you made. With the sort of falling spray of jewels . . .'

'Really?' Jo said in surprise.

'Of course I liked it!' Miri exclaimed. 'Anyone could see I loved it! It was exactly the sort of thing I would have chosen if it had been in a shop.'

That was a lie. She'd been quite uncertain whether to say yes to the design until Ivan had admired it. But Jo let it go.

'So what I was thinking,' Ivan went on, 'was that perhaps you could still make it for us, eh?'

'I . . . of course, the design is still . . . Are you saying, use the synthetic stones? Or . . .?'

'No, no, no! They've gone in the safe until I see about bringing the court case.' He was shaking his head in rejection but then paused and drew a deep breath. 'Synthetics, no! Miri loves the design but she doesn't want bling, you know. What we were thinking was, how about making the necklace with new rubies? You could do that, couldn't you?'

Lindora, sitting at the reception desk, was frowning at Jo and giving tiny nods that meant, Say yes. And beneath the pouting expression on Miri's face, there was muted eagerness.

But it wasn't quite as easy as that.

'It would cost a lot to buy forty good stones.'

'I understand that, but I'm hoping in the end to get back the money I spent on the fakes. And to make it up to Miri for all the

55

disappointment she's had, I'm willing to spend quite a bit more. After all, it'll be a good investment, won't it?'

'Oh yes.' An investment. She was used to this way of thinking, for other clients had come to her with that in mind. She never replied, 'It will be a work of art'. Now she said, 'You must understand, Ivan, rubies from Myanmar are rather scarce. We'd be thinking about perhaps Sri Lanka – though they're paler than Mogok stones.'

'What does that mean, paler? You mean they wouldn't look as good?' Miri put in at once. 'I don't want anything that's not going to have a good effect when the wedding photos come out.'

Jo held up a hand so as to have a moment to think. 'When is the wedding?'

'Well . . . you know . . . when the house is ready. Some time around Christmas, perhaps, or the New Year.'

She shook her head.

The others stared at her.

'What? You can't make it in that time? I thought you said it was OK when we first discussed—'

'Ivan, it would have been easy, using the stones we had. But it would be quite impossible to find forty well-matched stones in time to make a new necklace.'

He looked with anxiety at Miri. She pulled a little face but after a moment said, 'We-ell . . . let's say we put it off till the spring. March, April.'

But Jo was still shaking her head.

'Well, how long would it take you, for Pete's sake?' cried Miri, her voice rising.

'A year. Perhaps longer.'

'*What?*'

Lindora looked as if she would like to throw something at her sister-in-law. She rose from her place to hurry to Miri's side. 'Don't you fret about it, Miri. I'm sure Jo can think of some way to work it out.' She gave Miri's shoulder a friendly pat and remained hovering.

'Yes, I'm sure you can, Jo,' Ivan agreed. 'They don't have to be new stones, do they? There must be rubies in old pieces that could be used? I mean, like the Fieldingley necklace but genuine.'

'Of course there are rubies out there, already set, but you must understand, Ivan, to get stones that match would be incredibly difficult using that method. And the cost of finding them would be high.

It would mean making inquiries everywhere – and wasting a lot of time looking at stuff that wouldn't be suitable.'

'Perhaps you could use something else instead,' offered Lindora in a bright tone. 'Diamonds, maybe? There must be plenty of diamonds around.'

'Yes, sugar, how about that?' Ivan appealed.

'Diamonds! Everybody has diamonds! I've told everybody I'm having this *special*, gorgeous ruby necklace . . .'

'Besides, I wouldn't want to make the piece using diamonds,' said Jo. 'It wouldn't have the same effect.'

Miri sprang up, colour in her cheeks, her eyes sparkling with annoyance. 'You just don't care! All you're doing is making difficulties! You've ruined everything and I can't stand it any longer!'

With that she rushed to the door, which wouldn't open because she didn't have the code. She burst into hysterical tears, beating on the door with her fists. Lindora went quickly to her, put her arms about her, and murmured soothing words.

Jo was aghast. Ivan hurried to Miri's side, but she refused to accept his caresses. She turned to bury her face in Lindora's shoulder.

'There, there,' murmured Lindora. 'Come along now, dear, come back and sit down.'

'No, no, I can't talk about it any more. It's so d-disappointing, it was going to be so lovely, having this heirloom thing to w-wear and everybody admiring it, now she's sp-spoiled it all . . .'

She refused to let Ivan touch her. He was so distressed he was almost in tears himself. Lindora looked over Miri's shoulder at Jo, grimaced, and gave a little jerk of the head which meant, Make yourself scarce.

So Jo went out of the studio and upstairs to her flat, where she stood looking out of her kitchen window at some pigeons on a neighbouring roof.

To tell the truth, aside from the fact that she had now lost the commission and the enhanced reputation it might have brought, she was glad there had been a fracas. She'd been feeling she ought to get out of it. She had thought she might be on a good wavelength with Miri, but this childish tantrum had thoroughly disillusioned her.

Unless . . . Was it all an act? An act to make Ivan feel more and more guilty, and thereby get something more valuable out of him? A new necklace, new stones, costing a king's ransom?

Well, if that was the case, she wanted even less to do with Miri.

She was sorry now that she had wasted her time on a design for her. At the moment when she first saw Mrs Fieldingley's flower sketch, she'd seen rubies replacing the blooms and had imagined them against Miri's beautiful skin. But now the idea seemed absurd.

Miri had never deserved the Fieldingley Rubies, she told herself.

By and by there were sounds on the staircase and Lindora put her head round the door. 'I'm just showing Miri to the bathroom so she can wash her face,' she explained. 'Would you put the kettle on for a good strong cup of tea?'

She withdrew. Jo could hear Miri being steered along the passage. Shrugging to herself, she filled the kettle and switched it on. Then she went downstairs to see how Ivan was faring.

He was gone.

Probably he'd decided that absence was the best tactic. Leaving Miri to recover in Lindora's kindly hands might have seemed like a good way out.

She rang him on his mobile. He replied at once. 'I'm on my way home,' he explained. 'Ring me when Miri's calmed down and I'll come and fetch her.'

'She seems better now . . .'

'She gets upset,' he muttered. 'I didn't handle it well, I suppose.'

'You mustn't blame yourself.'

'Oh, I should have had more sense. If I'd thought about it I ought to have realized you couldn't conjure up replacements at a moment's notice. Sorry about that, Jo. It looks as if the whole thing's a no-go.'

'That's how it looks.'

'Send me a bill for the work you've done so far. I suppose I have to pay that guy who found out the stones weren't worth anything?' There was grim humour in the question.

'I'm afraid so.'

'Huh. Well, it's a case of grin and bear it, isn't it.' A pause. 'You said Miri was better?'

'Lindora's prescribing a strong cup of tea for her.'

'Is she . . . Is she still angry with me?'

'I don't know, Ivan. My sister-in-law's the one you'd have to ask.'

'Well . . . tell Miri that . . . you know . . . I'm sorry. Tell her I want to do anything I can, you know, to make it up to her.'

'Right.'

'I've got to go, I shouldn't be speaking to you on a mobile in this traffic, so long for now.'

Jo went into her workshop. Not to do any work; she went there for the comfort of its familiarity, its practicality. She picked up a miniature file, fitted a handle to it, took the handle off, and laid it aside. She screwed and unscrewed a drill. Then, most comforting of all, she took out of a drawer and unwrapped a bracelet she was making, semi-precious stones, a try-out for a precious piece she might enter in a competition next year.

By and by she felt she ought to go up to the flat to see how things were going. She had to pass on Ivan's message of apology. She went reluctantly, because she wasn't used to dealing with hysteria.

The kitchen was empty; no tea had been made, the kettle had boiled and switched itself off. She put her head round the living-room door: no one. She could hear voices from the bedroom used by her brother and his wife, so she went on and tapped on the door.

'Yes?' It wasn't exactly an invitation but she went in.

Miri was sitting at the dressing table using Lindora's make-up to repair the damage that tears had caused. Lindora was sitting alongside on a chair she'd drawn up. They were both gazing studiously at the mirror, assessing the work Miri was doing.

'I think you need a touch more eyeliner on the lower rim,' Lindora said. 'And below, coming right up to the rim, the honey-beige shouldn't fade out, you still have a bit of a tear-stained look.'

Miri obeyed instructions. 'Say, that does look better. You know, Lindora, I think you know more about it than the make-up expert at the salon.'

'Well, theatre, you see . . .' Lindora said modestly. 'It's a theatrical art.'

'Miri,' Jo began, 'I've just been speaking to Ivan and he wanted me to say—'

'Yeah, yeah,' said Miri. 'If he thinks he can hurt my feelings like that and just get away with it.'

'He said to tell you he'd—'

'I'm not interested! I'm sick to death of listening to him.'

'Please, he wanted me to let you know he'd do anything you want to make it up to you.'

'That's what he says but it always comes around to doing what *he* wants. You think *I* want to go to these stupid classes and learn "manners and decorum"? What the heck's decorum anyway and who cares about it? And altering the tone of my voice – what's that about? He wants me to sound like a newsreader? I'm sick of it and it's time he knew it!'

The tirade flew through the room like a storm-wind. Jo was silenced. This had blown up into more than a quarrel about a necklace.

'There, sweetheart, I think you've really worked magic there,' Lindora said to Miri in a quiet, soothing voice. She laid a hand on the one that held the cosmetic brush. Something in her manner redirected the girl's attention to the mirror. 'If you're ready, then, we might as well go down.'

Miri smiled in satisfaction at her reflection and got up obediently. 'I sent for one of the cars,' she explained to Jo. 'I feel OK to head for home.'

Lindora was picking up a jacket and her handbag. Jo frowned at her in surprise. Miri said, 'I've asked Lindora to come with me. That's OK, isn't it? I feel I . . . There's things to say to Ivan, and I don't feel up to saying them on my own.'

Jo was aghast. Within the space of about sixty minutes, had Lindora become confidante and friend to this girl?

She longed to get her sister-in-law alone and tell her not to meddle, but there was no chance of that. They all trooped downstairs together, Lindora in the lead, Miri behind her, and Jo helpless at the rear. Lindora tapped in the code to release the outer door and opened it. A handsome maroon car was waiting outside. Within minutes the two of them were whisked away; Jo was left in her doorway, anxious, uncertain.

She remained in that condition until mid-evening. At that time her brother Donald came home, too late for the meal she'd prepared.

'That's all right,' he said in a generous tone. 'I had a bite to eat with Miri and Lindora.'

'What?'

A smile spread over his bluff features. 'We had a sort of mini-conference. The poor girl's faced up to a big crisis and come out of it really well.'

'Donald, what on earth are you talking about? You don't even know Miri!'

'Oh, that's all changed now.' He was glorying in this moment of success. 'Lindora called me – they needed a business head to advise them.'

'A business head? Miri doesn't need—'

'She's still in a bit of a whirl, of course, but this is a big moment for her, she's going to do well out of it.'

'Out of *what*?' Jo almost shrieked. 'What's happened? She's going to do well out of *what*?'

'Her new life. Everything's going for her at this moment: big publicity opportunities, exclusives in the papers, all that sort of stuff. Couldn't have a better springboard for her new career.'

'Career? As what?'

'Actress, of course. It's what she really wants; she doesn't want to spend the rest of her life as just a pretty face and a sexy body on TV.'

'But she was going to spend the *next* part of her life married to Ivan Digby – and *he's* all the business advice she needs.'

'Oh, that's all over. *Bi-i-ig* bust-up! I gather it was tremendous. Ended with her packing a bag and walking out. Lindora helped her check into a good hotel and rang me. I've just come here to collect a few books and papers, to show her what we might be doing in the future to help her get launched.'

'Donald . . .'

'I just wanted to tell you – don't try to contact Digby over making any jewellery or anything, that's gone out the window.'

He marched off in a purposeful way to get documents out of the bureau in the bedroom. A few minutes later he put his head round the door of the living room to say, 'We might be late home tonight, Lindora and I, so don't put on full security, will you? I'll do that when we get back.'

'Donald, I don't think you should be interfering.'

'I'm not interfering, I was invited to help. You'll see, everything will work out fine.'

When he was gone she listened to the echo of those words in her mind.

Fine? It seemed to her everything was becoming too complicated to live with. She was going to find it hard to be civil to her brother and his wife. Lindora had rushed in where a whole choir of angels would have feared to tread.

She was beginning to feel very sorry for Ivan Digby. He might be foolish, lacking in discrimination, and vengeful towards the Fieldingleys, but he didn't deserve what was happening to him now.

Seven

Jo was sleepless most of that night. In the early hours of the morning she heard her brother and his wife come home, trying to be quiet, creeping about, stumbling on the stairs, whispering and giggling as if they'd been out at a party.

She was late getting up. She had an appointment with her accountant to bring the workshop finance files up to date, so went out after merely a cup of tea. After a couple of hours studying files of figures she felt in need of lunch so found a quiet restaurant. From there she rang her office number. No one answered. It seemed that Donald and Lindora had gone out.

When she got back to the studio she found the place empty and a note propped up against the office computer. 'Out on business, hope it's not inconvenient re customers but none noted for this morning. Answering machine switched on before I left. I took a few calls, please see telephone numbers to ring back. Lindora.'

One of the numbers was Ivan's. With great reluctance she pressed the buttons. He answered immediately. She said her name, and he rushed into speech.

'Is Miri there? Let me speak to her ...'

'No, she's not. She left not long after you did, yesterday.'

'I *know* that, she came home to have a big scene and then she stormed out. I was sure she'd be back again when she calmed down, but she's never appeared.' He was breathless with anxiety. 'I thought she'd be with you because she was with that sister of yours.'

'She's my sister-in-law.'

'Can I speak to her'

'She's not here.'

'Well, where is she, then? I want to know what the devil she's been up to with that woman.'

'So do I, Ivan. I've had no contact with Lindora since yesterday's upheaval.'

'She's not been back?'

'Well, yes, but I haven't—'

'Come on, Jo, don't clam up on me. What's happening? That woman's walked off with my poor little sweetie, all in an uproar about how mean I was to her and stuff like that! What right's she got to step in between the pair of us? Where is she? And where's my poor baby?'

Jo was touched by his utter desperation. Loath though she was to be mixed up in his affairs, she realized she couldn't just shut him out.

'I haven't seen Lindora,' she explained. 'But my brother – Donald, you know, her husband – he came in about nine o'clock last night saying he'd been called in to give Miri advice.'

'Called in?' It was a cry of bewilderment. 'What's he, then? A doctor? Counsellor? What's this about?'

'He's a theatrical producer . . .'

'What?' There was a sudden noise as if Ivan had jumped to his feet and perhaps damaged something – knocked his chair over, perhaps. Next came a confused stream of sound, scrabbling intermixed with muffled curses. She realized he'd thrown his mobile across the room and was trying to find it.

She waited. At length he spoke again, relatively calm. 'Sorry about that. I'm in a bit of a state, Jo.'

'I understand.'

'Let's go back. You said your brother is a – what? – theatrical producer?'

'Right. He tries to put together little companies of actors. He puts on shows. He had a business in Spain for some months, staging plays . . .'

'I don't see how his advice . . .?'

'He handles business affairs for whatever enterprise he's engaged in at the time.'

'And what's he engaged in at the moment?'

She hesitated. She couldn't very well utter either of the two replies that came into her mind. The first was: He's not engaged in anything, he's 'resting'. The other was: He's trying to get some advantage out of you and your girlfriend.

In the end she said, 'I suppose Lindora called him in to help Miri because she couldn't think of anyone else.'

'But what's this idea that Miri needs "help"? Help with what?'

'I'm not entirely sure. Donald was talking about "her new life"

63

last night. He said she had . . . what was it? A springboard for her new career.'

'What new career?'

'You'd have to ask Miri about that, I'm afraid.'

'But where is she? She's really not there with you and Lindora and everybody?' He was pleading for her to say his adored one was there.

'No.'

'Then where is she? What have they done with my poor little girlie?'

She sighed. 'I gather she's in a hotel somewhere.'

A silence. After a long interval during which she could hear his uneven breathing, he said, 'Which hotel?'

'I've no idea.'

'I'll find her. There's only two or three places she'd go.'

'Good luck, then.'

'This isn't the end of it,' he threatened. 'You'll be sorry you tangled with me . . .'

'Ivan, it's nothing to do with me.'

'They're your people, aren't they? Meddling in my affairs!'

'They're meddling, I can't deny that, but it's no wish of mine.'

'Why don't you stop them, then?'

'I've scarcely *seen* them! And if it comes to that,' she found herself saying, 'keep your quarrels to yourself! You come to my workplace, let your girlfriend behave like a bad-tempered baby, chicken out of it when it comes to dealing with her tantrum, and then you say *I'm* to blame?'

'Hey!'

'Find her, and drag her back if you want to, but stay out of my hair! Goodbye.' She put down the phone.

It rang almost immediately, but she didn't answer. After a few rings the machine picked it up. It was Ivan.

'Say, what's got into you, Jo? That's no way to talk. Come on, now, help me to work out where your sister's taken Miri . . .'

She didn't pick up. Ivan went on coaxing for a few more minutes than ended with, 'All right then, be stubborn! But this isn't over.' He disconnected. She didn't know whether she'd just heard a threat, or not.

She walked out of the studio. It took her all the rest of the afternoon to get over the upset.

Around five she decided to make herself a cup of tea. She was

64

feeling less edgy. She decided it was time to get in touch with her brother or his wife, so she tried first Donald's mobile, then Lindora's. Lindora answered from somewhere that sounded busy.

'Yes?' That was Lindora in her 'businesswoman' mode.

'It's Jo. Listen, Lindora, you've got to tell me what's going on. I had a dreadful clash with Ivan this afternoon.'

Linda made an impatient sound. 'That man's got to get over the idea that he owns Miri. This is the twenty-first century – slavery was abolished long ago.'

'That's just speechifying, Lindora. You're not on stage now. Tell me where you are and where's Miri.'

'It's none of your business.'

'All right then, whose business is it? A young woman has disappeared and her friends can't get in touch. Should I call the police?'

'The police?' Lindora's voice rose in alarm.

'Well, you're apparently hiding her, keeping her from hearing from her friends.'

'That's not the case; Miri is with us willingly and—'

'All right, let me speak to her.'

'She's busy.'

'Doing what?'

'If you must know, she's having a session with a publicity expert so as to—'

'Lindora! What are you up to?'

There was a hesitation, then Lindora said, 'I can't talk to you now—'

'Talk to me, or I'll go to the authorities and—'

'No, it isn't convenient. Besides, it's Donald who should lay it out for you.'

'And where is he?'

'He's in a meeting. Not here, somewhere else. Look, I've got to go.'

'Lindora, if you hang up now I swear I'll start a fuss—'

'Why are you being so difficult? This is a great chance for Donald and me . . .'

'And what is it for Miri? How does she benefit from what you're doing?'

'I can't go into it now.'

'When? When am I going to get an explanation?'

'This evening. Yes, this evening, Donald should have things tied up and . . . OK, let's say this evening. We'll put you fully in the picture.'

'Is that a promise?'

'Oh, yes, yes! Stop being such a pest, Jo! Can't you tell I've got a lot on my plate at the moment? Donald will explain everything to you later. Just stop nagging me now – I've got to go.'

Jo made her tea, drank it, and reconciled herself to the idea that something very important was going to be revealed to her later – and that she was almost certainly not going to like it.

She was right.

Around nine o'clock she gave up waiting for her relatives to appear for the meal of cold food, and cleared it away. Instead she made herself a sandwich. Around ten she was beginning to get sleepy; she'd had very little sleep last night. At some point after eleven she heard the chirping of the security system as it admitted her brother and his wife.

At once she was wideawake again. A mixture of anger, anxiety, and reproach sent adrenaline running through her. She heard them come upstairs, heard them murmuring to each other as they took off coats and jackets.

They seemed in an odd state – triumphant yet a little apprehensive. Donald was carrying his briefcase as if it was a newborn child, something very precious, holding all his hopes for the future. Lindora was flushed and smiling. Clearly their evening had been more enjoyable than Jo's.

'So . . .' Donald began. 'It's show-and-tell time, eh? Well, we have something worth "telling", haven't we, dear?'

'We certainly have! Everything's signed, sealed and delivered. And Miri is a new woman, free to see herself as a person in her own right.'

'What exactly does that mean? Jo demanded. 'Who's signed, and what?'

'We've signed exclusive management contracts with Miri. She's setting out on a career that could lead her to the top of the entertainment tree.'

'Donald, wait a minute. You're going to manage Miri's career? In what way? She walks on in a quiz show to hand over make-believe money prizes. How's that going to—'

'Oh, we're going to get her out of that contract. It pays quite well and it gets her exposure, but not the sort she deserves.' Donald was opening the briefcase. He took out a stiff document to flourish at his sister. 'See? We've already started the ball rolling in that direction – the show's producer is talking to us about that; this is the provisional agreement for her withdrawal.'

'And tomorrow there will be a big spread in the *Banner* about why she's making the change, and a piece in the *Financial Times*.'

'The *Financial Times*?'

'Well, it concerns Ivan Digby as well, doesn't it? We heard that there was quite a little tremor in the City today because he left his office unexpectedly.'

'He's been trying to find Miri, that's why.'

'Exactly. We talked it over with our publicity consultant and he said it would be good to cover that angle – no point in letting the financial biggies worry about something that's really a matter of the heart, and other papers are sure to pick it up.'

'You think there's something to be gained by dragging in Ivan?'

'You don't understand, Jo, publicity is a big aspect of being a success. We've got to make every point we can while the news is hot.'

Jo found her brother's attitude repellent. She tried to think of a way to make him see his actions from another point of view. 'Look, Don . . . I not only live here, but it's my place of business. My clients are often investing a great deal of money in jewellery, but often they don't want to advertize the fact. I can't have you putting this place into the spotlight.'

'Oh, don't worry about that. Lindora and I are moving out. We haven't actually found a place yet so we're going to put ourselves up with Miri at her hotel for a few days until we get settled.'

'And where exactly will that be? Where's Miri at this moment?'

'Aha, you think I'm going to tell you so you can pass on the news to that power-crazy tycoon!'

'Good heavens, think what you're saying! Ivan is just a man in love, that's all.'

'He's a money-bags with too big an opinion of himself! Thinks he can take that poor girl and turn her into a dowager in a stately home! All that nonsense about a big house in the country – what about what Miri wants? What about *her* ambitions?'

'Which are what? How do you know you—'

'She wants to be an actress,' Lindora put in. 'She wants to get some experience so that she can land a decent part in a film. And with her looks and her talent there's no reason why she shouldn't.'

'So you're encouraging her to break up with Ivan on the basis of this pie-in-the-sky ambition . . .?'

'She's broken up, she's already broken free!' Donald declared in theatrical tones. 'And she's put her trust in us, and we know just how to help her!'

Jo could see that arguing was useless. Donald had convinced himself that he was taking on a noble quest, freeing the captive princess from the selfish ogre. Lindora had accepted a part in this myth, but Jo suspected she had always had her eye on the main chance for herself and Donald.

She took a deep breath. 'Very well, since you seem to be committed to this project, I want you to understand that I disapprove entirely. You say you're moving out, well, I'd like you to be gone before the end of tomorrow.'

Her brother shrugged. 'We're going, we're going! Who would take us seriously if we're working out of a converted garage in the boondocks? We'll just pack enough for the next day or two then send for the rest when we're settled.' There was irritation in his voice, as if he were dealing with an unreasonable child.

Donald had always had this attitude of superiority. Their parents, dead almost a decade ago in a landslide accident on a mountain holiday, had always indulged him. They had been sure he would be a star of the theatre world. In fact, such money as the family owned had been left entirely to Donald. He had lost it all, in various enterprises. He'd believed in those failed ventures as strongly as he seemed now to believe his fortune was made with Miri Gale.

He strode out, carrying Lindora along with him like a small craft in the wake of a battleship. Jo sank into a chair and almost sank her head into her hands. Did her brother really think he could launch Miri into the world of serious acting?

Then she pulled herself up. Who was she to judge? In days gone by, Hollywood talent spotters had found stars working as waitresses or driving trucks. The trouble was, she didn't think Donald had any real experience in talent-spotting.

Well, it was clear that it was outside her power to do anything about it. She went to bed. Another virtually sleepless night.

Next morning the whole household was up and about quite early. Suitcases were soon in the downstairs vestibule. A taxi arrived. Jo released the locks, the little side door was opened, and the cases were carried out.

'Well . . . so long then,' Donald said awkwardly.

She smiled and nodded.

'Come along, Donald, we've got people waiting for us,' Lindora prompted.

If she had expected at least some slight thanks for giving them their board and lodgings for the past few months, she was soon disillusioned. They bustled off.

Yet Jo felt in her heart she hadn't heard the last of them.

Eight

Jo didn't know the publicity campaign had begun until she got a phone call from Ben Webber.

'What's all this in the *Banner* this morning about Miri Gale and her "new career"?'

'Sorry?'

'It talks about Miri Gale and how badly she's been treated over a necklace she was to get for her wedding gift. "Misled" and "been treated as if she were a business prospect" and "heartless"—'

'Who's heartless?' Jo interrupted, startled.

'Her former fiancé. He isn't named in this piece, but he's "well-known in the City" and regarded as "one of the most notable entrepreneurs of the financial world".'

'Oh dear.'

'What exactly is going on, Jo? There's an implication that somehow an inferior piece of jewellery was going to be foisted off on her. Now we both know that's not true.'

'Of course. And Ivan will probably set the record straight.'

'But what's going on? How did this stuff get into a rag like the *Banner*?'

She sighed. 'I'm afraid my brother Donald is responsible for that.'

'Donald?'

'Yes, and his clever wife and business partner, Lindora.'

'Well, how does it come about that they've got it all so distorted? Lindora was around while we were trying to sort out the history of the necklace; she must know perfectly well that no deceit was intended.'

'But that doesn't make such a good story, does it? Donald has engaged a publicity consultant, and I gather that this is his version . . .'

'Engaged a publicity consultant? Wait a minute. Are you saying that Donald is somehow . . . I mean, this is some sort of business set-up?'

'Sort of, is the phrase, Ben. He and Lindora have become business managers to Miri.'

She went on to describe the happenings of the last day or so, interrupted from time to time by protests from Ben. She ended with, 'I don't know that we come into it at all. It seems the story is being manipulated . . . so that it looks as if Ivan has somehow tricked Miri . . . Well, I don't know . . .' She was shaking her head as she spoke. 'The thing is, although it seems Ivan isn't named in this piece, the press are sure to have lots of pictures of Ivan and Miri together, and their wedding was going to be the celebrity event of the winter . . .'

'I call it totally irresponsible!' Ben exclaimed. 'How could you have let your brother do a thing like this, Jo?'

'Oh, for heaven's sake! Not you too! Ivan Digby was on at me yesterday as if I were to blame and now you think I ought to have stopped Donald! You've no idea what it was like when he and Lindora were here talking about it. They were aglow with enthusiasm at this big opportunity to get into the public eye, I simply couldn't stop them.'

'I'm coming round to speak to them—'

'They're not here, Ben, they packed up and left for pastures new this morning.'

'Oh, I see. Well, you have to get in touch and tell them—'

'I've no idea where they've gone. They're off with Miri somewhere, in a hotel. Mind you, you can bet your life they're going to have a smart new office and all that sort of thing before you can say Jack Robinson. It's no use, Ben, there's nothing we can do about it.'

He expressed himself forcibly about her brother and his activities but eventually calmed down enough to ask if she thought they should put out a rebuttal. 'The necklace was genuinely thought to be of great value,' he pointed out. 'We should tell the newspapers—'

'I don't intend to do a thing. I'm going to stay out of it.'

That proved impossible.

Her telephone began to ring just before lunchtime. 'Have you got photographs of the necklace that Ivan Digby was going to have remodelled?'

'I never discuss any work I'm doing for a client.'

'This was a necklace known as the Fieldingley Rubies and is a famous thing?'

71

'You should look the subject up in the art history books.'

'Oh, we've done some research. Can you tell us what value you put on the necklace now that it's been proved to be a fake?'

'I never discuss any work I'm doing for a client.'

The next caller tried a different tack. 'Ben Webber tells us that the Fieldingley Rubies are actually synthetic. Is that true?'

'You must refer to Mr Webber on that point.'

'Do you think Ivan Digby knew they were fakes when he bought them?'

'You must refer to Mr Digby—'

'Oh, come on, the guy's supposed to be a top-rank wheeler-dealer! Was he taken in by a bunch of fake stones?'

'I never discuss anything to do with my clients.'

'Were *you* taken in by this scam?'

She put the phone down at that point. It rang again almost immediately. She disregarded it for as long as she could and then she disconnected the office phone completely. Only those who knew her private mobile number could get in touch now.

But that proved no use, because in the early afternoon reporters began to ring the bell on her studio door. By teatime there were four cars lined up along the kerb. By nightfall there were some seven journalists grouped outside, some of them sipping coffee from plastic beakers. They finally packed up and left around ten.

Next day Jo went out very early to buy a collection of tabloid papers. The story was covered quite extensively. She was dismayed to see that they mostly had the facts wrong. Perhaps she should have answered some of the questions the reporters had been asking on the telephone, so as to at least get some truth into the accounts.

No reporters turned up outside Jo's studio. It seemed they'd gone elsewhere today. She later understood why. Ivan's solicitors had announced that there would be a statement read out at their offices. An attentive band turned up with microphones, notebooks and television cameras at the ready.

Jo saw it on the lunchtime news. They seemed to be in the firm's boardroom. 'On Mr Digby's behalf we are investigating the possibility of taking action against the vendor of the Fieldingley necklace. The necklace was bought on the assumption that it contained a matched string of natural rubies from Mogok in Myanmar, formerly Burma. There are two aspects to the case: either that the rubies were sold with the intention to deceive, or that the vendor was unaware of their true value.'

The reporters had had enough of legal speak. 'Does that mean that the Fieldingleys were tricked at some point? Did somebody steal the real necklace and replace it with a fake?'

The solicitor sailed on without taking notice. 'In the latter case, if Mrs Betsey Fieldingley was not aware that the stones were false, our action may be brought on the grounds of lack of diligence on her part: the Sale of Goods Act implies that goods must be appropriate for their purpose and these stones were certainly not fit to be classed as gemstones.'

The reporters found all this very dry and not at all to their taste. Their shouted questions had little to do with the Sale of Goods Act. Until this gathering, Betsey Fieldingley's name had never actually been mentioned. The newspapers had used the term 'the Fieldingley family'. Now her name had been put into the public arena. The reporters loved it. Betsey – what a great name to play about with in headlines. 'So Ivan didn't get much of a Bargain from Betsey? Is he going to claim a refund or is he going to Bust Betsey?' they cried. 'Is he going to allege Betsey's responsible for the Break-up?'

And then, at last remembering the 'heart-breaking tragedy' of Miri Gale's broken engagement, 'What does Miri say about this?' one of the women cried.

The solicitor rejected the notion that Miri Gale had anything to do with what he was announcing. 'This is a purely business matter,' he insisted, preserving a wooden dignity in the face of their babble. When they persisted in wanting to talk about Miri, he made his escape to an inner office.

The tabloid treatment of this interview wasn't very sensational – in fact it was muted. The press had wanted something more personal, something about Ivan's fury at being cheated or at least something about his abandoned wedding. However, there was considerable glee at the idea of a business tycoon being 'hoodwinked' into buying what amounted to glass beads. One wit had actually written a little poem about it: Rubies are red, Ivan is blue. He lost on the deal so he's going to sue.

On seeing the double spread in the paper she'd bought, Jo felt very sorry for him. He'd done nothing wrong yet he was being treated as either a fool or an Artful Dodger.

Donald's publicity stunt continued next morning. He put Miri on show for the television cameras. When Jo saw it on the lunchtime news, it was clear to her that Miri had been carefully coached.

73

Moreover, she'd also been carefully made up – presumably by Lindora – so that she looked pale and fragile.

First she made a little speech. She explained that she and Ivan Digby had been more than friends for a long time and had been engaged for about six months, but were no longer. 'I've returned his ring, of course,' she said, looking sad and displaying her left hand so they could see the ring finger lacked any adornment.

'And the wedding's definitely off?'

'Of course. I couldn't go on once I realized that I'd been misled . . .'

'You thought the rubies were real?'

'Yes, Ivan had all this historical stuff about them, it was very convincing.'

'Who do you blame for the confusion?'

'You feel a trick was played on you?'

'What about the castle in the country, Miri, are you disappointed by that?'

She looked to the minder who had been supplied by the publicity consultant. This was a young woman, a former reporter herself, so she understood how to steer Miri away from making accusations about trickery or blame. She whispered to her, and Miri took up the query about the country house.

'I'm really sorry about the life we were planning to live together in the country,' she said, much to Jo's astonishment. She'd heard Miri exclaim that she'd hated the idea of being cooped up with country types. But it was part of the plan that Miri should look as if she'd been deprived of almost everything she'd held dear: her engagement, her fairy-tale future in a castle, her faith in mankind.

At this point the excerpt ended on the television news but there was more the next day in the tabloids. Photographs of Miri, photographs of the house, photographs of the 4x4 they'd intended to buy.

Jo consigned all the newspapers to the recycle bin and went to oversee a tricky piece of work being done for her at a fine-metal works near Birmingham, a personalized bracelet for a commercially-made watch.

She returned home late at night. Next morning she was surprised to hear her studio doorbell at seven o'clock. Just out of the shower, she switched on the entry phone from upstairs. 'Who is it?' she demanded, expecting it to be a delivery of some kind.

'Who's that? Is that Jo Radcliffe? This is Tim Fieldingley and I want to speak to you about the way you've been trashing my grandmother's reputation!'

'What?'

'Open this door this *minute* or I'll take my boot to it!'

'Mr Fieldingley, please, calm down. Hold on a minute, I'm just getting up . . .'

'You'd better get down here and open this door if you don't want me to kick it in!'

'I'm coming, I'm coming!' she cried. 'Give me two minutes to put some clothes on, for heaven's sake!'

There was no sound of anything being kicked, but the bell rang again every few seconds while she pulled on slacks and a sweater. She ran downstairs in bare feet and through into the studio. When she released the locks and let him in, she saw that he was indeed wearing boots, quite capable of at least making marks on the surface of the security entrance.

He looked a little taken aback when he saw her hair still wet from the shower and pushed carelessly behind her ears in a tangle. He looked beyond her to the studio, which was dark because she hadn't wound up the shutters or switched on the spotlights. He hesitated, as if he might be realizing he'd come rather early.

'You'd better come up to the flat,' she said, in a very unwelcoming tone. Without waiting for a response or switching on a light, she led the way upstairs.

The rising sun was coming in through the windows she'd had installed in the old building. The staircase of beech wood was gleaming in its rays. She went straight on to the kitchen, to fill the kettle and switch it on.

Her back was to him. She heard him hesitate in the doorway, taken aback perhaps at the size of the place and its architectural elegance. The kitchen was simple and functional but bright in its detail: the table was yellow, the chairs were cushioned in blue, the cooker was bright steel with a yellow trim. Her visitor was moving about restlessly, looking for a spot from which to launch his attack.

'How dare you say that Grans pulled some sort of trick on that Stock Exchange celeb!' he challenged. 'You've no right to say she sold those confounded stones knowing they were fakes! She had no idea – none of us had any idea – the whole family is absolutely aghast!'

Jo let him rant for a minute or two, still not quite ready to take

75

him on. At last, to break through the tirade, she turned to ask, 'Would you prefer tea or coffee?'

'What?'

'I'm having coffee, but I've got tea bags ...?'

'I don't care a jot about tea or coffee! I'm here to make you retract the things you've been saying about Grans!'

She took the lid off the coffee jar, spooned coffee into her small cafetière, and poured the hot water on it. A delicious aroma filled the kitchen. She said, as she put the lid on the cafetière, 'In the first place, I've said nothing to anybody about your grandmother. In the second place, I'm as sorry as you are that her name is being bandied about ...'

'Now that's a lie! I saw in the papers, somebody called Radcliffe is handling the girl's affairs now, and Radcliffe, that's you!'

'Radcliffe, that's my misguided brother Donald. I tried to prevent him launching himself into this, but I failed.' She pulled a chair out from the kitchen table. 'Sit down and calm down. It's a few minutes after seven in the morning and I got home from Birmingham about two o'clock. I'm not fully awake, I'm hungry and thirsty, and you're giving me a headache.'

He stared, frowned, looked perplexed, then sat down at the table. The growing light of the morning was full on his face. He was tanned, or perhaps weather-beaten would have been a better word, she thought. He had thick brown hair that looked as if he didn't give it much attention, very dark-brown eyes under thick brows now drawn together in irritation, and a wide mouth set in determination. His clothes, chinos and a windcheater, were crumpled and perhaps had never been entirely spick and span.

'Would you like some toast?' she inquired. 'I'm going to make some.'

'Of course not! I came here to tell you that you've got to retract all of those insinuations!'

'I've made no insinuations and I'm not going to reply to another word you say until I've had a cup of coffee.'

'Confound it, I didn't come here to get involved in your breakfast arrangements.'

She shook her head at him, poured coffee into a mug, and took a hearty swallow. He watched her with a glowering attention, which gradually faded first to bewilderment and then to something like admiration.

'You're a cool customer,' he acknowledged.

She shrugged, then took another reviving mouthful of coffee. Next she opened a cupboard, took out the bread, cut two thick slices and put them in the toaster. He watched in baffled silence.

After her third swallow of coffee – which more or less emptied the mug – she sat down. 'Now,' she said. 'Let's go back to the beginning. You accuse me of saying bad things about your grandmother. I assure you that I've said nothing to the press about your grandmother. In fact, I've refused to take any part in what's been going on.'

'But you implied that Grans sold the necklace knowing that the stones weren't real . . .'

'I did not.'

'But you had them tested!'

'Yes, so as to know whether there were any natural defects that might be enlarged when I had the stones taken out of their setting.'

'You thought there was something wrong with them – I can't see why you'd do it for any other reason.'

'Look here, I didn't have any doubts about the stones. I'd never have taken on the job in the first place if I'd thought there was anything dubious about them.'

'But now you're saying Grans tried to pull off some swindle . . .'

'I'm saying no such thing. I was as astonished as you are when Ben Webber told me.'

'Yes, and that's another point! I gather he's some pal of yours. If you thought there was something wrong, why not go to an independent expert?'

'Ben *is* independent.' But as she saw his stubborn shake of the head, she knew mere words couldn't convince him. 'Wait,' she said. Getting up, she hurried downstairs. Her bare feet on the staircase felt cold and vulnerable. She took Ben's report from the safe in her workshop. Back in the kitchen, Tim Fieldingley was standing up again, examining a pad hanging on a cupboard door for reminders about shopping. There were little sketches and scribbles on it, ideas that came to her when she was doing chores such as stacking the dishwasher.

'What's that supposed to be?' he inquired, tapping out an outline.

'It's a jewelled band for a man's wristwatch. A special customer asked me to make one for him.'

'Good Lord! People actually want things like that?'

She shrugged. He took the sheets of paper she offered, then folded himself on to the kitchen chair again.

'I'm going to put on some slippers,' she said. 'My feet are freezing.'

He gave her a glance in which there might have been something of apology at his abrupt intrusion. When she came back, she set about making more coffee, since the remains in her mug were now cold.

He was reading still. He finished the last sheet then turned back to the first. She could see that the anger had died from his expression. He cleared his throat. 'So, he's . . . er . . . saying that in those days they didn't have any tests to tell natural from synthetic?'

'Yes.'

'And that my great-great-grandfather was cheated when he bought the necklace?'

She sighed. 'Mr Fieldingley, it's impossible to say at this late date whether the maker of the necklace was aware he was using synthetic ruby. It's quite possible that the firm of Castellani bought those stones in good faith. They might have been cheated.' She was about to empty the grounds out of the cafetière when she paused. 'Really, won't you have some coffee? You can see I'm making fresh, and it's just as easy to make for two as for one.'

'Oh, well . . . Yes, thank you, I wouldn't mind something. I dashed straight here from Heathrow.'

'Flying back from where?'

'Moscow.' He grimaced. 'You can't imagine what it's been like trying to get the hang of what's been going on. British newspapers don't reach Moscow until late the day after they're published, and when I had Grans on the telephone it got crackly and disjointed so I couldn't make out much except that she was terribly upset.'

'I'm very sorry. It's been terribly distressing for everybody. I expect you've gathered that the rubies were intended as a wedding present but now the couple have had a row and broken up.'

'I got some sense of that, but that's not my main concern. I want an apology to Grans . . .'

'Who's supposed to apologize?' she asked.

'Well . . . this millionaire guy . . . the one who's been saying he's been tricked and Grans has been up to no good.'

'Good luck,' she said, shaking her head and pouring hot water into the big cafetière.

'But he must!' He shook the papers she'd given him, then threw them on the table. 'This clearly states that there were no tests at the time the rubies were first used to make the necklace.'

78

'But I think what Ivan is implying for his court case is that *she* could have had them tested – before she put them up for sale, you see.'

'But who would she have got to test them? She had them valued, but by a local jeweller – and how much scientific equipment do you think you'd find in a jewellery shop in a market town?'

She understood perfectly. A necklace so old, so well-known . . . Any jeweller in his shop would have cast an eye over them with a loupe, just as she herself had done at the bank. Relying on their reputation, he would have given what he thought was a valuation that suited today's fashion and taste.

Tim went back to studying Ben's report while she set out clean mugs together with sugar and milk, then poured the coffee. At length, he sighed. 'Well, I can see how it happened. Everybody was under a misapprehension until this bloke did his tests.' Then he frowned at her. 'But why on earth didn't you let Grans know what was happening?'

She had to admit to herself that she had no good answer. 'It all happened so fast,' she apologized. 'One minute I was telling Ivan and Miri that the rubies were synthetic, the next minute Miri was storming out of the restaurant with Ivan dashing after her, then within the next twenty-four hours they had a big fight and my sister-in-law . . .' She faded into silence.

He gave a little shrug of understanding. 'Not your sort of scene?' he suggested.

'Well, no, I'm not good at having a row with anybody, and besides, I didn't really understand what Miri was on about. She was saying Ivan had treated her badly, but I didn't quite see how that was true, and . . .'

'But this Ivan character? I read in the papers that his solicitors had issued a statement making Grans the baddie?'

She stifled a groan. 'Yes, he's going to sue for the return of the purchase price, one way or another.'

To her surprise, he grinned. 'He'll be lucky! Grans put it down as part payment for this new place she's bought. Sheltered housing, you know.'

She was silent, shaking her head in perplexity.

'Well, look,' he contended, 'he can't get the money back if Grans hasn't got it any more.' As she said nothing to this, he said, 'That's logical, isn't it? He can't get what she hasn't got.'

'He'll try. You haven't met him. He's a man who's used to

winning.' She pictured Ivan, baffled and angry at what had happened. 'I'm very sorry for him,' she added. 'It seems to me he's lost, all round, and of course he's very upset.'

'Hmm . . . Well, talking of being upset, how about my grand-mother? The way the story's being told by the press, she's an old fraud! I'm sorry I came charging in here breathing fire and brim-stone, but you know, she's an old lady, and she's used to a quiet life.'

'I can only say I'm sorry. I wouldn't have this happen for the world.'

'If you're still sort of in touch with Ivan Digby, could you let him know that it's no use suing Grans? It'll get him nowhere, honestly. She hasn't got any money. It'd be pointless.'

'I don't expect to see Ivan Digby again,' Jo said. 'I imagine he never wants to see me again as long as he lives.'

She was wrong there.

Nine

Ivan turned up about mid-evening. He rang to ask if he could come to see her, and when she said yes he told her he was outside calling on his mobile. She opened the door that led to the flat, and there he was in a sparkling new Audi.

'Am I being a nuisance?' he murmured as he entered.

'Not at all.' She led the way up the stairs. She'd been in the middle of eating dinner in the kitchen but ushered him into the living room. Somehow she felt he needed the comfort of warmer colours, softer contours and the welcome of cushioned armchairs.

The evening was cool; she'd switched on the heating earlier. She said, 'Something to drink? A glass of wine?'

He shook his head. 'I've been hitting the hard stuff a little too much these last few days. It's time to back off.'

'OK then, tea, coffee, hot chocolate?'

He smiled. 'Hot chocolate! My ma used to offer that as the remedy for everything. No, really, thanks, I just came because I wanted to . . . to sort things out a bit.'

'All right, let's do that.'

He was silent, leaning back in the big armchair with his head a little tilted in thought. He looked tired, rather haggard.

'Everything going all right on the Rialto?' she asked.

'Pardon?'

'Sorry – that's from the *The Merchant of Venice* – means the place of business.'

'Showing off, eh?' He summoned a smile, then sighed. 'Shakespeare, I suppose. I missed out on all that – Shakespeare, stuff like that. Seemed a waste of time to me. I was always out making a little deal of some kind. Yes,' he reiterated as she looked surprised. 'Oh , yes, even at school. "I can get you the batteries for your Walkman at fifty pence less" or "I know how to get tickets for the show at Olympia" Always a player, that's me.'

'So how are things playing now?'

'In the wings, quite a bit of chuckling's going on, you can imagine. Ivan the Terrible comes a cropper.' He sat up, straightened his shoulders. 'I suppose I had it coming. But what I don't really understand is . . .' He broke off. 'Why am I talking to you about this?'

'I'm not somebody you come across on the Rialto, perhaps.'

'Could be. But I think it's more that . . . you know . . . you seemed to get close to Miri and I wondered if . . . if you knew . . . I mean, Jo, what did I do that was so bad?' It was a cry of desperation.

She leaned across to lay her hand on his, clenched on his knee. 'You didn't do anything wrong.'

'But I must have, or why does she . . . why does she keep on saying I was mean to her? What did I do?'

'Nothing. None of it is real, Ivan. It's all part of a publicity scheme – put together to turn Miri into a star.'

'But why has she gone along with it? We were so happy – at least I thought we were. I thought she . . . she wanted . . . well, she liked to have nice things, and that's why . . . And the necklace, I thought it would please her, something with history behind it and these wonderful rubies, but they're fake, just like everything else.'

He shook off her hand so as to cover his face. Jo got up and sat on the arm of his chair. She put a protective arm around his shoulders.

'Don't,' she murmured, 'don't take it to heart so much. It's not really Miri that's doing this. It's my brother and his wife and their publicity man. They tell her what to say, and she says it.'

'But why? Why doesn't she tell them it wasn't really like that?' It was a muffled protest from behind his hands.

Jo had no answer for that. Instead she leaned over him and put her cheek against his. 'It will all die down,' she said. 'There's always something new in the headlines, they'll turn to something else soon.'

He made no reply, and she felt him relax. By and by he half-turned towards her. They were looking into each other's eyes.

'You're so nice,' he murmured. 'I just knew you'd understand . . .'

It seemed right that their lips should meet. The kiss was meant to comfort him. At first. But he put his arms about her and pulled her down into the chair with him, and they were somehow wound into each other, her breasts crushed against him, her weight binding them closer. The kiss became full of desire.

82

When at length they moved apart, it was only far enough so that Ivan could speak. 'Is this real?' he murmured.

She smiled. 'It's real enough.'

'But . . . how could it happen?'

'We're just lucky, I suppose.' Her tone was light. If he wanted to back out, she would do nothing to stop him. But he had come to her this evening, and he had initiated the change from friendly consolation to passion.

He kissed her again, lightly. Then he said, 'And what happens next?'

'Do we need to plan it out in advance?'

He pulled her hard against him, and they clung for a long moment that they both knew was a prelude to something important. Then there were no more words, no more banter, only the urgent need to satisfy physical longing. They clung together as they made their way to her bedroom. They undressed each other with trembling eagerness.

Then there was the pursuit of physical happiness, an interlude of learning and knowing, and at last rapture.

Later they lay, arms about each other. Jo was happy. To tell the truth she'd expected him to be overcome with guilt at so quickly betraying Miri, but instead he began to talk to her about his boyhood.

She learned that he'd been brought up by his mother alone after his father walked out. He'd always felt he must be responsible for her, since there seemed to be no one else to care. She'd always wanted to live in the sunshine so he earned the funds to buy her a place in Majorca. Thus his obsession with making money, which had served him well up till now.

'Never thought I'd get caught in a dodgy deal,' he sighed. 'I can't help thinking Fate's caught up with me at last. Had a run of good luck all my life up till now.'

'But this deal isn't dodgy, Ivan. It'll all be sorted out . . .'

He sighed. 'I just feel my luck has changed. You can believe all you read in the financial columns if you like, but a lot of what goes on in the City is like the lottery, really.'

'And here was I, thinking it was all done by scientific analysis! But really, love, you mustn't be gloomy about everything. I know this has been a rotten time for you, but it will pass.'

'Think so? Certainly the outlook's better now than it was a few hours ago.' He hugged her closer. 'I never dreamed of anything like this. You're a wonderful girl, Jo.'

And so they murmured and chatted until it was time to make love again, this time with less haste but with more understanding and heed for each other. They slept then, enfolded together in a sweet gentleness that was like a coverlet of silk.

When she woke, daylight was beginning to creep into the room. He was gone. Propped on the bedside table was a page torn out of his diary: 'Had to leave you, precious – it's a very early start for us money-makers.'

She smiled to herself and scrambled out of bed. It was late-ish. She had to start her day. But while she was making her morning coffee she rang Ivan's mobile. He answered at once. 'Up at last, sleepy-head! *I've* been at work for hours. Everything OK with you?'

'Certainly is! And you?'

'Couldn't be better. Listen, Jo, what about this evening? Come to my place and have some dinner and we can . . . well, we can talk and then we'll see what we feel like doing, what do you say?'

'I'd like that.'

'I'll send a car for you.'

'Good heavens, I can find my way—'

'No, no, I want to.'

'Ivan, I'm a big grown-up girl. I'll come on my own. What time?'

'Soon as you can. You know I finish my day early, so I'll just be hanging about waiting for you.'

'All right, soon as the day's work is over, I'll be there.'

So she found herself at the beginning of a relationship that she didn't know how to categorize. She couldn't even understand how it had happened. She had leaned over him last night, to comfort him. Had she intended to go further? Had she invited him?

However it had happened, she didn't delude herself into thinking it was likely to last. He had turned to her because he needed someone, and for her part, she'd always found him appealing, intriguing, something outside her normal run of life. A financial star, a millionaire, young, good-looking, physically attractive – who wouldn't be happy to have him in her arms?

She had never belonged to a life of that kind. Of course she met rich people, went to events where rich people gathered – but that was because of her art, her talent. When she met them it was as clients, not as friends. Sometimes she got letters of appreciation, gifts of flowers or wine, but on the whole it was a business relationship. Her friends were people from art college, from the fraternity of jewel-craft and its science. She had to acknowledge that she lived a rather reclusive life.

And now that she was launching herself into an affair with a business tycoon, she mustn't make too much of it, she told herself with wry humour. They had made love, they were going to make love again tonight – and after that, who could tell?

All the same, she was smiling to herself as she went about the tasks of the day. Since now she had no receptionist, there were calls to answer, e-mails to respond to, dozens of little tasks that Lindora had undertaken. But she had managed without Lindora in the past and she knew how to manage without her now.

Then there was the watch bracelet she was designing: semi-precious stones set along a band of fine gold links, not too opulent yet good enough to match the worth of the watch itself, a Chopard. She spent a happy hour or two on the computer, working with the dimensions of the design until she thought she had got it just right – less gold, more topaz and onyx, but in narrower strips. This piece was intended as a wedding anniversary present to a man who already had everything. She hoped he would approve.

In the late afternoon she began to think about what she would wear. The weather was cold so she decided on a long-sleeved silk jersey dress under a fine wool coat. As she sat in the Tube heading towards Ivan's flat, she hugged herself with delight. No matter how short a time it lasted, this romance was giving a new piquancy to her life.

The first cloud appeared on the horizon a couple of weeks later. Ivan cancelled a date with her one afternoon. When they met the next evening he explained. 'I had to go to a meeting with Sayles and Bergen. It was unexpected because of the Sessions calendar.'

'Sorry?' she said, at a loss.

'The calendar for court cases. Of course there's a long queue, but Mr Bergen says they've managed to slip into a gap where someone's withdrawn their action.'

'I'm still not with you,' she protested.

'The case? To get my money back from the Fieldingleys?'

'Oh.' They had avoided discussing the Fieldingley necklace. It had come up occasionally – how could it not? – but they hadn't wanted to mar their blossoming relationship with unpleasant matters.

'When I say we've slipped into a gap, it's still months ahead. I was explaining to Bergen that he should make a point of that when he's putting the case – that I've been deprived of the use of that money in my business.' He paused and shrugged. 'It's not much in market terms, really, but the jury isn't going to know that.'

'Ivan . . .'

'What?'

'You're not going to go on with that, are you?'

He frowned at her. 'Of course I am.'

'But . . .'

'Look, sweets, I was made to look an idiot. I can't let that happen.'

They were in a fashionable wine bar in Piccadilly, on their way to a film premiere. It was a date that Jo was both looking forward to and feeling nervous about. For the first time, they were 'going public' – attending an event at which there would be cameras and reporters. There would be questions, challenges – the press people wouldn't know who she was; they would be trying to identify her for their gossip columns.

So for that reason she was wearing a new dress, which had cost her a lot more than she usually paid for her clothes. Ivan had wanted to pay for it but she had adamantly refused that offer. So the dress was off the peg, but it was off a very prestigious peg in a designer boutique. Hazy blue to set off her dark looks, diaphanous, yet – she hoped – not too figure-revealing.

Ivan was in dinner jacket and black tie. She knew they made a handsome pair. And, until this moment, she would have gloried in that fact. But now she felt a little chill, as if a cool draught had touched her bare shoulders.

She collected herself so as to deal with what he had just said. 'Ivan, listen. It's no use suing Betsey Fieldingley. She hasn't got any money.'

'She's got my forty-five thousand,' he said with a thin smile.

'No she hasn't.'

He stared at her. 'Don't be silly, Jo. Of course she got it – in full, the minute she handed over those confounded fakes.'

'Yes, she got it, but she's spent it.'

'How the devil do you know that?'

'Because her grandson told me.'

'Well, she better have spent it on something she can sell again quickly, because I'm going to have my money back.'

'Ivan, she can't. She used it as a deposit to buy a flat in a sheltered housing complex.'

There was a moment's pause. Then he said, 'There's no problem in selling sheltered housing these days. It's a lucrative market. She might even make a profit.'

'But you can't—'

'Who says I can't? That's my forty-five thousand she's living on, and I'm having it back.'

'But you must see that if you go on with this, she'll be homeless.'

'No, she won't. She can go back to the place where she was living before.'

'But that was a cottage in Herefordshire or somewhere. She sold that, I feel sure. I mean, she couldn't have relied on just the money she got for the rubies to buy the new flat . . .'

'The money for the phoney rubies, you mean.'

'Ivan, listen to me. Betsey Fieldingley is an old lady who's had to sell up and move into sheltered housing.'

'Don't give me a sob story. She's got money that belongs to me and I want it back.'

'She's not terribly well off, I feel sure. She used to be . . . I think she was a floral artist. What I'm saying is, she probably doesn't have much of an income, and she probably couldn't get a mortgage to buy the flat so . . .'

'You're under a bit of an apprehension here, lovey. I don't care about her financial situation. I care about the fact that she made me look ridiculous.'

'It wasn't Mrs Fieldingley that made you look ridiculous.' She stopped short. She had been about to say, It was Miri. But that name was unmentionable between them.

All the same, it hung in the air above them as if she had said it aloud. And Ivan could hear it.

The silence between them lengthened. In the end Ivan said, 'The car will be here in a minute, so drink up.'

'Yes.'

They went to the premiere. The reporters badgered them. They brushed it off, went to see the film, attended the post-premiere party, then started out for home.

It had been their intention to go to Ivan's flat. In the car, Jo said, 'I think I might go home and have an early night, Ivan.'

'Oh?'

'I feel a bit under the weather.'

'OK.' The fact that he didn't try to talk her out of it told her that

87

this was a serious moment. He got out of the car when it reached his building, kissed her briefly on the cheek, then instructed the driver to take her to Wembley. 'Goodnight,' he said.

'Ivan . . .'

'I'll be in touch.'

She slept badly. She didn't know what to do about what had happened. Had she any right to interfere in his business affairs? Well, no. Yet she couldn't somehow reconcile herself to the idea that he was going to badger an old lady for money that she couldn't possibly produce.

Matters were not improved the next day when she heard Tim Fieldingley's voice on the telephone. 'Ms Radcliffe, could I come and see you today? I'll be in London by about noon – could I drop by?'

'Umm . . . What's it about, Mr Fieldingley?'

'About the rubies, what else! And the action being brought by Digby. Grans needs a bit of expert help, but we don't know how to find it. Could we have a chat about that?'

She couldn't refuse.

When he arrived he was full of gratitude for her agreeing to speak to him. She had opened the studio door to him, and now he sauntered around looking at the exhibits. When he'd arrived on the previous occasion, she hadn't lit up the place, so now it was all new to him.

'My word,' he murmured. 'This stuff is gorgeous. Sorry I was a bit snippy when you said you were making a bracelet or something. I'd no idea you went in for things like this.'

She smiled and let it go by. She had work to do today, so she didn't want to spend too long on this. 'What was it you wanted?' she prompted.

He had a manila envelope in his jacket pocket. He took it out, opened it, and produced what looked like correspondence.

'These are from Grans' solicitor. He's . . . well, you know, he's a country solicitor, he does mostly conveyancing and wills. All this stuff is new to him and he's a bit overwhelmed.' He proffered the pages, but she shook her head.

'I can't get involved in the evidence in the case between you and Ivan,' she said.

'But you agreed to talk about—'

'I can give you my opinion on a gemmologist, but that's all. I'm sorry, but I don't know how this thing is going to go. I'll probably be called to give evidence if it gets to court.'

'Look, all of that is absolutely not on. Grans can't afford solicitors and barristers – besides which she can't refund the purchase price even if Digby wins his case. She hasn't got it any more.'

This was the point she'd already quarrelled over with Ivan. She said nothing.

Tim Fieldingley looked disappointed. He hesitated, then went on, 'About the jewellery expert – one of the things that's important to us is, how much would it cost? What sort of fee would he expect?'

She was beginning to feel sorry for him. It caused her a moment's ironic amusement – she seemed to feel sorry for everybody in this quandary.

'It would depend on what you wanted from him – or her, because of course they're not all men. Mary Enderby is very good. But it's a very specialized career, so of course you have to pay for it. Ben Webber isn't cheap – I can tell you that, but of course he's probably appearing for Ivan.'

'What sort of money are we talking about? Tens? Hundreds?'

'Well . . . if you wanted him or her to appear in court, it could be thousands.'

'Oh, Lord.' He sighed. 'But does it have to get to court? Can't Digby be persuaded to see sense?'

At that moment the buzzer sounded on her studio door. She was surprised: she had no business appointments for this morning.

She smiled an excuse to Tim then went to the door. She was too preoccupied to look at the image on the closed-circuit camera. She opened the door.

There on the threshold was Ivan Digby, a huge bouquet of hothouse flowers in his arms.

'I've come to say I'm sorry!' he began, offering her the flowers. 'I was absolutely rotten to you last night.'

He was coming in, and of course she certainly couldn't stop him – even in her surprise she knew it would be a bad move to try to prevent him. So he walked into the studio, and there was Tim Fieldingley.

He had no idea who he was. Tim, on the other hand, recognized Ivan from the newspaper photographs.

'Sorry,' Ivan said, polite though disappointed. 'I didn't think you'd have a client.'

Tim was staring at the huge bouquet. It seemed to amaze him. Jo saw that he hadn't understood until then that Ivan was anything more to her than a purchaser of her design.

Discomfiture had rendered her almost speechless. She pulled herself together and began, 'Ivan . . . This is . . . er . . . This is Tim Fieldingley.'

'Ficldingley?' Ivan echoed.

'Er . . . yes. He came to ask about finding a gemmologist.'

'Tim Fieldingley? One of the family?'

'Yes. He's trying to find—'

'Why is he asking *you*?'

'He . . . well . . . it's a specialized thing; you don't easily hear of an expert in—'

'But why is he asking *you*?' Ivan repeated, his voice rising. 'Why is one of the Fieldingley clan asking *you* for advice?'

'Well, you see, I telephoned Betsey Fieldingley early on, when I was trying to get some photographs to help me with the design . . .'

'But this is now, not early on, and I want to know why one of our opponents is—'

'Don't shout at her!' exclaimed Tim.

'You mind your own business! I want an explanation, Jo!'

'I'm trying to explain! Just calm down and listen for a minute, Ivan.'

'All right, I'm listening! Let's hear it!'

'Tim just wanted to ask me what sort of money he'd have to pay for an expert to look at the stones, you see.'

'Why do you keep avoiding my question? Why is he asking *you*, Jo Radcliffe, for advice. How does he come to know you?'

'She doesn't have to explain herself to you, for heaven's sake,' Tim intervened. 'But since you seem to be so obsessed about it, I'll explain. I called here a couple of months ago to hand over some old photographs. That's all. So can we be a bit civilized about it?'

Ivan glared at him. 'How does it happen that you feel you have to defend her? Stay out of it!'

'I'm speaking up because you're behaving like a barbarian!'

'What's it got to do with you how I behave? I—'

'You march in here and carry on as if you're the King of Kandahar! Didn't anybody ever teach you any manners?'

'No, I came up the hard way, and you're going to find out what that means if you don't clear off and let me talk to Jo.'

'I'm not leaving her here with you while you're in this state!'

'*Will you be quiet?*' It was said in the loudest tone she could summon. They both stopped abruptly and turned to stare at her. It was almost as if they'd forgotten her existence, as if she were some creature of myth they were quarrelling over rather than a human being.

Tim recovered first. 'I'm sorry,' he apologized. 'I'm causing you a lot of trouble.'

'That's true. But you didn't mean to, I know that. As for you –' she turned to Ivan – 'what's got into you?'

He hunched his shoulders at the rebuke in her voice. 'I didn't know you were . . . on terms like this . . . I mean, they're the opposition, Jo! You shouldn't be talking to them.'

'Consorting with the enemy, eh?' She couldn't keep the sarcasm out of the words. 'That's not how I see it. I was just being . . . you could more or less say I was being mannerly. And I certainly don't expect a shouting match in my home.'

He still hadn't apologized. His mouth was set in stubborn lines. 'He shouldn't be here,' he grunted.

'I say who can come here and who can't, Ivan.'

'Oh, come on, Jo, you surely know I wouldn't want any of the Fieldingleys here!'

'It's never occurred to me that you have any right to say who I talk to.'

'Well, I didn't exactly mean that.'

'No, I'm sure you didn't. Perhaps you should go away and think about it.'

'What?'

'And take your flowers with you.'

'Jo!'

Tim made a move. 'It's my fault, I'll go.'

'Yes, by all means. I'd like both of you to go.'

There was an awful silence, while the two men waited to see who would move first. She went to the studio door and opened it. Tim came first, pausing as he went out to murmur, 'I didn't mean anything like this to happen.'

He strode off down the street. After a moment, Ivan came to the door. He too stopped on the threshold and seemed at a loss. 'I don't think I handled that too well,' he said with a baffled shake of the head.

'I agree.'

Since she sounded unforgiving, he went on a step or two. Then he said, 'I'll call you.'

She shrugged and closed the door. She stood inside it, and heard him drive away.

Then she turned back into the studio. She saw that he'd left the luxurious bouquet on the reception desk.

Ten

She left the flowers where they were. She went slowly upstairs. In the kitchen she got a bottle of mineral water from the fridge, poured it into a glass, and drank it thirstily. Then she went downstairs to her workshop.

After an hour or two of concentration on her computer, she realized she was hungry. It was well past lunchtime. Shrugging on a jacket, she went out to a local coffee bar, where she ordered black coffee and a fish sandwich. The place was rather empty, but it was cheerful with the sound of muted conversation; she felt she'd made contact with the normal world.

Back at her studio, the first thing she saw as she came in was the great bouquet of flowers. She was struck with remorse. She'd been ignoring them because she was angry with the giver. Poor things, it wasn't their fault.

She took them upstairs, ran warm water into a big jug, and plunged them in for a drink. She'd arrange them later. Though in what, she couldn't quite imagine – normally the flowers she put in the living room and studio were simpler than these, more in keeping with the calm elegance of her décor.

She went downstairs to resume work. The light on the telephone was blinking to signify a new message. She switched it on.

'Hi.' It was Donald. After weeks of ignoring her, he'd decided to get in contact. 'Lindora and I have been a bit tied up but things are a little easier now. So it's catch-up time. Thought you'd like to know we've got engagements for Miri on two or three of the popular chat shows. Money-wise we've had some good offers for her.' A slight pause. 'Saw pics of you and Ivan in the papers after that big premiere.' Ah, so that was why he was calling. 'Are you close, you two? Might be good to meet – I mean you and I and Lindora – to see if there's anything we ought to know about the court case. For instance, is he still going on with that? Get in touch when you have a moment.' He recited the address of their new office, then its telephone number, his mobile, Lindora's mobile.

She noticed that he didn't leave a number for Miri. Clearly, if anyone wanted to speak to Miri, it had to be with the permission, or at least the agreement, of the new managers.

She made a note of the address and phone numbers. But she hadn't the slightest intention of using them, except for sending on some mail that had collected since they'd left her flat.

She wished her parents could have lived to see this move into the world of success. They had always believed that Donald was intended by fate to be a star, especially his mother. She sighed inwardly. It would have been comforting to be able to ring them and chat about it. They had died six years ago, and though they had never doted on her as they had on Donald, she found she missed them at this moment.

Later in the evening, while she was wondering what to eat for supper, the kitchen phone rang. She debated whether to pick up, thinking it might be Ivan either trying to repair the damage of the day or carrying on the argument.

It was Tim Fieldingley.

'Is it all right to call you now?' he began, in a doubtful tone.

'Yes, quite all right.' For her part, she was curious. Was he so determined to get advice on the matter of finding an expert that he'd come back to her after that angry scene?

'I just wanted to say . . . I could tell you were very distressed . . . I didn't know, you see, that you and he were . . . Not that it would be any of my business.'

'That was all very . . . unexpected,' she said.

'I was going to send . . . I thought of flowers but you didn't seem too impressed by those *Strelitzia*.'

'Is that what they are?' She gave a little grin. 'I've sort of forgiven them now. They're in a jug across the room.'

'Oh then, I'm sorry I didn't . . . Well, I only wanted to say, I'm really sorry I caused you so much trouble.'

'Just one of those things, I'm afraid. And I didn't handle it well.'

'I thought you did fine.'

'Thank you.'

'And I hope it didn't bring about . . . What I mean is, I wouldn't want to be the cause of a break-up.'

He waited. She wondered if that was a leading question. Did he want to know whether she and Ivan had split up?

She said nothing, because in fact she herself didn't know.

'At any rate, you're OK?'

'Yes, thank you, fine.'

'Well . . . I'm glad. Have a good night.'

'Thank you.'

'So. Goodbye, then.'

'Bye.'

She was thoughtful when she replaced the receiver. Had she broken up for ever with Ivan? She tried to recall the parting. She'd more or less thrown them both out. Ivan had lingered a few moments after Tim walked off. What had he said? She'd been too angry to be listening. She seemed to recall something about getting in touch.

But so far, he'd done nothing.

Should *she* call *him*?

A glance at the clock told her it was just after ten. He'd be in bed – she had learnt that a man who had to leave the house at four in the morning doesn't keep late hours. But perhaps he was lying there sleepless. Perhaps he was thinking about her, and regretting . . .

She began to dial. Then she stopped.

She said to herself, Listen, you fool. You told yourself at the outset that it wasn't serious, that it probably wouldn't last. And it seems you were right, because he hasn't made any move to patch things up.

But an argumentative voice within her was saying, Give him time. It all happened just a few hours ago.

So she did nothing about repairing the damage. Instead she watched some television and went to bed. To her own surprise she fell asleep at once.

She was busy the next day. The client for the watch-band came to look at the design, adored it, and wanted her to start work at once. As it needed stones different from the very precious materials she normally worked with, she spent the next couple of hours telephoning to find good suppliers. Then she went out for a lunch appointment with a friend from college days, who was anxious to grill her about the Fieldingley affair. She spent a busy time laughing and fending off her questions.

So when she returned home she was reinvigorated.

She'd had her mobile switched off in the restaurant. As she put down her handbag she remembered it and switched it on again. She saw she had a message. And it was from Ivan.

Kiss-and-make-up is always wonderful. They flew into each

other's arms an hour or so later. The world was bright and beautiful once more.

The next day, to her surprise, brother Donald got in touch again. 'Thanks for sending on the mail, Jo. And look – it's silly to be distant with each other, don't you think?'

'I suppose so.'

'I mean, after all, what's done is done. We have to acknowledge that Miri has a right to a life of her own, don't you agree?'

'Yes, of course.'

'So Lindora and I were thinking, how about getting together?'

She took time before answering. Perhaps it was wrong of her, but she couldn't help thinking he wouldn't be giving this invitation unless he wanted something.

'Getting together how?' she asked at length.

'We're giving a little party tomorrow evening. Nothing too formal, just drinks and a group of friends from the theatre. John Memling, you might remember him, he used to design for us when we were running that little theatre group in Torquay.'

'Oh yes.'

'And Lindora's old drama coach. And de Groot.'

Willem de Groot was a man whose name she remembered. In the past he had financed one of Donald's projects, so Jo deduced that he was being approached again. So was she invited as a hint that de Groot wasn't the only wealthy contact, that his sister was connected to someone even richer? She didn't know whether to be angry or amused. Really, Donald and his schemes . . .

She waited to hear what else he had in mind. He went on, 'I won't ask you to bring Ivan. It wouldn't be a good thing, because of course Miri is going to be there so it would be awkward, wouldn't it.'

'Beyond a doubt.'

He hesitated. He'd heard the sharpness of her tone. 'But do come, Jo,' he urged. 'The year's drawing in, Christmas will soon be here, families ought to be together at Christmas.'

It almost made her laugh aloud. It was years since he and Lindora had wanted to be 'together' with her at Christmas. But she guessed that it was necessary for Donald to make a good impression on the money-man, and she, the girlfriend of Ivan Digby, was impressive; she clearly moved in the right circles and by inference, so did Donald.

She realized she herself was quite interested in seeing Miri. She found herself wondering what they had done with her. So she said, 'I'll let you know.'

She wanted to find out what Ivan's plans were for the following evening. When she explained that her brother had invited her to a party, he looked at first confused, then a little offended, and then rather inquisitive.

'Do you feel you want to go?' he muttered.

'We-ell . . . It would be interesting.'

'Who would be there, exactly?'

'I don't know *exactly*. But yes, Miri will be there.'

'Ah.'

She let it lie there, a great question that they'd always avoided.

In the end he solved his problem by saying, 'Do what you like.' Which she took to mean that he wanted her to go because he wanted to know what was happening to the girl he'd once idolized.

The party was at Donald's new flat. A very pleasant place it proved to be, in an old but elegant block in Chiswick. Jo took care not to arrive too early so as to avoid any big pretence of rapprochement between herself and her relatives. Once she did arrive, she was given a quick hug by Donald and a rather formal handshake by Lindora.

They were both looking very well. Lindora wore a 'little black dress' that probably had a very good label in it. Donald looked sleek, well-barbered, and had invested in a new dinner jacket. He offered her his arm to lead her on into the drawing room, where the rest of the guests were chatting.

'This is Emily Patterson, Jo. She's giving Miri a bit of guidance, you know. Emily, my sister Jo – she designs jewellery.'

Ms Patterson had grey hair and an old-fashioned frock, but there was authority in every line of her face. 'Ah, yes, I've heard Donald speak of you. Clearly the creative impulse figures largely in your family.' She smiled. 'Creative people are always so interesting. I tell Miri she must cultivate her creative side.'

'Oh, I remember, Donald said you were—'

'Yes, giving her some coaching. A lovely child,' she surged on. 'Beauty of both body and face, but the voice, you know . . .' She was shaking her head. 'But she's improving, yes, improving.'

'I seem to recall that Miri had been having lessons before . . .'

'So I was told, yes, elocution, deportment . . . But for the stage, you understand, there must be more than words well-pronounced. The voice must convey emotion, power when it is needed, there must be a tonal range . . . you follow?'

97

Jo listened to quite a prolonged lecture about voice production before she was rescued by the offer of little snacks on a tray. She turned away to choose, and managed to insert herself into a group standing nearby. This included the important Mr de Groot. When she introduced herself he held her hand a little longer than necessary, saying earnestly, 'I think you have been in touch with someone I admire, Ms Radcliffe – you know Mr Ivan Digby, am I right?'

'Quite right.'

'Oh, Digby,' said another of the group. 'Yes, wasn't he the . . . the *friend* of our beautiful Miri?'

'Exactly,' said de Groot, looking at Jo. She knew he was cataloguing her as Miri's successor. 'And are you interested in the theatre like your brother?'

'Only as a member of the audience.'

The conversation turned to recent theatre productions. She listened and was quite happy to take little part. She felt de Groot's eye on her more than once. By and by he had worked his way to her side, so as to say in a confidential murmur, 'You know, I belong to the financial world. I have admired Mr Digby since he first began to make a name for himself. It would delight me if you and he would come to one of my little get-togethers, some time.'

She smiled. 'I can't speak for Mr Digby, I'm afraid.'

'No, of course not, but you would allow me to send you an invitation, perhaps? I put on little entertainments at these evenings – a reading by some well-known actor, someone from a big show to sing for us – would that interest you?'

'Sounds delightful,' she said, without having the slightest intention of ever going. Her suspicions had been confirmed. She'd been invited to please this possible theatrical backer.

To her surprise, she was rescued by Miri Gale. She was looking even more beautiful than ever. It seemed that Lindora had persuaded her to dress for elegance rather than for sexual display.

She too was in a 'little black dress'. It didn't have a plunging neckline to show off her bosom, but clung gently to her curves without being obvious. Her hair was piled up in a little top-knot so that her neck and throat, slender and somehow vulnerable, were shown to advantage. Her make-up gave her a fragile quality. The words 'English rose' came into Jo's mind.

'So there you are!' Miri cried, seeming quite friendly. 'Don told me you were coming. How are things going back at the ranch?'

'Not bad, thank you. How about you?'

'Ooh, still having lessons, only this time it's a bit different and old Pattie isn't so snooty as that duchess in Hampstead. And of course, Lin's marvellous – she really *knows* what it's like being on stage, she's given me ever so many hints.'

'So it's going to be a stage career, then, is it? That's what you always wanted.'

'Right, and now I'm with the right people to help me. Don's full of ideas, and he keeps me clued up so that I can see where we're heading. He's got me on a couple of good TV chat shows . . .'

'Yes, he mentioned that.'

'Well, you see, it's so that I can let the public know what I'm going to do. He's been giving me hints on how to bring in my ambitions when I'm interviewed. And old Pattie says it's always a good thing to aim high, so I'm going to say my ambition is to do Shakespeare – how about me as Titania, eh?'

'Can't be bad,' Jo said. And indeed, Miri had all the beauty needed to play the Queen in *A Midsummer Night's Dream*.

'So how you doing, yourself?' Miri asked with a giggle. 'I saw you in the papers, with Ive. At that premiere. You holding his hand, eh?'

Jo smiled and shrugged.

'It's good, you know. At first he kept on trying to get at me. I had to get a new mobile with a new number, so as to avoid him ringing me. But that's stopped, I'm glad to say.'

Two or three of the male guests now descended on them to drag Miri away for a signing session with photographs. Accepting another drink from the waitress, Jo edged her way towards the door. She'd done what was expected of her – been sweet to the important Mr de Groot, been non-combative with Miri. She found Lindora and murmured her farewells.

'But Jo dear, I haven't had time to catch up with you!'

'Well, you're busy being hostess, and I've been mingling with your guests. We can have a chat some other time.'

'Of course. I'll ring you, Jo. Now that we've patched things up, we must keep in touch.'

'Of course.' And perhaps she would be included in another of Lindora's parties. It seemed she had a certain usefulness.

When she got home the light on her answering machine was flashing. She knew, before she picked up, that it would be Ivan.

'Let me know how you enjoyed the party. I hope you've patched up everything with your brother now,' was the message.

What he meant was, how was Miri?

And since it still wasn't so very late, she rang to tell him.

'There was a man there who told me he admired your ability,' she began rather teasingly. She told him about de Groot, but he wasn't really interested. So she quickly went on to the other guests and then mentioned Miri.

'Oh yes?' he said, extremely casual. 'How's she doing?'

'She was talking about acting in Shakespeare.'

'Good Lord!' He needed a moment to take that in. Then he ventured, 'Do you think she was serious?'

'I couldn't say for sure. But Donald and Lindora have sent her to a voice coach.'

'But she'd done all that already with that teacher—'

'But this is for pitching your voice on stage, you know. It's part of being an actor.'

'Hmm . . .'

She knew he was longing to ask, 'Did she mention me?' So to put him out of his misery she said, 'We didn't talk for long. You must understand, Ivan, there were about thirty people there, and I think she was supposed to circulate so as to introduce herself to those who might do her some good. This man I mentioned, the financier – I think Donald hopes to get him to back some production or other.'

She heard a stifled sigh. 'Well . . . If that's what she wants . . .'

They said goodnight.

As she put down the receiver she was thinking, He's still in love with her.

Eleven

Christmas came. Jo was able to avoid any 'family get-together' with Donald and Lindora by going abroad with Ivan. They spent three relaxing days in a superb hotel in Dubai, the sort of thing Jo would never have thought of doing herself. She found the modern décor in the hotel very interesting: it set off all kinds of ideas about future jewellery design.

The New Year brought sheaves of invitations from people she scarcely knew. It seemed that being seen as Ivan Digby's partner made her popular. Ivan too had invitations. They went to various events, began to be taken almost for granted as a couple. However, Ivan still couldn't bring himself to go anywhere where he might run into Miri. So when Jo let herself be persuaded into yet another of Donald's parties, she went alone.

This time it was a Sunday brunch and there were fewer guests. Jo found herself in conversation with John Memling, the set designer. He seemed to take it for granted that she knew what he was working on.

'Extremely portable,' he remarked. 'So that it can be set up without disturbing the school timetable.'

'School timetable?'

'Oh yes, you must remember, the school hall is always used for morning assembly so—'

'Your scenery's going to be put up in a school hall?'

'Quite a challenge, what? But I've nearly cracked the problem, except for the bit where Paulina opens the curtain and shows the statue.'

'What statue?' Jo begged, her mind seeking after the connection with the name Paulina. It came to her after a moment. 'The Winter's Tale? Donald's putting on The Winter's Tale?'

'Oh, I thought you knew.'

It took her totally by surprise. 'Is this . . . is this for Miri?'

'Of course, yes, letting her into the classical style in an off-stage sort of way. Abbreviated, you know. Because even sixth-formers aren't likely to want to sit through a whole Shakespeare play.'

'Let me get this straight,' Jo said. 'Donald is putting on a production of *The Winter's Tale* for schools?'

'Yes, it's the set book for one of the examining bodies, you see, so he's got at least seven bookings so far and there's sure to be more.'

'He's touring it?'

'Yes, hence my quick-put-up-and-take-down scenery.'

'And Miri's in it?'

'Yes, Donald suggested it to her last year when he took her on. You must remember – she mentioned it on one or two TV interviews. And then this schools project came up so Donald went for it – you know he's always been a bit of a go-getter.'

Jo recalled her conversation with Miri. She'd said she wanted to play Queen Titania. An awful thought came to her when she recalled the plot of *The Winter's Tale*. 'She's not going to play the Queen of Sicily, is she?'

'No, no, of course not, she's playing the daughter,' Memling laughed. 'Lovely costume designs, and not too expensive, because they're mostly muslin – she'll look fabulous.'

Jo was speechless. She'd never really believed that Miri would play Shakespeare. She'd thought that was only something Donald had cooked up to tell TV interviewers, to make her sound deserving, honourably ambitious, something more than just a pretty face and a sexy body.

She was determined to speak to Donald about this plan, but it so happened that Miri came to sit beside her while she was having her second cup of coffee.

'Saw you talking to Johnnie. Did he tell you about me doing Perdita?'

'Yes, he did. He said the designs for your costumes were lovely.'

'Yeah . . . I suppose so, haven't actually been made yet.' There was a long pause, during which Jo tried to think of a way to ask if she knew what she was getting into. Miri forestalled her.

'You ever see it?'

'What? The play? Yes, I've seen it a couple of times.'

'My part doesn't start until sort of late into it.'

'Yes, you have to grow up in exile before you can be in the play,' Jo said, making light of it.

'I don't know. It's a weird sort of play, really. It's not easy, you know. Pattie says it's all about unfairness and learning about truth, but it all sounds so quaint. "I'll queen it no inch further" – who's going to understand that, I ask you!'

'Well . . . you're sure to understand it better as you learn the lines. And your coach will help you.'

'Of course, you'd think so, but she . . . I don't know why she thinks I ought to know about all this stuff already.'

'She belongs to a profession that takes it for granted you've been steeped in Shakespeare all your life, I imagine.'

'Drama school! She keeps wailing that it's a pity I never attended drama school. Well, who ever told her I did? And as for Don! It was his idea in the first place, this Shakespeare thing. He keeps saying it only needs hard work to make a go of it.'

Jo let a moment go by, then said, 'When you used to say you wanted to be an actress, what kind of parts did you have in mind?'

'Oh, something with a bit of fun in it – something in one of the soaps, even. Just something that I could at least get the hang of!'

'When do you actually have to perform?'

'Don says after Easter. "The Easter term", he says. Going out to schools! He's keen but it doesn't sound much fun to *me*.'

'But I imagine he feels it would be easier than starting out for the first time on a proper stage.'

'Oh yeah? In front of a hall full of schoolkids? I don't know what his school was like, but the one I went to, we'd be calling out rudies after the first five minutes.'

As they talked Jo became convinced that Miri hated the whole idea. She sought out her brother so as to put this to him.

'Oh, that's just cold feet,' he protested when he'd heard a few words. 'These are rural schools we'll be going to – manners are pretty good there. And as to the part being difficult, good heavens, it's one of the shortest parts in Shakespeare for a female lead. All she's got to do is get her head round it and . . . well . . . of course that needs a bit of commitment on her part.'

'But she doesn't even like it, Donald. I mean, it was your idea to have her tell people she wanted to do Shakespeare.'

'I know what I'm doing, Jo. She was always regarded as nothing but a bimbo, and if she's ever going to get anywhere in the theatre she's got to prove that she's more than that.'

'But Shakespeare's like throwing her in at the deep end.'

'Oh, mind your own business, will you? You always take a dismal view of anything I'm doing. This is going to give Miri a chance

103

to find her feet, and then I've more or less got a promise from de Groot for a chance to direct a new play by Dave Underwood.'

He turned away to give attention to another guest, and she knew that she'd done no good. He was determined that his present plan would land him the financial backing to put on a play by one of the most promising young writers. She sighed inwardly. Donald would do almost anything for a chance like that.

She left soon after.

Some ten days later she was meeting Ivan for a Valentine's Day dinner. He greeted her at the restaurant with a kiss as usual yet she thought he seemed preoccupied.

During the first two courses they chatted about everyday things, but at last he said, 'You'll never guess what happened today.'

'No, what?'

'I . . . er . . . I got a call from Miri.'

She was surprised, but didn't exclaim about it. She murmured, 'Oh yes?'

'She was saying . . . You know, today being St Valentine's, it made her think . . . Last year, we went to Venice.'

'A perfect place for St Valentine's.'

He gave a deep sigh. 'I could hardly believe it when my secretary said she was on the line. I was in two minds whether to take the call.'

'But you did.'

'Well, I . . . Do you think I should have refused?'

He seemed to be asking for her permission to go on with what he was trying to say. She said, 'No harm in being polite.'

'Right, that's what I thought. And I'm glad I did, Jo, because, you know, she seemed very down.'

'In what way?'

'This acting thing. She's got to go on tour in a couple of weeks, doing Shakespeare. She said she talked to you about it at that Sunday thing you went to.'

'Yes, she did.'

'You never mentioned it!' He was reproachful.

'I told you we had a word or two.'

'But you didn't tell me she was so unhappy about it! Shakespeare! No wonder she's got the jitters about it.'

'She did tell a lot of people that she wanted to do Shakespeare.'

'And who put that idea into her head?' he demanded, indignant at the harm it caused. 'Really, that brother of yours, he must have been out of his mind to suggest it!'

She blew out a breath, feeling he was right. 'Donald has always had a tendency towards the grandiose.'

'Why didn't you stop him? Why did you let Miri get into his clutches?'

She let a moment go by, then said in a cool tone, 'If you remember, Miri threw a tantrum in my studio and flung herself into the arms of not Donald, but my sister-in-law. What did you expect me to do, drag them apart?'

'Oh!' He was startled by what to him was unexpected sharpness. 'I'm sorry, of course it wasn't your fault, I shouldn't have said that.'

'That's all right. I'd just like to say that I really don't want to discuss Miri's acting career.'

He understood he was being rebuked. He looked down at his plate, pushing his dessert around with a spoon. 'It's just that I can't help being worried about her,' he muttered. 'You see, she hasn't got anybody to turn to.'

'She's got family – parents – somewhere in the Midlands, hasn't she?'

'They seem to be very strict. They washed their hands of her when she started wearing those skimpy clothes on TV.'

Jo sighed inwardly.

'Could you maybe speak to your brother about it? Get him to put off this trip she's supposed to make. I mean, until she feels less scared.'

She was really beginning to feel she'd had enough of this. 'Ivan, the tour is for schools that have the play in their examination schedule. It would be no good doing it in six months – the exams would be over by then. Either she pulls herself together and goes on schedule, or it's a wash-out.'

At last it seemed to come home to him that she didn't want to have this conversation. He nodded at the waiter, who brought coffee.

Afterwards they walked in silence to his car in the parking lot. As they drove off Jo said, 'Drop me at Leicester Square Tube, would you?'

'Aren't you coming back to the flat?'

'I think I'll just go straight home.'

He didn't put up any argument. 'I'll drive you—'

'No, honestly, Ivan, just take me to the Underground.'

They were at traffic lights. He turned to look at her in their glow. 'You're peeved, aren't you? I spoiled our Valentine's dinner.'

He sounded like a little boy caught with his hand in the cookie jar. She felt, once again, that impulse of pity for him. Rich and clever in his own circle, he seemed inept at handling human relationships.

'It's all right. You were worried about her. It's only natural, because at one time you had a big thing going between you.'

'Yes.' He was very subdued, very despondent.

'So it's best if you go home and get over your anxiety about her. It's not your concern any more, Ivan.'

'I suppose so.' He accepted without question that she was parting from him now simply because he needed time to himself. He'd at once given up the thought that she might be offended.

She gave him a kiss on the cheek as she got out quickly at the Tube station. Travelling home, she debated with herself whether she'd done the right thing in letting him go home alone to brood. But she had felt wrong-footed when they were discussing Miri. She couldn't say what she really thought – that Miri was an amateur gold-digger who was unfortunately something of an air-head. Unrealistic ambitions about acting had caused her to make a decision that she now deeply regretted.

What on earth did she expect to do now? She'd let Donald plan out this imaginary career. She was supposed to learn her job the hard way – on tour, with audiences less than enthusiastic, speaking the lines of a playwright who loved words and meant them to be spoken beautifully. If she backed out, the whole scheme would fall to the ground.

Turning to Ivan for help was absurd. Except, of course, that she didn't expect him to 'help'. Jo was almost sure that she was looking to him as a way of escape. An escape back to the carefree life of leisure, of credit cards to use in exclusive boutiques, of party-going, of romantic trips to Venice . . .

The evening had depressed Jo. She was still feeling rather disconsolate next morning, but her day brightened when she found among her mail a letter from the chairman of a well-regarded jewellery firm. He was asking her if she would be willing to meet with him, to discuss a proposal that he had in mind for her.

It piqued her curiosity enough to ring him and ask what it was about.

'Well, I thought it would be nice, dear lady, if we could meet and have a chat. Are you free any time soon?'

'My time's my own, Mr Tchekari.'

'By any chance, could you come to the office this afternoon? I could offer you tea and an interesting idea.'

'This afternoon?' This is sudden, she thought.

'I don't want to hurry you,' he said, although clearly he did.

She agreed to go to tea with him, and that afternoon at four she found herself in a beautiful first-floor room in Bond Street, above the flagship store of this respected firm. Omar Tchekari shook hands warmly when she was shown in.

Tea was waiting, and tiny cakes from an Arabian shop. It was clear that Mr Tchekari enjoyed cakes; he had several double chins.

'Now, my dear colleague, I expect you are wondering what this is about,' he said. He twinkled at her. 'I hope you will be responsive to what I am going to say. You designed a replacement for the famous Fieldingley necklace, did you not?'

'I did, yes, to my regret.' She gave a wry smile.

He smiled in acknowledgement. 'A very unfortunate set of circumstances, yes, yes. So now I ask, Ms Radclliffe – the design – did Mr Digby actually buy it?'

She frowned. This was almost an impertinent question. What went on between herself and her clients was confidential. But then she recalled that Ivan wasn't her client any longer.

'No, he paid for preliminary work and *approved* a design. But we never got to the contract stage.'

'The revelation of the facts about the rubies prevented the sale of the design, in other words.'

'Exactly.'

'So it is still yours.'

'Of course.'

He beamed. 'This is what I thought. I am most pleased. Ms Radcliffe, I would like to buy that design—'

'But—'

'Or rather, I would like to buy the rights in that design. You must understand, dear lady, that the Fieldingley necklace has become an object of much interest to the general public. People who know jewellery would have liked very much to see what you meant to do with the rubies.' He paused, looking at her attentively.

'Thank you,' she said.

'Several customers of mine have mentioned that they would like to have the design that you worked out for Mr Digby,' he went on.

'Not, of course, in rubies. There are forty synthetic rubies in the old necklace, no?'

'Yes, but they're part of the evidence in what may be a court case. They're not available.'

'Well, we could buy in other rubies. It would be perfectly simple to obtain handsome synthetic stones. And then we might also have it made with different gemstones – not of course in the high-value range, but of good quality and always using eighteen-carat gold.'

He finished his statement, picked up another sticky cake, and bit it with enjoyment.

Jo was astonished. This businessman hadn't even seen the design yet he was making her what sounded like a very lucrative offer.

She had never worked for a firm that had nationwide branches. Of course, this one was long established, had shops in only very prestigious locations, and sold excellent products. But so far all her work had either been commissioned or had been made for competitions, where prize-winning entries were often bought at very high prices.

Did she want a dozen women to be wearing copies of her necklace? Or perhaps more than a dozen – fifty, perhaps?

'How many copies are you thinking of?'

He waved a hand. 'That would depend on demand. But it would be a limited edition. The cut-off point would be a hundred.'

She gained some time for thought by sipping her tea.

'This is a new idea to you,' he resumed. 'Perhaps I should tell you a little more about my plan. I have had a request to see it made with synthetic rubies or perhaps garnet, and of course amethyst springs to mind. But much would depend on what you show me.'

Opal, Jo thought to herself. It would be lovely to see the design carried out with opals of a good colour and not too large. She recalled the watercolour sketch done by Betsey Fieldingley, the one that had inspired her in the first place. *Thunbergia mysorensis,* the flowers were called; not bright flowers, rather dark, unassuming.

'I see you are interested, dear lady,' Tchekari said. 'It would be very helpful to have some idea of your feelings for my plan.'

'I'm interested. It's something I've never done, but . . .' She was still uncertain.

'It would be financially rewarding, Ms Radcliffe. I understand that money has not always been your first concern, but I can promise considerable benefit and also assure you the work would be done by my makers to the very highest standards.'

'Let me think about it.'

He stifled a sigh. 'Can I persuade you to agree now? To give me an early sight of the design?'

He was too eager. And it suddenly occurred to her that there was someone else who wanted to do what he was suggesting.

The world of jewellers is a small one. Threaded through by gossip, it was a clan in which it was almost impossible to keep anything confidential. She wondered whether Tchekari had stolen this idea from some other maker, and hence his eagerness to make a deal with her as quickly as possible.

'It's a new thought to me,' she parried. 'I couldn't commit myself without thinking it over.'

They parted in the end with a promise on her part to let him know in a day or two. On her way home she called Ben Webber on her mobile. He greeted her with warmth.

'It's ages since we were in touch. How are you?'

'Pretty good, thanks.' They exchanged items of news. He didn't ask after Ivan Digby or the court case.

Shortly they got to the point she wanted to make. 'Ben, have you heard anything about interest in the Fieldingley design?'

'Ah.'

'You have?'

'Who's been in contact?'

'Tchekari of Virgilio.'

'Yes, I heard that. And Simenoff. They were asking around as to whether you could be approached.'

'Really?'

'I'd have told you, but you were off enjoying the high life with your money-making friend so I thought you wouldn't be interested in a commercial scheme like that.'

She hesitated. 'I'm not against it, Ben. I've got this design, and it's just sitting there in my computer.'

'But you don't do commercial designs.'

'No, but this would be a bit different, wouldn't it . . .?'

'Jo, you know that the moment anybody brings it out with good stones, the chains will have copied it in glass and abalone shell in six weeks.'

'Mmmm . . .'

'You mean you wouldn't mind if every second woman in Britain were wearing it?'

She couldn't answer that, for the moment. Her work had always been exclusive so far; she couldn't tell whether she would be upset to see it on general release.

Ben went on, 'I know one of the guys on the board of Simenoff. D'you want me to mention to him that you're approachable?'

'I wouldn't mind.'

'Well, well, whatever next. OK, I'll have word with him.'

'You're a dear, Ben.'

'Yes I am, but it doesn't get me anywhere.'

Next day her studio phone rang at a few minutes past nine. 'Ms Radcliffe, this is Alfred Eades of Simenoff. Ben Webber mentioned to me that you wouldn't mind if I put an idea to you.'

'That was quick,' she said, smothering a grin.

'Would it be possible to have a meeting about it? Whenever it would suit you.'

'I'm busy at the moment,' she said. She was working on a brooch and earrings set for a thirtieth-anniversary present. She could, of course, have put it aside to meet Mr Eades, but it had become clear to her that she ought to take her time over the projects being offered to her.

They made a date for lunch in the following week. In the meantime she was going to do nothing about Mr Tchekari. She returned to her pearl and platinum earrings.

A few days went by, and she worked, answered business correspondence, paid bills, and didn't allow herself to worry about not hearing from Ivan.

He rang her on a bright, cold Friday morning. 'Can I come and see you?' he asked.

'Of course. Any time.'

'This afternoon?'

'Fine, whenever you like.'

'About three-ish, then.'

'Look forward.'

'Yes, see you.'

He sounded odd. It unsettled her.

He rang the door buzzer at the appointed time. She looked at the security camera before she keyed in the release for the door, and saw that he had the driver of his car at his side. The driver was carrying an enormous basket of flowers. Ivan looked up at the camera lens and gave a weak smile.

She knew then why he had come.

It was to tell her that he and Miri were getting back together.

Twelve

She opened the door to her visitors. The chauffeur walked in, looked around for a place to set the flower basket, and could see only the low table where clients could sit for a drink and a chat. He placed the basket there and went out.

Now, if she asked Ivan to sit down, they would have this enormous bouquet – this consolation prize – between them. So she leaned against the reception desk to ask, nonchalantly, 'Is this going to take long? Should we go up to the flat?'

'No, no – or at least – well, I don't know.' He stopped. He looked extremely uncomfortable. It took him a moment to start again. 'I . . . I was going to write you a letter. But then I thought that would be a rotten thing to do, because you've been so lovely to me and I want us . . . I don't want us to be bitter about this.'

She decided to help him out. 'About what? About Miri?'

'Oh!' Shock made him draw into himself for a second. 'What makes you say that?'

'Woman's intuition.' She was trying to lighten the occasion. 'It's all right, Ivan. Go on.'

'I told you she had been in touch. I couldn't stop thinking about it, how worried she was. So when she rang again, I . . . I told her to come and talk to me and so . . . Well . . .'

This time she waited him out. All he had to say was, 'We've come to the parting of the ways.' But he couldn't bring himself to do it.

Instead he stammered: 'I . . . I . . . She's everything to me, Jo. And she . . . well . . . she feels the same way about me. It was all a big mistake, she got carried away about those stupid rubies, but she's forgiven me for that now, and understands it wasn't really my fault.'

'I see.'

'And when she lost her temper that day, I should have been more understanding, of course. I should have been there for her, in all that muddle and disappointment. But I was thinking about my

111

money, wasn't I, as if money matters compared with . . . compared with . . .'

'I understand.' She was thinking of a song she'd heard in the past: *Money Can't Buy Me Love*.

'I've realized now that I have to make allowances. She's an actress, isn't she, although this Shakespeare thing really *has* been a mistake. But she's an actress and she's got the artistic temperament.'

'Is she going to go on with the acting idea?' she inquired, really quite interested to know Miri's plans.

'We-ell . . . Not for the present. She needs a good long rest after all she's been through, poor love. I'm carrying her off to Mustique for a few days and then we'll just take things quietly at home.'

'That sounds a good idea.'

'Then there's the house, you remember? Chembard? In all the upset of the past few months, funnily enough, the builders have just been getting on with it and so now, you know, it's time to think about furnishing. Colour schemes, curtains, that sort of thing. I was going to hire some interior decorator but Miri seems to think she could do something herself. And it seems a sort of quiet, easy thing for her to do.'

She nodded.

Now he began to suspect that he was going on and on and not actually saying what he'd come to say.

'I wanted to tell you,' he resumed, 'that I'll always be grateful to you for everything you've given me. I don't know if we could have made a permanent thing of it, but it seems Miri and I are . . . we were meant for each other so I have to say that . . . that you and I . . .'

'It's goodbye for us.'

'Yes.' He threw out a hand. 'Don't hate me for it!'

She took his hand in both of hers and pressed it. 'Of course not, Ivan. Don't worry about it.'

'And we can still be friends?'

'Why not.'

They shook hands, he kissed her lightly on the mouth, and then rather hastily he went out.

For quite a while she stayed where she was, leaning against the reception desk. Then she looked at her watch. Four o'clock.

She got her car out of the garage at the back, brought it round, and loaded the basket of flowers into the passenger seat. She drove to her hairdresser.

'Would you like these for your treatment room?' she asked.

'Good heavens! Where did these come from?'

'A friend gave them to me. But it's far too much for my flat – too sumptuous.'

'You think my facials are sumptuous, do you?' she said, chuckling. 'OK, I'll give these flowers a home. Let me give you a hairdo in exchange.'

So she spent the rest of the afternoon being pampered. At home afterwards she was restless for a while, walking from the living room to the kitchen and back, switching on the television, switching it off.

She was a little bit hurt, a little unhappy. But she kept telling herself to snap out of it. She had never expected the affair with Ivan to last. They were too unlike each other in temperament and taste.

And she had always known he was still in love with Miri. The mere fact that for a long time they'd avoided the very mention of her name had told her so.

She'd had forewarning that they were about to part. When he said at the St Valentine's Day dinner, 'I had a call from Miri', at that point, she had known it was going to end.

Had she loved him? Really loved him? She had liked him, felt for him, found there was more to his character than mere money-making. But she had to agree within herself that her heart wasn't breaking. She would recover.

Only, for the moment, there was this sense of missing him.

At breakfast next morning she found herself totally disinclined to work. She decided to give herself the day off. She began by ringing a few friends to meet at a lunch-and-lecture in Soho. After the talk they lingered for a while, arguing about the subject, which had been Etruscan jewellery, and laughing at how little they had taken in.

She then went on to some retail therapy. She convinced herself she needed something special to wear for her meeting with Mr Eades of Simenoff, which was the following day. So she spent a happy hour or two in Sloane Street among the designer boutiques.

While she was there she took the opportunity to look at what was on offer in the branches of the jewellery stores. She'd often studied their advertisements in fashion magazines, but now she took the time to examine their wares in some detail.

113

There was nothing there to be ashamed of, that was for sure. Fine workmanship, good quality gems, a high standard of design. Perhaps there was a tendency to go for 'the trend', but that was only to be expected: shops wanted goods that were almost certain to sell, not experimental pieces.

She was tired by the time she reached home. She still felt no impulse to get on with the pearl and platinum earrings, but she was stimulated by what she'd heard at the lecture and seen in the shop windows. She sat down with a glass of wine and a sketchpad. When she looked up again, it was nearly midnight. And she hadn't once thought of Ivan since she left the flat at ten in the morning.

The meeting with Mr Eades was all business and no frills. He offered no cakes, no compliments. Small in stature and very neat, he laid his offer neatly on the line. He wanted the design she'd done for the Fieldingley Rubies. He intended to bring it out in various semi-precious gems as birthstone presents – he already had sources for good supplies of garnet for January, spinel for May, peridot for August, and had inquiries out for some others.

'I'll have the rest sorted out in a couple of weeks,' he declared. 'I'd like to launch in time for Christmas with high-type zircon, which of course is the December birthstone, and in the blue version, if you think that's right for you.'

She nodded. She'd always rather liked blue zircon, which she found warmer than some blue sapphires.

They discussed money. He was prepared to send her a contract within a week if she would come to terms within the next few days. 'But you haven't even seen the design,' she protested.

'I have faith in you,' he said.

On parting she promised to be in touch soon. In a nearby coffee bar she rang Ben Webber. 'I've had very enthusiastic offers from both people, Ben. I'd like your opinion. Could we meet and talk it over?'

He was delighted. They agreed to have dinner together in town. He listened to her account of her meetings with the two men then sat musing over his thoughts.

'You seem to have been quite taken by Mr Tchekari,' he murmured.

'Oh yes, he's a darling.'

'That's important, if you're going to be doing business with him over a period of time.'

114

'But Eades was more down-to-earth, had his plans laid out.'

'What do you prefer – a nice chatty guy with cakes, or a more organized type with plans?'

'I don't know.'

'Well, let's do it from the financial point of view. Which is going to make you the most money?'

'I haven't worked that out yet.'

'Perhaps you should be talking to your accountant, not me.'

As they were preparing to leave the restaurant Ben said to her, 'Jo . . . have you seen the evening paper?'

'No, why?'

'There's a photograph in it. Ivan and a friend at Heathrow en route to Mustique.'

'Ah.'

He hesitated. 'You're not surprised?'

'No.'

'So, what . . . er . . . happened?'

'Let's not talk about it, Ben.'

'OK,' he said, looking penitent.

She took Ben's advice, contacted her accountant, then spent three or four days debating with herself. She had three choices: go with Tchekari, go with Eades, or refuse both. In the end she contacted Eades and, with the advice of her accountant, she struck a very profitable bargain.

She said to herself, Now I could afford to go to Mustique too. But she was shaking her head at the idea as she thought it. She had far too much to do to go swanning off to tropical islands. Besides, she didn't even like tropical temperatures.

Tim Fieldingley called her. 'Ms Radcliffe, my grandmother and I are in town for a few days. She was saying that she'd like to meet you, so I was wondering . . .?'

'Oh, I don't think that's . . . What about the court case?'

'Well, what about it? Grans isn't going to lead you astray!' She laughed.

'I told her, you know, that you'd admired her watercolour – what was it, it was a *Thunbergia* of some kind, wasn't it?'

'Yes, it was. I liked it a lot.'

'There you are. She likes it too – the plant, I mean. So you and she should meet. We're at the Taberner, and it's got a rather nice bar. How about drinks one evening? Or lunch, or something.'

The Taberner Hotel, she knew, was in Bloomsbury. As she wanted to go to the British Museum at some point to do some further checking on Etruscan design, she decided to accept the invitation. She could combine it with a museum visit. And besides, she rather wanted to meet Betsey Fieldingley.

The meeting took place next day. Mrs Fieldingley was settled on a velvet-padded bench in a corner of the bar, sipping Amontillado. Her grandson had a glass of dark beer in front of him. He rose as Jo came in.

'Ah, been working?' He was glancing at the sketchpad that peeped out of her handbag.

'Only a look-see at something.'

'Grans, this is the famous Jo Radcliffe.'

'Good gracious, I'm not famous . . .'

'We're all famous, dear, because of those confounded rubies. Sit down, what would you like to drink – Tim, dash about.'

He grinned, nodded at Jo's request for a glass of white wine, and took himself off. His grandmother studied Jo unashamedly. 'You're younger than I thought,' she remarked. 'I looked you up, you've done well in some exhibitions and stuff, so I thought you'd be in your forties at least.'

Jo managed a smile. 'Is it good or bad that I'm not in my forties?'

'Good, of course, because Tim seemed so impressed with you and if anything's going to come of it, I wouldn't want him to choose someone older than himself.'

'Mrs Fieldingley!'

'Oh, call me Betsey, everybody does mostly.' She wrinkled her nose and sipped sherry.

She was pale and there were lines in her face that spoke of hardships, but there were crinkles round her dark grey eyes, which still held a lively sparkle. Her hair was silvery white, badly cut so that it had to be held back by an old-fashioned tortoise-shell clasp. Her clothes were tidy but had a slightly outdoors look, rather like her grandson.

'Is this why you wanted to meet me?' Jo inquired, amused. 'To inspect a future granddaughter-in-law?'

'Well, he's off abroad so much, it's difficult to fix him up with anybody suitable and I certainly don't want him coming back with a bride from somewhere that they speak some language nobody's ever heard of.'

116

'Does Tim know what you were up to when you got him to invite me here?'

'Of course, but he's got the good sense not to say so. You mustn't mind me, dear, I've always been one to look at things and then do something about them. Couldn't have travelled so far on so little money when I was younger without being quick off the mark.'

'I gather you went everywhere in those days. Were you in search of specific plants?'

'Oh, that's so well-mannered!' She gave a little chuckle. 'You don't really want to know about my travels, Jo, but it's nice of you to ask. I was very pleased when Tim said you liked my *Thunbergia*. That was a good piece of work, I do think.'

'I really liked it. Not one of those glorious, admire-me flowers, but it had something.'

Betsey sighed. 'It was probably somewhere there that I picked up this bug that seems to have damaged my ticker. I was in a fever for days. Stupid twit – I'd got low on funds and I was on my own by then, poor darling Geoffrey having gone to the big plant-house in the sky . . .' She sighed. 'He always made me stock up on drugs but this time I hadn't brought enough mepacrine . . .'

She broke off, shaking her head at herself as Tim came with Jo's drink. 'You arrived just in time to prevent me being a bore, my boy,' she told him.

'You expect me to say you're never a bore, but I'm not going to. This is Graves, is that OK?' He handed the glass to Jo.

'Yes, lovely, thank you. You said you were in town for only a few days?'

'Yes, Tim has to see his scientific director about this next trip, and I –' Betsey paused and held up a hand for attention – 'I am going to look at my paintings on show in a gallery in Mayfair.'

'Really?' Jo was surprised and pleased. It always pleased her when some neglected artist had a success.

'A whole gallery!' said Betsey. 'Mind you, I think it's only about a hundred square feet – one of those little private places in a chic location.' She laughed. 'Do you know, it's over twenty years since any of my work's been on show?'

'So how did it come about?' Jo asked, genuinely interested.

'Well, it's those blasted rubies again! Nobody hears about me or my work for decades, and then all of a sudden the public's a bit interested so some bright spark decides to put on a show.'

'I had to get the paintings out of store,' Tim put in. 'You won't remember, but the first time you ever telephoned I was up in the attic at the old cottage getting her stuff down and packing it. Most of it went into one of those storage lockers.'

Betsey nodded in satisfaction. 'Air-conditioned, insured, all that kind of thing. Good value.'

'But, of course, nobody was ever likely to see any of it,' Tim said, 'until this chap Gedberg pops up and says he'll hang her stuff in his gallery on commission.'

'Thrilling!' cried his grandmother. 'Pushing on towards eighty and still capable of being thrilled.'

'Grans, I think you've had too much to drink.'

'Nonsense, one glass of sherry. Days gone by, I used to be able to knock it back with the boys and never have a hangover.' She looked regretfully at her empty glass. 'I'm only allowed one glass now – doesn't agree with the wonder drugs I have to take.'

'You must let me have the address of the gallery.'

'We'll be heading off there later. It's the preview for favoured customers.' Tim hesitated. 'I suppose you wouldn't like to come with us?'

'I certainly would!' Then she thought about it. 'I'm not dressed for a thing like that.'

'Nonsense, we're not dressing up – are we, Tim?'

'But Mayfair?' Jo protested.

'Oh, pooh to that,' Betsey cried. 'And besides, dear, you look charming.'

Since Jo was wearing jeans and a shirt under a denim jacket, this couldn't possibly be true, but they were so insistent that she gave up arguing.

The gallery proved to be small, as Betsey had foretold. That meant it would be crowded with an attendance of forty people, and as more than a hundred had turned up, there was a queue outside and the press were there.

Tim led the way through the crowd. There were some protests but he announced airily, 'This is the artist, please let her pass.'

The press cameras were immediately pointed in their direction.

'Mrs Fieldingley! Mrs Fieldingley! Does Ivan Digby still have the rubies? Is he still going to sue you? Mrs Fieldingley, how do you feel about being a sell-out before you even open?'

Anton Gedberg came bustling out. 'Now, now, friends, please let my star come through. Mrs Fieldingley, how lovely to meet you

118

in person. And this is . . .?' He led them inside, introductions were made, and drinks were handed round.

The gallery was indeed small so that the wall area was not great, but by clever placing of standing screens Gedberg had managed to display about ninety paintings, watercolours and oils. It wasn't quite true that it was a sell-out, but many of the cards naming the plants and their habitat had red dots.

'Good Lord,' muttered Betsey, half-shaking her head. 'What's got into them? This is about twenty times what I sold in the old days.'

'My sweet, you're news, that's what it is,' Gedberg explained.

'Oh, so it's not my artistic talent.' Her tone was ironic.

'Ah, bless! You're an idealist! Never mind, dear heart, you know and I know that these are authentic works of art. And money is always useful.'

'Huh. If I'd been able to sell like this last year, I wouldn't have had to put those confounded rubies up for sale.'

'C'est la vie. Now come along, pet, I want to introduce you to Hallydale. He's a publisher, art books, you know? This way. Rupert, Rupert! Here she is!'

He urged her away to go further into the gallery. Tim hesitated. 'A book? Should I go after her? If it's a business offer, you know, she's not good at that.'

She gave him a little push. 'Go on, then. And I'm going to make myself scarce. I shouldn't be here in public hobnobbing with you, you know.'

'Why not? Oh – the court case. Oh, look here, it can't matter all that much.'

'Go on, your grandmother is being hit by a charm offensive! She'll sign away everything she owns if you don't protect her.'

He sighed, took her hand, and pressed it between both of his. 'Can I ring you again? Not soon, I have to be in Hamburg for a couple of days but when I get back . . .?'

'Whenever you like,' she said lightly.

She threaded her way out to the street. The cameramen were still active, but they were interested in art-loving celebrities in high fashion clothes, so she was able to edge her way round the gathering unnoticed.

A few days later, she herself was the centre of interest. She arrived at the offices of Simenoff Jewels in Clerkenwell to sign the contract for the reproduction series, to find that Mr Eades had invited the press. However, on this occasion it was only journalists interested in the jewellery trade and a few from expensive fashion magazines. There was no hassle, no impertinent questioning. She submitted to a photographic session, thankful that she was wearing a decent silk blouse and a tailored skirt. She'd brought with her a folder containing printouts of the original design, and was invited to hold it up.

'But please make sure it stays closed!' warned Eades, thinking about the exclusive deal he had made. He'd said he intended to have a big launch party when the first version of the necklace came out.

Jo laughed and obeyed. But she found it less amusing when the general press tried to do a follow-up the following day. She knew their interest would die away, but for the day she resorted once again to disconnecting her office phone and relying on her mobile. It was on her mobile that she received a call from Ivan.

'Hey, what's this about you selling my design?' he challenged. He sounded amused yet rather cross.

'It isn't your design. You dropped out.'

'You might have let me know you were going to sell it.'

'You were off on some tropical island.'

'That was only for a few days. I was around.'

Not as far I could tell, she thought to herself. And then it occurred to her that she was dealing with him in a very self-possessed way. No muffled sighs, no quavering of the voice. It might almost have been thought that she'd never had sleepless nights about him.

'I wouldn't even have known,' he complained, 'but Miri has a chum on one of the magazines that went to your signing thing. So that's now I heard about it.'

'Next time I sell anything I'll send you a text message.'

He let that go by a minute, then said in a muted way, 'You think I'm being interfering, eh?'

'Somewhat.'

'Well, you know . . . I'm always going to be interested in what you do. You said we could be friends.' Now he was reproachful.

'So is this a friendly call to congratulate me on a good piece of business?'

'Huh!' Then he said, quite briskly, 'As a matter of interest, what sort of money are you getting?'

'Not much compared to what you deal with. But I'm pleased with it.'

'So it's not such a bad thing, being friends with me and designing things for me.'

She made a non-committal murmur. She had a feeling this was the prologue to something.

'You know, Miri and I ... you know we're getting married ... probably June. And Miri's been saying, you know, hearing about your deal with Simenoff, she thought it would be great if you'd design something for her for the wedding.'

Jo was startled. Whatever next?

'Oh, I don't think so, Ivan. I'm busy.'

'But it's not wanted till June. You could fit it in somewhere, couldn't you?'

'I'm pretty well booked up with commissions.' And that was certainly true. She'd become very much in demand, one way and another.

'Miri thought you'd be interested,' he persisted. 'She says she showed you once – little headdresses, pretty little things she sometimes likes to wear in the evening, something like that, only in white, of course, and I said she must have diamonds in it, so what do you say?'

'I really can't, Ivan. I'm sorry.'

'At least think about it.'

'No ... really.'

'But we're still friends, aren't we?'

'Of course.' Anything to get rid of him.

As she switched off, she was shaking her head. Had he always been so insensitive? Or had she been stupid to fall in love with him?

Stupid, she thought. Stupid, stupid!

Thirteen

Jo telephoned Betsey Fieldingley to thank her for the drinks and the invitation to the preview of her exhibition.

'But you didn't see anything, darling child,' Betsey cried. 'You vanished out into the night while my back was turned.'

'I thought it better not to be seen.'

'Yes, so Tim explained.'

'How many paintings were sold, if you don't mind my asking?'

'Mind? I love it. Gives me a chance to boast. By the end of the evening about half of my masterpieces had been sold. Not bad, eh?'

'Marvellous!'

'And the fellow in publishing? He wants me to contribute to a book about South American alpine plants. Words by Sir Bernard Lermonth, illustrations by Betsey Fieldingley. I've got about eighteen watercolours I did on a trip to the Andes. So it's back to the storage lock-up to sort them out.'

'Well, it couldn't happen to a more deserving painter,' Jo declared.

'I totally agree. So now, I'm in the likelihood of making a bit of an income and it occurs to me . . .'

'Yes?'

'Jo, you know this Ivan Digby character quite well, don't you?'

'You might say that.'

'Could I ask you to arrange a meeting with him?'

'Ah.'

'Ah, yes of course, or Ah, I can't?'

'Well, I *could* . . .'

'But you don't want to?'

'Hm . . . Let me think a minute . . .' There was silence between them for a space. Then she said, 'Ivan and I more or less said goodbye to each other, you know?'

'Not exactly, but go on.'

'However, we agreed to remain friends.'

'Oh.' There was understanding in the word. Betsey then said, 'You have to forgive me, dear. I don't read the gossip sheets although plenty of people reported all the bits about the rubies. If there was something . . . I mean . . . But you're saying it came to a sticky end?'

'Glutinous, I think is the word.'

'Sorry. I shouldn't have asked, then.'

'No, wait. After all, we did say he and I would "still be friends" and . . . Look, I wouldn't let it mean too much – it would be a business contact. To ask if he'd meet you, I see nothing against that.'

'It's like this, my dear. I can't pay back the whole purchase price. The earnings from last night's exhibition were good, but you know, watercolours never raise anything like the same money as oils.'

'I suppose not.'

'But if he'd agree to take it in instalments, you see. I'm going to be earning a bit, and though I don't expect all this popularity to last, it ought to increase my bank balance for a couple of years, with luck. So if he'd agree to discuss the idea of, say, quarterly payments, it would perhaps be a solution.'

Jo was silent as she considered this.

'You don't think it's a good idea?' Betsey asked, in a disappointed way.

'I haven't a clue. What does your solicitor say, Betsey?'

'I haven't asked him yet. I just got the notion this morning.'

'Don't you think you should?'

'Why? It's got nothing to do with him what I do with my money.'

'But don't you see? It's like admitting you were to blame in the first place, if you start offering Ivan money.'

'But if it would get him off my back? This court case is going to drag on and on, and the lawyers' fees are going to be something horrid '

'That's probably true, but . . .'

'I'll ask Mr Anstruther,' Betsey said. 'But he's a frightful bore, and he's going to put up all kinds of objections. Just for the sake of objecting, I mean. He's an objecting sort of man.'

Jo smiled. 'But you hired him to advise you in this business, didn't you? Seems to me you ought to get his opinion.'

'Humph!' Clearly, this wasn't what Betsey had hoped to hear. 'Oh, all right then. But if he agrees, can I come back to you about having a word with Mr Digby?'

'Certainly.'

A few letters had come for Donald. She sent them on while she was attending to business matters that morning, but was surprised to get a thank-you phone call from her brother a couple of days later.

She'd made no effort to contact him after Miri's desertion. She felt he was probably too angry and disappointed to want any words of comfort from her. To her surprise, he was quite buoyant on the phone. When she asked how things were going, he replied with some self-satisfaction.

'Oh, a bit of a downer when Miri said she was walking out. But we had a contract, of course, so we had a haggle with Mr Moneybags and we came out of it rather well.'

Jo hadn't thought of that. 'I'm glad to hear it,' she said, and meant it. 'And the schools drama tour?'

'Well, that's still on. Got someone to replace her. After all, lots of actresses would jump at the chance of playing Perdita. But some of the schools backed out, because they particularly wanted Miri Gale in the cast.'

'Really?'

'Teenagers, you know,' he explained, huffing a little, 'they'd have been enthusiastic if they were going to see a celeb, but some of the schools said they couldn't justify spending the money on something that most of the kids wouldn't attend.'

'So are you going to lose money on that?'

'Nooo, de Groot is picking up the tab.' Donald gave a little grunt of amusement. 'He's got a little friend he wants to launch into the theatre. She's taken on Perdita.'

She was shaking her head as she heard him out. To her mind, it was a complicated way to earn a living.

They parted with good wishes on both sides. She was relieved that it had turned out so well. Apparently Donald was launched yet again on a theatrical course, but this time with a fair wind behind him. And better yet, he and Lindora were settled in a flat in Chiswick and sounded as if they wouldn't be returning to live with her.

Tim Fieldingley came calling that afternoon, after ringing to ask if it was convenient. 'It's about Grans,' he explained.

He was rather travel-worn. 'I only got back from Hamburg last night,' he said. 'And Grans comes up with this daft idea about paying Digby by little dribs and drabs.'

'Yes, we talked about it.'

'So she told me.'

Jo had offered him tea and biscuits. He stirred sugar into his cup rather vigorously. She had a feeling he'd had a quarrel with his grandmother.

'The whole thing's preposterous! That confounded necklace was sold for forty-five thousand, and she's proposing to refund the money at a couple of thousand a year!'

'My word. The arithmetic isn't attractive.'

'You can say that again! And besides, she *shouldn't* be paying him anything.'

'I agree.'

'She told me you were against it. And so is Anstruther – he's the solicitor. His view is that she sold the necklace in good faith, and that's what he put to the barrister who was going to handle it in court.'

Jo nodded.

'But now she's saying she's only got so many years left on this earth and she doesn't want to spend them worrying about a court case, so she's determined to make this offer to him.'

'It's a mistake. I know Ivan. He wants his money, all of it. He's not going to agree to this little-by-little arrangement.'

Tim sighed deeply. 'Well, really, the reason I'm here is to ask you to speak to Digby and get him to come to a meeting.'

'Wouldn't it be better if Mr Anstruther did it?'

'He refuses. He says his duty as a solicitor is to give her what he calls "best advice", and he says to make this offer is to admit she feels guilty.'

'Well . . . don't you think he's right?'

'Of course I do. But she's so pig-headed!' He sat back in his chair, glaring at one of her showcases. 'Look, Jo, it's like this. She asked you to make the approach to Digby, and if you don't, she's going to do it herself. She'll ring him up and before you know what's happening she's going to apologize and tell him she just wants a quiet life, and he'll take advantage of her.'

She was quiet, and he waited. After a bit she said, 'I'll ring him. What shall I say?'

'That Grans has a proposition to put to him.'

'Shall I say what it is?'

'No, let's leave that until the meeting. He's probably going to ring his own law man about it, and if we let him know she's offering payment, it gives them an advantage from the start.'

125

'Ivan's going to be angry, having to drag himself down to Hereford for what he'll think is a waste of time.'

'No, it's going to be London. I told you, Anstruther has refused to be a party to this, so Grans is coming up to London, and Anstruther's relented enough to get a colleague in Gray's Inn to supply the meeting place.'

Jo was rather ashamed at her unwillingness to take part. Her instinct was to stay out of it. But Tim was looking so troubled that she said, 'Do you want me to ring him now?'

'Well, would you? If you could do that, I could go and have a look at this office where the conference is supposed to take place. I mean, this sounds silly, but if it's all going to happen on the second floor, has it got a lift? Grans can't manage stairs; it makes her heart go pit-a-pat.'

'OK. Just a minute.' She picked up her mobile and took it into her workshop. She somehow didn't want Tim to know that she could ring Ivan without having to look up his number. Nor did she want him to hear whatever preliminaries there might be, stumbling explanations that might imply . . . she didn't quite know what they might imply. She only knew she didn't want Tim to hear them.

Ivan answered at once, but asked her to hold. There was a lot of noise in his office. It sounded like a celebration. When he came on line again he said, 'Sorry about that, we've just landed something we've been after for a while. So, what's the score?'

'I'm calling because, I've been asked . . . Mrs Fieldingley was wondering—'

'Mrs Fieldingley? The ruby swindler?' From satisfaction his tone changed to annoyance. 'What about her?'

'She's asking if you would like to meet her.'

'Only in court! And that's not going to be for months yet.'

'But Ivan, she's inviting you to a—'

'Inviting me? To a dance, eh? Costume ball? Lynching party?'

'Ivan, will you be quiet and listen to me?' she cried, as annoyed now as he had been. 'I've been asked to invite you to a meeting at an office in Gray's Inn, to see whether some arrangement could be made . . .'

'I'm not making any arrangement with that old fraudster.'

'Ivan, please. Mrs Fieldingley has a plan she'd like to put before you, and she'd just like to meet you and see what you think.'

'No.'

126

'What harm could it do? Neutral ground, just a friendly conversation.'

'I'm not friendly with her and never will be – she's made me look a fool.'

'But if she has something interesting to say . . .'

'Nothing she says could interest me.'

She groaned inwardly. This was going even worse than she'd expected. 'All right,' she said. 'I can see you're not even going to listen, but how you ever expect to live without paying heed to other people's ideas, I can't imagine.'

'What d'you mean? I listen to other people all the time. That's how I get to make money.'

'But outside your office you don't listen.'

'I certainly do. Why, Miri and I . . .' He paused. It seemed to occur to him that the relationship with Miri wasn't a good example.

'It's just a meeting for a chat,' Jo said, seizing her opportunity.

'But we're on opposite sides in the court case.'

'Are you afraid she'll lead you astray?' she asked, recalling Tim's phrase.

'Me? I'm not afraid, I'm just not in favour.'

'Half an hour. What harm could an old lady do to you in half an hour?'

'She's done me enough harm already.'

'But what if she wants to do something to repair the harm?'

'What?'

'It's up to her to tell you.'

'Why isn't her lawyer doing this soft-soap job?'

'You can ask her that when you see her.'

He was silent for quite a long moment. 'Hm . . .' he said. 'Is she thinking of giving up her defence?'

'Meet her and find out.'

'OK. Let's say I might.' It was a doubtful assent. 'When and where?'

'I'll get Tim Fieldingley to tell you that.'

'Fieldingley? How does he come into it?'

'He's here, he came here to ask if I'd speak to you. So now let me hand you over.'

She thought Ivan made a sound of protest but she didn't wait to hear the rest. She walked back into the studio to hand the phone to Tim. She then retreated back to her workshop. She didn't want to be there if a noisy dispute was going to begin.

Ten minutes later Tim tapped on the workshop door to return the mobile. 'All fixed up. I'm not sure whether I've done a good thing or a bad thing. He sounds a bit of a brawler.'

'Well, he's no push-over where money's involved. I don't think your grandmother knows what she's taking on. You were saying, her solicitor won't be involved in this?'

He was anxious about it. 'I'll go with her, of course. Thing is, I'm not much of a help. I might lose my temper and take a sock at him.'

'Are you all the family she's got?'

'Good heavens, no! There are Fieldingleys in all corners of the globe – I expect I could summon up one or two to be there as moral support.' He nodded to himself. 'Yes, that's a good idea. Then he'll see he's not just got an old lady to browbeat, won't he? Good idea, Jo!'

Was it a good idea, she wondered, after he'd given her a hug and hurried off. Only if one of the Fieldingleys was a hard-headed business type.

Although Jo felt she knew Ivan quite well, she'd never seen him in action in the world of finance. But she gathered from items in the newspapers that he could be very ruthless.

Were the Fieldingleys likely to be able to handle ruthless?

About six the next day Betsey Fieldingley telephoned. 'My dear, I won't keep you, I expect you're off out somewhere for a nice evening. This is just a thank you for your help and all that.'

'That's all right, glad to do anything.' She hesitated. 'Tim said he was calling in the far-flung Fieldingleys. How's that going?'

Betsey gave a little sigh and an apologetic chuckle. 'Tim was a bit optimistic there, I'm afraid. I mean, not everybody leads the kind of footloose life that he does.'

'Oh dear. So who's coming, then?'

'Only Hugo. He's the handiest, you see – he's only got to come from Lewis.'

'Lewes in Sussex?'

'No, no, the Isle of Lewis, in the Hebrides. He's an ornithologist. Runs a bird preserve – sea-birds, you know? Works for a scientific organization – well, it's a bit complicated, he's having to arrange for somebody to take over while he's away, they were in the middle of counting gannets or something.'

Jo listened to this in dismay. 'Is he good with money? Does he manage accounts, hire and fire staff, anything like that?'

'Well, he's good at statistics, to do with the birds, you know – how they're surviving, what's happening to their food sources . . .' She fell into silence. Then she went on, 'I thought I'd be able to talk Peter Anstruther into coming along, but that didn't work. I feel I've perhaps bitten off a bit more than I can chew.'

'Perhaps you should cancel.'

'No.' Betsey was stubborn and annoyed. 'Mr Digby will think I'm a dithery old lady if I cancel. I've a perfectly reasonable business plan to put in front of him, and I'm going to do it.'

'But it's not something you've ever done before, is it?'

'No.'

'And you don't *know* Ivan.'

A very long pause. 'My dear, would *you* come and hold my hand?'

Her first impulse was to cry 'No!' loudly and emphatically. But she checked herself. It would be like allowing Daniel to walk into the lion's den blindfolded.

Betsey went on quickly, 'I'm sorry. I shouldn't have asked.' Then she said, 'But I can't think of anyone else who might be a help.'

So that was how it came about that Jo was entering the premises of Collyer Bates in Gray's Inn on a late March afternoon a week later.

Fourteen

The room they had been allotted was nothing special, clearly an office not in use that particular afternoon. The Fieldingleys were already there when she was shown in. Tim leapt up from his chair to greet her.

'Hello there.' His grandmother beckoned her to a chair at her side. 'This is my cousin Hugo,' Tim said, directing her first towards a burly man standing by the window. They shook hands, Jo thinking he looked uncomfortable in a suit that he didn't fit into very well.

Tim was wearing a suit too. She guessed the two men had decided their normal garb was too unsophisticated for this occasion; these were probably the suits they wore to weddings and funerals. As to their grandmother, she was in a dress and jacket that had a Sixties look. Jo smiled to herself.

Ivan hadn't yet arrived. Betsey said with some irritation, 'Us Fieldingleys acted like a bunch of country bumpkins – we got here too early.'

'Now, Grans, don't get tetchy. It doesn't matter about arrival times – we're not a train timetable.'

'Tim tells me you're a designer,' said Hugo, making conversation. 'Dresses? Furniture?'

'Jewellery. I was going to turn the Fieldingley Rubies into something more up to date.'

'Hugo, I told you that over the phone,' Tim groaned. 'Do pay attention.'

'Sorry, sorry, the connection wasn't good.' To Jo, he said in explanation, 'I only got here from the Hebrides at lunchtime. I'm still catching up.'

'You've had a problem getting away?'

They made conversation, until Ivan was shown in fifteen minutes later.

There could have been no greater contrast to the members of the Fieldingley clan. Ivan was wearing a suit by Paul Smith, a dark

130

red shirt from Jermyn Street, and a tic of muted grey silk. The only thing that indicated he'd come from his office was the fact that his tie was rather loosely knotted, as if he'd been pulling it about during some difficult negotiation.

'Mr Digby,' said Betsey, rising from her chair and holding out her hand. 'We met only briefly when you collected the necklace. These are two of my grandsons – this is Hugo, and this is Tim.'

'How d'you do,' murmured Ivan, nodding at them. To Jo he said, 'Didn't expect to see you here, duchess.'

Tim cleared his throat. 'Er . . . Are we expecting anyone else? Any colleague of yours?'

Ivan gave him a shrug and a rather scornful smile. 'I reckoned I could handle this on my own.' He paused to survey those present. 'Didn't bring a lawyer?'

'Mr Digby,' said Betsey, 'what I had in mind was an informal, friendly discussion. If we come to an agreement, at that point we could bring in our solicitors.'

He shrugged, not in acceptance but indicating she should go on.

'I'd like to say first,' she said, 'that there was never any intention to deceive you. I believed the rubies were genuine, and so did the jeweller that I showed them to—'

'Let's cut to the chase,' Ivan said. 'You're here to offer me something in the hope that I'll back off from suing you. So, what's on the table?'

'It so happens that my financial situation has improved a bit since I had to sell the rubies. I don't suppose you've noticed, but there's been some interest in my paintings—'

'Yeah, yeah,' Ivan interrupted, waving a hand in irritation. 'Bit of a crowd at your show, bit of glitz among the customers buying your stuff, it comes to what? Four or five thousand, eh?'

Tim cleared his throat. 'Mr Digby, it would help if you'd let my grandmother finish a sentence.'

'I'll wait her out to the end when she starts talking in hard cash.'

Betsey coloured up. She pursed her lips before saying, 'Very well. I think I could probably pay off the cost of the rubies in quarterly instalments. Would you agree to that method of payment?'

'Instalments of how much?'

'That would depend . . . er . . . depend on how much my work brought in each year. I've given it a lot of thought and it seems to me I could offer a total of, say, two and a half thousand per annum.

131

Certainly for the next two or three years, while my work is in demand.'

There was a small silence. Ivan was frowning. 'Two and a half thou?'

'Perhaps more this year and next. Then it might have to diminish a bit.'

'Diminish! It's so little it would disappear if it diminished.'

'But I have a proposal to deal with—'

The corners of his mouth were turning up in contempt. 'Done your arithmetic? By your calculations, it's going to take you twenty years to pay me off – and I don't mean to be hard hearted, lady, but do you think you're likely to last that long?'

Jo gave a gasp of protest. 'Ivan, show some respect!'

'Respect? If I can hear some sense, I'll give it the respect it deserves. I've got forty-five thousand tied up in a bunch of glass beads, and that money should be out earning dividends. Even if we tried this idiot idea, what about the interest I'm losing? Add that on, she's gonna be paying me off when she's dead and buried.'

'Ivan!'

'It's all right, Jo,' Betsey said, waving a hand at her. 'He's right, and of course it's quite true I mightn't pay off what I owe him—'

'Grans, you don't *owe* him anything,' Tim interrupted.

'That's right,' agreed Hugo, who had watched and listened in astonishment to the discussion so far. 'And he's so rude about it, I think you should just walk out!'

'Hugo dear, it was my idea to have this meeting,' she said. 'And I really have thought about it, and I want Mr Digby to hear me out.'

'Ivan,' Jo begged, 'please try not to sound so harsh.'

He drew in a deep breath and blew it out. 'She doesn't understand anything about finance. I can't take this seriously.'

Betsey sighed in agreement. 'That's right, I don't understand finance. All I'm trying to do is sort this out so that it's not hanging over me for months and months, perhaps even years.'

'Shouldn't have unloaded your phoney heirloom on me, then.'

She refrained from protest at that. 'You were saying I wouldn't last long enough to pay you off – well, it's true, and I've thought of that. You probably don't know that I put the money I got for the rubies towards buying a flat in a sheltered community.'

He grimaced in irritation at that, but made no comment. It seemed to Jo that he was determined not to be softened by words like 'sheltered community'.

132

'What I thought was, I'd make a will, leaving the flat to you, so that one way or another you'd get your money.' Betsey lifted her chin rather defiantly to wait for his reaction.

He was totally taken aback.

'Grans!' exclaimed Tim. This was clearly news to him.

Ivan smiled at his reaction. 'See? That's not going to go down too well with the family, is it? No, no, I'm not agreeing to anything that's gonna involve me in a legal battle with your heirs. That's just not on.'

'It's a genuine offer,' Betsey insisted. 'I think the place will hold its value and the selling price would take care of this point about losing interest over my instalment idea.'

'I've had enough grief from that stupid necklace!' Ivan exclaimed. 'You think I want the media laughing at me because I'm waiting to put on a dead woman's shoes? You must be living on Planet X if you think I'd agree to this!'

Hugo had risen from his chair, his body tense with anger. 'Your manners are really appalling! Show a little courtesy!'

'Courtesy, respect, be a little gentleman,' Ivan mocked. 'Save it, it gets you nowhere in the business world!' He too had risen, and was turned towards the door. 'I only came here 'cause Jo talked me into it, but I always knew it was a waste of my time. Goodbye!'

He walked out. Hugo made as if to go after him and drag him back, but his grandmother rose so as to stand in his way.

Tim shook his head at him. 'No rough stuff,' he said.

Betsey ran a hand through her untidy hair. 'That didn't go well,' she sighed. And then, with a faltering smile, 'Please don't say I told you so.'

Tim put a comforting arm around her. They all trooped downstairs, arriving at the vestibule in time to witness Ivan driving off in a maroon Mercedes.

After thanking the office manager for the use of the room, they went out and hailed a taxi. In the lounge of Betsey's hotel they sat down to talk things over. Tim ordered tea, looking anxiously at his grandmother.

But she was absorbed in what had just gone by. 'Could you speak to him, Jo?' she asked.

'I don't think so.' She was sorry not to be able to help any further, but Ivan's attitude had shocked her.

'I thought the money side of it was quite good,' Betsey sighed.

The impossibility of explaining the real problem depressed Jo.

133

Betsey was truly naïve about finance, but there was something even greater that stood in her way. She'd never met a man like Ivan before.

'It's not about the money,' Jo began. 'It's about his image. He's been made to look silly, and he wants a public victory to repair the damage.'

Hugo was still trying to catch up with the details of the case. 'He wouldn't necessarily win in court, would he?' he queried. 'Grans didn't do anything *wrong*.'

'I don't feel I did, Hugo dear, but it *is* my fault in a way. I should have taken the necklace to a specialist for valuation before the sale took place. I see that now. Relying on a jeweller in a shop was silly of me.'

'How on earth were you to know?'

'Apart from all that,' she swept on, 'it's taking ages to go through all the legal how-d'you-do, and it's really so . . . distracting . . . and *depressing*, to say nothing of what it's costing in ongoing legal fees!'

They talked for an hour or so, ending with the reluctant agreement on Betsey's side that she would make no further efforts.

Jo went home thinking that she was the only one who understood Ivan – but not well enough to know what might move him to cancel the lawsuit.

Spring brought international exhibitions of jewellery design, some of which Jo felt she must attend. She had something of her own to submit later in the year and it was important to see what influences were at work, and also to keep contact with the owners of great jewellery firms, whose customers might order some special piece. She was abroad intermittently, and busy in between times with work on hand.

In May she went with a group of friends to the opening day of a big annual antiques fair. Her interest was to see what jewellery was on sale there, what was appealing to the general public, what influences were at work. For others, this was one of the great occasions to see and be seen.

Among the visitors she noticed Ivan and Miri. She was startled at first, but on second thoughts realized it was quite understandable. Ivan was probably looking for items – or perhaps merely ideas – for the furnishing of Chembard, his stately home in the country.

She intended to avoid them. To her surprise, Miri sought her out. 'I spied you when you first came in,' she announced, taking her by

134

the arm. 'Been trying to get at you for half an hour, but your pals have been taking up your attention. What brings you here?'

'Oh, the antique jewellery, of course. And you're looking for furniture, I expect.'

'Yep, some, though a lot of that is ever so dark, isn't it? I like the French things, you know, sort of old ivory look with little painted scenes, but our decorator says they're only suitable for bedrooms.'

'Are you doing the entire house in period pieces?'

Miri shrugged. 'Who knows? Meredith says we mustn't make the place look like a museum.'

'Meredith is the interior designer?'

'Some pal of Ivan's in the City recommended him. I'd have liked one of the guys I used to know when I was on TV – he worked on some of those house-improvement shows, you know? But Ive said he was too lightweight.'

Jo thought he was probably right. She moved the subject along a little. 'When will the house furnishing be finished?'

'July, we think. Suits us quite well, 'cause Ive says everything starts to go a bit quiet in the City in July and August. So we're thinking the "Great Day" could be August.' She gave a rueful smile. 'Got to fit our lives around what goes on in the City.'

'There you go,' said Jo. 'Even weddings have to take account of earning a living, Miri.'

Miri nodded. 'I don't kid myself. If me and Ive are going to make a go of it, it's got to be handled so that he can concentrate on what he's good at. And that's making money. But sometimes . . .'

'What?'

There was a long hesitation. 'That business with the old girl, Mrs Fieldingley.'

'What about her?'

'Ive's really got it in for her! He told me about that meeting – the one in the law office. I mean, she made him a decent sort of offer, but it just made him angry.'

Jo didn't want to say that she thought Betsey's plan had always been a non-starter. 'Ivan doesn't like to make concessions of any kind,' she remarked, in a neutral tone.

'Right. And you know what? People are sort of teasing me about it. They're saying he's a real old meanie.' She pouted. 'After all, what does the money matter to him? He can make that sort of cash in a day at the office! But he just won't let it go.'

135

'It's to do with prestige, Miri. He doesn't like to think he was made to look foolish.'

She groaned. 'I wish this whole court case thing could be sort of wished away. Those rubies are like a sort of ... what's it called? . . . hanging over us!'

'*Bête noire*?' Jo suggested.

'Yeah, sort of a dark cloud. You know, he often has to put papers away in the safe at the flat, and there it is, the necklace, in that flat jewel case.'

'He ought to get rid of it, then.'

'Ha! Who'd want it? Bunch of rubbish!'

Jo frowned. 'It's not exactly rubbish, Miri. The necklace was made by a master designer of the nineteenth century. It's worth something.'

'Not to *me*,' Miri dissented. Her attention was called away to something at the other side of the hall. 'There's my lord and master waving at me. Gotta go, Jo.' She smiled at her little rhyming phrase, patted her on the arm, and began the process of working her way through the crowd towards Ivan.

Jo was home by early evening. While she was getting herself a meal, her thoughts turned back to the conversation with Miri.

The rubies *were* worth something. Their provenance was good, although the stones themselves were not valuable. The name of the designer, Giacinto Mellillo, was highly regarded by those who were experts in the jewellery world. The design was an excellent example of late-Victorian style, worth preserving for that reason alone – Jo had always felt rather guilty at the idea of breaking it up. Moreover, the recent publicity earned by the necklace had made it something of a by-word. Surely that ought to count in assessing its present-day value?

In the morning she still thought there was something to be done about the Fieldingley Rubies. She rang the number for Ivan Digby's flat, hoping that he would still be at his office. The phone was answered by the Filipino manservant, who said Madame was at the building's health club.

'She comes back after healthy lunch, afterward going out to little rehearsal of friend in theatre show.'

She left a message, asking Miri to ring her. The call came through on her workshop phone a couple of hours later.

'Hello, Jo, say, whaddya know?' Miri carolled.

'Hello, Miri, thanks for getting back to me.' They exchanged a few words of chit-chat, then Jo said, 'Remember what we were talking about yesterday at the antiques fair?'

'Er . . . What? Ive and his bad temper?'

Jo chuckled. 'No, the reason for that. The Fieldingley Rubies.'

'Oh, them.'

'Yes, Miri, listen. I've had an idea about them. I think it might help to make Ivan feel better.'

'You do? Let's hear it then, for Pete's sake!'

'I think he should put them up for auction.'

Fifteen

Miri argued a little. She was convinced nobody would bid for what she called 'a load of old fakery'. She refused to put the idea to Ivan.

'You know what he's like,' she moaned. 'Anything he's involved in, it has to work so he makes a profit. Who's going to make an offer on that stuff?'

Jo tried to explain that there were collectors in the world who weren't primarily concerned with intrinsic value. 'What interests them is the history of the piece. The story behind it, that sort of thing.'

'Huh. And d'you think Ive is going to be convinced when I start telling him stuff like that?'

Perhaps not, Jo said to herself. Aloud she said, 'How about you tell him I have this idea, and I'm going to ring him and explain?'

'How about you come here and do your explaining one on one?'

'Well . . . All right.'

She agreed to arrive for drinks at about six thirty. If Ivan was furious at her idea, she was to make her escape as soon as she could. If he was interested, she'd accept an invitation to stay for dinner.

When she got to the flat at the arranged time, she found the pair of them out on their lovely terrace. Evening sun shone on a vista of towers and pinnacles and domes. They were drinking Singapore Slings; the manservant hurried to pour one for her. Ivan had been home since about three in the afternoon, had had a session in the gym and a massage, and was in a good mood.

Jo opened play by asking how Miri had enjoyed watching the rehearsal of that afternoon.

'Oh, gosh, one of those weird plays, everybody has to wear an outfit made of canvas and only four characters – talk about cheap! But Dulcie's keen, she's into that sort of fringe stuff. She thinks it's gonna be her big break.'

Ivan laughed. '*You're* never going to appear in a play where you have to wear canvas, princess, are you!'

'I should say not! And I'm never gonna be in Shakespeare, either!'

He shook his head at her. He said to Jo, 'So what's all this that Miri's been on about?'

'Has she explained anything?'

'Some scheme to sell that stupid necklace. I thought she must have got it wrong, she usually does. And anyhow I don't want to part with it because it's needed as evidence in court.'

'Not necessarily, Ivan. The report that Ben supplied is evidence enough. And if you accept my idea, there would be another test done – by the auction house.'

He gave her a hard stare. 'So Miri's right. You're actually suggesting I should put it up for sale?'

'Yes. I think you might do well.'

'Don't be daft,' he grunted. 'It'd be a dead loss. Your pal Ben Webber gave me the impression that the whole thing's only worth about four thousand, and that's mostly for the gold.'

'That may be true if you value the components merely as minerals,' she began. 'But as works of art . . .'

'Huh!'

'The components are worth a lot more than that.'

'Works of art!' There was only scorn in his response. Miri frowned a warning at Jo.

Jo refused to be put off. 'Listen, Ivan. You were looking for a wedding present for Miri and you heard of these famous rubies. Yes?'

'But they're not rubies . . .'

'No, they're synthetic. *But* that in itself makes them famous. They may well have been the very first synthetic rubies used in a piece by a great designer.'

'By some crook, you mean!'

'No, there's no proof that Mellillo had any idea he was working with a form of aluminium oxide. And that too is an aspect that makes those stones valuable. Don't you see? They're part of history, part of a *drama*.'

He sipped his drink, staring out at the view. 'So they're maybe worth more than four thousand?'

'Yes.'

'How much more?'

'A lot, I'd guess.'

139

'Yeah, but how much is a lot? Are they worth ten thou? Fifteen? What?'

'I don't know. At the antiques fair where you and Miri were looking at furniture, some of the antique jewellery on offer was selling for very large sums. Did you see the green Beryl ring? The asking price was eight thousand pounds. Now the stone in the ring was worth very little – the ring was valuable because it had belonged to Sarah Bernhardt.'

'Who's Sarah Bernhardt?' he grunted, irritated.

'Oh, Ive!' Miri rolled her eyes. 'She's ever so famous, she was an actress from olden times.'

'Learned about her while you were doing your Shakespeare, did you?' But he was less irritated. He waved a hand at Jo. 'Didn't see this cheapo ring.'

'You think eight thousand pounds is cheapo?' she challenged.

'Are you saying those forty-five so-called rubies are worth eight thousand?'

'I'm saying they could be worth more. Because they're early specimens of the synthetic process. To a collector, that's important.'

'More than eight thousand. So you mean what? Ten, twelve? That's still no go. I'm not taking a loss of over thirty thousand because some collector might want pieces of man-made ruby!'

'Ivan, that's not the way to look at it. Nobody in their right mind would want to dismantle that necklace for the separate pieces of synthetic ruby.'

'Good grief, Jo, I wish you'd make yourself clear! You were talking about this cheapo ring – somebody wanted that because it had belonged to this old actress.'

'Yes, and the rubies are famous now partly because they belong to *you*! The necklace has got star value, don't you see? It was made by Mellillo, it's in a design that's part of the history of jewellery – that's to say, Classical Revival style. And then, remember what a sensation it caused when Ben's report came out – it was on TV and in the papers—'

'You don't need to remind me,' he interrupted, getting to his feet and turning away. She guessed it still made him flush in shame to think he'd been taken in.

But Miri took a different view. Something like a smile of pleasure touched her lips as she recalled the furore.

She too rose, and followed Ivan to the parapet, where she put

140

an arm round him while they stood looking out at the roofs of London. Jo could see that she was murmuring to him.

By and by they came back to the table, but didn't sit down.

'Dinner's coming out soon,' Ivan said. 'Want to stay and talk about this a bit more?'

The meal was served in the dining room. Jo went through the points that she felt would have importance to him. 'The auction house would value the necklace again, taking in all the things they feel are relevant – the press interest in the jewellery, the likelihood of the big collectors taking part.'

'Big collectors? Such as who?'

'Oh, I don't know . . . There are people who are interested in the artistic side, and then there are quite a few who look at the stones from a scientific point of view. There are a lot of history buffs, they might want the necklace because of its place in the development of modern techniques. That's important, you know. Synthetic stones are used now in all sorts of ways – in industry, in science. A lot of scientific instruments have synthetic gemstone in them somewhere.'

'You know any of these collecting guys?'

'I know *of* them. I see them mentioned in the technical magazines. But the auction houses know them all. They send out invitations, you see.'

'And another thing,' Miri put in. 'The press are bound to be interested.'

'Well, that's no inducement!' he countered. 'I hate all those creeps.'

'But, Ive, it depends how you treat them. You can get them on *your* side. Give them a bit of advance warning, let them make a story out of it – you know, I learned a lot from the man Donald hired for me.'

Ivan glowered, and Miri fell into an abrupt silence. Ivan had no good memories of the publicity agent who had handled their break-up.

Luckily the manservant appeared to clear plates and refill wine glasses. Miri had a short conversation with him about the dessert, which she suggested they should take on the terrace.

When they were settled there again, Ivan said, 'Let's get real about this. What kind of money are we talking about here?'

Jo took her time laying down her spoon and swallowing her mouthful of fruit conde. 'That I can't tell you,' she confessed. 'A lot depends on who takes part in the auction. There could be agents acting for overseas buyers at the sale, and there are telephone buyers, and so on. But the auctioneers could give you some idea.'

'I'd get back my forty-five thousand?'

'Oh! There are no guarantees!' she warned. 'But if the valuation at the auction house isn't up to what you hope for, you don't need to go on with the idea of selling.'

'Huh.' He wasn't enthusiastic.

They discussed it intermittently until she felt it was time to take her leave. On her way home in the Tube she told herself the idea had failed to attract Ivan.

But about a week later Miri phoned. 'Ive has put the Fieldingley necklace up for sale,' she announced with some triumph in her voice.

'Really?' Jo was truly surprised. 'I thought he didn't take to the idea.'

'Oh, you don't know him. He likes a bit of a gamble – that's how he makes all his money, Jo. He got one of his staff to do a bit of research on prices for jewellery at auction, and some of the things have gone for enormous sums – quarter of a million, that sort of thing.'

'But, Miri!' Now she was alarmed. 'That would be for very famous pieces! I mean, something that had belonged to the Duchess of Windsor, or had been part of the crown jewels of France or Italy . . .'

'Yeah, well, OK,' Miri laughed, 'I was only joking. Ive isn't expecting a quarter of a million, but he got interested in the whole idea after we talked it over a bit. So he's had a conversation with Remmingson's and they say the necklace could make between fifty and sixty thousand.'

'That much?'

'Good, isn't it? Ive would really like it if he made a bit of a profit on it.'

'Has he actually entered the necklace for a sale?'

'There's one coming up next month. "Important Gemstones", Remmingson's are calling it.'

'Oh, I see.' Jo felt some relief. Had the necklace gone into a general sale of jewellery, the title would have been something like 'Pieces by Famous Jewellers'. She thought she ought to explain the difference to Miri so went on, 'It's a special sale intended for gemmologists, people who are interested more in the history of the stones than in the art work.'

'Well, that's OK, isn't it?' Miri interrupted. 'You were saying the history of the necklace is interesting to some people.'

'Yes, it has a lot of appeal, so let's hope a lot of collectors are interested.'

All the same, she could have wished that Ivan hadn't moved so fast. Jewellery auctions were quite regular in the commercial calendar. To wait a little and get some idea of the market would have been a good idea. But Miri had explained the necklace was a constant reminder of how he'd been made to look a fool. She could understand why, seeing a way of getting rid of it profitably, he wanted to go ahead.

After a few days items began to appear in the gossip columns of the newspapers. 'Rumour has it that two well-known love birds are selling the famous necklace that broke them up . . .' And a little later, in one of the popular celebrity magazines: 'TV beauty Miri Gale is saying she'll be glad to see the Fieldingley Rubies find a new home.'

It turned out that Ivan and Miri wouldn't be able to attend the sale. 'Got to go to a conference on corporate finance in Singapore,' Ivan explained. 'And of course Princess wants to go to Singapore – shopaholics heaven, isn't it?'

'Dresses of Thai silk made in a day,' breathed Miri, 'in hundreds of colours . . .'

'Just as well to be somewhere else,' Ivan said with a shrug. 'If we'd gone to the auction, the press gang would have leapt on us, wouldn't they?'

They were in the bar of a hall in Hammersmith where a grand charity concert was about to start. Miri had invited Jo, and though rather surprised, Jo had accepted. It seemed Miri wanted to keep up a vague friendship with her, at least until the troublesome jewellery was disposed of.

'You're satisfied with the auction arrangements?' Jo asked. 'You've put a reserve on the necklace?'

'One of my assistants is going, just to keep an eye on things. The auctioneer asked me about a reserve price, but . . . well, you know, the necklace has got so famous there's bound to be a lot of bidders.' He shrugged. 'I didn't know where to put the price so he and I agreed he should just use his discretion.'

The warning bell for the opening of the concert rang in the bar.

Everybody began to drift towards the exit. Jo was parted from Ivan and Miri. The rest of the conversation was lost in the business of finding their seats and settling in.

Ben Webber had mentioned to Jo that he was going to the auction, not to buy anything but to be in the company of those who might need his services. She asked him to let her know how it went.

He dropped in on Jo the morning after.

'I thought you'd like a first-hand report about your troublesome rubies,' he said, grinning a little. 'They were successfully sold off last night after quite a little bit of a battle. By telephone, to a Mr Grukescki, who I think is a history specialist collector in South Africa.'

'Thank goodness for that! They made a decent price, I hope?'

'Thirty-five-and-a-half thousand.'

'What!'

Ben was surprised. He frowned at her. 'You sound put out. What's wrong?'

'Ivan was expecting to get something like fifty.'

'Thousand?'

'Yes.'

He stared a little, shook his head at her. 'No . . . They started rather low, as a matter of fact. Nobody was putting up any money until the auctioneer got up to a simmering point of twenty thousand. Then it all woke up, but in the end everybody dropped out except Mr Grukescki and some bidder in the room, who gave up at thirty-five. So Mr G's extra five hundred got him the necklace.'

'But, Ben, the auction house's valuation of the necklace was something between fifty and sixty!'

'Well,' he said, thinking it over, 'they might have turned out to be right, but everybody was probably saving their money for the benitoite. You know the Getnor stone?'

She'd heard of it. One of the very rarest gems on the planet, more valuable than any diamond or ruby.

Benitoite had first been discovered early in the twentieth century in the valley of the San Benito River in California. Its colour could vary but the most desirable was a lovely azure blue, found only rarely. The Getnor stone weighed fourteen carats, which for benitoite was very large. It had been cut as a round brilliant, and its colour was said to be perfect.

'That was in the sale?' She sighed.

144

'Yes, and that was what everybody was waiting for. So the big money went on that, and Digby's necklace just averaged out.'

She could understand it. The Fieldingley Rubies were well-known and worth acquiring, but they were completely outshone by something so rare and so extremely beautiful.

Ivan's assistant was to have been at the auction. He or she was someone who didn't even know her, so wouldn't have called her. But surely he would have called his employer with the news? She was amazed that she hadn't had a furious phone call from Singapore.

A moment's calculation told her that it was early evening now in Singapore. She had the name of the hotel, so directory inquiries furnished the number. At first she was blocked at the hotel's reception desk. 'We are asked to screen callers.' When she gave her name, she got a cool, 'I will inquire, madam.'

She waited, looking at Ben in anxiety. He said, 'Why are you looking so upset? None of this is your fault.'

She could only sigh and feel miserable.

The call was put through to Ivan's suite. Miri was on the other end.

'So it's you,' was the ungracious opening.

'I just heard about what happened here last night, Miri. I'm sorry the necklace didn't meet its expectations.'

'Not by a long shot! Ive got the message when he got up this morning. Fine start to the day, I can tell you!'

'I'm so sorry, Miri.'

'He's been really cranked about it all day. At first he wanted to get on the phone to Remmingson's but of course they were closed for the night 'cause we're so ahead of you here on the clock . . .'

'Why was he trying to ring Remmingson's?'

'. . . And he's had to go to the conference; he's on some sort of special little committee about exchange rates or something. But when I dropped in on them at the lunch break, he was still looking like a thunderstorm and what he's going to be like at this formal dinner tonight, I can't imagine.'

This tirade was delivered in a tone of angry reproach. Jo could just imagine what Miri was having to put up with.

'I'm sorry. It was bad luck that the necklace was in competition with the benitoite.'

'Yeah, whoever heard of *that*?'

'Well, it isn't well-known, but it's so very rare.'

'Oh, we found out all that from Tommy Bayning, he emailed us a picture of it. It's just a blue stone, and I thought it was just like any sapphire I've seen, yet it's supposed to be very extra-special – load of scientific rubbish!'

Ben could hear a faint version of all this. He raised his eyebrows at her dismissal of the benitoite.

'Ben is here. He was at the sale and told me the benitoite got all the attention.'

Miri gave a little snort of annoyance. 'I don't see the sense of it. This picture we got, the stone isn't even in a ring or anything, it's just a stupid stone in a box.'

'It's not something you wear. It's a collector's item. It's usually in a glass case.'

'If it was going to attract all the big money, you should have warned us!'

'Miri, I didn't even know it was in the sale. If you remember, you and Ivan took the bit between your teeth.'

'You saying it was *our* fault? You're the one suggested we should sell!'

'I know, and I apologize for the fact that the rubies didn't attract the kind of money—'

'No, well, Ivan's going to sue the auctioneers.'

'He can't do that, Miri! He told me he'd asked the auctioneer to use his discretion.'

'Discretion! For a lot less than he promised us?'

'He couldn't *promise*, Miri. Really, you've got to tell Ivan the sale was perfectly in order. Thirty-five-and-a-half thousand is a good price for a set of synthetic rubies.'

'But you told us they were special! Don't deny that you said that to us!'

Ben, who had been standing by, now seized the phone from Jo's wavering hand.

'This is Ben,' he said. 'Listen, Ms Gale, tell Ivan to grow up! Everybody knows that auctions are a gamble and he's got no grounds for taking action against the auction house. In any case, does he want to make himself look a fool again?'

Jo heard Miri's exclamation of surprise at that last question.

'He put the rubies up for sale and got a decent price,' Ben surged on. 'But that's not enough for him so he's going to sue Remmingson's. He's already suing Mrs Fieldingley. The newspapers will love that.'

'Ben!' Jo cried, and got the receiver back from him. 'Miri, I'm sorry about that, but Ben's right.'

'Ive's got to do something,' Miri interrupted, almost frantic at what Ben had said. 'He can't just sit down under a loss like that!'

'But he hasn't *lost* anything! Good heavens, let's be logical. What he's had is a disappointment, not a loss! He thought the rubies were worth about four thousand, he got thirty-five thousand plus for them; by anybody's calculation that's a good result.'

'Ive doesn't think so.'

'He's got to see sense. What's done is done.'

'You seem to be saying we'll just have to get over it,' Miri groaned. 'But Ive is *really* peeved.'

'I'm sorry,' Jo said, for what seemed the hundredth time.

'So you should be,' Miri retorted and put the phone down.

Ben was shaking his head at her as she replaced her receiver. 'Why did you keep on apologizing? It really was not your fault.'

'In a way it was, Ben. I suggested the idea of the auction. But I didn't expect them to dash into it so quickly, without keeping me in the loop. And I was busy myself, so I didn't keep an eye on what else was going to be in the sale.'

'I knew, of course,' he confessed. 'I had the catalogue.' He looked regretful. 'But we don't keep so much in touch these days, do we, Jo?'

She smiled in acknowledgement of this reproach.

'And besides, I didn't know they were counting on the rubies making such a big price. Fifty thousand? Who put that idea into their heads?'

'The valuer at Remmingson's.'

'Ooh . . . That was optimistic. I wonder who they engaged to value the items? To tell the truth, I thought the necklace did rather well.'

'Yes, but you see, I idiotically encouraged them to think collectors would bid up for them,' she groaned.

'Poor you. Luckily you don't really have to care what they think about the result. That thing you had with Digby – that's a thing of the past.'

This was perhaps true, but nevertheless Jo went on feeling guilty about the outcome of the auction. She should have kept in contact, she should have been aware that there was something else very important being put up for auction that evening, she should have warned Ivan to withdraw the necklace. On some other occasion, the necklace might have reached the target mentioned by the valuer.

She let a couple of days go by. Luckily the newspapers showed little interest in the event: although to gemmologists the outcome had been fascinating, they were a very small readership indeed.

She'd hoped that the rubies would sell for enough to convince Ivan that he might give up the court case against Mrs Fieldingley. She'd hoped that thereby the cloud that hung over Betsey would be banished. She still hadn't put her in the picture, so she rang her, just so that she would know Ivan was still on the offensive.

'An auction?' Betsey repeated. 'Really? I had no idea.'

'It didn't get much publicity. Sometimes, if record prices are reached, the media get interested, but this time it was an auction of rare stones. That doesn't appeal to the public as much as paintings by Van Gogh that go for a couple of million.'

'All the same, those old rubies of mine seem to me to have done quite well.'

'Unfortunately, not as much as Mr Digby expected. He thought he was going to get back all the money he paid to you, and perhaps even more.'

Betsey laughed. 'It's like the pot of gold at the end of the rainbow, isn't it? I thought I'd got a lot for them, yet it's turned out not to be gold but trouble and strife.'

'I'm so sorry, Betsey.'

'Not your fault, dear. I suppose Mr Digby's in a rage about the result, eh?'

'So I hear. He was in Singapore while the auction took place so I rang, and Miri – that's his partner, you remember? – she said . . . well . . .' Jo had been going to say that Ivan was sulking, but that seemed too unkind so she let it go.

'Still, to me thirty-five thousand pounds seems a lot of money, Jo.'

Jo thought, Unless you've been told you'll get fifty. Aloud she said, 'I'm afraid it has only . . . exasperated Mr Digby.'

'I understand what you were trying to do, my dear. You thought if the rubies fetched a good price, it would cancel out what Mr Digby lost on the purchase. I see that. But he's still ten thousand out of pocket.' She gave a wry chuckle. 'And that's not counting the interest he feels the money should have been earning.'

'Money is important to him,' Jo explained, 'because of the status it brings him. He's *got* to be a winner.'

'And so he's never going to give up the lawsuit until he's been shown to come off best – yes, I understood that, after we had our little friendly chat! He just doesn't think beyond himself – he doesn't realize what it's costing me in legal fees . . .' She sighed. 'Well, I thank you, Jo dear, for trying to sort it out. A great pity the auction didn't go as well as you expected.'

Jo had now apologized to Miri and to Betsey, but that didn't seem to ease her feeling of guilt. It nagged at her for the rest of the day.

She reckoned that Ivan and Miri would be back from Singapore by now. She sat down and wrote to Miri. A formal letter, without a mention of the Fieldingley Rubies.

Miri was at her doorstep two days later.

'Jo, *darling*, you're an absolute *angel*! Ive is so *pleased*! He wants me to say he's ever so grateful and he's never going to say another word to you about those awful rubies, because he says what happened at the auction probably wasn't your fault, and you're to come to dinner this evening if you're free, so we can have a real chinwag about everything.'

And all of this because Jo had offered to design a hair ornament for Miri to wear at her wedding.

Sixteen

Jo didn't really want to design a hair ornament. Had it been a tiara, that would have been different – there was something magical about a tiara, a diadem. Jo had designed two in the past, for prima ballerinas about to dance *Swan Lake*.

But a hair ornament for Miri meant it had to go with her wedding dress, and would probably involve veiling.

She was taken by the bride-to-be to her dress designer's studio workshop in an enviable position in Soho. Jo had expected someone wreathed with measuring tapes and a pin cushion strapped to his wrist. She found a tubby little man in a business suit. This was Desmond.

'So you're going to do the hair thing,' he said to Jo in a very irritated manner. 'What's wrong with my headdress, I'd like to know?'

'Nothing's wrong with it, Dessy, don't be cross about it,' Miri said after kissing the air at the side of his cheek. 'It's just that Jo's so – you know – so special, and she was going to do my necklace, but you know how that turned out, so she's making it up to me, aren't you, love?'

Jo smiled and nodded and felt uncomfortable. Miri had never mentioned that the dressmaker would be offended. 'Miri was *very* disappointed about the necklace,' she murmured. 'If you and I were to get together, perhaps we could turn out something that would please her and be—'

'Glitzy?' Desmond put in. 'Glittery? I put a lot of toil and sweat into her headdress. I never bargained for any jewels being put on it. I'm not pleased.'

'Well, it'll have to glitter a *bit*,' Jo said in a placating tone. 'That's what jewels do, after all. May I see the headdress you've designed?'

'It's still being made in the workroom.'

'Come on now, Dessy, don't be difficult,' coaxed Miri.

'Don't call me Dessy!' He glared at her.

'Oh, all right then, *Mister* Desmond – is that all right? Come on, let Jo see the headdress.' She took his arm and pressed it fondly.

'She can see my sketches,' he said, relenting a little as she leaned against him and smiled into his face. He pushed her away. 'You're a little minx! You go behind my back like this, and then you expect me to be ready to change my work. Come on, let's go into my office, I'll let you see the design.'

They left the handsome studio for a cluttered office. He unlocked a file cabinet, pushed a few files around, and came out with a folder which he handed to Jo.

Jo leafed through them. She felt a sympathy with him when she saw his work. Early sketches were rather plain but had been developed later into various flower themes: lily-of-the-valley, camellia, roses. The one stamped 'Accepted' was drawn in large detail with the various fabrics noted alongside. It was a bandeau of ruched voile intertwined with silk ribbon and gardenia blossoms of velvet. From this descended a short veil speckled with what the note called 'gardenia petals.'

She was horrified.

For a moment she extended the silence in which she'd made her inspection. Then she looked up from the folder. Desmond was watching her with his brows drawn together in what she saw was a warning.

She understood. He had been trying to produce something that Miri would accept, and in the end Miri had accepted this. But it wasn't what Desmond had had in mind when he started. And he didn't want any more trouble.

She turned to Miri. 'Listen, Miri, I don't think I can do flowers.'

'What d'you mean?'

'I never do representational jewellery. I never try to pretend that a group of gems put together is a violet or a rose. For me, the stones have to speak for themselves as stones, as beautiful things in their own right.'

'Well . . . OK . . .' Miri hesitated. 'You don't want to do imitation violets, I get that. But I mean, you could put some diamonds or something in among Desmond's flowers, couldn't you?'

'No.'

'What?'

'No. I couldn't do that. And Desmond wouldn't want me to.' She glanced at him, and he, hesitating, nodded. He was watching and listening with interest.

151

Miri said uncertainly, 'You wouldn't want her to, Des?'

'No. You and I had a hard enough time coming to an agreement on this design. I don't want to go through all that again, Miri. You want a Jo Radcliffe headdress, that's what you're going to get. Let me step out of it.'

'Oh,' said Miri.

Jo flashed a glance of thanks at the dress designer. To Miri she said, 'It won't be floral. No rubies pretending to be red roses, no sapphires pretending to be forget-me-nots. And no velvet gardenias cluttering up the place.'

'Well, for heaven's sake, don't be so bossy!' Miri was pouting. 'Of course I always knew you might want to do something a bit different to this . . . I understand that, you've got to be artistic. OK, we can start all over again, if that's OK with you, Des?'

There was relief on his face. Also, there was a defensiveness for his earlier work. 'It can't clash with the dress!' he warned. 'I've spent months on that dress!'

'May I see it?'

He looked to Miri. The gown had been a tremendous secret, something to be unveiled on the great day and to take everyone by storm.

'Oh yeah, yeah, she's got to see it, for goodness' sake, let's give her a look.' Miri was irritated, out of her depth, and perhaps wishing now she'd never accepted Jo's offer to make the headdress.

Desmond conducted them now to a workroom. Huge cupboards lined one wall, all carefully locked. A lady in a smock over a very smart skirt and high heels hurried up. Several seamstresses looked up from their work-tables with interest as she produced keys and, at Desmond's orders, opened one of the cupboards.

The interior was filled to its capacity by a wedding-gown with an enormous skirt, almost like a crinoline except that it had no hoops. It was made of a silvery silk taffeta. When the overseer took it out, it shimmered and glinted in the bright light streaming in from the Soho square outside.

Jo had great difficulty in preventing herself from groaning aloud. It was so much *not* the kind of thing she wanted to deal with. It had a neo-Victorian air about it, and while she had nothing against the Victorians, she didn't want to have to design after their style.

'What d'you think?' cried Miri with a delighted eagerness. 'Isn't it great?'

'Very fine,' Jo said. That was true. It was very fine.

'This was the final product after weeks – months – of revision,' Desmond said. Something in his tone told Jo he had had more than enough of Miri's wedding.

'What do you think you should do, Jo?' Miri asked. 'Ive says expense no object.'

'I was going to suggest something without a veil,' Jo said. 'But now I see the dress, I see there has to be a veil.'

Desmond nodded with fervour.

'Let me think about it,' she said.

'But you'd brought some sketches to show . . .'

'None of those are suitable. I've drawn little things that lie close to the head – I was thinking along the lines of those little hair ornaments you showed me when we looked at your clothes, remember? But this is too . . . too voluptuous for something as small as that. Let me go home and think about it.'

Desmond supplied photographs of the dress. She took them home and later that day spread them out on her dining table.

The design was so unlike what she'd expected that she had to make herself go back to square one. She'd thought Miri would have wanted a gown that clung to her so as to show off those famous curves, that gorgeous cleavage. Instead she'd chosen a glamorized version of a Victorian maiden's garb.

All the same, like a Victorian maiden, she was going to show a large expanse of upper bosom and shoulder. Above the enormous skirt and the nipped-in waist, that display of beautiful flesh needed a flourish. She had to start thinking quite differently.

She scanned one of the photographs into her workshop computer. She turned it and moved it and studied it from every angle.

She had no idea what would look right on the head of the wearer, except that it had to counterbalance somehow the challenge of the voluminous skirt.

She had to put the headdress aside during the next few days, to work on other assignments, but it was always somewhere at the back of her mind.

She woke up one morning with an idea in her head. It harked back to her original doubts about doing a hair ornament. Floating about in her mental vision were old sketches she'd done for the ballerina's headdress.

She rang Miri's mobile, and found her in the health centre at the flats.

'How are you getting on with my wedding thing?'

'I'm beginning to see something, Miri. Tell me – are you going to wear a necklace?'

'Yeah, sure, Ive and I are looking around for one. Nothing antique,' she added hastily. 'Ive and I have had enough of *antique*.'

'So if you're going to have a necklace . . . I was thinking, would you like me to design that too?'

'Eh?'

'I've got the beginnings of an idea for the headdress. But I don't want attention distracted by anything too splendiferous at your neck-line.'

Miri gave it a moment's thought. 'What about that design you were going to do with the fake rubies? I liked that.'

'No, no, I've sold the rights in that to a commercial jewellers, and in any case it wouldn't be right for what I have in mind. Could I do some try-outs on my computer for you to look at?'

'Gee whiz! You're all set to go, aren't you! Of course, Jo, do what you feel would be good. When could I get a look at your ideas?'

'How about this afternoon?'

'As fast as that? Of course, I'd be absolutely thrilled . . . We'll come as soon as Ive has sorted himself out after the daily grind, if that suits you.'

'Look forward,' Jo said, and disconnected.

She looked up reference books. She wanted just a hint, a little arrow of guidance. In the end she found an example of the shape she had in mind, a photograph of a dancer as the princess in a ballet called *The Firebird*. The dancer was wearing a knee-length tunic heavily embroidered, and on her head a diadem that looked like a low-peaked arc of solid gold.

Jo had no intention of saddling Miri with a solid gold headdress. But the shape was right: a gentle pointed arc from one temple to the other, with sufficient solidity to counteract the dress and to anchor the veil.

She imagined it as she put the book on her work-table. She picked up a pencil, got out some sheets of paper. Instead of solid yellow gold there would be strands of white gold and then yellow gold, to make it light and delicate. At the top of each strand a diamond would gleam – not jutting out, but forming part of the arc, and not great heavy stones but brilliants of about half a carat.

Matching it, at the throat, a choker necklace about an inch deep made of strands of white and yellow gold, criss-crossed like a gentle lattice. At the front, a medallion of brilliants of the same size as those in the headdress, and shaped to match the diadem.

All she had to do was to get it down on paper and then translate it into a figure on her computer.

She sat down around mid-morning. She rose from her chair at three in the afternoon, bleary-eyed, shoulders aching, mouth dry. She tottered upstairs to drink a gallon of water before lying down on her bed to let her body recover. Then she went into the shower where she soaked the weariness out of her muscles. Afterwards, she ate quickly in her kitchen to restore her energy: biscuits and cheese, an apple.

She got downstairs only a few minutes before the arrival of her clients.

'Hi!' carolled Miri, hurrying into the studio. 'Can we see – is it in the workroom?' She dashed onwards. Ivan came behind her wearing a tolerant smile, and nodding in an unexpectedly friendly way to his hostess.

'She's really thrilled to bits that you're doing all this,' he said, taking her hand. 'And you know what she said – expense no object.'

'We'll talk about money later, Ivan. But this isn't an expensive piece.'

'No? You mean it's not gonna have any appeal for the magazine? She's set on looking gorgeous for the magazine.'

'This will look good, I promise. Come along, have a look.'

Her finished work was awaiting them just as she'd left it an hour ago – a computer-generated human figure wearing Miri's wedding gown. On its head was Jo's diadem with the wedding veil descending behind it to the waist, and on the figure's neck shone the band of filigree gold with its eye-catching centre-piece against the throat.

Miri was sitting in front of the computer, dabbing with her finger at the keys that made the model turn slowly so that she could see the effect from all sides. She was utterly entranced.

'What do you think?' Jo asked.

'It's like . . . It's like a *crown*! It's just so different from those flowers that Desmond and I sorted out between us. I just think it's . . . Oh, Ive, isn't it *gorgeous*?'

It was clear to Jo that Ivan had no real opinion of his own. He looked at Miri, not at what was on the screen.

'Well, so it *should* look like a crown,' he said with a touching adoration. 'It's for my princess, isn't it?'

'I love it! I love it! Oh, Jo, I'm so glad you offered to do this for me! It's just so . . . I'd never have thought of anything like this but it's just so right, isn't it. Oh, thank you!'

She leapt up to hug Jo with fervour. Jo patted her on the back. She was too tired to do any enthusiastic hugging.

'Ah . . . Well . . .' Ivan wanted to say something, so they broke off their embrace and turned to listen. 'The wedding's in August. Can you get this made in time?'

'I'll do it myself.'

'Really? I thought you handed out stuff to some commercial firm.'

'On this occasion I'll do it myself. It seems to need the personal touch.'

So a few days later the gossip columns had mentions of: 'Awarding-winning designer of jewellery is working on a secret set of jewels for the wedding of TV favourite Miri Gale.' Miri was on an afternoon chat show enthusing to the host about her gown and the beautiful modern-style headdress she would be wearing.

'I can't tell you any more, it's a secret,' she murmured with a teasing smile. And for good reason, for the exclusive rights to the first photographs had been sold to *Lookee Here* magazine.

The materials Jo needed were easy to acquire, the design in itself was simple. Moreover, she'd always enjoyed the practical work. Everything was going forward well.

Tim Fieldingley telephoned her around lunchtime one day in July. 'I'll be in town later today, Jo, I wondered it we could meet again, if you're not too busy.'

'No, as it happens, I've a bit more leisure time at the moment.'

'But I thought you were heavily engaged on the wedding design for Miri Gale?'

'I'm just waiting for the jewel-box to be made so as to deliver them to her.'

'Well, that sounds marvellous. I bet it looks great, whatever it is.'

'Would you like a look?'

'But I thought it was all a tremendous secret, according to the little hints I've been shown in the papers? Grans cut them out to show me when I got back.'

'Well, it is, but you're not going to come with a hidden camera and then sell the pics to a newspaper, are you?'

He laughed. 'I've *got* a miniature camera but I promise not to bring it. Instead I'll bring the pictures of Grans's paintings. I've been bringing them up to the photographer's studio in batches as Grans sorts them out, and now they've been photographed ready for the printer. Would you like a look?'

'Of course! How many are going into the book?'

'The botanist made his choices – she's had to do a few extra from his own samples, from things in pots, you know. That's never as good as painting them in their natural habitat. But now twenty-four are accepted and the captions are written, so it's going to the printer.'

'I'd love to see them. Bring them along.'

'How about around seven-ish this evening? And then we could go out for something to eat?'

'That would be good.'

She had some business calls to make in the afternoon, which somehow seemed more tiresome than usual. She really must find some help for the office work. Since Lindora's departure she'd been handling things on her own, but now that she'd linked up with a commercial outfit, there seemed to be too many letters and reports. And besides, she now had a steadier income. She could even pay for a daily help to do some of the housework, which she hated.

But the main reason for her distracted state of mind was contemplating what she should wear that evening. After all, it was just a casual arrangement. They'd probably go to a wine bar. Nothing too dressy. But on the other hand, not jeans and a shirt, her usual workwear.

When she went upstairs to review her wardrobe, it struck her there was a gap in its provision. She had plenty of slacks, plenty of shirts and sweaters. Then there was a big jump to dinner dresses because generally, when she went out in the evening, it was to some public event: an award giving, a symposium on the work of some great artist or designer.

The trouble with you, she told her reflection in the wardrobe mirror, is you don't get out enough.

It had happened so gradually she hadn't noticed. But she'd become immersed in her work, had let herself drift away from even old friends and acquaintances. When she travelled abroad to conferences, she made notes of names and telephone numbers, but now it struck her that she almost never followed them up. Living as she did rather off the radar of the fashionable world, she was losing the knack of being a social creature.

Well, now she was preparing to spend an evening with Tim Fieldingley. And it seemed that here was someone she wasn't going to drift away from.

The realization surprised her. But it was a pleasant surprise. Because, she thought, Tim had taken the trouble to keep up their friendship.

That must mean something, surely?

She certainly hoped it did.

Seventeen

The wine bar they chose was in a busy spot in Harrow. A quiet enough place, because it was early in the week. They had a table to themselves near a window looking out on a patio full of roses in full bloom. Dusk was closing in, the restaurant area was lit by candles.

'You said earlier on that you were back from somewhere?' Jo said in inquiry.

'Oh, yes, back from Moscow again. You know, there are a lot of tycoons there these days. Some of them are very interested in minerals in out of the way parts of the old Soviet territories.'

'Do you live with your grandmother when you come back, or have you a place of your own?'

He grinned. 'You'll be surprised to hear that I do actually have a home. I have a flat in Strasbourg.'

'Strasbourg?'

'Because I was offered it cheap, that's all. And it's handy, in a way. The European Parliament has debates about assets and exploration and that sort of stuff, and I'm quite happy to hear any gossip about new projects. But, to tell the truth, I'm not there very often.'

'No, you seem to spend a lot of time in transit,' she suggested.

He nodded, looking around the candle-lit room with approval.

He was wearing what Jo thought of as his 'meetings' suit. When he turned up on her doorstep, she was rather glad she herself had been thoughtful about what to wear. She'd decided against the boutique clothes she'd bought when she first got involved with Ivan and his high-powered circle. The dresses had been brought out for one or two events recently, but they were inappropriate for a quiet evening far from the West End.

Instead she'd chosen a simple black skirt and a summery top. She felt at ease and rather optimistic. Perhaps something good was about to happen.

Their wine was brought. Jo was no expert so had left the choice to Tim. When she'd tasted it he asked for her opinion.

'It's not like anything I've had before, but it's good.'

'It's from Alsace. When I'm "at home" in Strasbourg, it's regarded as the local drink.' He shook a warning finger at her. 'Mind you, it's fairly strong stuff.'

'Thanks for the warning. When I drink anything strong, I get loquacious.'

'Feel free to say anything that comes into your head.'

'Ah . . . Thinking about that . . .' She paused. She'd been rather disappointed in his reaction when she showed him Miri's jewellery. She ventured, 'It seems to me you didn't have very much to say about the things I'd made for Miri Gale's wedding.'

She meant it as a joking invitation to be complimentary about her work, but he looked uncomfortable. 'Oh, well . . . That sort of thing isn't in my line, Jo. I'm not much in the company of women who wear high fashion. But I could see it was . . . well, very beautiful.'

'But?'

'But, well, I don't really know anything about Miri Gale except what I see in the newspapers – Grans keeps me cuttings and photographs that she collects so as to keep me up to date.'

'And so?'

'Well, I'd have thought . . .'

'What?'

'Aren't those things too austere . . . too dignified for her?'

She was quite taken aback. After a moment she said, 'That's very perceptive. Yes. You're right, they aren't at all in keeping with Miri's lifestyle. But these two things are for a very special occasion, for which she's going to wear a very special gown. The diadem and the necklace go with the gown, not with Miri.'

'So what's she going to do with them afterwards?' He seemed irritated, his tone had become rather sharp.

'Sell them, I should think. And for a good profit.'

'And that doesn't disturb you? That you're doing something that's absolutely meaningless, simply for this silly woman to show off how much her money-grabbing bridegroom has spent on her?'

Jo sat back in her chair. 'Hold on!' she exclaimed. 'If you felt like this about it, why did you say you'd like to look at the jewellery?'

'I didn't say that. You said you'd show it to me in return for a look at the paintings.'

'But you were interested.' She tried to recall the conversation.

'You just said Betsey showed you cuttings about them. She wouldn't bother if you didn't pay attention to them.'

'Of course I'm *interested*. I'm interested in how someone with money to throw away on stuff like that – stuff that girl's only going to wear for one day – is still threatening my grandmother with a court action!'

'Oh, but surely . . .' She broke off, wanting to sort things out in her mind. 'Ivan has been in touch since the auction, hasn't he?'

'No.'

'But he . . . The old necklace sold for quite a good price.'

'We know that,' he said impatiently. 'You were good enough to let Grans know. So after she thought about that, she asked her solicitor to get in touch. She imagined that Ivan Digby's view of the affair would be different.'

'And it is, surely?'

'Not in the least. The only response from his law firm is to say that unless Grans is proposing to return the purchase price any time soon, they'll see her in court.'

Jo was almost speechless. 'But . . . but, he got back about three quarters of his money! If your grandmother can be said to owe him anything, it's only something like ten thousand pounds now.'

'I'm afraid you're under a misapprehension.' Tim's expression had something like contempt in it. 'Nothing has changed as far as that extortioner is concerned. He still wants his full pound of flesh.'

At that moment their food arrived. The waitress fussed with all the side dishes then left them in the strained silence that had developed between them.

After a long pause Tim began again, 'I must say I was surprised that you were doing this jewellery set for the bride. Of course business is business, but I did rather think you'd be disinclined to do any special favours for Ivan Digby.'

'You don't understand. He was so disappointed after the auction.'

'Disappointed? You just said he got a good price.'

'But not as much as he expected. Unfortunately the auction house was over-optimistic.' She stopped, trying to put together some words that would explain Ivan's view of the matter, and finding it hard. 'He hoped he'd be . . . he'd be seen as putting one over on your grandmother by selling the stones for more than the price he gave her. If he'd done as well as he expected he'd have let the press know.'

'How admirable.'

161

'No, of course it doesn't show him in a good light.'

'It seems to me it would be quite difficult to do that.'

His attitude baffled her. 'Why are you being so angry at me? My idea was that when he sold the synthetic rubies he'd do well, and that he'd drop the case against Betsey. That was why I suggested the idea in the first place.'

'And now that you know he hasn't?'

'Well . . . I can't do anything about that,' she said with an inward groan.

'No, instead you're getting yourself involved in this vulgar celebrity wedding.'

'You've no right to be so judgmental about it.'

'Oh, that's right, and I apologize,' he said with irony. 'It's just that I thought you'd have a reasonable explanation for taking any part in it.'

'I don't owe you any explanations,' she said. 'In fact, I think you owe *me* a proper apology instead of a polite pretence. It seems the only reason you came to see me was to carry out a cross examination of my motives.'

'You must admit it's all turned out very odd. When we all met in the solicitor's office I got the impression you thought Digby's behaviour was all wrong. Next thing I know, you're playing up to him so as to make money out of this stupid wedding business.'

'Listen to who's talking! Aren't you the man who's working for a bunch of tycoons so they can exploit something in some wilderness part of Russia and make even more money? Everybody knows they're nothing but a bunch of bandits!'

'At least I'm not toadying to them by making expensive rubbish for their girlfriends.'

'Oh, now we're getting your real opinion of my work. Rubbish, is it?'

'It may be good in itself, but it's for a rubbishy purpose.'

'Are you saying I have to ask for your approval in how I run my business?'

'Oh, I wouldn't dare. You clearly know how to get by in this tricky world. Designing things to make that silly girl look like royalty – it's nothing but the most sickening flattery.'

Jo pushed her plate of food away and stood up.

'Goodbye,' she said.

'Hey, wait a minute—'

'Thank you, no. It's been delightful, but I think it's time to go.'

She stalked away. She didn't look back, but heard him rising to prevent her. A hovering waiter stalled him. She heard: 'Is something wrong with the meal, sir?'

She was out of the wine bar in seconds. A bus was drawing up at a nearby stop. She ran for it and got on. She didn't look back to see whether Tim Fieldingley had emerged. She got off at the next stop because she was going in the wrong direction. She walked through a few side streets until she found an Underground station.

Soon she was back on her home ground. She let herself into the studio, engaged the security system for the night, then went upstairs.

At first anger and resentment prevented her from thinking about what had happened. Her reaction was simply: How dare he, how *dare* he! She could hear only the echo of his words, the reproof and anger in them.

He thought he had the right to judge her? Without even knowing why she'd decided to join in Ivan's wedding plans? It apparently didn't occur to him that she had a motive that wasn't self-seeking, mercenary, or mean-minded.

Showing her the photographs of Betsey's work and the invitation to dinner had been nothing but a ploy. He'd wanted an opportunity to raise the matter of the court case. He'd wanted to challenge her about Ivan's vengeful attitude, Ivan's determination to screw every penny he could out of Betsey.

Perhaps he'd meant to ask her to try once again to act as intermediary. But his distaste at her part in the wedding had overtaken him.

And because her work was so important to her, she began to be anxious. Was her diadem wrong? Pretentious? Over the top? Had she let herself get carried away by the chance to demonstrate her skills?

She went down to her workshop, opened the safe, and took out the tray on which rested the headdress and the necklace. She cleared a place on her work-table and set them there. For a long time she stared at them. Then she walked round the table, tilting her head to get a varying view. At length she picked up the headdress to turn it in her hands.

She tried with all her mind to be detached. What she saw was a fragile, gentle ornament. It glittered, yes. It had the shape of a crown so there was perhaps something regal about it. But it wasn't demanding, it didn't shout for attention. It was a framework through which light could travel, a delicate tracery of fine wire tipped with an arc of bright little diamond stars.

And what's more, she said to herself with returning assurance, it goes with the gown. That's the important point – it's right for its moment of drama, it makes a triumphant comment on the scene.

As for the necklace, she regarded that as one of her most successful pieces. There was nothing like it anywhere else in the world of jewellery, so far as she knew. She felt pride and satisfaction as she put the jewels back in the safe.

Tim Fieldingley was wrong, she told herself. What did *he* know? Off in places in the back of beyond for long stretches at a time, working always in the harsh world of exploration and machinery; what could he know about the art of making jewellery? He'd said it himself: 'I'm not much in the company of women who wear high fashion'. His opinion of her work meant nothing.

So she would stop bothering about it.

All the same, he'd said other things. She tried to recall his criticism. Was she toadying to Ivan Digby? Was she going along with all this wedding nonsense because of ambition?

She tried to look at her actions dispassionately. She'd offered to make a hair ornament. But within a few minutes of seeing the wedding gown she's gone off at a complete tangent – envisioning something greater and grander than would do her credit.

Well, was that wrong? She was a designer. She couldn't design something she knew was unsuitable, inadequate.

Of course not.

The shape that had leapt into her imagination had been the right one. Yes, she thought it would earn her credit in the design world. There was nothing wrong in that.

As to trying to make Miri Gale look royal, that was untrue. Everything about Miri was to do with pop culture, with showbiz. For the occasion of her wedding, Miri was assuming the appearance of a rich young Victorian woman – and Jo was helping her to succeed in that.

Once the wedding day was over, Jo could imagine the whole outfit perhaps going on display somewhere for a time. Then Miri would get rid of it. She couldn't imagine that the gown and its accessories would be laid away and treasured as many wedding gowns were, to be brought out years later for a daughter or a granddaughter.

She'd said to Tim that she was reasonably sure the jewellery would be sold off. She was almost certain that would be the fate of the diadem. There were few occasions likely to occur in Miri's life where she'd want to wear a diadem again.

Having argued and reasoned with herself for hours, Jo came to the realization that it was well past midnight and that she was very tired. She went back upstairs. As she made preparations for bed she shook her head in dismay.

This wasn't at all the result she'd hoped for from this evening.

Eighteen

Next morning she woke with the feeling that everything would turn out all right. Tim would ring or come in person. She'd get an apology. She'd accept it, of course, after a little reluctance.

No such thing happened. Every time the phone rang she leapt to it, but it was never Tim.

Once, in fact, it was her brother Donald.

'I saw the stuff in *Lookee Here* about the headdress,' he said. 'Good work! I take it you'll be going to the wedding?'

'Yes.'

'I wonder, Jo, could you get us an invitation?'

'Why on earth would you want to go to Miri's wedding?' she asked, surprised. 'You and she parted on bad terms.'

'That's exactly it. Could you explain to her that it was all a mistake, that we didn't show enough understanding about her timidity.'

'Timidity?'

'Well, Shakespeare scared her. I should have cottoned on to the fact that she really didn't want to do it. You know, it's often difficult to know with people in the theatre – you can't be sure when they're being modest and when they're just putting it on.'

'I can't ask Miri to invite you,' Jo said. 'She and I aren't really that close.'

'But you agreed to do this headdress thing,' he objected. 'I know you well enough to think it's not the sort of commission you'd really want. She ought to owe you something for that.'

'No, Donald, I'm not going to ask her. And I can't think why you want to go, anyhow.'

'Well, it's going to be a big affair – everybody who is anybody is probably going to be there. It would be nice to get in there, do a bit of networking.'

'I'm sorry. If you want an invitation you'll have to get in touch with Miri yourself.'

He hesitated. 'Well, I *could* do that. After all, we were colleagues for quite a while, weren't we. What does she feel about me?'

'Your name never comes up,' she said bluntly.

That was so direct that it stopped him. 'Oh, OK,' he muttered, and rang off.

A week went by. Jo admitted to herself that she wasn't going to get an apology from Tim.

A letter came, beautifully handwritten, from Betsey Fieldingley.

> Dear Jo,
> I'm beginning to get the impression that there has been some argument between you and my grandson. If I'm wrong in this, please forgive this intrusion. But if something has gone awry, I should very much like to set it right. I wonder if you're likely to be in my part of the world at any time? You know I have moved into a retirement community and it is quite a pleasant setting. I should very much like to offer you lunch or a cup of tea, and show you some of my work. And perhaps we could have a chat.

The address was from a village outside Worcester. Jo said to herself, Why would I be going to Worcester, for heaven's sake. Then, a couple of hours later, I could call in on Hechman's, to discuss my sketch for Mrs Dorsey's ring, and take a look at how those sapphire earrings are getting on, they're due to be delivered soon.

The manufacturer was in Birmingham. Birmingham was quite near Worcester.

She dithered for a day or two. Would it be almost like admitting something if she went to see Betsey? That she cared whether Tim had quarrelled with her?

She telephoned.

It was mid-morning. There was a delay before the phone was answered. 'Ah, Jo my dear, how nice to hear you! Sorry to be so slow – I had paint on my fingers.'

'I'm sorry, you're at work.'

'No, no, nothing important, I'm painting a spray of *Aruncus* from the communal garden.'

'What's *Aruncus*?'

'My love, I'm sorry to tell you that its common name is goat's beard, but it's got a fascinating plume of . . . Oh, well, you don't want a botany lesson. How are you?'

167

'I'm fine, I'm fine. I'm thinking of calling on a firm that makes things for me when they're beyond the range of my workshop.' It all came out in a rush. She stopped, took a breath, and went on in a more mannerly fashion, 'I thought about dropping by, as you suggested. The day after tomorrow. The firm's in Birmingham, so . . .'

'Ah, you're taking up my invitation.'

'I thought I would, if the day suits you?'

'Oh, Jo dear, my time's my own, I've no rigid rules about which day I do what. Come to lunch.'

'I can't manage that, Betsey, I'll be at the factory till past noon. But I'll take you up on your offer of tea, if that's OK.'

'Splendid, only make it more like three o'clock tea rather than four because if I'm going to show you my paintings we want the light to be good.'

'Three-ish, then, on Thursday.'

'It's a date. Now, to find me, you leave Worcester across the bridge and along New Road, and so on until you see signposts for . . .' A detailed set of directions followed. She asked Betsey to repeat it while she took notes.

'Got that,' she said. 'I'll see you for tea.'

'I look forward, dear.'

She hadn't had the courage to ask why Betsey thought there had been a disagreement between herself and Tim. She longed to know what Tim had said, whether he had seemed regretful.

Well, she only had two days to wait.

Betsey in a sleeveless, shapeless print dress was waiting for her on Thursday afternoon at the imposing gates of an estate that looked quite extensive. She was wearing a battered panama crammed down on her white hair, and leather sandals that might have come from an Indian shoemaker long ago. Jo felt rather ashamed of her designer jeans and silk shirt – they seemed too dressy by comparison.

Betsey got in beside her to give directions to her apartment. The place had the air of being almost a little village in itself.

'Used to be the estate of a china manufacturer,' Betsey explained. 'The owners have done quite well, I think, using the main house and the outbuildings and barns and so forth. Here we are.'

Jo obediently drew up outside what was a converted barn. They went in through a wide arched entrance, to a door at one side. Casting the panama at a peg on the wall and hitting it, Betsey led the way into a small lobby and upstairs. Jo understood at once why she'd wanted this flat – it had good light, from big modern windows with a northern aspect.

The living room was furnished with items from Betsey's former home, worn but comfortable. Jo offered the flowers she'd brought. She'd chosen well – old-fashioned marigold-like blooms, from a stall in Worcester market. Their tawny yellow went well with the faded upholstery.

'Oh, thank you dear – *Rudbeckia hirta* – we don't have them in the garden here, the gardener doesn't go in for annuals.' She led the way into the kitchen. 'Let's just find a vase to give them a drink and I'll put the kettle on. I've only got shop-bought scones, but they're from a little local bakery and the jam is home-made from a church sale.' She was fussing about rather nervously.

Jo took over finding a vase for the flowers. Betsey took a little tray out of the refrigerator to reveal the scones, jam, and clotted cream. She trotted into the living room with it. When she came back the kettle had boiled. She made the tea, then led the way to a low table by one of the windows.

The outlook was on the garden, where shrubs and a sloping lawn dreamed in the July sun. 'This is a lovely place,' Jo said.

'Oh yes, and it was a lovely price too, let me tell you. Lovely for the owners, I mean. But I'm not going to be unkind about them because I really like it here and some of the other places I looked at, well, you know, for your money you got a skimpy living room, bedroom, kitchen and bath – where was I going to paint, I ask you? But here I've got a spare bedroom that I use as a studio.'

'I'm looking forward to seeing your work. Do you know it was one of your watercolours that gave me the idea for the design I was going to use for the Fieldingley Rubies?'

'Yes, the *Thunbergia mysorensis* – I gave that to Tim for you.' The mention of the name made them both stiffen a little. 'Have a scone,' said Betsey, offering the plate.

They each chose a scone and busied themselves with cream and jam. Betsey took a bite, then waved her scone in the air for attention.

'I'd better get on with what I wanted to say, but first, dear, I have to ask you not ever to tell Tim that I interfered.'

'I promise,' said Jo, hiding a smile.

'He's a darling, you know, I think the world of him, but he can be so pig-headed sometimes! He went stamping off to catch his plane last week with a great big cloud hanging over him, and as everything seemed to have gone extremely well with the book's art editor and the photographer, I thought it had to be that . . . well, something had gone wrong when he saw you.'

Jo nodded.

'What happened, dear? Because I'm certain he never intended . . . well, it looked as if it had been rather serious. Was it?'

Jo let this faltering query die away while she considered what to say. She didn't want to be a telltale. 'Let's just say we had a disagreement.'

'But *what about*?'

Jo shrugged.

Betsey made a tutting sound. 'It's that awful Mr Digby. It was, wasn't it? Tim really dislikes that man! And it bothers him . . . it bothers him that you and Mr Digby . . . you know.'

'But that's all in the past, Betsey.'

'Ye-es. Only it says in the papers that you're doing these jewels for the wedding and it makes it seem . . .'

'What? That I'm going to be "the other woman" in that marriage?' Jo laughed. 'No, no. Really, that's not on the cards at all. I'm just making a headdress and a necklace for the bride, that's all.'

'But after all the fuss over the rubies, Tim would have thought you'd steer clear of him – even in a business sense – unless . . . unless you felt something for him.'

'No, no, it wasn't that.' She hesitated. 'I'll tell you why I decided to do the headdress.'

'Yes?'

'It's difficult to explain. You remember I called you and told you the rubies had gone up for auction.'

'Oh yes, of course. And I got on to my solicitor, but it didn't do any good over the court case, you know. So disappointing.'

'That's a shame; I'd hoped . . . Well, anyway, Ivan was really terribly let down over what he got for the rubies. He'd expected a lot more. And I'd suggested the idea of selling them, so I felt a bit responsible. So to make it up to him I offered to design Miri's diadem.'

'Good gracious!'

'And when it comes to presenting the bill,' she went on, 'I'm only going to charge him for the materials. I'm going to ask him to consider my fee for the design as making up the loss on the rubies.'

'You can't do that, Jo! You've your living to make.'

'That's true, but if you look at it strictly commercially, I've done well out of being connected with Miri and Ivan, so . . .'

'My dear girl, why should you lose out just because I was silly enough not to have a proper check-up before I sold them.'

'Betsey, no one's to blame about the rubies. Everyone was taken in – if you want my opinion, even poor old Mellillo back in the 1900s thought they were genuine stones. But Ivan has this view of life . . . It's a big flaw, but he's *got* to be a winner. I hope that when I hand him my bill he'll feel that he's got ahead of the game.'

'You mustn't do that. I absolutely forbid it!' Betsey cried. 'There must be some way *I* can make it up to Mr Digby.'

Jo was shaking her head. 'Only by losing the court case,' she sighed. 'That's what Ivan thinks of as his public vindication. No, Betsey, let's try my idea. That way he might soften enough to let the matter drop.'

Betsey sat with her hands in her lap, looking distressed. 'Oh, bother!' she cried. 'Oh lordy! Why did I ever get that boring old necklace out of the bank?' She glanced about. 'And now the tea's gone cold, and I'm being a terrible hostess, and I feel rotten about the whole thing!'

Jo stretched a hand over the table to take one of hers and press it firmly. 'None of it is your fault,' she murmured in comfort. 'Ivan is the one to blame, so stop letting it upset you, and as to the tea, that doesn't matter. How about showing me your paintings, eh? That's something to be happy about, the success you've been having, now isn't it?'

After a minute or so Betsey allowed herself to be persuaded. They went into one of the rooms off the little vestibule. Here there was a big work-table cluttered with jars, cleaning rags, tubes of paints, and canvases in the process of being stretched on frames.

A canvas propped on an angled work frame stood there also, with a sprig of blossom in a jam jar alongside. A partly finished portrayal of the flower was already to be seen on the canvas, a delicate tracery of grey as an outline, with the colour growing within those confines. The flower was a spire of scarlet, to Jo's eye rather like a lily.

'*Schizostylis coccinea,*' said Bestey. 'What a name for such a pretty thing, eh? It's for a group of four on commission for somebody who's keen on moist-condition type plants. I'm doing spring, summer, autumn and winter. This is summer, of course. What d'you think?'

'It's lovely. What on earth grows in a soggy sort of place in winter?'

'Snowdrop, of course, what else! You're not a gardener, are you?' She chuckled, then led the way to shelves along two of the walls.

'These are the work of past years,' she commented. 'I've been painting since I was about eight years old, but of course not seriously until I was nearly twenty. A lot of it is dispersed around the family – I went through a long period when nobody wanted to buy my stuff so I gave it away to anybody who'd take it. This collection here is partly what got "saved" and what I've been doing recently.'

'Which end do I start?'

'Doesn't matter. It's all stacked there any old how. Just dip in and see if anything attracts your attention.'

Jo did as she was told. Most of the plants were neatly identified in small black letters on the back. *Philipendula purpurea* was the first one she looked at, a feathery-looking bloom. Next came a fearsome-looking thing called *Euphorbia milii,* with spines all over the stem and a tiny red flower. After that came *Primula siamensis,* which she thought was some kind of primrose, only purple.

'Wouldn't it be better if these were sorted out into some sort of category?' she suggested.

'Yes it would, well spotted, dear! But you see, just as I was moving we had all this terrible hoo-ha about the rubies and then the threat of a court case, and then I began getting requests for new paintings, and honestly I haven't had time to get down to sorting them. Besides which, I need help to do it and Tim isn't here all that much.' She waved a hand at a folding bed in the corner of the untidy room. 'Tim sleeps here when he's home,' she added.

'Good lord!' Jo cried before she could stop herself. Then she added, 'I'm sorry. But it really doesn't look very comfortable.'

'Oh, Tim sleeps in a sleeping bag when he's off on one of his safaris, or in a bamboo shack, or a trailer attached to a truck. He's used to roughing it.'

Jo thought it was extremely good-hearted of him to put up with conditions like this when he left what she supposed was the wilderness. Speaking for herself, she'd have wanted something a lot more civilized. She went on with her inspection of the canvases, and paused at one she found some yard or so further on. 'This is pretty!' she exclaimed.

172

Betsey came to look. '*Foeniculum purpureum*,' she said. 'That's fennel.'

'Fennel? What, fennel that you eat? That vegetable?'

'Yes, why?'

'But it's got that beautiful feathery leaf and these lovely little yellow flowers!'

'Of course. Most plants have a flower, Jo. Almost everything you eat. Potatoes flower. Melons flower, so do peas and beans and apples and pears and almonds.'

'I never thought of that,' Jo said, astonished.

'You like the fennel painting?'

'Oh, I think it's gorgeous. I seem to notice that you like to paint these delicate things.'

'Quite right. And since you have the good sense to like delicate things too, I want you to have that one.'

'But Betsey, you already gave me one.'

'Yes, *Thunbergia mysorensis*, so now you can have the fennel to keep it company.'

'I couldn't, really – I didn't come here to cadge something from you.'

'Nonsense, nonsense, it's just sitting there with its back turned to the world. You take it home and put it up so the flower faces out.'

'Let me buy it from you.'

'No, no.'

'Yes, I couldn't just take it.'

'All right, then how much is it worth?'

'Ah . . . A thousand?'

'Of course not. Special discounts to a friend.'

'Five hundred?'

'You've no idea, really, have you? And nor have I. I couldn't sell that ten years ago for love nor money. And you didn't come on a visit to me to spend hundreds or a thousand on a painting you suddenly see. So please take it, and be fond of it, and that's what I'd like.'

In the end she gave in.

Once home, she cleared a space on a bookshelf in her living room. She set the painting there. It pleased her and she thought she'd get it framed so as to hang it properly.

August came and with it the wedding. Jo had been invited to come on the day before, and to stay that night and the next.

173

Ivan arrived to drive her to the house in the new sky-blue 4x4. He was wearing Burberry casuals – but was not in a casual mood, happy yet nervous, like an actor before a first night.

The day was warm but cloudy. August had begun with a few thunderstorms but they seemed to be rolling out to sea. 'I hope the sun comes out,' Ivan muttered. 'Of course everything's happening indoors, but it would be nice to have some shots of Miri and I in the grounds. Wait till you see the garden! That's really something.'

The garden, when they arrived at Chembard, proved to be a vast new lawn with, in its centre, a fountain spouting spray from four dolphins.

'What do you think?' he asked as they came up the drive and Jo saw it for the first time.

'Oh, I love fountains,' Jo said, avoiding a direct answer. Though it clearly belonged to the right period and suited the house, she thought it ponderous and stodgy. But she knew better than to say so. There had been great pride in his voice when he pointed it out.

Miri, in a pale yellow T-shirt and matching slacks, was waiting to greet them in the porch. 'So there you are! Lunch will be served in about half an hour, so let me show you to your room at once, Jo.'

A manservant picked up Jo's travel bag. They crossed the great marble-floored hall, went up the wide oak staircase, and along a passage in which there were several doors. Jo's bedroom was the third along the way.

The room into which she was shown was papered in a pale Chinese silk. There was a chandelier. The bed had a canopy of light-blue striped voile. The furniture was eggshell blue with Fragonard-style paintings.

The window looked out on to the fountain. 'Thought you'd like the view,' Miri said. 'Now if there's anything you need, just ring.' She touched the bell-pull of blue tapestry hanging near the bedhead. 'Come down as soon as you can, there's a soufflé for lunch and Cook's very temperamental – if it falls, she may walk out on us.'

She smiled and shrugged in apology. She was playing the part of the capable hostess. 'We're eating in the conservatory,' she added. 'The flower arrangers are in the dining room at the moment.'

In a way it was understandable that Cook was being temperamental, for the house was in turmoil. Caterers and florists were everywhere. There was a young woman with a clipboard in charge of it all, introduced to Jo as the wedding organizer.

The meal was delicious, the soufflé with which it opened a perfection of lightness. Almost as soon as it was over, Miri disappeared to supervize some part of the arrangements for next day. Ivan took Jo on a tour of his property.

There were six main public rooms on the ground floor. The conservatory opened off the billiard room. 'Do you play billiards?' Jo asked as they passed through it on their way to the hall.

'Sure, and I'll polish up my game now I have a table of my own,' he said proudly.

The wedding was to take place in the entrance hall. It was a very large hall, stately and imposing, but softened now by the summer garlands that were being hung along its dark panels. Chairs were stacked waiting to be put in place for the next day. Giving them a quick appraisal, Jo judged that the happy pair were expecting about fifty guests.

The dining room, as Miri had said, was in the hands of the organizer. She was having little tables set up which tomorrow would be covered by fine white linen and decked with little nosegays. 'The flowers will be pale pink roses,' she told Jo, cupping her hands to show their size. 'And there will be pale pink ribbon loops to go round the edge of the tables, and garlands of white lisianthus and lilies between swathes of white silk hanging from the picture rail.'

Something about the way she glanced about the big room told Jo that she thought it needed as much lightening-up as she could supply. And it was in fact rather sombre. In a desire to fit in with the period of the house, the decorator had painted it an impressive dark green. The fact that there was a leafy pergola outside the French doors made it seem somewhat dim, even though the doors were open to the August afternoon.

The tour ended with Ivan's study, where he couldn't resist switching on his computer so as to see how the stock market was going. Jo amused herself by looking at a file of photographs, copies of which were already distributed for advance publicity: the house, the fountain, the gates of the estate, the wedding gown spread on a sofa with Desmond standing by, and the diadem.

'Ah,' Ivan said when he'd finished with his review of current prices, 'that reminds me – the jewellery – you ought to let me have your bill for that.'

'Well now, Ivan, I thought it would be a good idea not to charge you for designing that. Just for the precious metals and the stones, but not for my work.'

'Oh, making it a wedding present?' he cried. 'That sounds great! That'll go down a treat in the magazine – Famous Designer's Gift – and then head shots of Miri wearing it – it ought to make a nice special in the later pages of the spread.'

Jo was taken aback. She had a wedding present in her travel bag – a pair of eighteenth-century silver candlesticks by Ebenezer Coker, found for her by a friend in the antiques business.

'No, wait a minute, Ivan, that's not what I mean. I had the idea that if I didn't take anything from you for my work on the jewellery, it might go to make up the difference —'

'The what?' Puzzlement replaced the pleasure. 'What are you talking about now?'

'I'm talking about Betsey Fieldingley. I thought that if I could make up the difference between what you got for the rubies at auction, and what you paid for them, you might forget about taking her to court.'

'What gave you that idea?'

'Well, one way or another you'd have got back what you paid for the necklace. It seems to cancel things out.'

'Oh, you think so, do you?' There was astonishment and irritation in his voice. 'You weren't the one that looked like a fool in public.'

'Come on, Ivan, that's an exaggeration.'

'Guys in my office still snigger about it behind my back!' He hit his desk with his fist, and she was startled. 'I want satisfaction,' he insisted, 'and I want it in public!'

'But surely you must see, it's going to look like revenge.'

'That's what it is! Of course it is! I want to equal the score.'

'Good lord, Ivan,' she pleaded, 'she's a nice old lady leading a blameless life in a retirement home.'

'I don't care! And let me tell you, I don't want *your* money, I want *hers*.'

'But she hasn't *got* any.'

'So you say, but I want a judge to make a statement that she owes me that money, and her snooty family will have to rally round and help her pay me if she hasn't got it herself.' He paused a moment then added, 'She must have earned some with all those paintings she's sold and that book.'

'Ivan, listen to yourself. She's got to live, you know – she needs money for that. I don't suppose she ever had a good enough income to invest in a pension. And you're beginning to sound almost paranoid about it.'

'Oh, so you're a psychologist now, are you? Paranoid? Get that from a TV programme, did you?' He thrust his face forward in a glower. 'And anyhow, what right have you to meddle in my affairs? Who asked you to come to the rescue of that old twister?'

She was silenced for a minute or two. Then she nerved herself to say, 'I didn't make the wedding diadem and the necklace as a wedding present. I intended it as paying off the balance of what you think Betsey owes you.'

His expression set as if in iron. 'Then we can't accept it.'

'We? What do you mean, we? Miri will never forgive you if you don't let her have that headdress.'

'Blackmail now?' Now he was smiling, but it was more like a sneer. 'Miri will blame *you*, when I tell her you've decided to take it back. And I hope you enjoy what the press will say. Killjoy sounds about right. There might even be something about how you're getting your own back on her because of the past.'

She understood at once that he was talking about their short-lived affair. It would be easy for anyone to think that it rankled with her, to watch Miri simply take Ivan back when she wanted to.

She stared at him, totally at a loss.

He said, 'Now, listen to me, Jo. You don't want to do this. Your reputation as a businesswoman is on the line here. You can't suddenly withdraw a piece of work at the last moment.'

'I never said I was going to do that! You were the one who—'

'If you don't mean it as a wedding present, that's OK. I'll pay you for it as I expected to. I know we haven't had a proper contract over this but fair's fair, and Miri wants to wear it. I can't have her hurt. But the long and the short of it is, it's not to have anything to do with that old woman. If *she* comes into it, I don't accept the jewels.'

He waited.

She couldn't bring herself to say that she agreed. All the same, she knew she had lost.

'Right,' he went on briskly. 'Everything's back to square one – agreed?'

She sighed and nodded.

'And listen, sweetie-pie, Miri doesn't hear a word about it. Nothing's going to spoil things for her. Is that clear?'

'Yes.'

'Now you're showing sense,' he said, and led the way out of the study. In the hall he summoned a manservant. 'Show Ms Radcliffe the grounds,' he commanded. He walked away without another word.

Nineteen

It seemed they were no longer on speaking terms. Luckily, the house was so full of people and activity that no one noticed.

Some of the wedding guests arrived during the afternoon and evening. Among them was Ivan's mother, a plump, sun-tanned lady in expensive clothes, who spoke very little except to praise everything she saw. The rest of the guests came from the world of finance or show business.

Dinner that evening was a buffet set out in the conservatory, served to not only guests but to organizers and helpers. During the night Jo could hear work going on in other parts of the house: hurrying footsteps, hammering, creaks and bumps.

Next morning was taken up with a rehearsal of the wedding ceremony, Miri coming down the grand oak staircase two or three times with a bedspread tied round her waist to represent the dragging skirt of the wedding gown. The flower arranger waited at the foot of the stairs to hand her a bunch of dahlias standing in for the wedding bouquet. A friend from Ivan's office read through the wedding service. It seemed to go on for hours.

At three o'clock in the afternoon the great event took place in reality. Miri looked superbly beautiful; Ivan was calm and elegant in his morning suit; the minister's voice resounded round the beams of the great hall; cameras flashed; TV equipment whirred, and Mrs Digby Senior wept quietly into a lace handkerchief.

Next there was a photographic session both indoors and out: photos of signing the register, kisses, handshakes; the happy pair and the guests at the front of Chembard, by the fountain, the rose arbour, on the slope of the lawn in front of the old cedar tree – to Jo it began to seem like a ten-mile hike. Then there were the 'specials', snapshots of important guests, of the groom's mother kissing her new daughter-in-law, and of sightseers outside the gates staring in.

When they at last sat down to the wedding breakfast in the

prettily decorated dining room, Jo was already beginning to droop with weariness. Yesterday had been difficult, she'd had a nearly sleepless night thinking over Ivan's outburst combined with the noises of work going on downstairs. Now she'd spent ten hours being polite to people she didn't know.

She laughed at the jokes in the speeches, raised her glass for the toasts, but chiefly she longed to get away somewhere quiet. But before then she had to be interviewed by the journalist from *Lookee Here* magazine, to tell her about the diadem and the necklace she'd designed.

'Amazingly effective,' cooed the journalist.

'Glad you like it.'

'Ivan tells me it's your wedding present to them.'

'Yes.' The Ebenezer Coker candlesticks were still in her travel bag. 'At least, the design is. He's paying for the materials.'

'And how much does that come to?'

'Oh. I don't think I can discuss that.'

'Where did you get the idea for the design?

She explained about the princess in the ballet.

'You're a ballet fan?'

'Not especially. I'm just interested from the design point of view.'

The questions seemed to go on forever. She felt she wasn't responding well.

Yet when the magazine came out the following week, she found herself quoted as a great lover of ballet, who went often to Covent Garden and used themes from the world of dance as her inspiration.

Well, so much for that, she thought. Luckily most of the magazine was filled with photographs of everything else to do with the wedding, and shots of the bride, the groom, and the important guests.

But it had its effect. She began to get inquiries from prospective clients, among them some very well-known jewellery chains.

Donald and Lindora invited her out to lunch. Donald said he just wanted to 'catch up'. What he really wanted was a blow-by-blow account of everything that had happened at Chembard.

'Was de Groot there?'

'Yes, he was.'

'What did he say?'

She thought back. 'I can't remember ever exchanging a word with him.'

Her sister-in-law stifled a groan of exasperation.

'Did you get the impression there was anything in the air about going back to the theatre? For Miri, I mean.'

'No, not that I recall.'

'Were you asleep all the time?' Lindora demanded.

Jo laughed. 'More or less. You've no idea how exhausting it was.'

Donald was frowning. 'There's some rumour Miri's ready to go back to work,' he murmured. 'Someone told me she doesn't see herself as a full-time wife and hostess.' He waited. 'What do you think?' he urged as Jo said nothing.

'Well, for the moment I think she's enjoying all that,' she replied. 'It's still very new, you know. And there's so *much* of it – the house, the furnishings, the grounds, the fountain . . . Ivan loves the fountain.'

'Huh!'

So they parted, Jo feeling that she'd disappointed them.

About a week later, Miri telephoned to ask if she could drop by for a chat one morning. Surprised, Jo agreed at once. She wanted to keep up contact with Miri and Ivan. She kept hoping there could be some way to deal with the court case.

Miri arrived next day, delivered to the door as ever by a chauffeur in a maroon sedan. She was looking as beautiful as always, and fresh from the ministrations of her hairdresser – new highlights, a smoother look. Jo was reminded that she ought to make an appointment to do something with her own short but shaggy crop.

'I'm not interrupting your work, am I?' Miri asked as she came in. 'But mornings are best for me if I want some girl talk. Afternoons aren't easy; Ivan comes home when he feels he's done enough in the markets.'

'No, it's lovely to see you.' They settled with coffee in Jo's living room, Miri refusing the offer of Belgian chocolate biscuits.

For a while they looked back on the wedding celebrations. 'Everybody adored my dress and the tiara,' Miri enthused. 'I'm going to wear it again – the tiara, I mean. We're going to a thing overseas, in Mexico City, and there's to be one of those grand dinners with everybody from high up on the diplomatic ladder and all that. So I thought it was a good opportunity to show it off again.'

'Quite right.' She nodded, then added, 'Wear your hair up.'

'Really? All right, if you say so.'

By and by she came round to what it was she'd come to ask.

181

'Your brother Donald got in touch,' she remarked. 'It's rather sweet, really. He wrote us this nice letter, and what do you think? As a wedding present he's asking if we'd like some special fish for the fountain.'

Ah, thought Jo. She couldn't help but admire her brother's neat thinking.

'And are you going to accept?'

'Oh, sure thing! Ive's all for it. We're consulting an expert so as to get the right brand – no, I mean species.'

'That sounds a good idea.'

'So it means I'll be in touch with Donald and Lindora again and, you know, what I wanted to know is, do you think they've got something in mind for me?'

'In the acting world, you mean?'

'Yes. Not immediately,' she added, rather hastily. 'Ive probably wouldn't like me to go swanning off until we've got the house perfect and there's still quite a bit to do.'

'That's a big responsibility. What more do you plan to do?'

'Well, we're extending the garage so's to build a flat above it for staff. And I wouldn't mind having an indoor pool. Then, of course, there's the dining room.'

'What about the dining room?'

'Well, one or two people we've had to dinner have mentioned that it seems kind of gloomy. It's that green paint, you know. It's an authentic Victorian colour but somehow . . .'

'I know what you mean. It's because of that rose arbour outside – the overhead trellis obstructs the light.' She considered. 'You could have that taken down.'

'No, no, that's part of the whole effect, a rose pergola to walk out under once you've had dinner. No, we couldn't do that.' She looked irritated. 'We had some big mirrors designed to make the room seem lighter, but then you see, you glance up and you see yourself chewing your steak – and nobody looks good chewing.'

Jo laughed. 'That's true. So you've taken down the mirrors?'

'Yes. And now we've got big green walls again.'

They were sitting together on a sofa in Jo's living room. Opposite was a bookshelf. Here Jo had cleared a space for Betsey Fieldingley's watercolour of the flower of the fennel plant. She was looking at it now.

She said, 'I could suggest an idea, but I don't know whether you'd go for it.'

182

'What sort of an idea?'

'How about a series of paintings, say about ten of them – not too big, but all on the same sort of theme?'

'Huh?'

'Six on the long wall opposite the windows, and two on each of the others – something like that.'

'What kind of paintings'

'Paintings of flowers.'

'Oh, that's kind of . . . old-maidish.'

'But these would be the flowers of things you eat. Vegetables, like peas and beans. Herbs, like . . . like rosemary or . . .' Jo wasn't much of a cook or a gardener. She rose to fetch the painting of the fennel flowers. 'Like this, Miri.'

Miri looked at it with her lips in a disbelieving smile. 'This is a vegetable?'

'Yes, it's fennel.' She turned over the canvas to show her the lettering on the back. 'That's the Latin name for it.'

'Well . . . It's sort of nice.'

'There could be nine others.' She tried to summon up the names Betsey had mentioned. 'Melons have flowers. I think vanilla has a flower – I think I heard somewhere that it's an orchid. And peaches and strawberries have flowers.' She sought about for something more exciting. 'I expect guavas and mangoes have flowers. That Mexican cactus that gives you tequila, I bet that has a flower.'

'Mm . . . Well . . . Could be quite fun.'

'And different. I bet nobody else would have that kind of thing.'

'Yeah . . . Yeah I think Ive might go for something like that.'

'He would, especially if you said *you* liked the idea.'

'Well . . .'

'Oh, you know you could talk him into anything,' she teased.

'Well, almost anything. Yes, I think he would like it. It's sort of refined, isn't it?'

'Yes. That's a good word for it.'

'So where did you buy this, Jo? I'd like to have a look at some more.'

Now was crunch-point.

'Miri . . . Betsey Fieldingley painted this.'

Miri set down her coffee cup with such a bang that the liquid slopped out. She gazed down at it, mopped it with the napkin Jo had provided, then muttered, 'Oh, well! *That's* a no-no. One mention of that old biddy, and Ive is in the grumps for the rest of the day.'

183

Jo waited a moment before replying. At last she said, 'I tried to talk to him about her a while ago. Some of the things he said . . . Honestly, Miri, it's time he let it go.'

'He won't!'

'He should listen to himself some time. If he talked like that to the press, they'd adore to give their readers a few quotes of some of the nastier things—'

'Oh, that doesn't bother him, you know, he likes his reputation as a hard man.'

'But, Miri, if *you're* on a chat show, say, wouldn't it bother you if they asked you about your husband's attitude? If they wondered about his vindictiveness?'

Miri looked uncertain. 'We usually agree beforehand about what we're going to cover.'

'Do they always stick to the rules? Especially when the case gets to court – you're bound to be asked for your opinion, don't you think?'

Miri sighed. 'That stupid court case! I'm dreading it. I can't be called as a witness, thank heavens, at least that's what the solicitor says because Ive bought the necklace as a surprise, so I never knew anything about it, but the fact is, Ive is going to be in court and he's going to be so cross all the time.'

Jo said nothing.

'All the same,' Miri went on, 'I'm not trying to get him to forgive Mrs Fieldingley. That's just not on.'

'The way I see it,' Jo said, 'he doesn't want to forgive her. He wants not to look a *fool* over what happened.'

'Well . . . yeah . . .'

'He needs some way to get his money back, to come out of it having lost nothing.'

'More or less. But, you know, it's got to be something public. He's never going to be satisfied if somebody just comes along and says, "Here's the balance of the money, now drop it".'

Jo was a bit surprised at the perceptiveness of this. She said, 'You're right. And if you think about it, Miri –' she tapped the painting – 'this is a way to do it.'

'I don't get you.'

'You want something to brighten up your dining room. You like the idea of a set of paintings to do with the flowers of food plants. Betsey Fieldingley could provide you with them. Let's say Ivan agrees to commission them so long as they're regarded as the final payment of what is owed to him. The press get advance information, you all get your picture taken looking at one of Betsey's paintings and smiling.'

'How's that's again?' faltered Miri.

She went through it several times, each time simplifying the process. Miri listened to it all, looking doubtful most of the time but sometimes nodding.

In the end Miri said, 'Well, if it could work, it would be great. The last thing I want is to have folk saying I'm married to a guy who's being rotten to an old lady.'

'So you'll have a try with my idea?'

'I'll ... I'll see how it goes. But listen, I'm not going to be a hero about it!'

'No ... Perhaps it wouldn't be a good idea to try for it all in one go. And you know, Miri, I don't want to be the cause of a serious fight. If it doesn't look like working, you can just drop it and say it was all my idea in the first place.'

'There's always that,' she agreed, laughing.

After that they went back to the subject of possible acting projects from Jo's brother. Jo felt she had to give a word of warning. She knew from experience how seldom his projects came to anything. 'Is there anyone else you're in contact with, about being in a show?'

'Only glam things, on TV. I've had two or three offers, but I've finished with that. Donald once said something about putting together a one-man show, something with a bit of humour about, you know, the kind of thing I used to be on, wearing tight dresses, showing off my cleavage. But it would all have to be in good taste, of course. Donald used to say he knew someone who could write it for me , . .' She sounded wistful.

'He's thinking about Shakespeare,' Jo teased.

'Oh, don't! I don't ever want to go through that again.'

'But there are plenty of good writers, Miri. Surely you could find someone yourself?'

'Me?'

'Why not?'

'But I don't know any writers.'

'But there are organizations – sort of trade unions – you might try getting in touch with one.'

'But where are they? I mean, how do I find out their phone number or anything?'

'Ask in the library for a reference book about writers.'

'Oh, that sounds a bit sort of nerdy. I don't know if I want to do that.'

'Well, do you go to any clubs where there's comedy? At those big dinners you and Ivan go to, is there sometimes an after-dinner speaker?' She herself had been to many such events. 'I'm sure there are people who write the scripts for them, you could try asking around about that.'

'But then what?' Miri said, looking perplexed. 'It would be easier to leave all that to Donald.'

'What about your publicity man? Do you still have one?'

'No, but, he's still there . . . in his office, I mean. I *could* ask *him.*'

'There you go!' cried Jo.

She reflected afterwards that she'd probably done her brother no favours. But she really and truly didn't want Miri to get involved in any of his schemes. Better that she find someone else to steer her acting career, if she were ever to have one.

She was busy with her own affairs for the next week or two. She received the sapphire earrings from Hechman's, sent them by courier to be exhibited in a show in Boston, attended a two-day conference in Milan, and interviewed one or two applicants for the receptionist job.

She was still answering her office phone herself when to her astonishment she received a call from Ivan Digby.

She said, rather unconvincingly, 'How nice to hear from you. How was Mexico City?'

'Huh,' he said. 'What do you care? You know for a fact that I'd decided never to speak to you again after that little session we had in my study.'

'Well . . . yes.'

'You put her up to it, didn't you?'

'What?'

'Miri. She's been on at me about these terribly desirable paintings until I'm ready to brain her.'

'Ivan, that's no way to talk—'

'The worst of it is, she's got the interior designer to agree with her. They're both nagging at me to get something to brighten up the dining room, and when I say let's just have it repainted, Meredith looks as if he's going to faint.'

'I'm sorry,' she said.

'No you're not, it's what you wanted to happen. But for some reason I can't fathom, Miri thinks you're the best pal she ever had, so when I call you names she gets upset. And I don't like Miri to be upset.'

'No, quite right.'

'So can you come and bring this confounded painting of yours to the flat so I can see what I'm supposed to think is so great?'

'Well, of course, I'd be very glad to.'

'Don't sound so delighted about it.'

'Well, you seem so angry . . .'

'I *am* angry, and you know why! You and your do-goodery are making me miserable! I never knew I had a weak spot until Miri started this campaign about the dining room walls.'

Jo had a hard time not chuckling aloud. Here was this master of the financial world, brought to his knees by the tears and sighs of a beautiful wife.

'When would you like me to come?'

'The sooner the better.'

'Well, I'm interviewing staff tomorrow. How about the day after?'

'What time?'

'That's up to you. When would you —'

'Oh, come to lunch, for heaven's sake, and we'll make peace over a drink or two beforehand.'

'I'd like that.'

'Right then. One thirty. I'll send a car.'

She didn't protest that she was perfectly capable of travelling to the City by herself. For the time being she was going to agree with Ivan Digby as often as she could.

It was late September, still quite warm but with a breeze that warned summer was over. She put on a knitted jacket over her poplin shirt, patted her newly-styled hair, settled the canvas of the fennel painting in a special carrier, added the watercolour sketch of the *Thunbergia* spray in a large manila envelope, and was ready when a maroon BMW drove up.

Miri was alone when she reached the penthouse flat. To Jo's surprise, she gave her a hug.

'It's so nice to see you again, Jo, there's such a lot I want to tell you. We've got a bit of time before Ivan comes home, there's some delay over a translation or something at the office, he's closing some deal or other.'

187

She was looking very bright and beautiful today. Velvet trousers, ivory silk top, still something left of her summer tan – the picture of health and happiness.

She led the way out to the terrace, where a pitcher of pale liquid with pineapple and orange floating in it was waiting. 'This is just a champagne cup,' she said. 'Biku is good at making it.' A little gesture indicated Biku was someone in the staff quarters.

They sat down in chairs sheltered from the breeze by a barrier of evergreens in ornamental pots. 'Shan't be able to sit out here much longer without bringing out the heaters,' Miri said. She pointed at the carrier Jo had propped by the table. 'Is that the painting?'

She nodded. 'Ivan's phone call was quite a surprise.'

Miri smiled to herself. 'It took quite a while. He can be as stubborn as an old mule. But I wanted to do something for you, Jo, because you know, that hint you gave me about finding a writer, it turned out to be a real winner.'

'Oh, that's good. Who is he?'

'It's a she ... It's so great, because she used to be an actress too, so she understands what I'm hoping to get, and she's full of ideas, and she's done it herself.'

'Done what?'

'The one-man-show thing. And you know, when I tell her little things about what's happened in the past, she turns it round so that it comes out ever so funny, and I'd never even have thought of looking for her if you hadn't put me on to it.'

'She's writing something for you already?'

'Well, so far it's just a trial thing. When she's done, say, four or five pages, I'm going to ask a guy I know from TV, try the stuff on him and see if he laughs.'

'It's going to be comedy, is it?'

'Well, that's what Viv is doing, but you know there's going to be some contrasty bits – my hard times before I struck it lucky, but we haven't got to that yet. And Lennie is just the sort of guy who'd be able to steer that in the right direction, because he's produced sit-com, and that has to have sort of ups and downs, you know?'

Jo listened as she talked on, full of enthusiasm. Only time would tell if anything came of all this, but at least Miri wasn't going to entrust herself to Donald, who'd probably want to put her in a play by Ibsen.

By and by Miri's plans and schemes had been dealt with, and she was brought back to the purpose of Jo's visit. 'He's still not very keen,' she warned. 'When I said he was going to look bad in front of the press he growled and groused, said he'd stand up to 'em. Then I just happened on the right thing to say.'

'And what was that?' Jo asked, intrigued.

'I said to him, I said, "How'd you like it if someone was treating Ella like this?".'

'Who's Ella?'

'*His Ma!*' Miri cried in dramatic tones. 'It's weird, you know, when she's around he finds her a dead bore, but he's ever so protective about her. Turns out that she had all kinds of trouble with the house she wanted to buy in Majorca, nearly had a nervous breakdown over it, and he had to keep going out there to deal with the authorities and that.' Miri smiled tolerantly. 'He's not all steel and concrete after all, you see!'

Jo nodded in acceptance of that. She knew it from experience: she had seen the state he was in when Miri first broke up with him.

'So, anyhow, I let it go at that for a bit and then I began to wonder what to do with the dining room walls if we didn't try the idea of the paintings. He really lost his temper, called me a terrible nag and that night, what d'you think? He slept in the guest room! So next day he didn't come home from the City until ever so late and really, Jo, I was terribly worried, I *mean* it. Because you know, his day finishes early compared to other people – he usually packs up by lunchtime, and sometimes he decides he's done enough by, like, eleven in the morning, because of course he starts so early.'

She paused to take a big swallow from her glass of champagne cup. Then she said, 'Well, so then, when he got in at around midnight I was in floods of tears and we just grabbed each other and hung on, and after that it was all kiss-and-make-up.'

Jo could picture it. She gave her an enquiring glance. 'All this was a bit risky, Miri. Did you really go through all that just to do me a favour?'

'Ha!' A little startled laugh. 'That's not very grateful, is it?'

'Sorry. But it sounds like you were quarrelling for days on end.'

'Look, lovie, Ive likes to win. It's a big thing with him and I understand it. But you know, if he wins all the time I'll end up like a doormat, won't I?' She stared in challenge at her listener. Then she went on, 'And in any case I really want the house to look good and your idea about the watercolours *is* a good one, and Meredith's all for it, so I thought I'd just push it along until I got my own way.'

'So he's really agreed.'

'He's agreed to take a look at the old lady's stuff. I don't know what'll happen after that. He muttered something about making an agreement, but then he seemed to take it back. I dunno, Jo, we'll just have to see.'

Distant sounds heralded the arrival of the man in question. He was still clad in business clothes. Miri hurried to him, linked her arm in his, and drew him to the table on the terrace. 'Just a nice little drink to revive you, lover, and then you have to get into something more comfortable.' She laughed at the oft-quoted words, then waved at Jo. 'Jo's probably dying of hunger by now, so hurry up.'

'Hello, Jo,' he said. He didn't smile, but neither did he seem unwilling to be in her company. In fact there was something smug about him.

'How'd the Chinese thing go?' Miri asked, pouring him a drink.

'Couldn't have been better. Just got to get the legal interpreter at their end to verify the wording and the contract's as good as signed.'

'You're doing something in China'? Jo asked, surprised.

'Me? Nah. I'm just selling them shares in a building firm.' He drank from his glass, gave a great sigh of appreciation, then went on, 'The building boom in China's going to make money for everybody. You should get in on it, Jo.'

'No thank you. In any case, I haven't any shares in a building firm.'

'Neither had I until a coupla months ago. And I only bought them so as to sell them on. That's what arbitrage is all about, buying in one market and selling in another.' He drank off the remains in his glass then turned away. 'Back in ten,' he said to Miri. 'Tell Biku to get the food on the table, sweetness, I'm starving.'

When he was gone, Miri winked at Jo. 'He's had a big success. He's in a good mood,' she pronounced.

Biku came a few moments later to say that the first course was ready. They went indoors to the spacious dining room. Jo glanced about at it; there couldn't have been a more striking contrast to the dining room at Chembard.

'Yeah, different, isn't it,' said Miri, catching her look of assessment. 'Of course, it's all done by a designer – not Meredith, we hired him special for Chembard because the Victorian era is his thing. And you have to admit, Jo, except for the dining room, Meredith did all right.'

They were discussing the merits of the various rooms in the country house when Ivan returned, showered, refreshed, and in slacks and jersey by Armani. When they'd sampled the pear salad and sipped the Sauternes, Ivan said, 'So . . . You're still on about cancelling out Mrs Fieldingley's debt, are you?'

She was about to say, 'Mrs Fieldingley doesn't have a debt,' but checked herself. Instead she said, 'If you're interested in breaking up this gridlock, I think it could be done.'

'And these paintings she does – you really think they'd look good?'

'I'm sure they would. Don't you remember, Ivan, when we went to that preview of her work at the little Mayfair gallery, the paintings were nearly all sold already.'

'Don't recall much of that. I don't pay attention to arty things.'

'And her book will be out around Christmas,' Jo went on, 'It's sure to do well.'

'She's got a book coming out?'

'Oh, you didn't know? A book about flowers that grow in the Andes region – some famous botanist has written the text and she supplied the watercolours.'

'Huh! Who's gonna buy a book about plants in the Andes!'

'Gardeners, of course. People who grow rare Alpine plants. And people who want to make money.'

'Eh?' he said, surprised. 'How d'you make that out?'

'There are wicked people who buy art books, Ivan, who cut out all the illustrations, frame them, and sell each of them for a good price.'

'They do?'

'They certainly do. Libraries are always complaining about people stealing the illustrations from important books.'

He shook his head. 'What a world,' he said, grinning

He was certainly in a good mood. He waited until the main course was brought then began again. 'Well, OK then, let's say I agree to have, say, ten paintings by the old girl. Your theory is that I should take that together with what I got for the fake rubies, and say I've got my money back.'

'Yes.'

'So how much would these paintings be worth, then?'

'I'd say about a thousand pounds each. And prices for her works are going up, Ivan.'

'A good investment then?'

'You're the expert on investment. But apart from that, it would let everybody off the hook.'

''Specially the old lady,' Miri put in. 'And you'd look good.'

'I don't care about that.'

'But I do, Ive! I don't want people saying I'm married to a rotten old meanie!'

'Oh, you,' he said fondly, and shook his head at her.

When they returned to the terrace for coffee, Jo opened the artwork carrier still propped against the table. She produced the canvas showing the flower of the fennel plant. Ivan took it, held it out at eye level, and pursed his lips.

'And this would be worth a thousand?' he wondered aloud.

'Ask around among the gallery owners. Prices might vary, depending on the subject.'

She took out the watercolour sketch of the *Thunbergia*. 'This isn't a finished work. I think I could get between four and five hundred for it.'

He raised his eyebrows. 'Is she some sort of Old Master type?'

'No,' she said, laughing. 'But she's fashionable at the moment.'

'So if she goes out of fashion this –' he shook the canvas he was holding – 'could be worth nothing much?'

'It will always be worth something. A botanist who could afford it would always like to buy a Betsey Fieldingley, I think. But the value might go up, not down.'

'You mean it's a gamble.'

'How can it be a gamble?' she challenged. 'You're not going to pay her for them.'

'Ri-i-ight,' he drawled on a speculative note.

By the time they'd drunk their coffee he'd decided he would agree to take a set of watercolours for his dining room so long as he liked the look of them. He would cancel the suit for misrepresentation.

'There's only one little problem,' Jo said.

'You what?' Now he was indignant. 'I'm going along with everything you just suggested.'

'But Mrs Fieldingley might not.'

There was a shocked silence.

'Don't be daft,' said Ivan. 'Why would she say no?' He frowned fiercely at Jo. 'Now you're gonna say she'd want to be paid.'

'I don't know. I haven't discussed this with her at all. But there's the possibility she might not want to take it on for a different reason.

She might think she was being asked to provide something that was just interior decoration, not art.'

'Oh, for Pete's sake! She's been practically begging me to drop the case and now you say—'

'She's an independent-minded lady,' Jo said. 'You better be careful how you go about all this.'

'Oh, you're going to ask me to apologize to her. Not a chance.'

Biku came to clear the coffee cups. They sat in silence until he had finished. When he had gone Ivan said, 'You're pally with her. You can tell her . . . well, you could say I sort of want to put it all behind us.'

'That could work,' Jo acknowledged.

Twenty

Betsey Fieldingley seized Jo and hugged her very tight for a moment. Then she let go, sank down on her chair, and fanned her face with her fingers.

'Wooh!' she gasped. 'Don't say things like that! It gives me a set of the tizzies!'

'I'm so sorry. I didn't mean to shock you with it. Are you all right? Drink some tea, you'll feel better.'

'I couldn't feel better! It's like having a great big sack of stones taken off my back. My dear girl, you've no idea what it's been like!' She gazed up in wonder at Jo. 'You really mean this awful man is going to take ten of my paintings and call it quits?'

'Well, he said he had to like the look of them. But he will . . .'

'He might not!'

'His wife will make him see that they're beautiful.'

'Really?'

'Trust me. When I had a look through your studio a few weeks ago, I saw a lot of things that Miri would like.'

'Dear soul, I'll paint new pictures for her – for him – whoever! I'd paint their front door for them, if it will only put an end to this interminable expense of lawyers and telephone conferences.' She leapt up and sought for a book on her bookshelves. 'Where's that plant dictionary? Oh . . .' She seized a hefty, worn volume and came back to her chair.

She flicked over a few pages. 'Ten food plants – it's easy, the world's full of plants that provide food. *Actinidia deliciosa* – that's kiwi fruit. *Allium sativum* – garlic. I could find ten under just the letter A!'

They were in Betsey's living room. Jo had asked if she might come with some news. 'Good news,' she'd agreed when Betsey nervously challenged her, but refused to say more over the telephone. Now the announcement was made, with perhaps too much effect on the hearer.

Betsey got up again to look for a pencil near the telephone. She came back with it, and the telephone pad. 'Beets,' she was muttering, 'of course only insignificant flowers but the leaves . . .' She paused to appeal to Jo. 'Would they like leaves? Or only flowers?'

'You'd have to ask them that yourself.'

'What?' An abrupt pause and a definite lessening of joy. 'Meet them? Meet him again?' Now her confidence was fading. 'Oh no . . . That time in the London office . . .'

'It would be different this time, Betsey. He likes to please his wife, and, you see, Miri is quite in love with this idea of having your paintings in their dining room. She thinks it would be "refined".'

'Refined?' Betsey raised her eyebrows, and broke into a chuckle. 'Is garlic refined? Well, never mind.' She sat silent for a while, her hands loosely holding the pencil and pad, her mind elsewhere.

When she spoke, she was calmer. 'Dearest Jo,' she said, 'this is really going to put an end to the court case? No more demands for money I haven't got?' At Jo's nod she continued, 'I'd do almost anything to see it dropped. So if I have to, I'll meet Mr Digby. So long as there's somebody else there – his wife, I suppose. Is she nice?' Without waiting for a reply she began scribbling plant names on the pad. 'What should I do, provide them with a list of possibles, or sketch a few so they can get an idea of what we're talking about?'

'It's no good asking me, Betsey. You'll have to ask Miri which of those ideas appeals to her.'

'Well, yes. Ask her. Why not? Should I write to her? Or telephone?' The mere idea seemed to set her in a flutter once again.

'Calm down,' Jo said. 'You've been asked to undertake projects before. Just do what you usually do.'

'But the people I deal with usually are botanists. Or at least plant-lovers. I don't know how to handle a glamour girl.'

'You'll soon get the hang of it,' Jo assured her, thinking to herself that Miri was probably a little more difficult than Betsey's usual clients.

'Well then . . . I suppose it would be best to telephone. If you could give me her number?'

'How about if I ring her now and say you'd like to speak to her?'

'Oh. Right now? I don't know . . . I need to sort of . . . get myself ready.'

'Why? Now come on, Betsey, be sensible. She's a young woman who wants to buy some of your work, that's all.'

'But she's married to that fearsome man!'

'So she is, and she's not the least bit like him. So shall I ring, and get this show on the road?'

'Well, I suppose so. Oh, golly, I wish I was wearing a better dress!'

Jo laughed at that, and after a moment so did Betsey. 'I'm a silly old bat,' she said. 'Go on, ring her.'

She used her own mobile to ring Miri's. Miri came on after a slight delay. 'Oh . . . Jo . . .'

'Is this inconvenient?'

'No, I'm with Desmond. Hang on a minute, Desmond, I want to speak to someone. Well, take out the pins . . .' After a sound of rustling and snipping, she came back on line. 'OK, I'm listening.'

'Miri, I'm with Mrs Fieldingley, and you'll be glad to know she's delighted at the idea of doing some work for you. Shall I put her on?'

Miri was clearly a little taken aback but burst out with a rather insincere, 'Oh, super! Good for you, Jo. Sure, love to speak to her.'

She handed the mobile to Betsey, who took it gingerly and said, 'Mrs Digby? Yes . . .' She kept her eyes fixed on Jo, as if for comfort. 'Of course not, I think it's a fine idea. Yes . . . How nice of you to say so.'

Jo wagged a hand to signify she thought she should leave her to her conversation. Despite Betsey's glance of appeal, she wandered out and into Betsey's studio. There she found a water-colour on an easel, drying in the afternoon air. It portrayed the branch of a fig tree, the beautiful leaves glowing as if in full sunlight, one of its fruits half visible. Quiet, almost detached, but full of life. The subject was drawn from a fig tree outside the window a few yards off.

The whole room was a testament to Betsey's love of her work. It seemed she could never stop painting. So for her, to be asked to undertake a series for Miri and Ivan was no hardship, and even though she wouldn't receive any money, she would be happy in the undertaking.

By and by Betsey came bursting into the room. 'Well, she's quite a surprise! Very unassuming about her knowledge of art. She wants me to see the room where they – the watercolours – are going to

196

be hung. This great big house of theirs . . . It sounds enormous. *He* won't be there, will he?'

'I don't know, Betsey. When's this going to happen?'

'Tomorrow. She's going to drive up from London, collect me, and take me on to Chembard.' She hugged herself. 'It's all going so fast, it scares me a bit. But she *says* the husband won't be there.'

'You know, you're going to have to meet him again one day. One of the things they want is for you and him to be photographed.'

'Oh no! She never said anything about that.'

'Well, it's part of the plan, and why not?'

'But . . . but . . .'

'It'll be all right. He'll be on his best behaviour. He wants the press to see him accepting one of your watercolours and shaking hands or something. To show that you've made amends for all the trouble over the necklace.'

'Yes. Of course. I see that. Am I to look apologetic?'

'If you could manage that, Betsey, it would be all to the good. He wants to come out of this as having proved his point.'

Betsey grimaced, but nodded. 'Well, that's not going to happen immediately, is it? So long as he doesn't start putting on his war feathers!' She ran a hand through her untidy hair. 'Good heavens, I've faced African snakes and Amazonian Indians in my time. I should be ashamed of myself for being afraid of one angry man.'

'Not a bit. But I'll tell you what, Betsey.'

'What?'

'Put on your best dress and have your hair done before you meet Miri. She's so perfect to look at, it's disheartening.'

Betsey managed a shaky laugh. 'My best dress is twenty years old.'

Jo expected to hear from her the following evening, after their meeting. But a silence ensued. She began to get worried. Had something gone wrong?

Not at all. On the Friday, soon after Jo had opened up for the day, Betsey arrived on her doorstep. She was wearing a rather good-looking but elderly tailored dress and shoes with heels.

'Good gracious, what are you doing here so early in the morning?'

'I'm just dropping by,' Betsey said with a wide smile. 'Look!'

Beyond her was one of Ivan's favourite maroon cars. 'I'm being driven home to set the scene. You've no idea, Jo, it's been like a sort of whirlwind.'

197

'Come in, sit down, get your breath back,' Jo invited.

'Well, only for a minute. I've got to get back to my studio to pick out a few canvases. The photographers are going to meet us there.'

'Photographers, eh?' Jo clapped her hands. 'So you've summoned up your courage?'

'Yes, I'm feeling quite intrepid. Miri is so pleased with everything. Do you know, when I got to Chembard to see the famous dining room, she made me stay overnight – I wasn't prepared for that, of course, no nightie or anything but she supplied me with whatever I needed from her own collection – my *dear,* what a collection! So many clothes . . .'

'How did you like your bedroom? Did you get the one with the Fragonard furniture?' Jo asked. She had clear memories of the over-furnished room.

'Oh, you've seen that? It's so over the top. But anyhow, after that, she brought me up to London, and . . .' She paused with a finger in the air for emphasis. 'I've *met* Ivan the Terrible. I was scared stiff at the whole idea but Miri insisted on me driving up to town with her and somehow I couldn't get out of it. And that place they've got on the top of the world! Do you know, the bathroom attached to my bedroom had gold taps? It's a whole other way of living, Jo.'

'You spent the night at the penthouse flat?'

'Yes, I *did,* and it was fabulous. And there was Ivan, and after all he's not so very scary when you get to know him, although, to tell the truth, I don't think I could ever be bosom pals with him.'

They laughed, and Betsey patted Jo on the shoulder. 'My dearest girl, I owe all this to you. Everything is smoothed over, we're going to have a photographic session today, "in the artist's studio", you know.' She giggled. 'And Ivan's given instructions to *his* solicitors to get in touch with *my* solicitors so there should be something in tomorrow's papers.'

'That's great! I wish you weren't in such a rush. We ought to celebrate, though it's too early in the day for champagne – and anyway I haven't got any.'

'Just as well! In these last two days of *la dolce vita* I've had more wine than is good for me. And anyhow I've got to dash. Miri and Ivan are to be at my place soon after one, and the cameramen will be there before that to set things up.'

'Off you go then. And I'm really delighted.'

They hugged, she let Betsey out, the uniformed chauffeur opened the car door, and she was swept off giving mock-royal waves at Jo from the car window.

True to her prediction, photographs of Betsey and the Digbys appeared in the next day's tabloids. Jo bought all of them, and wondered how Betsey felt about being called 'a little old lady with a marvellous talent' in one of them.

Jo's new part-time receptionist, Lucille, was thrilled at it all. 'You actually know Miri Gale?' she marvelled. 'I used to see her on TV – in that quiz show, you know.' She sighed. 'What I'd give for a figure like that.' A middle-aged mother whose children had flown the nest, her chances of having a figure like Miri's were about a hundred to one.

Some details of the peace-making were given in the papers. 'Mrs Fieldingley, former owner of the troublesome Fieldingley Rubies, is to provide financier Ivan Digby and his lovely wife Miri Gale with paintings for one of the rooms in their fabulous country home, Chembard.'

The story of the fake rubies was re-hashed. Miri was quoted: 'When we've hung Betsey's paintings where we plan to, they'll just be so wonderful! I feel that, with them, we'll have something richer than rubies.'

Jo was pretty sure that the little speech had been written for her by her publicity expert. In fact, the whole thing seemed to have been beautifully stage-managed. A mention of Miri's plans to appear on-stage by and by in a one-hander was included in the report. The photograph varied from paper to paper but each showed Betsey holding up one of her watercolours with Miri and Ivan looking on in admiration.

Peace had been declared, the *affaire Fieldingley* was over. Jo celebrated with Lucille by ordering in a special lunch from a nearby Italian restaurant. The restaurant couldn't supply champagne, but Asti Spumante was adequate for the occasion.

'Dear me,' murmured Lucille, 'this is a really lovely job!'

She was even more impressed the next day. A great basket of flowers arrived from Ivan, roses and ribbons and streamers. The card simply said: 'Thanks.' When Miri rang later, Lucille was almost speechless with awe as she passed the receiver to Jo.

'Get the flowers?'

'Oh yes, Miri, thank you, they're gorgeous.'

'I suppose you saw the papers yesterday, did you?'

'Of course. Betsey forewarned me so I bought them all.'

'Yes, I think it was a slow news day so we got good coverage. And do you know, your brother rang while I was still eating break-fast! He's offering to manage my show for me.'

'What did you say?' Jo asked, alarmed.

'Oh, I said no. No offence, Jo, but Viv can put me on to someone with a lot more know-how.'

Jo was reassured. 'So it's actually going to happen, the one-man show?'

'Looks like it. Listen, why don't you drop by and I'll let you look at the script Viv's putting together.'

'Ah, I'd love to come, Miri, but don't expect me to give an expert opinion on the script.'

'No, that's OK, you don't have to read it if you don't want to. Thing is, Jo . . . Why I really rang is . . . I was wondering . . . if you could design something special for me? Ivan wants to give me a special present to make up for never getting the rubies.'

'But Miri, I thought the wedding jewellery was the amends for that?'

'Well, yes, of course. Yes, it was, you're quite right. But you see . . .'

'What?' Jo prompted.

'The tiara isn't really something I can wear just for a first night or an evening out, now is it? It's too . . .' She sought about for a word. 'It's stately, is that what I mean?'

Jo nodded to herself. 'Yes, I know what you mean. It's not a friendly piece of jewellery. It really only goes with a dress like your wedding dress.' And the person you were pretending to be at that time, she added mentally.

'And I'm not going to wear that dress again, am I?' Miri went on to detail the difficulties of managing the long, exuberant skirt and the corset constricting her waist. She came at last to the point. 'Tell the truth, one of the TV production companies has asked to buy it for a costume drama they're putting on.'

No sentimentality there, thought Jo. 'So will the diadem go too?' she asked.

'Funny you should ask that,' said Miri, hesitant and apologetic. 'Ivan's saying we ought to sell it – not to any showbiz company, of course, 'cause it's high-class, isn't it.'

Yes, thought Jo, it is. And of course I did expect you to sell it.

Hearing no protests from Jo, Miri went on, 'He's thinking we could use the money to have something made to match the gold-and-diamond choker. He likes that a lot, and so do I – every time I wear it somebody tells me how elegant it looks. You could do a bracelet and earrings, mebbe, along the same lines. What do you think?'

She was pleased to be asked yet Jo found herself sighing a little. She'd felt sure the diadem would be sold, yet it was sad to think of it changing hands so very quickly. As it if were unloved . . . But that was silly.

The more serious aspect was that she'd still have to be in contact with Miri and Ivan. Once the problem over the rubies was solved, she'd hoped to detach herself from them. It had something to do with the idea that they just weren't her kind of people. And perhaps to do with the fact that Tim Fieldingley had reproached her about her affair with Ivan.

'Let's just leave it to simmer for a while, Miri,' she suggested.

There was disappointment in her voice when she replied, 'Right, no problem. It's not urgent.' After a pause, she added, 'But you know, if anybody notices that I'm selling the tiara, it might be good publicity to say you're making me something else instead.'

'I see.' She stifled a sigh. Always the publicity angle. 'Well, I could give it some thought.'

'Splendido! Do some of those sketchy things on your computer, eh?'

'I'm rather busy, Miri.'

'No hurry, no hurry! I'll leave it to you. So, OK, bye now!'

When she hung up, Lucille was hovering. 'Are you going to make something new for Miri Gale? Isn't that great? I'd no *idea* when I applied for the job . . .'

'Don't get excited, Lucille,' Jo sighed. 'I might not do it.'

To which Lucille responded with a stifled gasp of amazement.

Yet later that day, Jo's imagination was showing her little glimpses of a bracelet that would match the choker necklace. Unsought, almost unwished-for, her designer's instinct was suggesting what might be done.

She spent the afternoon catching up on correspondence with Lucille's help. Lucille was a great improvement over Lindora: she could take dictation, she didn't mind doing the filing. Two hours of concentrated work made a great improvement in Jo's office's administrative efficiency.

When they finished and her new helper put on her jacket to leave, Jo was weary. The last few days had been full of activity and surprises. She went upstairs, poured herself a drink, and decided that she must get on with yet another piece of recruitment: she must find a reliable daily help so as not to face a living room that needed dusting and a dishwasher full of unwashed dishes.

The surprises of recent days were not at an end. Her office phone was ringing when she went downstairs on her way to an evening meal in a restaurant.

It was the organizer of the Excellence in Gems exhibition in Boston, William Michel.

'Ah, Ms Radcliffe, forgive the informality of a phone call, we've emailed also, but a formal letter is on its way. I'm delighted to tell you, Ms Radcliffe, that the judges have just finished giving their verdicts on the various categories in our exhibit. You have won the Award for Best-in-Show for the small-ornament section! Your earrings really delighted them.'

'Really?' She sat down in the desk chair, breathless with delight.

'Yes, Reimund Keller and Emilia Tonini were especially taken with them. The technique required from your factory technicians at Hechman's was innovative, so they too are receiving an award, for Excellence in Production Methods.'

'That's absolutely great. Hechman's are invaluable to me. I'm so glad the judges understood – the main gemstone had to be raised and extended forward . . .'

'Yes, yes, our technical panel was very taken with the styling. Now listen, Ms Radcliffe. You'll know, of course, that the medals are awarded at a separate function, which is in fact tomorrow evening, a grand dinner. Cecil Grant from Hechman's is already here, as perhaps you know. I *do* hope you're going to be with us to receive your award, Ms Radcliffe?'

'Oh, well, it's such short notice, I hadn't thought of attending.'

'Please do, if you can. Mr Keller is very anxious to have a word with you.' Unsaid was the fact that Reimund Keller was a very influential man in the world of jewellery.

'Oh, in that case . . . I could . . . Perhaps I could get a flight early tomorrow morning.' She made rapid calculations. Taking off around seven, arriving at Logan Airport in the early afternoon European time, mid-morning Eastern Seaboard time – yes, it was certainly possible. 'I'll see what I can do, Mr Michel.'

'Will you let me know if you're able to come? An email would be great.' He dictated his address. 'I'll have you met at the airport and we already fixed a hotel for you. Lovely, look forward then. I have to go, the press are waiting to interview me about the judging. See you soon, I hope. And congratulations.'

It took her an hour to find a seat on a plane. That done, she emailed Michel then telephoned Lucille at her home, to explain she wouldn't be able to let her into the studio next day. Lucille was, as seemed her way, thrilled by the news.

A sleepless night for Jo. Her mind was whirling with designs for Miri's bracelet, images of the sapphire earrings that had won a medal, Betsey Fielding's flower paintings, and worry that her alarm would fail to wake her the next morning.

The flight was uneventful. A young man holding a placard saying 'EXCELLENCE' met her and conducted her to his car. The hotel was close to Boston Common and only a few blocks from the exhibition hall. As she was ushered through the lobby she could see many people wearing badges using the word EXCELLENCE as a sign that they were part of the jewellery world.

Her room gave her a view of the common. The trees were that heavenly mixture of gold, amber and ruby-red that makes New England the best place to be in the fall. She stood for a long time gazing out, letting the sight calm her after the hectic journey to be here.

She'd been given a schedule of events at the reception desk. She found she was expected at 'an informal lunch and drinks party' at some other venue in a couple of hours. 'Informal', she knew from experience, meant that it was being given by some influential member of the jewellery world, who'd be offended if she didn't turn up.

She unpacked, hung up her Rive Gauche dinner dress to let the creases fall out, then showered and changed. She travelled in jeans, a jersey, and trainers, but now she put on high heels, a slim skirt and a silk top. She did her face rather hastily, but a glance at her watch showed her she had some minutes to spare. Her escort was to collect her from the front desk in good time.

The phone in her room was winking with message lights. She sat down to listen. Reimund Keller welcoming her to the exhibition, hoping she would make time to have a little talk. Mr Michel of the organizing committee, reminding her that she'd be expected to say a few words in response to the award. And so on, friends she often met at events like this, from France, from Germany, from Scandinavia.

When she'd finished noting down numbers and names, she found herself wondering if any of the European magazines had caught up with the news of her award. She called up the answering machine in her home office.

The first recording was the London correspondent of *Joaillerie Moderne* asking for an interview for the November issue. The editor of *Gemme* had called from Milan to say he would like photographs of the 'prize-winning object' as soon as possible. Then, so unexpectedly that she gave an audible gasp of surprise, the voice of Tim Fieldingley.

'Hello, I'm outside your studio door but you're clearly off somewhere gadding this morning. Sorry to miss you. This is Tim Fieldingley, by the way, passing through London so I thought I'd look you up, perhaps take you out for a drink, but no reply at your door. Better luck next time, eh? Well, so long.'

She stared at the receiver as if it were some star that had suddenly fallen from the heavens into her hand. Then she hastily pressed buttons to have the call repeated. She hoped to catch something she'd missed first time around – a telephone number where she could reach him.

No, she'd heard it all correctly. She replaced the receiver in dismay.

She thought, I'll ring Betsey. He may be staying with her, or at least she'll have a number for him.

But Betsey's number wasn't in the address book she'd brought with her. She had two – one in the office for business contacts, one usually in her handbag for friends and relatives. But on this trip she'd brought only the business book, of course.

She'd get the desk to find the number through international inquiries. But her phone rang as she was about to pick it up. It was in fact Mr Dukowsky, her escort, calling from the front desk to say their car was outside. The hotel commissionaire was asking that they either get into it or move it away, as it was blocking access.

She found she was panicking. She'd had too little sleep, she was trying to do too much in too little time.

Later. She'd get Betsey's number later.

She stood up, took a look at herself in the mirror over the bureau to make sure she was presentable. It was early afternoon and she

204

was going out to meet a lot of very influential people. She mustn't keep her escort waiting.

All the same, she stood still for a moment to struggle with the distress welling up within her.

'Tim is in *London*,' she said to the empty, uncaring room, 'so what am I doing *here*?'

Twenty-One

The day seemed long. The award at the grand dinner was the climax, enjoyable because it was proof that her work was understood and appreciated by her peers. Yet she was glad to return at last to the sanctuary of her hotel room.

She felt exhausted, disorientated. She fell into the chair by the bureau, knowing there was something she wanted to do, something important. Not about her award – a handsome gold medal in a velvet case – that she had had put in the hotel safe. She considered it as in the past now. No, this was something about the future, some action she intended to take.

After some moments of sitting listlessly in the chair, it came to her. She wanted to telephone Betsey Fieldingley, to ask if Tim were there, and if not, how to get in touch with him.

Her brain seemed stuffed with cotton wool. How did she find out Betsey's telephone number? She'd intended to ask the reception desk to do that for her. She glanced at the digital clock that was part of the bedside equipment. Ten past one in the morning. She screwed up her eyes, trying to do the mental arithmetic. It was about six o'clock in the UK.

Would Betsey be awake so early?

And then another thought. How would it look if she rang from Boston to ask to be put in touch with Tim? Wouldn't it seem a bit, well, over-eager? Almost desperate, in fact?

She was too tired to have any judgement. She let her mind wander for a moment or two then resigned herself to going to bed.

As a result of too much stimulation, too much activity, and too much uncertainty, she slept too long. She was wakened by the buzzing of the telephone. It was the front desk.

'Ms Radcliffe, Mr Dukowsky is here, he expected to meet you in the lobby?'

'What?' The fog of sleep was slow to lift.

'Alex Dukowsky. He's here.'

Now she remembered. She was supposed to be at a morning reception across the river in Cambridge at eleven. She groaned. 'Would you please tell Mr Dukowsky that . . . that I'll be there in fifteen minutes.'

So the day went. She never seemed to keep up with her schedule. She was to catch a late-night flight that would get her home at around lunchtime in London. Once in her flat, she intended to sit quietly in an armchair for the rest of the day, until her internal clock put itself right again.

But it wasn't to be. When she reached home, she found a long queue of messages on her office answering machine. The editor of *Gemme*, thanking her for the photographs of her prize-winning earrings was asking for a quote to go with them, Miri Gale inquiring why she hadn't been in touch, her brother Donald saying he'd ring again, Ben Webber congratulating her on the award.

More importantly, there was a call from Mr Eades of Simenoff, the commercial jewellers. The copy necklace, from the design she'd originally done for the rubies in the Fieldingley necklace, was due to go out on sale before Christmas.

His tone on the machine was easy, almost paternal. 'I'm calling just to remind you that the launch party for your piece is Thursday of next week. I know you have it in your diary, Ms Radcliffe, and we've emailed you a guest list. All the thrill of your Boston trip might have put this out of your mind so I thought you wouldn't mind just a little nudge, eh?'

She rang him at once, to assure him she was back and well aware that there was a party a few days off.

'I do congratulate you on your medal, Ms Radcliffe,' he said. 'The manager of our New York branch was at the symposium, but he didn't get an opportunity to speak to you.'

'No, it was all a bit of a whirl . . .'

'Apart from everything else, your prize comes at such a good time for our publicity campaign. You won't mind if we combine the two elements, the award and the new necklace?'

'Of course not. I want the necklace to be a success.'

'Oh, I hope we'll have other successes in the future. But we'll discuss that some time. My board are quite hopeful that you might do some exclusive designs for us, from time to time.'

'No – well, I've never worked in that way . . .' Her voice trailed off. 'You have to excuse me, Mr Eades.'

'Alfred. If we're going to be colleagues, perhaps you could call me Alfred.'

'Well, then, Alfred. I'm suffering from jet lag, I really can't think straight for the moment.' They parted with good wishes on each side. She wondered vaguely if she should have returned his friendly gesture and asked him to call her Jo.

It was all too much to deal with. Her head still seemed in a whirl.

Her office phone kept ringing. She let the machine take the calls. She also switched off her mobile. But the phone in the flat rang while she was trying to decide what, if anything, to do about lunch. It was her brother Donald.

'Why don't you answer your telephone?' he complained. 'I've been leaving messages for days!'

'I've been in Boston.'

'Boston? Boston in Lincolnshire?'

'No, Boston in Massachusetts. I was accepting a prize for one of my designs.'

'Really? Oh, well done then. But listen, I want to ask you about Ivan Digby. That idea about a wedding present for him and Miri fell through, so I want your help in thinking of something else.'

'I'm sorry, Donald, this isn't the right moment.'

'Oh, come on, just suggest a couple of things, perhaps for this famous house of theirs.'

'What went wrong with the first thing? Wasn't it something like, fish for their pond?'

'For their fountain. But we consulted an aquarium expert,' he explained, sounding important and dignified about it. 'He tells us that the fountain's in a bad position, right in the middle of a lawn, no shade, you see, and the downward force of the water is too strong, so he doesn't recommend putting fish in it. But as you've been to Chembard I thought you'd give us some idea. Because, of course, we've only seen magazine photographs.'

Jo's mind was in such a hazy state that she took in almost nothing of this long explanation. When he stopped she said, 'I'm sorry, Donald, you'll have to talk to me about this some other time. Goodbye.'

With that she hung up, and then after a moment called up her newly-hired receptionist. Lucille was only too pleased to be asked to come in, even at short notice. For the rest of the day she fielded all the interruptions.

Next morning, feeling much more like herself, Jo studied the list and began to return her telephone calls. First came business contacts, which took her until lunchtime. Then she wrote short thank-you notes or emails to non-urgent messages, mostly to her friends in the jewellery world. Meanwhile Lucille was handling incoming calls, trying to decide which were to be passed on to Jo and which could be put off with polite excuses.

Alfred Eade called again. 'My dear Ms Radcliffe . . .'

'Oh, please call me Jo.'

'Thank you, then, Jo, are there any names you'd like to add to the guest list for the party? Because, of course, our publicity manager has asked jewellery bigwigs and members of the trade press, but we'd certainly like to have some of your personal friends.'

'Oh, Ben Webber, of course,' she said at once. 'And Edward Notting, from Hechman's.'

'Yes, if you'll just check, you'll see we already have the Hechman's people. Ben Webber, of course, I never thought of him. I'll add him. And Jo, we've already included Ivan Digby and his wife.'

The name startled her for a moment. She'd thought this party would be only for people in the world of jewellery, but if Simenoff's wanted to extend the public interest, then the Digbys were always newsworthy.

Of course. It was good publicity to have them there.

She stifled a sigh. She herself would never have suggested including them. But to ask to have their names taken off the guest list was too . . . uncivil, too pernickety. She said rather slowly, 'Yes, certainly, why not.'

'Anyone else? Reimund Keller? You know we had a staff member at the Boston show, he said Keller was showing a great deal of personal interest in your work.'

'But Keller is in the States.'

'No, he's back in Frankfurt now. He flits about a lot, I'm sure he'd come. Would you like us to invite him?'

'Well . . . Yes, I would . . .' It made good sense. Keller was a banker whose dearest interest was jewellery; he wrote learned papers about antique or historical pieces, he judged at competitions, he supported struggling designers – in a word, he was a man worth having as a friend.

'Good, we'll telephone him at once just to make sure he's expecting his invitation.' Other names were suggested; she made no demur. It was Simenoff's party so let them make the decisions. And of course, it was always wise to issue plenty of invitations. There are always people who have prior commitments.

She rather hoped Ivan and Miri would be too busy to accept. A feeling was growing inside her that somehow she'd like not to be too involved with them any more.

When at last she felt she'd caught up with the absolutely essential contacts, she came to the one she'd been longing to make. It was after six and Lucille had gone. A good time for a social call. She rang Betsey Fieldingley.

'Ah, Jo, how lovely to hear from you! Tim was in London a few days ago, said he missed you.'

'Yes, I was in Boston. In America.'

'Good gracious! Business or pleasure?'

She explained about the award. Betsey at once broke out into hearty congratulations. 'How marvellous. No wonder your place looked all shut up! What's the award like – sort of an Oscar for jewellery?'

'Oh, it's not one of the main awards, Betsey – I only entered a pair of earrings, that's not entitled to anything big. The award is a medal, you know, quite nice. Neat, not gaudy, as Shakespeare says somewhere.'

'Next time I'm in London, may I pop in and have a look?'

'You're not going to be in London next week, by any chance? I've got a piece of work being put out by Simenoff's. I don't know if you know them, they're rather high-class jewellers.'

'Oh!' It was a laugh of surprise. 'Well, I see their advertisements sometimes, in the glossy magazines at my hairdresser!'

'Well, this necklace that they're going to put on the market, I think it would interest you, Betsey. They're replicating the design I did for your ruby necklace, only they're bringing it out in various less precious stones.'

'Really? What a good idea! Some good is coming out of that blessed thing! I hope it makes a lot of money for you, dear.'

'Simenoff's are giving a party. It's next Thursday. Would you like to come?'

'Thursday? Oh . . .' Her tone was doubtful. 'Well – is it a very *high-class* thing? What would I have to wear?'

'Early evening sort of thing, Betsey – cocktail dress, you know?'

Betsey chuckled. 'I really haven't got a cocktail dress, my love. And, you see, I've got quite a lot of work – Miri Gale keeps asking me how I'm getting on with her watercolours, she keeps wanting to come and have a look.' She paused, her thoughts elsewhere for a moment. 'Really, it's a bit of a nuisance, you know. She's so . . . so *bothered* about having the paintings. As if her world wouldn't be complete without them.'

'Oh yes.' Jo caught her meaning. Neither of them wanted to say aloud that Miri's view of the world was rather shallow. She said, 'Miri is coming to this party.'

'Really?'

'Simenoff's have invited her.'

'And the husband?'

'Yes, him too.'

'In that case, I think I'll say no to your invitation. But I hope you have a lovely time. Tim will be really amused to hear I've been asked to a thing like that!'

'Are you in touch with Tim regularly?' Jo said, coming at last to the question she really wanted to ask.

'Goodness, no, only when he can spare the time and the satellite phone is working!'

'Satellite phone? He's off on one of his big trips, then?'

'When *isn't* he! Always on the move.'

'I was just thinking I'd reply to his phone call. He left a message on my machine.'

'Oh, I'm afraid that's hardly possible. I always have to wait until *he* calls *me*. What a shame.'

'Never mind, it doesn't matter. Next time he's in touch, you might tell him thank you for dropping by.'

There was a little pause, as if Betsey were trying to catch some nuance from her words. She said, 'You could do that yourself. Leave a message on the machine at his flat.'

'His flat? Oh yes, in Strasbourg, I think he said.'

'I'll give you his phone number,' Betsey said. 'Got a pencil?'

When they had disconnected, her first impulse was to ring the Strasbourg number. But as she was doing so, she found herself wondering what message she could leave: Sorry I wasn't there when you called, I was in the US . . . Was it, after all, worth doing? What sort of impression would it make? And anyhow, he was in the wilds of Siberia or somewhere. It might be weeks before he heard it.

So she replaced the receiver.

Things didn't get back to normal. There was the usual run of work, items she was making herself and items to be got ready to go to

Hechman's. In spare moments, she was interviewing possible home helps from an agency, which was difficult. There was always the matter of security. Her studio, her workshop and her home had plenty of the usual safeguards, but when you allowed someone into your personal space it was different. She was hoping to find someone she could like, and moreover, who would be approved by her insurance firm.

Then there was the fall-out from her American visit. She had several customers competing for copies of the prize-winning earrings. She'd always worked directly with her clients in the past but now she began to think she ought to have an agent.

She needed to get her hair done. She really ought to buy a new evening dress.

So the days seemed to fly by, and suddenly it was time for the Simenoff's launch party. A bright, busy affair, well attended, in the sparkling new Solaire Hotel. Two separate versions of the Radcliffe necklace were on show in the banqueting room, one with peridot, one with red spinel. Little groups formed to admire, to utter sighs of admiration and, particularly from the women guests, of desire.

After all the announcements and little well-wishing speeches and toasts, Ben Webber caught up with Jo for a moment's talk. 'Nice to be invited,' he said. 'Simenoff's haven't used my good offices much but I had a little chat with Eades, something may come of it. So how are you? On top of the world?'

'To tell the truth, I'm feeling a bit worn,' she acknowledged. 'It's been non-stop since I was told about the award.'

'Ah, the award, well done – I hear the earrings are gorgeous. And as to being "worn", nonsense, you look great.' He gave a big sigh, looking at her with affection. 'We don't see each other often enough, Jo. The last time we were in touch there was all that stupid kerfuffle over the rubies.'

'I know. Sometimes I wish I'd never heard of them! I can't seem to get rid of the Digbys.'

'That's odd, really.' He stared past her, at a point in the room where Miri was holding court, glowing with delight at being the centre of interest. Miri, catching his eye, blew a boisterous kiss towards Jo.

It surprised him. 'You'd think Digby's missus would want you kept well away, considering, you know, how things went between you and him. But she seems to like you?'

'No, no, I'm no competition and she knows it. Besides,' she shrugged, 'that was just one of those silly mistakes.'

Ben looked pleased. 'Glad to hear it,' he remarked, and raised his glass to her in a toast.

She was drawn away from him by Reimund Keller, who murmured that he'd like to discuss a little matter with her. The little matter proved to be an invitation to give a talk at a gathering in Frankfurt after Christmas.

'Me?' she said in amazement.

'Yes, of course, you. Don't you know that you are a rising star in contemporary style? You could explain your method of collaboration with the technicians you use – very important.'

Next day there was coverage of the launch party in one or two of the tabloids. Jo found she didn't figure much. It was Miri and Ivan who got most of the attention. Nevertheless, Alfred Eades rang to congratulate her. 'It went very well,' he proclaimed. 'The main fashion magazines will be featuring the new necklace in their New Year issues. We should do well with it.'

Jo was still uncertain about it 'going commercial'. Her career had begun in making jewellery with semi-precious stones, pieces that had been sold in small boutiques and at craft fairs. From that she'd progressed to being commissioned for work with costly stones, and to winning prizes that brought her further clients. She didn't know how she'd feel about seeing her necklace all over the place.

There were messages of congratulation all morning. Flowers came from the publicity department of Simenoff's. Would-be customers dropped in to look at the work on display in the studio, taking away illustrated leaflets for consideration. Then in the afternoon, she came to the more mundane matter of interviewing an applicant for the cleaning job. As she saw her out, her brother Donald drove up to the door.

He stormed in. 'Why didn't *we* get an invitation?' he demanded. 'First I hear of it, it's in this morning's papers!' His voice was loud with indignation. His bluff features were tight with hostility, dark brows almost menacing.

Lucille, alarmed, had got up from the reception desk. Jo waved her back. 'It's all right, Lucille, I'll handle this.' To Donald she said, 'Come on through.'

She led him into her workshop. There she faced him. 'Don't dare march in like that again! You scared Lucille.'

'And who the devil is *she*, anyway? You never bothered to have

213

anyone on the desk until Lindora took it over and organized it for you!'

'Stop shouting! It's not convenient to have you here. I'm expecting a client.'

'Oh, I'm not good enough to meet the elite types who come to buy your stuff, is that it? Not good enough to be asked to that thing last night when you *know* how useful it would have been to us!'

'Donald, it was all about jewellery!' she said, her own voice rising. 'You're not connected to the jewellery trade.'

'Miri and Ivan were there. You're not saying *they're* connected to the jewellery trade?'

'They *buy* jewels. Next time you pay me thousands of pounds for something I make, I'll see you get on the invitation list.' As soon as the words were out, she regretted them.

He went red. 'Oh, so that's it! It's all about money, of course. All about how you can get your name in front of glitzy shoppers. You never think of helping Lindora and me, oh no – although you know that the chance to meet up with Miri again would have been such a blessing to us!'

'You should make your own arrangements about contacting her.'

'Do you think I haven't tried?' he cried despairingly. 'It's all over the grapevine that she's planning some sort of show, and for that you must know she needs a writer, and I could put her in touch—'

'I think she's found a writer for herself.'

'She doesn't know any writers! She's just an innocent—'

'I think you'll find you're wrong there; she's found someone.'

'Well, who? You seem to know all about it, who's writing her script?'

'You'd have to ask her that yourself. Or your famous grapevine could supply you with the information, perhaps.'

'But don't you see,' he scolded, 'if you'd asked us to that party last night, I could have asked her there.'

That checked her. The fact was, it had never occurred to her to ask her brother and his wife. And she had to acknowledge that if it had occurred to her, she'd have ruled it out.

He caught her self-doubt. He tried a coaxing tone. 'Now next time there's an opportunity, Jo, promise me you'll put me in touch with her. It could be very important to Lindora and me.'

'Surely Miri Gale isn't the only prospect in your life, Donald?'

she replied, depressed by his dependency on contacts and cronyism. 'You want to be a theatre manager, then you should find other ways to manage—'

'Oh, you don't understand! Money is so scarce these days! Unless you're Andrew Lloyd Webber or Richard Eyre, nobody wants to know you. And Ivan Digby's got money, pots of it, and a wife who wants to be a success in the theatre.' He sighed, recalling better days. 'The worst thing that ever happened to us was when Miri decided to go back to being a wife and sweetheart. But now she's realizing that she made a mistake there, because she's planning something and if I could only get her to listen to me, just meet with me and have a chat – Jo, it isn't much to ask!'

She shook her head. 'It's no use, Donald. I can't and I won't.'

'It would only take you a minute to ring her.'

'No, sorry.'

'But why not? *Why?*'

'Because I don't really like being involved in Miri's affairs, I'm trying to distance myself.'

'But you're making this new thing for her, it was in the papers, about that headdress thing she's selling, you're making something to replace it.'

'She's a customer, that's all.'

'Oh, I get it! You want to keep her all to yourself! I should have known, you've always been self-centred, never cared about anything except your own stupid career. Making sparkly things for silly women.'

'That's enough, Donald!'

But he was fully launched, pent-up resentment spilling out. 'You're just a selfish money-grabber, that's what it is! I must have been crazy to think you'd put out a hand to help me.'

Jo had had enough. 'Stop roaring at me like a madman! How dare you do this? Shut up and get out!'

'Oh, you don't like to hear the truth? I could have said this a long time ago.'

'Yes, a long time ago, while you've been brewing up one silly project after another! I've put up with it long enough! I don't want you here!'

'Oh, of course not! Anybody telling you home truths is mad.'

'Go, will you? Turn around and go! If you don't, I'll have you thrown out!'

'Or, what? Hit the panic button? Have the security force rush in

215

in their fancy uniforms? Don't bother, I'm going. I don't know why I wasted my time on a sister who's always turned her back on me!'

He marched out. Jo followed him, close at first and then stepping back to make sure the entry was secure after he'd gone.

'Who on earth was that?' Lucille asked in horror.

'That was my brother, Donald. If he ever comes to the door again, don't let him in. If he telephones, put the phone down.'

'You bet,' Lucille said.

Twenty-Two

A fterwards, she hated herself.

She'd quarrelled with her brother, the only relative she had in the world. She ought to telephone at once, and say she was sorry.

But although she was sorry, she didn't feel she could do that. What she'd said to Donald about the Digbys was true. She didn't want to be too closely connected to them any more.

Her reasons were complex: partly she felt that although it was good publicity to know them, it wasn't seriously good for her image, her prestige as an artist. She didn't want to be known as 'that woman who makes things for Miri Gale'. And then, partly it was because of the history between herself and Ivan. She looked back now and had to acknowledge that she'd made a fool of herself there.

If she were to apologize to Donald for losing her temper, the first thing he'd say was, 'Then will you put me in touch with Miri Gale?'

He's got to stand on his own two feet, she told herself. But it made her smile ruefully. He was a big grown-up man, wasn't he? Heading towards his forties. Too late to be told he had to stop living in a dream world.

She'd seen him act in plays. He was a capable actor, and if he'd only stick to that, she thought, he'd do quite well. But his ambition was to produce and direct, to have his own theatre company. Those were ideas that belonged to days gone by, before cinema, long, long before television.

She felt she oughtn't to do anything that would encourage him in those ideas. He mustn't keep calling on her for help. If they were to be reconciled, Donald had to reconsider his ambitions and make the first move. He would have to accept that she had her own view of life, that she couldn't be called upon to behave as some sort of Miss Fix-it.

That might take a long time because he believed himself to be

217

always in the right, and Lindora always supported him. As she thought of her sister-in-law, Jo sighed. She could just imagine how indignant she felt about Jo's behaviour – failing to invite them to that important party, ignoring them, letting Donald down.

At the office desk, Lucille kept glancing up and watching her for the rest of the afternoon. Full of silent concern for her, she stayed longer than usual, washing wine glasses used by clients, tidying papers, checking off tasks on a notepad. To tell the truth, Jo was longing to be alone. She sighed in relief when at last she locked up after her.

She went upstairs to her flat. Lamplight from the street was shining in, but otherwise it was dark. And empty. Tears pricked under her eyelids. She paused in the doorway, leaning against the jamb for a moment, as if nerving herself to go further into that silent, dim world.

Come on, stop being an idiot, she scolded herself. Everything's fine. You've just won an award. You had a big exhilarating party last night. You've been asked by an important man to speak at a meeting in Frankfurt. You're a *success*.

But she didn't feel successful.

She must do something to cheer herself up. She ought to go out and have a nice evening. With someone. But who?

Well, there was always Ben Webber.

She rang him. 'Are you doing anything this evening, Ben?'

'Er . . . Well . . . No, nothing special. You?'

'No, so I wondered if you'd like to, you know, go out and have a bite to eat somewhere.'

'Good idea.' He sounded very pleased. 'Got anywhere in mind?'

'Somewhere quiet. Life's been a bit of a Monte Carlo rally for the last week or two.'

'How about Corsalino's?' This was calling up the good old days, the days when they were close, bound together in a relationship that they'd thought would last for ever. With a little laugh he reminded her of that time. 'We don't have to choose the students' menu. We could have the special *ragu* with pheasant and things. That's if you feel like Italian food?'

'Why not? With lots of red wine.'

'Sounds good. Shall I book?'

'Yes, for about eight. I'll meet you there, shall I?'

As soon as she'd put the phone down, she wished she hadn't done it. She'd start bemoaning her life to him, and bore him to

218

death, and he was such a good old friend he'd put up with it. But then if she rang back and cancelled, he'd think she was crazy. Or he'd be hurt, and she didn't want to hurt him, dear old Ben.

So she went to her bedroom to get ready to go out. Normally, for a date with Ben, she wouldn't have bothered too much. But this was a cheer-yourself-up event so she chose a long-sleeved V-necked tunic of cyclamen silk over a dark-red skirt. She took some care over her make-up, styled her short hair with some glossy gel. When she'd finished, she rather thought she'd overdone it; trying too hard, she told herself. But she couldn't be bothered to change to something less partified.

Corsalino's was not far from the university. She smiled as the taxi set her down at the familiar old façade with its windows already a little steamed up in the winter night.

Ben was already there, at a quiet table in a corner. She saw that he too had taken unusual trouble over his appearance; his burly figure was clad in a good suit worn with a dark-blue shirt and a pale-blue tie. His broad brow was furrowed as he inspected the menu.

She tucked herself in beside him. 'I see you've already ordered the wine,' she teased.

'"Be Prepared," I say. You do look nice.' He was surveying her with a smile of appreciation.

'Thank you. I thought it was time to make a bit of an effort.'

'Oh? What does that mean?'

She shrugged. 'I got fed up with myself. Have you ordered?'

'No, not yet.' The waiter hurried up at his nod, offering her a menu. When they'd decided he poured wine for them. 'Well, here's to you,' Ben toasted. 'You're really on a roll these days, and I want to thank you for thinking of me and inviting me for last night. I think I did myself some good.'

'Oh, splendid, in what way?'

'Mr Eades rang me this afternoon. He's buying some stones in Amsterdam, he's asked me to go over and take a look before he finalizes the deal.'

'Diamonds?'

'No, gem-rough aquamarine. You know how careful you have to be about varieties of beryl – it's easy to be charmed at first glance. So he wants to choose out only the really good shades – he's got an agent over there of course, but these are special stones and he's going to give me a colour-match stone to work from. It's

219

really interesting, I love looking at beryl, its colours are often so unexpected and these aquamarines sound really top grade.'

He went on for some time enthusing about Mr Eades' commission. If Jo was rather in the dumps, Ben was in good enough spirits for the pair of them. He explained that he hoped to do a lot more for the firm of Simenoff, that he wouldn't mind being under contract to them, and he speculated on what kind of terms he might agree to.

Jo listened with genuine interest. They had been good friends for years. They toasted each other's successes, they exchanged little titbits from each other's food, they shared a rich dessert that consisted mainly of peaches in cognac.

Ben offered her a sliver of fruit rimmed with cream from the edge of his spoon. When she accepted it, he leaned forward and kissed her on the lips. 'Mmm . . . You taste delicious.'

'That's not me, that's the peaches,' she giggled.

'You're my peach. Always have been. Dashing, flashing Jo Radcliffe – always a bright light to me and if you wanna know, I thought you were great last night at the party, prettiest woman there!'

'No, no, that's an exaggeration. But it's nice, anyhow. And I think a lot of you too, Ben, you know that, even if maybe . . . I . . . what was I going to say? Oh, yes, even if I don't say it.' She paused, hearing the echoes of her own words. 'I think I've had a little too much to drink, you know, Ben.'

'Nonsense, we're celebrating. We have a right to get a bit lit up on an occasion like this. We should've had champagne – why didn't I think of that before, stupid me.'

'What we ought to have is some strong black coffee, sober ourselves up,' she said, blinking hard to steady her gaze.

'Now I have just the thing,' Ben announced, wagging a finger at her. 'Just bought it yesterday. Thingamajig that makes pitch-black espresso. What say we go to my place and try it out, eh?' He waved at the waiter. 'I'll have the bill, my man, and if you'd be so good as to call a taxi for us, I'd be greatly obliged.'

The waiter gave him an indulgent smile. In a few minutes they were going out the door arm in arm, and were on the kerb waiting for the taxi.

The night air was very sharp and cold. Jo shivered, drawing her wool-cloth jacket about her. Where were they going? To Ben's place. Why? Because he had a new coffee-maker.

Now wait, she said to herself. What was that again?

The taxi drew up. They got in, Ben giving his address. As they took their seats he crowded up against her and drew her close. 'Ah, sweetheart,' he sighed.

'Oh!' She was taken aback. 'Wait a minute, what are you doing, Ben?'

'Just having a little kiss-kiss before we get to the main event, my angel. It's so good that you want to go back to what we used to be – you and me, we had a good thing going in those days.'

That was true. They had been happy, easy-going lovers. She relaxed into his embrace. Dear, kind Ben, always a dear good friend. She felt sentimental tears gather in her eyes. It was so lovely to have someone care about her.

'I got the message last night,' he went on. 'Everything finished, over and done with as far as the money-man's concerned. So it's time for a new start, but I wasn't sure until you called. You're so honest and good, Jo, so direct.'

Her brain was hard at work, trying to follow his train of thought. 'Wait a minute. What does that mean – I'm honest and good – I don't know what you're saying, Ben.'

'No need to be modest, sweetheart. You're more of a go-getter than I am, we both know that, don't we, so of course you'd take the lead, I accept that.'

'Take the lead. No, I didn't take the lead. Did I? How d'you mean, Ben?'

'Starting over. That's what we're doing.'

She heard the words, and through the haze brought on by the last hour or so she tried to make sense of them. She was starting over again with Ben? Yes, that seemed quite possible.

But wait. Ben was a friend. An old friend, a reliable comrade. But did she want to begin again where they had left off years ago?

'No,' she murmured, surprised, startled.

'What?'

'No, when did I say we should start over?'

'Well, that's what you meant, wasn't it? When you said it had all been a silly mistake with him.'

'With Ivan?'

'Yes, him, of course, who else d'you think I'm talking about?'

'Well . . . it's true I said . . . but Ben . . . That was just a statement of fact.'

'But I know what you really meant, of course.'

'What did I mean? What are you telling me?'

'Oh, come on, dear, why else did you ring me?' He drew her hard against him and kissed her as if to stifle conversation.

She struggled free. 'I can't do this, Ben. Stop the taxi.'

'What?'

'Please ask the man to stop.'

'But why? We're nowhere near . . .'

'I'm not going home with you.'

'But, Jo!' He fell back in the taxi seat, staring at her in the gloom. 'You're not making sense!'

'I'm sorry. I seem to have misled you somehow.'

'Misled me?' He was sobering up at her words. 'You rang me, asked me to dinner, after the things you said last night I understood you to be saying . . .'

'No, no, I don't really remember what I said last night, I'm sorry, Ben. But I never intended anything like this.'

'You can't suddenly change your mind and back out.'

'Yes, I can, because I never meant this to happen. I apologize, Ben, I'm truly sorry. But I . . . I simply can't.' The words ended on a sob.

He drew away from her. 'All right, all right, don't start crying.' He was mortally offended. 'If you don't want to make love, it's not going to turn into a wrestling match.' He leaned forward to tap on the driver's glass. 'We've changed our minds,' he said angrily. 'Stop at . . .' He turned to Jo. 'I'll get out, you can have the cab.'

'No, no – I should . . .'

'Oh, for Pete's sake!' To the driver he said, 'Stop at Euston Square.'

It was only a short distance. They sat in frigid silence. He got out at the station entrance, gave a brief wave, then walked quickly away to catch a train home.

'Where to now, miss?' the taxi driver inquired in a very neutral tone.

She gave her home address, and finished the journey in a flood of tears.

Twenty-Three

After her quarrel with her brother that afternoon, she'd thought she couldn't feel more wretched. Well, she was wrong.

She walked about from her workroom upstairs to her living room, then down again to the comfort of her work, her tools. Nothing seemed to help. She tried watching late-night television. She listened to some music. She sat down at the office desk and sent some emails.

At last, around three a.m., she went to bed.

Next day was quite busy. If Lucille thought her very taciturn, she kept it to herself. On Sunday Jo was committed to go to the opening of a star-studded Christmas auction for charity, to which she'd donated a piece of her work, an experimental brooch in silver and opals.

She didn't want to go, but Miri was to be there as one of the main attractions. It was Miri who'd got her involved in the project in the first place. She felt she had to attend.

The hall in Chelsea was buzzing with activity. Jo was shepherded off to the hospitality room where, to her astonishment, she found Betsey Fieldingley. Betsey was clad in what seemed to be her only good dress, and was sampling the Belgian biscuits.

'I know you were going to be here, Miri's been on about all this for days and days,' she cried. 'How are you, dear?'

'Fine, fine. And you? The paintings are going well?'

'Oh, marvellous – I'm really quite keen on them.' She winked at Jo. 'We got off to a shaky start. Miri decided she wanted something more glamorous than flowers of common or garden old British eatables, so I did quite a bit of research and made a trip to the tropical house at Kew, and now all the paintings are of exotic blossoms – banana, guava, ginger – it's really turned out to be great fun. Miri didn't like the painting of *Litchi chinensis*, so I've donated that to the auction.'

'I might bid for that,' Jo said.

223

'No, don't, the man who's running the auction says it ought to fetch a thousand. It's idiotic. Miri's donated one of the dresses she used to wear when she was on the television show, and do you know, someone's already put in a bid of four hundred pounds for it.'

They were interrupted by one of the organizing team, offering a plan of the stage and a timetable of events. 'Items donated by lesser-known people will be first, of course, and those that wish to be identified will be picked out in the audience. However, when we come to the bigger things, we're asking the donor to mount the stage and be present there while the bidding goes on.'

'No, no,' said Jo.

'Oh, but you must, Ms Radcliffe. It will help to raise the bids.'

'Yes, take it on, Jo. I'll be up there too, so we can hold hands.'

Miri was among the last of the celebrities to arrive. She waved a welcome at Jo and Betsey but was hurried away by a committee member.

'I'm staying overnight with Miri,' Betsey said as they watched her vanish into the main hall.

'Oh, I thought you'd decided to try to avoid Ivan.'

'He's abroad. Otherwise he'd be here, scaring everybody into bidding for her dress.' Betsey gave a wicked chuckle. 'They tried to inveigle me into staying with them over Christmas, but luckily I had a good excuse not to.'

Other 'celebrities' were ushered into the hospitality room. They broke off their conversation to view them. 'That's that politician,' Betsey said. 'You know, the one who backs some football team or other – Crystal Palace, I think.'

'And that's Annie Goodbere, I think she's going to be in the Lyceum Christmas show.'

Betsey smiled and shrugged, then turned back to study Jo with a keen eye. 'Sit down and have some tea, my dear. You look a bit pale and wan today.'

'Oh dear.' She obeyed, wishing she'd tried a bit harder with her make-up. A helper hurried up with fresh cups of tea and yet another plate of biscuits.

Betsey inspected the biscuits. 'I do love these,' she sighed. 'It's a terrible weakness.' She selected one with a thick covering of dark chocolate. 'Heard from Tim day before yesterday,' she remarked, nibbling. 'You know, those satellite phones are wonderful, but they fade off when the satellite passes out of range overhead.'

'Oh . . . How was he?'

224

'I don't think he said,' Betsey replied, frowning a little. 'He was talking mainly about the fact that his camera hadn't turned up. He'd ordered a special miniature camera for something or other, but it had got lost en route. Kamchatka, you know – postal services are never very reliable out on the edge of things.'

'Where's Kamchatka?'

'Oh, up there near the Arctic Circle but on the other side of Russia – I mean, not the European side, the bit that's north of Japan.'

'But that sounds terrible!'

'I don't think it's much fun, dear.' Betsey shrugged. 'But of course he's used to it. I told him you were sorry you missed him that day.'

'You did?' She hesitated. 'What did he say?'

Betsey smiled. 'I don't remember. You'll have to ask him yourself when he gets back.'

'But when will that be?' Jo burst out, unable to prevent it.

'To London? Who knows. But he's going to be in Strasbourg soon after Christmas – that camera, you know? It was supposed to go to an agent in Strasbourg who acts for the survey team, but it never turned up. He's tried getting at the supplier on the Internet and all that, but he's decided that on his next leave, he's going to have to pursue inquiries personally.'

Jo said nothing. She was recalling that Betsey had given her the phone number of the flat in Strasbourg. She could call, leave a message, say that she wished he'd let her know when he was going to be in London again.

Betsey was eyeing her with undisguised interest. 'So he won't be coming to London,' she continued. 'Not for quite a while.'

'No, I suppose not.'

'So I'm going to Strasbourg instead. I'm quite pleased about it, never been there, and I'll get a chance to have a little look at the flora of the Vosges mountains.'

Jo was so taken aback by the news that once again she was stricken to silence. Betsey, who seemed to be enjoying herself, munched her biscuit for a moment then explained, 'Of course, there won't be much to see in the way of actual flowers in January. But Tim says Strasbourg is nice, and there's a very interesting botanical garden attached to the university.'

'That sounds great.'

'Yes, doesn't it? The only thing is, I'm not very good at travelling these days.'

'You don't like flying?'

'Not keen, and the old ticker doesn't much enjoy airports and grabbing baggage off carousels and all that.'

'Perhaps Tim will come to Heathrow and then travel back to Strasbourg with you?'

Betsey gave her a little frown that seemed to say, You're being very dense. Aloud she said, 'He has little enough time to himself – I wouldn't want him to spend it travelling back and forth like that.'

'No, of course not.'

'Well . . .' Now the old lady was measuring her words before she spoke. 'I suppose you wouldn't like to come with me as a travelling companion?'

'What?'

'I wouldn't expect you to want to go into the mountains and look at plants. But I'd quite like a bit of a shopping spree in Strasbourg with you, if you fancy that.'

'But . . . but . . . you'll want to spend your time with Tim.'

'Not all the time. He's going to be busy trying to catch up with his missing camera. I'll probably only see him in the evenings.'

'You'll be staying at his flat?'

'Dear me, no. I think his flat is like a cubbyhole in some old building. It's all right for him to sleep on a camp bed when he comes to me, but I'm too old for stuff like that. He's getting me a hotel room. Not expensive, in the student quarter.'

'Oh.'

'He could easily book a room for you, if you think you'd like it.'

'Oh.'

'Stop saying "oh", my dear,' Betsey scolded. 'It's inadequate.'

'Oh, I mean, sorry, well, it's something I hadn't thought of.'

'Think of it now.'

'I'm thinking. Betsey, I *am* thinking.'

'Is there a problem?'

'No, not really although . . . After Christmas? When after Christmas? I'm speaking at a thing in Frankfurt after Christmas.' Aware that she was babbling, Jo fell silent.

One of the committee came to usher them on to the platform in the hall. Betsey said over her shoulder, 'See if you can sort it out. I'd really like some company on the trip.'

During the auction, Jo's attention was really taken up with thinking about Betsey's suggestion. She was committed to speak in Frankfurt, but that was on January 11. She was hoping that Betsey's trip might be before that. She longed to ask her but they were seated in a little line on the platform, and Betsey was three seats away.

The donor of each item was introduced by the chairman of the charity and then invited to get up and say a few words about the item being put up for sale. Jo groaned inwardly at hearing herself introduced as 'the designer of the beautiful tiara worn by Miri Gale on her wedding day.' Miri's name was greeted with quite a burst of applause.

When the dress she'd worn on *Catch My Drift* was brought on stage, the applause was even louder. The bidding was vigorous, Miri laughing and waving at the buyers as they put up their hands. Jo was interested to see that it wasn't women who mostly wanted the dress. It went at last to a male bidder for over seven hundred pounds.

The event ended at about six o'clock. Then there were press interviews about the prices gained by the items on sale. Jo's opal brooch had gone for a little over two thousand, Betsey's painting of *Litchi chinensis* made sixteen hundred. 'It's silly,' Betsey said as they escaped from the cameras. 'Two years ago nobody would have wanted that.'

They found a quiet corner in the entrance hall to resume the conversation they'd been engaged in. 'What date are you going to Strasbourg?' Jo asked, with an interest she did nothing to disguise.

'That's not settled yet. Tim has to fit in with the other men on the team; they have a rota, you know? But I think it's likely to be early January.'

'I hope it's not around the eleventh. I'm in Frankfurt on the eleventh.'

'I'll mention it to Tim,' Betsey said, with a little smile of satisfaction. 'I'm sure he can work it so as to avoid that.'

Miri came up, radiant with pleasure at the outcome of the auction. 'Come on now, Betsey,' she commanded. 'Time to head for home and a nice quiet drinkie before dinner.' She gave Jo a pat on the shoulder. 'Your brooch did awfully well, didn't it? Listen, what's happening about my bracelet and things?'

'Not much,' said Jo. 'I've been a bit distracted.'

'Well, I'll tell you what. I'll drop by tomorrow to look at what you've done. You'll have sketches and things, won't you? So see you then, let's say about eleven.'

'No, really, Miri, I've nothing to show you.'

'Course you have. Bye till then.' She swept Betsey off with her, to be driven away in a maroon Chrysler.

Jo thought of telephoning to put off the visit several times during the evening. She did at last nerve herself to do it, but was answered by a manservant. He said Madame and her guest were out, but spoke very poor English. She gave up trying to leave a message.

When Lucille heard the next day that Miri Gale was coming to the studio, she was thrilled. 'Oh, how lovely, to actually see her in the flesh – she's just so beautiful, isn't she! And she's going to buy something else from you? That's such a compliment to your work!'

Jo said nothing to that. She got on with the routine of the day. Miri arrived a little early, Lucille leaping to the door to let her in. Miri rewarded her with a brilliant smile then swept on past her through the studio and into the workroom. She was wearing bootleg pants with a sweater of knitted metallic thread, and looked startlingly beautiful.

Jo had meant to settle her at the visitors' sofa and offer her coffee. Taken aback, she followed her into the workroom. Miri was already picking up sheets of sketch paper from the bench, then letting them drop as she saw they were nothing to do with her jewellery.

'It's on the computer, is it?' she cried, turning towards it.

But the screen held a totally different image.

'Oh, haven't you set it up for me? Come on, Jo, let's have a look.'

'There's nothing to show you, Miri. Honestly.'

'But I asked you ages ago! Come on, you must have *something* to show.'

'No, really.'

'Nothing in your head? Just give me some idea. I'm dying to know.'

'Miri, I haven't done anything about your bracelet and earrings. I've been too busy.'

Miri gave a little laugh of irritation. 'Too busy to get on with something for *me*?'

Jo was tempted to point out that there were others in the world, but resisted. She wanted to achieve something important this morning, to get across an important message, and being impatient with Miri wouldn't help.

'I had to go abroad,' she said. 'Then there was the Simenoff's launch of my necklace.'

'Well, yes, I was there, remember?'

'And then I had family problems.'

'Family problems? Oh, you mean brother Donald, I suppose.' Miri shrugged dismissively. 'Well, yes, he is a bit of a problem.'

228

'And then there were other things ...' She wasn't going to mention anything about Ben Webber.

'Well, OK, I get all that, so come on, what sort of thing are you going to do? I just need a clue so I can tell people – I'm on a daytime chat show next week.'

'I don't think I'll have time to get to it at all, Miri. I'm going to be very busy.'

'Hey!' It was an exclamation of total surprise. 'What d'you mean, not going to get to it? We've got an agreement.'

'No, we haven't. You said you'd like me to show you some designs and I thought about it for a few days. But it all faded out of my mind, and I can see now that I'm going to be totally engaged in other things.'

'But I've told everybody you're doing this new stuff.'

'There are plenty of other designers, Miri.'

'But it was *you* that mattered. You made my wedding headdress.'

'I'm glad that was a success, Miri. I liked it when you said it seemed richer than the rubies you'd lost. But I feel I want to move on.'

Miri drew her beautiful brows together in intense concentration. 'I know what it is!' she announced. 'You're offended because we're selling the tiara!'

'No.'

'I thought you understood about that. You said yourself, it only matched up with the wedding gown.'

'I wasn't offended. Jewellery changes hands all the time. In a way it's a good thing because it lets the design reach a new audience. It's totally acceptable to me, I assure you. But I can't do anything about making pieces to match the choker necklace.'

'How can you say, you *can't*? That's what you do all the time. You invent ways of making jewels look ... pretty ... interesting ... *different*. I don't believe you can't think up something to go with my necklace.'

'I haven't got the time, Miri.'

'Good heavens, how long can it take to sketch out a few things? You did it for those stupid old rubies.'

'No, if you remember, that took me quite a while ...'

'Oh, yeah, that's right, you came and looked at where I lived and what I wore and everything. Well, good heavens, we can do that again! Come down to Chembard, spend a few days, a week, come for Christmas, Jo, we're having quite a house party!'

229

'I'm sorry, Miri, I've got other plans.'

'Oh, if you mean Christmas arrangements with Donald, trying to have a family gathering, you said yourself you and Donald have problems, so why bother?'

'It's nothing to do with Donald. I've got engagements before and after Christmas and then I'm going abroad.'

'Oh . . .' Miri drew in a long breath. 'Well . . . When you come back, eh?'

'No, honestly, Miri. I can't.'

Miri frowned and hesitated. Then she said, 'You . . . you don't *want* to?'

The question had a faltering sound. There was reproach in it, a sense of hurt.

Jo didn't know what to say. The truthful answer was no, she didn't want to.

At last she found a few words. 'You and I lead such different lives, Miri.'

'Yes, well, so what? It's good for you to get caught up with what's happening to me and Ive. Reporters wouldn't be paying nearly so much attention to you otherwise – now would they?'

'No, they wouldn't. But you see, I don't like that.'

'You don't like being in the papers?'

'No. It always seems to me like prying.'

Miri laughed. 'Oh, good heavens, all you need is a good publicity manager. I'll get Ralph to give you a ring.'

'No! Please don't. I really want you to understand – to listen to what I'm saying. The work I do needs peace and quiet – long periods when I think and wonder and try things out. I don't like interruptions, I don't like having to . . . to sort of dance to someone else's tune.'

Miri was staring at her in mystification.

Jo tried again. 'I don't really much like big events. I have to go to them – I felt I had to go to that thing in Boston because it involved a sort of tribute to the work I'd done, but in general I don't go after publicity.'

'You don't want to be a success?'

'Yes, but in my own world, not yours.'

'Oh.' A silence while Miri thought about it. 'And if you do my bracelet and earrings, I'll make a fuss about it? Is that it?'

'Something like that.'

'Well, but . . . I've already made a bit of a fuss about it. I told

230

everybody you're doing it. I mean, you can't back out now! You *said* you'd do it.'

'But I find somehow I can't.'

'Oh, come on, Jo. Do it for *me*.'

'No, I'm sorry, Miri.'

Miri's lower lip trembled. 'I thought we were friends?'

There was something so childlike in the question that Jo felt tears come into her eyes. She said gently, 'We have been friends, and we still are if you want us to be, but I think we're moving along different paths now.'

'I don't understand that,' Miri protested. 'I can always include you in what I do, and you can include me in what you do.'

'I don't think that will work.'

Sudden anger flared. 'Because *you've* made up your mind to change? I don't know why you're being like this, but I think it's rotten of you! After all I've done for you! Just to walk away without any real reason – that's the artistic temperament, is it? Well, I hope it's a big comfort when you're left all alone with no one to give a hoot what happens to you! Stupid, conceited, stick-in-the-mud!'

She whirled around and rushed out of the workroom. Lucille rose from her desk in amazement as she darted to the outer door. In a moment she was gone.

Lucille was staring as Jo came into the studio. A question was hovering on her lips. But one glance at Jo warned her not to ask it.

231

Twenty-Four

About half an hour later the office phone rang. Lucille had gone to lunch so Jo picked up.

It was Ivan, furious. 'What the devil have you been up to?' he shouted. 'Miri's just been on the line to me, practically in tears!'

Jo, astounded, drew her phone away from her ear, then said, 'Where are you speaking from?'

'What's that got to do with it? I'm in Madrid, if you must know.'

'Miri rang you in Madrid?'

'Of course she did! We share everything. And what I want to know is, what have you said to my little sweetheart to make her cry?'

Jo had to pause for a moment before she could bring herself to answer. 'I had a conversation with her about the bracelet and earrings.'

'And she tells me you're backing out of doing them. Now look here, chum, if you think you can do that to us without a by your leave, you've got another think coming!'

'Ivan, calm down. We have no contract, no agreement of any kind.' She let that sink in for a second then went on, 'So I've decided not to do any designs for items to match the choker necklace, as I'm not committed in any way.'

'Yes, you are, my lady, and you'll be sorry if you let us down.'

'Stop being an idiot! What'll you do? Tell your pals on the newspapers about it? They'll just say something cruel – that I've got better things to do than dance attendance on you and Miri.'

'What?' It was a faint gasp of surprise.

Jo knew that she had to give him some explanation and decided to come out fighting. 'The fact is, Ivan, Miri came here and acted like a spoiled child. I'd decided I didn't want to design anything for her, and when I tried to tell her she just had a tantrum, that's all.'

'What *is* this?' Ivan demanded. 'You were quite keen when she suggested the idea of—'

232

'I wasn't exactly keen. I saw it as a project, but since then I've had a lot on my mind and now I'd rather not go ahead with it.'

He took a moment to consider that. 'Well, mebbe we didn't have a contract, but you *promised*.'

'No I didn't.'

'Don't back out of it. You know you did!'

'Ivan, you weren't there when she suggested the idea. I didn't promise.'

'But Miri's told people that you're doing this, and her friendship with you is a big thing to the press, they like it that she's got this link with a prize-winning designer and all that – it builds her up a bit more.'

Jo stifled a groan. 'I understand all that. And that's one of the reasons I don't want to do this. I don't like being part of her publicity campaign.'

'Oh, get *you*!' It was a snort of ridicule. 'I didn't notice you being all that shy in the first place.'

'I didn't know what I was letting myself in for.'

'What's that mean? What are you trying to pull? You're high-minded and sensitive while Miri and I are a pair of thickies?'

'Now wait, Ivan, I never said anything like that.'

'I think back and I realize you came over all funny about the tiara, didn't you? Didn't like having it thought of as being a personal present, wanted to make it all business-like – all right, you were saying that you're an artist with all these finer feelings, superior to the likes of us.'

'Ivan, get a hold of yourself! How can it be that important to you? You can get someone else to make Miri's bracelet.'

'No, I can't, because Miri wants *you* and if you think I'm going to let you hurt her feelings you've got another think coming. There's such a thing as a verbal contract, you know! I'll make you keep your promise or take the consequences!'

Now she was as angry as he. She raised her voice. 'You can roar and rant at me as much as you like but I'm not going to be involved with her any more. Or with you. Or with your house, or your publicity machine, or your silly glitzy lifestyle!'

'Hey!' he cried. 'You can't speak to me like that!'

'I just have,' she said, and put the phone down.

It rang again almost immediately. She took it off the hook, pressed down the connection, then left it on the desk. She went upstairs for

233

a coat, set the security, and took herself out for a pub lunch. She took care to switch off her mobile before she set out.

When she and Lucille started work that afternoon, the first thing Lucille did was to scold her for leaving the phone off the stand. 'That's no way to run a business,' she said, shaking her head at her.

There was a message from Ivan. 'Don't think that's the end of it, girl!' he snarled.

'What?' Lucille cried in amazement. 'Who on earth is *that*?'

'Never mind,' said Jo.

The rest of her day went by in planning for the possible trip to Strasbourg. She had the usual pre-Christmas engagements in her diary: office parties, visits to colleagues, an invitation to Christmas dinner with a married friend from college days. She must set aside a day later in the week to buy presents. Her cards were already being printed, from her own design.

After Lucille had gone, she locked up as usual, then went upstairs to make her evening meal. Outside it was drizzling, the dampness making haloes round the street lamps. She put on an old disc of Kate Bush to give her something to think about while she tried out a new recipe from a cookbook, teriyaki kebabs. She was sitting down to eat when the door buzzer sounded.

Wondering who would be there at this hour, she went out to the passage and flicked on the outside surveillance camera.

There in the circle of light it provided she saw Ivan Digby.

She threw up her hands in dismay and drew in a deep breath. No use pretending there was no one at home since she'd switched on the camera. She pressed the communication button.

'What on earth are you doing here, Ivan? I thought you were in Madrid.'

'I was but we were winding up. I'm on my way home from the airport but I need to talk to you first.'

'I'm just sitting down to a meal, Ivan.'

'Oh, come on, this is important. Let me in.'

She hesitated.

'Come on, we've got to talk.'

'You don't talk, you shout.'

'I promise not to. Look, I'm going home, and first off Miri will want to know that I've sorted all this. I don't know what to say to her. I need you to explain what's happening.'

'Surely it's plain enough? I'm trying to disengage from the fuss and flutter that surrounds you and Miri.'

'But why? I don't understand why you've changed.' His upturned face was serious and perplexed. 'Come on, Jo, it's cold out here.'

With misgivings she switched off the camera then went downstairs to open the door to the living area. He came in, and she glimpsed behind him a maroon saloon car with a uniformed driver sitting in quiet attendance. Hardly cold, he'd just stepped out of a warm and comfortable car. What a manipulative soul he was; it was in his nature, he couldn't help it.

Well, she had let him in so now she had to go through with whatever he had in mind. She led the way upstairs, into her living room, switching on extra lights so that there could be no suggestion of an intimate tête-à-tête.

'Drink?'

'No thanks, I had a glass of wine on the plane.'

'I think I will, if you don't mind waiting a minute before you get started.' She went to the kitchen to make herself a cup of strong black instant coffee and to take a few deep breaths in case there was going to be a battle.

When she returned, he was standing looking at the watercolour by Betsey Fieldingley, now framed in a simple dark wood.

'Did you buy that at the auction?'

'No. Betsey gave it to me a while ago.'

'It all started with that necklace of hers.'

She said nothing, merely sipped her coffee and waited.

All at once he whirled to glare at her. 'This is your way of getting back at her, isn't it?'

'What? At who?'

'Because Miri and I got together again – I went back to her the minute she gave up that that acting thing – the Shakespeare and all that. You can't forgive her for splitting us up, you and me.'

The mere idea made her speechless. She sat with her mug of coffee halfway to her lips, meeting his angry scowl, amazement on her face.

Her expression was enough to give him pause. He became less menacing, and said after a moment, 'It wasn't that?'

'Of course not. I always knew you'd go back to her if she crooked a finger at you.'

'You what?'

'You were always in love with her. I knew that.'

'But you must have been . . . well . . . hurt.' He sat down, studying her.

'Oh yes, for a while. But I got over it.'

He was looking back, something like regret in his face. He sighed. 'We were a good pair for a while, though, weren't we? There was something real there for us.'

She wasn't going to allow him to become sentimental. She said in a cool but gentle tone, 'Don't get misty about it. You were only making up for the loss of your darling, and I was playing the ministering angel to your broken heart.'

'Oh, no, I really thought a lot of you, Jo.'

'All right.' Perhaps it was true. 'But it's got nothing to do with today. You and Miri have your life to live and I've got mine.'

'But why do we have to live them cut off from each other? Why do you have to hurt Miri's feelings like this?'

'I'd no intention of hurting her feelings. I was taken aback by the way she carried on. I told her I would be too busy to design for her and she got herself all worked up about it. But it's . . . it's unreasonable, Ivan. Just because we got thrown together over the rubies, it doesn't mean we have to live in each other's pockets for ever more!'

'No, well, that's true, but Miri felt there was something personal in it.'

'If you mean I had some sort of a grudge, she's wrong. And you know, Ivan –' she nerved herself to say it – 'she's often wrong. She made a fool of herself over Donald and the acting career.'

'Hey! Don't talk like that about her.'

'She made a fool of herself over her wedding dress – that thing was like something out of a period drama. I don't know if you ever got to see the veil and headdress she originally meant to wear with it . . .' She broke off. 'Of course you didn't, and it's neither here nor there.'

'You've no right to run her down like this.'

'I'm trying to explain to you that she and I are not on the same wavelength. We have almost nothing in common; nature never intended us to be friends. And if I'm honest with you, I think she only wants to hang on to me because she feels I'm useful.'

He was shaking his head in disbelief. 'You're so wrong about her! She hasn't got a sly bone in her body. That's why she needs me, she needs someone to look after her.'

Jo drank some coffee. He seemed to want her to make some comment, but she'd no desire to go any further. He said at last, in a helpless tone, 'What am I going to tell her, then?'

236

'Tell her the truth, the same as I told her. Or tell her I'm a crotchety old thing who wants to get on with her life in her own way.'

'You're determined? You're not going to make the bracelet for her?'

'No.'

'But how's she going to explain it to everybody? People think you're buddies and you're happy to be making her this new piece.'

'Why does she have to explain it?' demanded Jo. 'If she just doesn't talk about the idea of having new pieces to match the choker, the journalists will forget about it. It's no great thing to anybody except Miri. And nothing really seems to last more than a week or two.'

'Well, that's true.' For a long moment he sat in silence, then he sighed and shook his head. 'I was so angry with you, Jo! All the way home on the plane I was telling myself I'd come here and tear you into little pieces for hurting my girlie! But somehow . . .'

'You've changed your mind?'

'Yeah, and to tell the truth, now it seems kind of like intimidation, me coming here to bawl you out and you all on your own.'

'I wasn't exactly pleased to see you, if you must know.'

'Right. Aw, it's a shame, Jo. You ought to have somebody to look out for you, somebody special in your life.'

She nodded without speaking, and rose to let him know it was time for him to go. He kissed her gently on the cheek as she saw him out.

'Bye then. It doesn't look like we'll be seeing much of each other from now on.'

'Probably not.'

'Good luck.'

'You too.'

When he'd gone she didn't know what she felt. Relief, some satisfaction, a little bewilderment. And there was sadness too. She felt that it wasn't entirely a happy thing, to break ties with two people who'd had meaning in her life for a time.

She went to the kitchen to survey the food on the table. Cold now. Should she put it back under the grill to see if it would revive?

Too much trouble. She sat down at the table, and found herself on the verge of foolish tears. The phone in the living room rang. She got up slowly. Please don't let it be Ivan, wanting to come back and argue everything through again.

It was Betsey.

'Is this a convenient moment? Yes? Just thought I'd let you know, dear girl, that Tim's been in touch. He says he's almost sure to be in Strasbourg by January fourth.'

'Oh!'

'Can you make it?'

'Oh, yes. Yes. Of course.'

'So we'll be in touch about flight times and so forth – yes?'

'Of course.'

'It might be simpler if you do all that, do you think? I believe it's easy by Internet and I'm not good at that.'

'I can do it. Of course.'

'And I'll meet you at the airport but remember I've got to come up from the boondocks.'

'Yes, I'll remember.'

'So that's all for the time being. I've got to dash – my neighbour's coming in for drinks. We'll ring each other tomorrow, shall we?'

'OK. And Betsey . . .'

'Yes?'

'Thank you.'

Twenty-Five

S trasbourg looked delightful under the wintry sun. It was a city she'd never visited before, but Jo was prepared to love it.

Because it was here she'd soon meet Tim.

They queued for a taxi in the crisp afternoon air. They sped north along the autoroute past fields clothed in snow and studded with stands of tall evergreens, then into the southern approach to the city, past Belford and then across a patch of water by the Porte de l'Hopital.

'That's the river?' wondered Betsey.

'That's the canal, madame,' the driver said over his shoulder. 'And now we are on the Quai Fustel de Coulanges and soon we turn to the Rue de Lausanne and you are in our university district, but you would prefer perhaps not to go as far as this because now we wish to go to your hotel. But you see we go now through so little lanes where the buildings are so very old, much admired . . .' He threw out a magisterial hand to point them out.

He kept up a running commentary until he lined up to leave the traffic and turn into what looked like a mere passage. '*Voilà!* Hotel Erstein.' He parked almost up against the doorway of a building wreathed along its façade in garlands of greenery, left over from the Christmas celebrations.

A burly elderly man bounced out and at once took charge of the luggage. Betsey was asking the taxi driver how much she should give as a tip. He grinned, selecting a few coins out of the handful she'd collected at a bureau de change in the airport.

The hotel lobby was small but bright with a row of poinsettias. Warmth and comfort seemed to enfold them at once. Madame Wechner took them through the formalities in English and with brisk efficiency. She led them from the reception desk to the stairs. They had to climb up to their rooms; it was clear the building was too old to house a lift. Jo's room had furnishings only just

239

sufficient: bed, dressing table, night-stand with telephone and clock. The bathroom was at the end of the corridor. This was student accommodation.

Betsey's room was across the passage. 'Let's just dump our luggage,' she called. 'Let's get out enough to put on some warm clothes, and go out for a look-see. And coffee! I need coffee!'

They had eaten lunch on the plane, so they weren't actually hungry. But on visiting the riverbank café recommended by Madame, they found they couldn't resist trying the *Kougelhopf*. They sat with great thick cups of strong coffee and wedges of cake, staring out of the window at the lights of the barges on the River Ill in the gathering darkness of late afternoon.

'Where is Tim's flat from here?' Jo inquired.

'Dear child, I've no idea. But he's supposed to fly in some time late this evening and the plan is that he'll meet us for lunch tomorrow.'

'I see.'

Betsey smiled at her. 'It's a long trip for him,' she explained. 'He has to change planes at least four times, if I remember correctly. The dodgiest part is getting to Moscow, and from there he flies to Paris, and from Paris at last to Strasbourg. So you see he's a bit groggy by the time he gets here. I don't exactly know how many times zones he'll have crossed.'

'Of course. I should have thought of that.'

Jo was thinking of the map she'd consulted. Kamchatka seemed to have very few towns but a large number of volcanoes. 'What exactly is his team doing there?' she ventured.

'They're looking at the feasibility of using factories, installations, machinery – I don't quite know what. The thing is, under the Soviet regime, there were explorations going on in the region to see if they could find minerals worth digging for. It seems that it was all abandoned when Stalin died, so now the rich chaps in Moscow are wondering if it's worth going back there and starting it up again.'

'And that's what Tim is doing? Looking at old buildings?'

'It's a kind of surveying. Other members of the team verify maps and measure distances. Tim photographs parts of buildings – girders, or perhaps foundations – to see if they've stood up to the climate, or the swampy soil conditions, or something. Hence the camera he's chasing after. I think he's being lowered with it, down a cleft or a chasm or something. He doesn't tell me much about it. But he brings me some interesting photographs of plants from time to time,' Betsey added with satisfaction.

'It sounds dangerous!' Jo said anxiously.

'Oh, yes, it is,' was the blithe reply. Then, seeing the alarm on her face, Betsey added, 'But he likes that. He wouldn't do it otherwise, you know.'

'I suppose not.'

They went wandering along the riverbank, but home-going traffic made it noisy so they turned off into a more peaceful street and at last found themselves in the Rue de la Krutenau. 'Ah!' cried Betsey. 'This is the bit I remember from what Tim talked about – the boatmen and market gardeners used to live around here in days gone by and, do you know, he once brought me a photograph of a bean-flower, growing in a crack between paving stones – a poor little survivor from somebody's smallholding . . .'

She glanced about in the light of the street lamps, but there could be no little flowers peeping out in this weather. They walked so far that at last, tired and cold, they had to hail a taxi to take them back to the Erstein. The hotel had no restaurant so they showered, changed and went out in search of a good place for a drink and a snack. Inevitably the floodlit cathedral spire, floating in the night air, drew them to the city centre.

As yet the university had not yet recommenced after the Christmas break, so they found a café that was by no means busy. There they sat, drinking the wine suggested by the waiter, and after a while eating a meal that was a shared platter of delicatessen, so rich that they had to give up only halfway.

Jo slept as soon as her head touched the pillow. In the morning she came awake only slowly, amazed that she'd slept at all. All the way in the plane she'd been thinking and wondering what it would be like to be with Tim again. Did she really remember what he looked like? Would she still feel this restless attraction towards him?

The Café Erstein at the corner of the alley provided a wondrous array of croissants, brioches and breads. There was a conserve of dark fruit to go with them, which Betsey, after a first taste, announced to be *Vaccinium myrtillus*. 'In other words, bilberry. I believe they gather the berries growing wild in the forest,' she expounded, and went on to describe other fruits of the locality.

Jo wasn't listening. Madame Wechner had offered a slip of paper to Betsey as they went out, a telephone message received from Tim

241

after they'd gone to bed last night. 'Meet you for lunch at the Valency, Rue des Grandes Arcades, 12.30.'

Munching a mouthful of brioche, Betsey said, 'Now, as I recall what Tim says, the Grandes Arcades is the big shopping area, so that's nice, we can enjoy ourselves there until it's time for lunch. I'm looking for a good pair of walking shoes. How about you?'

Jo had no shopping ambitions. They wandered around the busy malls and department stores. Betsey found a specialist store where she bought sturdy shoes with ankle supports. As they strolled on and around a corner into the Rue des Hallebards, she caught Jo by the elbow.

'How about buying something here?' she suggested.

They were outside a lingerie boutique.

Jo glanced at the window display. Exquisite lace, diaphanous silk. No prices, which meant: If you have to ask, you can't afford it.

'I think all that's a bit outside my budget, Betsey.'

'Not even for a special occasion? I feel sure there's one in the offing.'

Jo felt herself going pink.

'You're blushing!' It was a cry of delight.

'You're a wicked woman, Betsey,' she protested.

'Good Lord, I wasn't always a wrinklie, my dear.' She stood looking into the window, head tilted as if picturing something from the past. 'Warm nights somewhere in the tropics, stars so bright and clear you felt you could reach up and touch them . . .' Then she chuckled and shrugged. 'Or sometimes in a cabin on a mountainside with a wild wind howling outside.'

Jo pointed an accusing finger. 'Wisps like this wouldn't have been much good there!'

'Darling child, it didn't matter. So long as Geoffrey was there.' Betsey's mind was far away. 'I had to fight off a lot of competition to marry Geoffrey. A wonderful man. I've never met anyone that was his equal.' She sighed. 'Although Tim is like his grandfather in some ways. Just as adventurous.'

They moved on, a little silence between them. They inspected the windows of one or two of the marvellous displays in the fashion shops. After a while Jo ventured, 'Has Tim always been a globe-trotter?'

'Oh, you must find out all that for yourself, my pet. That's what you're here for.'

She said it with calm assurance. Jo accepted the statement without demur. Yes, that was what she was here for: to spend time with him, to find out whether this was all some strange delusion or whether they were meant for each other.

Soon it was time to find the restaurant. When they presented themselves, the *maître d'hôtel* old them apologetically that they would have to wait for a table. They were nonplussed, then Betsey mentioned Tim's name. On consulting his list, the head waiter smiled upon them, handed over their coats to a cloakroom girl, then conducted them to a charming little booth with dark wood framing old mirrors that advertised old local beers and long forgotten cigarette brands.

'Very folkloristic,' commented Betsey. 'Tim clearly knows the right places.'

They ordered drinks, but had scarcely sipped them when they saw Tim handing over his outdoor coat to a cloakroom girl. He was shown to the table, apologizing as he came. 'Sorry, it took me a long time to surface this morning. Hello, Grans. How are you, Jo?'

He was clad in slacks and thick sweater; she noted signs of fatigue, his hair rather longer than usual from lack of a barber, his face still bore the signs of a long flight.

He shook hands with her, then bestowed a kiss on his grandmother. They settled down, exchanging travel news. 'My helicopter to Petropavlovsk was delayed because of bad weather, which is quite usual around there, so I missed my flight to Habarovsk.'

'These places have dreadful names,' Betsey complained. 'The long and the short of it is, you missed your connections until you got to somewhere more cosmopolitan.'

'Novosibirsk.'

'And now here you are. You look somewhat the worse for wear, but you'll recover, you always do.'

'It's kind of you to be so concerned,' he told her with a grin. 'How do you like your hotel?'

'Oh, it's sweet,' said Jo. 'The alleyway outside is so narrow the taxi had to park practically in the doorway.'

'So long as you think it's comfortable?'

They assured him they were happy, then inquired whether his body-clock had adjusted itself yet. He said he'd had a *café complet* at ten. 'That was breakfast, so this is lunch.' They ordered their food: a ragout of locally caught game, recommended by Tim, and an Alsace Riesling.

The talk was a sort of general catching-up. His grandmother knew a little already so prompted him with questions about the people with whom he worked. Tim had tales to tell, amusing although rather alarming, about the bands of thieves who visited the survey team's camp quite regularly.

'It's no wonder,' he remarked in extenuation. 'The old government took quite a lot of interest in the area, but since the new lot came in, they've been more or less left to survive as best they can. They don't have a lot of the things we take for granted, so it's natural that they come foraging. That's enough about me. What are you up to, Grans?'

Betsey described her problems with the ten watercolours. 'They're going well now,' she said, 'but Miri kept changing her mind at first.'

Tim looked across the table at Jo. 'Last I saw from the clippings that Grans collects, you were making something else for the famous Miri. What was it, a bracelet or something?'

'Oh, that's all cancelled now.'

'Really?' Betsey asked, surprised. 'I didn't know that.'

'No, it probably won't make any paragraphs in the gossip columns.'

'Of course it will! Everything she does seems to get into print,' Betsey countered.

'No, I sorted that out with Ivan. They're not going to mention it and the idea is that everybody will forget I was ever going to design it.'

'How is Ivan?' Tim inquired rather too casually. 'Still at the top of the financial tree?'

'Oh yes, I'd imagine that's second nature to him by now.'

'What interests me,' Betsey insisted, 'is why you're not making this special bracelet and earrings set. I mean, one of the magazines was describing it, I gathered it was supposed to match her wedding tiara.'

'No, it was to match the necklace I made at the same time.' Jo hesitated. 'She and I had a bit of a disagreement. Well, it was more of a quarrel, really. I found I just didn't want to do it and she got quite upset.'

'Oh, dear, I am sorry,' Betsey said.

'No, there's no need, really. I'd got to the stage where I just . . . I couldn't be part of that whirligig they live in.'

'I have to admit I'll be glad when I can back out of their circle of activity,' Betsey agreed. 'And as for the husband . . . He scares me.'

Tim grunted something under his breath.

'Yes, I know, dear, you think he's a dreadful man,' said his grandmother. 'And he is, of course. But until the paintings are finished and hung in their dining room, I have to put up with him.'

Jo didn't want to be a telltale, but felt she must make everything clear now, while she had the chance. She said, 'He came dashing back from Madrid in a fury to see me about disappointing Miri over the bracelet.'

'What?' It was a sharp exclamation from Tim.

She shrugged. 'You know what he can be like. But we talked it over, and he . . . he didn't exactly understand but he accepted my decision.'

'Which was what, exactly?' Betsey prompted.

'Not to be connected with each other in future.'

'What, not included in their house parties at Chembard? Not invited to donate things to their charity auctions?' Betsey was laughing as she itemized the events.

'And not to have my name dragged in when they talk to the press. That was my only real importance to them,' Jo said with seriousness. ' I was just another little point to make in their publicity handouts.'

Tim looked at her keenly. It was clear there was something he wanted to ask, but couldn't find the words for. His grandmother came to his aid. 'Are you saying that goes for both of them? Him as well as her?'

'Absolutely.'

'Because, you know, for a while you and Ivan were . . . good friends.' Betsey was trying to be diplomatic in her choice of words.

'We all make mistakes,' Jo said, as lightly as she could.

'Grans, will you stop cross-examining her,' Tim chided, although he was smiling.

She gave a little snort of amusement and offered her glass for more wine. 'Let's have a little toast,' she suggested. 'Here's to Miri and Ivan, long may they live and prosper – so long as it's not on our doorstep!'

Laughing, they drank the toast. 'Well, do we have plans for this afternoon?' she asked. 'It's a fine bright day outside, the city is waiting for us.'

'The city will have to get on without me,' Tim said with a sigh. 'I've got appointments to help me in the pursuit of my missing camera.'

'Oh, Tim, must you really?'

'I'm sorry, Grans – it's a very expensive piece of equipment and the lack of it is holding us back on the survey. I've got to see the paperwork at Ruckmann's office and then go with him to harass the specially-insured mail service.'

Jo hoped her face didn't mirror the disappointment she felt. Betsey frowned at Tim. There was a moment of hesitation all around. Then Jo said, 'Well, you and I will find things to do, Betsey. How about your Botanical Garden?'

'But my dear, you're not interested in—'

'Is it open at this time of year?'

'Of course.' She glanced at her watch. 'It will just be reopening now, after the lunch hour. I suppose it wouldn't be bad to have a quick look-see although it'll be getting dark soon.'

This became the plan. Tim was still apologizing as he paid the bill. They arranged that he should pick them up that evening at the Hotel Erstein, then he hailed a taxi for them and sent them off to the garden.

In the taxi Betsey said crossly, 'This isn't at all what I had in mind! Dear girl, I'm sure you'd rather go somewhere more to your own taste.'

'No, no, it's all right, Betsey. I'd like a look at the *Musée des Arts Decoratifs*, but I can probably do that tomorrow if Tim is busy.'

'Are you sure? Because, listen, I'd like to get out to the mountains tomorrow to look at the plants.'

'But will there be anything to look at?'

'Might see a *Leontopodium alpinum*,' Betsey said with a grin.

'A what?'

'Edelweiss to you, you ignoramus.'

Betsey's enthusiasm carried them along throughout the afternoon. 'Look, catkins coming on the hazel already! That's a fine *Campsis*. Now that's clever, that *Onoclea* is doing better than I expected on that slope.' And so on, until the sky darkened and some light flakes of snow began to fall.

They went back to the city centre to amuse themselves for the hour or so before it was time to go to the hotel to change for dinner.

Tim took them to one of the best-known restaurants, in the Place de la Cathedrale. He'd changed to a suit and tie, and looked much less travel-worn. He gave Jo an appreciative smile when he saw her moss-green velvet jerkin and slender skirt.

Betsey set out her plans for the next day as soon as they were settled at their table. 'I'm going to Mont Ste Odile tomorrow, Tim, so you and Jo can spend the whole day together.'

Jo felt herself colour up a little at this open manipulation. Tim looked startled. 'Oh! Well, that's put the damper on my plans!'

'Which were what, exactly?'

'I was going to invite you both to come to Stuttgart with me.'

'Stuttgart? Why on earth should we go to Stuttgart?'

'Because that's where my camera was made, and I've got to collect a new one from the manufacturer. Ruckmann and I spent all this afternoon going through his paperwork and phoning back and forth, and the long and short of it is, the camera is gone, nobody knows where. So the insurance firm has given a verbal agreement to pay for a replacement and I'm going to collect it tomorrow.'

His grandmother treated him to a long stare. Then she said in a considered tone, 'And how are you proposing to get to Stuttgart?'

'By air, of course.'

'Well, I hate airports and all that so I don't want to fly with you to Stuttgart. I shall go for my little clamber around Mont Ste Odile.'

Tim frowned at her. Then he turned to Jo. 'Ah . . .' He cleared his throat. 'Can I tempt you to get on a plane and go to Stuttgart with me?'

'We-ell . . . It so happens I know and like Stuttgart,' Jo said. Of course she was going to go with him to Stuttgart. She'd have gone to Timbuktu if he'd asked. 'I've exhibited pieces of my work there. So yes, I would rather like to go.'

'Good, that's settled,' Betsey said at once, picking up her menu. 'Now let's decide what we're going to eat.'

The conversation throughout the meal turned to the attractions of the city of Stuttgart, the excellent optical equipment turned out by its technicians, the opera house and its adventurous productions, and – from Betsey – the contents of the hothouses in Wilhelma botanical park. Since they were all intending an early start next day, they broke up soon after ten.

'I'll call for you at eight, then,' Tim said on parting from them at the hotel. 'Can you get breakfast early?'

'Oh, certainly, the corner café seems to be open almost day and night.'

Betsey was already going in through the hotel doorway. 'Just a minute,' Jo called. 'What about tomorrow evening? We meet up for dinner again?'

'Just as you like,' Betsey said over her shoulder, and disappeared.

247

'Is she cross with us?' Jo asked, taken aback.

'Who knows? Grans is a law unto herself.' They stood hesitating, then Tim dropped a light kiss on top of her head. 'See you in the morning.'

Jo tapped on Betsey's door to say goodnight. She would have said more if Betsey had seemed willing, but all she got was a muffled, 'Night.'

In the morning she found her waiting in the foyer. They went to the café for the essential cups of coffee. Betsey was clad in what looked like her mountain-clambering outfit, but Jo had put on bootleg pants and an elegant leather jacket. The old lady gave her a smile of approval.

'Well, now, my love, I've got something to say to you. I'm going for a walk in the mountains but after that, I'm off to Paris.'

'What?'

'When you get back from Stuttgart, I shan't be here. And in fact, if I were you, I wouldn't hurry back.'

'But Betsey . . .'

'When I asked you to travel with me to Strasbourg, I had no intention of hanging around making a threesome all the time. I hoped you and my stupid grandson would be off on your own.'

'Wait, wait, I'm still trying to catch up!' Jo cried. 'Why are you going to Paris?'

'Well, it's as good a place as any. And it has an orchid exhibition on in the Jardin des Plantes at the moment. And I can get there by train – it's true that I hate airports, although I was fibbing a bit when I said I couldn't handle the baggage carousel.'

'But you've only been here two days.'

'And I only came so as to get you here.' She waved a hand at the quiet café, and at the buildings beyond the window, beginning to be touched by the early sun. 'Strasbourg is a lovely town, I hope to see more of it some day. But Strasbourg can do without me for the moment.'

Jo was slowly recovering from the shock. She said, 'I told you you were wicked, and it was true.'

'Listen, my darling,' Betsey said, very seriously. 'I think you and my grandson are on the verge of falling in love. Now . . . It will either happen or it won't – but it *certainly* won't happen if the two of you are in two different places all the time. Tim has to go back to the other side of the world in a day or two.' She gave the table a little thump with her fist. 'Think about it.'

When they returned to the hotel after breakfast, Tim was just walking up the alley to meet them. He gave his grandmother a hug at parting, with the words, 'See you this evening.'

She didn't reply, but she smiled at Jo over his shoulder.

They took the *navette* to the airport. When they finally disembarked at Leinfelden, a car from the manufacturing firm was waiting to whisk them off to the factory. There they were given an escorted tour. 'I'm sorry about this,' Tim murmured, 'I didn't expect all this attention.'

'It's fine,' she said. 'I have work done on my designs by precision instruments, so this isn't unknown country.'

The manager insisted on giving them lunch. It was nearly two when at last they got away, with Tim's precious camera in a special little shock-proof carrier.

The firm's driver had expected to take them back to the airport. 'Could we be dropped at the Liederhalle instead?' Jo asked.

'Of course, madame!'

'What's the Liederhalle?' Tim inquired as they settled in the car.

'Oh, it's just the part I know best, that's all. We can go anywhere you like after that.' She paused. Then she went on, in a rather faltering tone, 'I have something to tell you. Your grandmother is probably on her way to Paris by now.'

'What?'

'She wanted to leave us on our own.'

She waited with some trepidation. To her surprise his reaction was a slow, smiling nod of appreciation. 'She's a wily old soul,' he said. 'I knew she was up to something.'

'I think it's called matchmaking.' And if he's troubled by that, I've been kidding myself for a long time, she added inwardly.

'Well . . . We ought not to waste all her hard work.' He took her in his arms and kissed her hard on the mouth.

Everything else in the world seemed to fade away. The only reality was this strong embrace. It was as if their very souls had dissolved into one another, in a sort of timeless glory, a golden glow.

Reality claimed them when their driver braked to await his chance to join the motorway. They inched apart, to smile at each other in acceptance of their discovery.

'I've wanted to do that almost from the first moment I met you,' he said.

She gave a little sigh. 'Only I was mixed up with Ivan.'

249

'Don't let's talk about him. Let's talk about us.'

The attempt to explain themselves to each other kept them enthralled while the car sped along the autobahn. They were startled when the driver drew into the car park of the Liederhalle. They emerged, almost at a loss, into the afternoon light of Stuttgart. It seemed a little milder here, but not by much.

'What we need,' Tim announced, 'is somewhere quiet and warm where we can talk and sort ourselves out.'

'I know just the place,' she said, and led him along Schloss Strasse into a quieter part of the city. The Hotel Pavillon's lobby was bright with lamplight, welcoming and peaceful. 'I stayed here when I came for the *Gemme Ausstellung* last spring,' she explained as she directed him through an archway into the *Weinstübe*.

There were a few customers in leather-upholstered booths reading the newspaper or chatting over a glass of beer. The seating was arranged so that each little compartment was separated with its own little overhead lamp. The plate glass window gave a view of a quiet street and, across the way, the green lawns and leafless trees of a little park.

They slid into a booth at the far side of the room. The barman approached at once, then paused. He studied Jo for a moment. 'Fraulein Radcliffe, *nicht*? *Wie gemütlich!* And you will drink our year 2000 Riesling, I think. And for you, sir?'

'The same for me.'

'Thank you, Emil.' They didn't really care what they drank. An hour slipped away, then most of another, as they confessed their doubts and perplexities and dared to express their hopes.

'I was so jealous I could hardly bear it,' Tim said with a sigh.

'And I was an idiot ever to get mixed up with a man like that,' she said. 'But he and Miri . . .' And she tried to paint for him a picture of that strange relationship.

By and by Emil came up. 'Excuse me, *mein Herr,* but in the kitchens there are preparations for dinner. Shall I bring a menu? Would you wish to dine here?'

Tim looked at his watch. 'Good heavens! We ought to be at the airport catching a plane back to Strasbourg!'

They stared at each other in momentary consternation. Then they both began to smile.

'We'll be having dinner here, Emil.' Then when the waiter had gone, Tim looked a question at Jo.

'Yes,' Jo replied.

250

He put a long arm about her to hold her close. She smiled up into his face. 'Since I know the receptionist,' she suggested, 'shall I go and ask for a room?'

'That sounds like an excellent idea.'

So it came about that later in the evening they arrived at the moment that they had been moving towards from their first meeting. They were in each other's arms, the first wave of passion carrying them towards their own private paradise.

The night had many hours until sunrise, but not enough for their love to be satisfied. They rose late, still so immersed in each other that they went through the formalities of paying the bill, summoning a taxi, and boarding the pane for Strasbourg still in a dream.

They went to Tim's flat in Strasbourg. As his grandmother had warned, it was tiny, but all they needed was to be alone together. They ate and drank when they remembered to think of it, they talked and kissed and touched.

Somewhere around the time when dusk began to fall, Tim said, gently but without preamble, 'Jo, I start back to Kamchatka tomorrow.'

'*No!*' It was a cry of desperation.

'I must. They need me and my camera. And until I get back, the next man on the rota can't go on leave.'

'But Tim . . .'

'I know.' He kissed her long and hard. 'But I'll be back.'

'When, though?'

'April, that's my next slot in the schedule. But I can call you on the satellite phone.'

'But your grandmother says she can hardly make out what you say!' It was a wail of misery. 'And I'll be in Frankfurt in day or two!'

'Doesn't matter where you are nor what I actually say. You'll know what I mean.'

'Yes . . .' She made a great effort and stifled the sobs that were trying to escape. 'When do you have to leave?'

'If I'm to catch all the connections en route, I have to leave for Paris tomorrow on the midday flight.'

'Then I'll go with you as far as Paris.' She looked at the bedside clock. 'We have something like eighteen hours until then, dearest.'

They seemed to fly by – and there were fewer than her counting, because she had to go back to the Hotel Erstein to pack and pay

251

the bill. She sat close to him in the taxi to the airport, the thought of parting like a lead weight on her heart.

They were totally absorbed by each other on the flight to Paris. They wrote out telephone numbers, she made notes of when and where she'd be, first at home then in Frankfurt, then home again.

Tim's flight to Moscow was first. They clung together in farewell until the last moment. She watched him disappear with the others through the departure gate.

There were plenty of flights to London. She let one or two go by, too steeped in misery to care. At length she boarded, and then she searched for her diary. She counted the days until April. More than eighty. She groaned inwardly. How could she live that long without him?

Well . . . She had to go to Frankfurt next week. And she had work waiting for her at home.

Something like a smile began to grow within her. Somewhere among the days ahead, she was going to find time to design and make a present for Betsey Fieldingley. Something unaffected and not too costly, something that would be to Betsey's simple taste.

It was to be a thank-you present, made with an everlasting gratitude and appreciation for what Betsey had done. Betsey had given her something richer than the rubies that had first brought them into contact. She had brought her the love of her life.

And April would soon be here, she told herself. Only four score days and she would see him again.